PRAISE FOR CARA PUTMAN

DELAYED JUSTICE

"*Delayed Justice* will hold you to the end . . . A very timely story!"

—SUSAN PAGE DAVIS, AUTHOR OF THE MAINE JUSTICE SERIES

"*Delayed Justice* is a timely and compelling legal thriller that will have you turning the pages in search for justice. Putman packs an emotional punch and tackles tough issues head on while demonstrating God's redeeming love."

—RACHEL DYLAN, BESTSELLING AUTHOR OF *DEADLY PROOF*

IMPERFECT JUSTICE

"This is the way legal thrillers are meant to be—compelling, intelligent, and deeply satisfying."

—RANDY SINGER, AUTHOR OF *RULE OF LAW*

". . . a frightening yet compulsive reading experience."

—*LIBRARY JOURNAL* STARRED REVIEW

"The second book in Putman's Hidden Justice series is intricately plotted and thoroughly engrossing . . . This page-turner is smart, thoughtful, and appealing to readers who enjoy legal thrillers and solid mysteries."

—*RT BOOK REVIEWS*, 4 STARS

"The hopeful ending will satisfy fans of romantic suspense."

—*PUBLISHERS WEEKLY*

"*Imperfect Justice* is solidly written with great tension and a feminine-yet-tough heroine."

—*CBA MARKET*

"A legal thriller that takes on a burning social issue and the role of faith and strength in meeting that challenge. Like all good storytellers, Cara Putman makes you care. She is ~~at the top~~ of her game with *Imperfect Justice*."

—~~B~~ESTSELLING AUTHOR OF *ROMEO'S RULES*

"*Imperfect Justice* tackles a gritty subject, and Cara Putman writes with finesse and delicate sensitivity. This legal thriller had me turning pages long after even lawyers have retired for the night, and the fine threads of romance and faith brought hope where often there is none. With a superior story of law and crime, the verdict is in: *Imperfect Justice* will stick with you long after you've devoured the last gripping page."

—JAIME JO WRIGHT, AUTHOR OF *THE HOUSE ON FOSTER HILL*

BEYOND JUSTICE

"With its menacing mood, crisp dialog, and quick pace, Putman's action-packed legal thriller highlights a complex political scene. Starring a determined female attorney who will stop at nothing to resolve her case, this title will please fans of Joel C. Rosenberg and John Grisham."

—*LIBRARY JOURNAL*

"Putman's new legal thriller is exciting from start to finish. The author builds suspense throughout, and, just like real life, it's not easy to distinguish the good people from the bad. This story is well thought-out and incredibly detailed. The author's expertise shines through and adds a tremendous amount of credibility to the story. Danger, adventure, and intrigue pour from every chapter."

—*RT BOOK REVIEWS*, 4 STARS

". . . a relatable and fascinating story . . . Remarkably akin to today's news headlines . . . a legal thriller that is intricately written to keep readers on edge."

—*CHRISTIAN MARKET*

"John Grisham, move over for attorney Cara Putman! *Beyond Justice* showcases Putman's deft hand with pacing and authenticity to create an unputdownable novel that kept me on the edge of my seat. I loved the peek into the workings of Washington's political scene as well. *Beyond Justice* is a spectacular novel, and I highly recommend it!"

—COLLEEN COBLE, *USA TODAY* BESTSELLING AUTHOR

"Cara Putman's legal background has definitely been put to good use in this nail-biter of a romantic suspense/legal thriller. The tension is gripping and the suspense rarely lets up. The story should come with a warning label: Expect high blood pressure and no sleep if you start this book. You won't be able to put this one down until the very end."

—Lynette Eason, bestselling, award-winning author of the Elite Guardians series

"Cara Putman's expert legal mind shines in *Beyond Justice* as she weaves a gripping, suspenseful tale of intrigue that takes on one of the hardest issues of our time. Hayden McCarthy is one feisty heroine who doesn't let anything get between her and the truth—no matter the cost—even if it's her own life. John Grisham should watch his back!"

—Jordyn Redwood, author of the Bloodline Trilogy and *Fractured Memory*

"*Beyond Justice* is a page-turning mix of action, mystery, and romance that wrestles with real-life issues. Cara Putman packs twists and turns into every chapter. I dare you to put this book down before you reach the end."

—Rick Acker, bestselling author of *Death in the Mind's Eye*

"Cara Putman's *Beyond Justice* is a great read featuring crisp writing, page-turning suspense, and a deeply satisfying ending. **Highly Recommended.**"

—Carrie Stuart Parks, author of *A Cry from the Dust* and *When Death Draws Near*

"*Beyond Justice* is a riveting read. I immediately connected with the heroine and devoured the pages of this legal thriller with many twists and turns, staying up way too late to finish the story. Putman is at the top of her game with this one—I recommend you don't miss this one!"

—Robin Caroll, bestselling author of the acclaimed Evil series

OTHER BOOKS BY CARA PUTMAN

Beyond Justice
Imperfect Justice

DELAYED JUSTICE

CARA PUTMAN

THOMAS NELSON
Since 1798

Published in Nashville, Tennessee, by Thomas Nelson. Thomas Nelson is a
registered trademark of HarperCollins Christian Publishing, Inc.

Thomas Nelson titles may be purchased in bulk for educational, business,
fund-raising, or sales promotional use. For information, please email
SpecialMarkets@ThomasNelson.com.

Publisher's Note: This novel is a work of fiction. Names, characters, places, and
incidents are either products of the author's imagination or used fictitiously.
All characters are fictional, and any similarity to people living or dead is
purely coincidental.

Library of Congress Cataloging-in-Publication Data

Names: Putman, Cara C., author.
Title: Delayed justice / Cara C. Putman.
Description: Nashville, Tennessee : Thomas Nelson, [2018]
Identifiers: LCCN 2018020488 | ISBN 9780785217916 (paperback)
Subjects: LCSH: Women lawyers--Fiction. | GSAFD: Christian fiction. |
Mystery
 fiction. | Legal stories.
Classification: LCC PS3616.U85 D45 2018 | DDC 813/.6--dc23 LC record
available at https://lccn.loc.gov/2018020488

Printed in the United States of America

18 19 20 21 22 LSC 5 4 3 2 1

This book is dedicated to my family. Life has been quite the roller coaster this year, but I wouldn't want to ride it with any other group. My heart belongs to you alone: Eric, Abigail, Jonathan, Rebecca, and Daniel.

PROLOGUE

TWENTY-ONE YEARS EARLIER

It's time to go, sweetie."

Jaime shook her head. Words collided in her throat, releasing in a squeak of protest.

Her mother frowned, eyes shadowed by another sleepless night. She didn't know that Jaime could hear her tossing and turning and crying through the small apartment's thin walls. It was why Jaime had learned to sob into her own pillow, blanket pulled over her head.

Her mother rolled her eyes, irritation tightening her mouth. "Jaime, I do not have time for this." She glanced at her watch, then held out her hand. "Come on. We have to go now, or we'll get caught in traffic."

Mommy hated traffic. She talked all the time about how the moment Jaime's father's tour of duty ended, they would move to a small town in Indiana and not fight traffic anymore. But for now she had to work at the hospital on these weekend overnight shifts.

Jaime didn't want to move to Indiana. It wasn't home. But she did want to be as far from Uncle Dane as possible. Just thinking about him made dark spots swim in front of her eyes and her hands slick with sweat.

She stomped her foot. "I'm not going."

"Jaime, you don't have a choice." Her mother's voice carried the do-not-mess-with-me tone. The one that meant Jaime would lose something important unless she corrected her ways. Her lower lip trembled, and she bit down hard.

"Can't I stay with you this time? Please, Mommy."

Her mother met her gaze with sad eyes. "Honey, while your daddy is gone, I have to take these shifts. We need the money. We're very fortunate your Uncle Dane is here to help. I don't know how I could do this without him." She sighed and brushed back a strand of hair that had fallen in Jaime's eyes. "I need you to be my strong soldier until Daddy gets home. It'll be better then."

Jaime saw tears welling in Mommy's eyes. In her head Jaime was screaming, but she didn't say anything aloud. She didn't want to make her mother cry. So she picked up her pink, heart-covered backpack from the couch and slowly followed her mother to the door as a ball of heaviness settled in her stomach.

CHAPTER 1

The October air held the bite of fall as Jaime pushed out a breath and entered the domain of the enemy. The Commonwealth's Attorney's offices in Arlington were located in a tall stone building near the courthouse Metro station just minutes down the road and across the Potomac from Washington, DC.

She'd spent time on the opposing side of each attorney in the Commonwealth's office. Would the person assigned to her for this conversation see her as the enemy as well? Or would the attorney be willing to dig deeper into the heart of Jaime's conflict?

She didn't know, and that had her moving with hesitant steps.

This appointment was her birthday present to herself. Rolling back two decades wouldn't be easy, but it was time. She crossed the lobby and rode the elevator to the Commonwealth's Attorney's offices. Unlike the public defender's office where Jaime worked, the walls here weren't painted an industrial beige, but a calming robin's egg blue. There was real carpet on the floor rather than cheap stick-down carpet squares, and the chairs for those waiting for an audience with the attorneys weren't seventies relics with duct tape holding cracked vinyl together.

How very different the resources were on the two sides of the criminal process. It was hard not to feel bitter. The only thing the public defender's office had going for it was the dedication of the men and women who practiced there, serving those who needed an advocate.

Now Jaime was on the other side, about to beg a prosecutor to believe in her enough to take a huge risk and launch an investigation that reached twenty years into the past.

No small task.

After giving her name to the receptionist, Jaime settled on the faux leather chair and glanced around, taking in the photographic images of courthouses located around northern Virginia and Washington. Jaime had litigated inside many of them. It was hard to think of herself as accessing one of those courts in the role of victim instead of the avenging defender. Her voice was her power, and now she had to trust someone else to take on that responsibility for her.

A short, thin man with a five o'clock shadow on his jaw came into the waiting area and, after a quiet word with the receptionist, strode toward her. Mitch McDermott? They'd been opposing counsel in at least half a dozen low-level felony trials. If she'd known she'd have to talk to him first, she wouldn't have come.

"Hello, Jaime." He stuck out his hand and shook hers firmly. "Good to see you. Let's go to a conference room."

Jaime eased to her feet, a wave of confusion flooding her as she prepared to follow the man she'd battled one month earlier. "Did the receptionist tell you why I'm here?"

"To join the right side?" When she didn't laugh at his weak joke, he nodded toward the door. "Let's head where we can talk."

"Okay." This was even more uncomfortable than she'd imagined.

She followed him through the door and down a hallway to a closet-sized room with a table and handful of chairs. This nonpublic part of the office looked more run-down and familiar.

He held the door for her, then followed her inside, where he gestured to a chair. "Let's sit, and you can explain what you're doing here."

"I really would feel more comfortable talking with one of your female attorneys. Maybe Adrienne Ross?" Ross was a bulldog on cases like this, and the kind of prosecutor Jaime wanted in her corner.

Mitch gave her a rueful smile. "You know how the system works. I'm afraid you get me." He studied her closely, just to the point of awkward, and said, "Why don't you go ahead?"

This was not the way Jaime had imagined the scene, but what choice did she have? She sank into the chair and felt the rough fabric prick her legs through her navy slacks. She set her bag in her lap and pulled out a battered cloth-covered journal.

"Here." She slid it across the table to him. "This is a journal I kept as an eight- and nine-year-old. I know it's not perfect, but it's the best evidence I have. If you don't believe what I wrote, there won't be any point wasting more of your time."

"All right." Mitch slid the book around and in front of him and opened the cover.

"Start where I put the Post-it note." She sat back and watched as Mitch frowned his way through her childish scrawls. She'd thought long and hard about bringing something so personal to this office, but she had few options.

Watching him read the intimate thoughts of her younger self was excruciating. She had envisioned a woman in this role, someone who would understand and champion her.

Could she trust Mitch McDermott to do that?

Did she have a choice?

The minutes dragged on. At least he was taking time to read it . . . or taking a nap with his eyes open, fingers flipping the pages every minute or so.

Finally he glanced up at her, his light green eyes slicing through her. Laying her bare. "Jaime, this happened a long time ago. Why haven't you acted before?"

She had anticipated the question. "I've spent the last eight years in therapy, coming to grips with what he did to me and how it impacted me." She rubbed her temple, wishing she could whip out her roller of lavender oil to ease the growing tension. "I've spent thousands on counseling, but it's only in the last year that I've become strong enough to ask the Commonwealth to consider filing charges."

She was losing him. She could feel it, and her heart rate spiked. "There's no statute of limitations, and I've recently been diagnosed with dysthymic depression. That gives us some fresh evidence of the harm."

"No counselor tracked back to the alleged abuse?"

She sucked in a breath. "Alleged? Really? How would you feel if you poured out your experience to someone and they used that word?"

"Jaime . . ." The way he drew out the word warned her to be careful.

She took a deep breath. She knew it was his job to probe, but couldn't he do it without the quirked eyebrow that communicated skepticism?

"It's an onion. One counselor peeled back a layer or two, then the next probed deeper, but it took years to get to the core." She leaned forward, closing the space between them and willing him to understand. "This isn't something I do lightly. It's taken me years to gather my courage." She met his gaze. "I don't know that my uncle has abused anyone else, but if I remain silent, I'm tacitly allowing him to harm others."

"Was your mother aware of the abuse?"

"No. I used to think she was, and I couldn't understand how she allowed it. But I was a child, and I didn't know how to explain what was happening. I'd throw a fit each time she took me to his house, but she thought I just didn't like going away, didn't want her leaving me."

"Never probed deeper?"

"I didn't know how to tell her."

And how she regretted that to this day. Would her teen years have been different if she hadn't believed she deserved to be abused, and tried to fill the holes in her heart with one unhealthy relationship after another?

It had been by the grace of God—not that she believed in Him—that she hadn't become pregnant or contracted an STD or become a victim of violence . . . It wasn't until a college roommate intervened and practically forced her into counseling that her life began to change, one hard-fought step at a time. She'd worked hard to pull herself out of the morass of ongoing pain she'd self-inflicted to add to Dane's abuse.

"Jaime, would your mother testify to any of this?"

"I don't know." She shook her head. "I don't think so."

Mitch leaned against his chair and crossed his arms. "You understand this will not be easy. I'll run it by the Commonwealth's Attorney, but she'll have to sign off on taking your matter. Even without a statute of limitations, cases like this are hard to prove." He studied her as if trying to weigh her commitment, his hand still resting on her journal.

"I understand."

"I'm not sure you do." He leaned onto the table. "When you go after people for crimes like this, the gloves come off. Things you never thought would come out do. Are you prepared for the defense team to dig into your history? You will be on trial as much as your uncle is."

Jaime swallowed. She'd witnessed exactly what he was talking about more often than she cared to admit. It was a classic defense strategy in sexual crimes. A defense attorney had to challenge the victim. Doing less than that could lead to an "ineffective assistance of counsel" charge lodged in the appeal or before an ethics board.

"I've lived that side of cases," she said.

"It's very different when you're sitting at the prosecutor's table."

"Thank you for your concern, but I know what to expect." Jaime squared her jaw and reached for her journal, hoping she could live up to her firm words. "Get the prosecutor on board. I'll do my part."

CHAPTER 2

The lights of DC twinkled across the Potomac through Jaime's window, a view that was worth every extra dollar she paid for it. The mantra of real estate in a city was "location, location, location," and her experience reinforced its importance. She could spend hours a day commuting with thousands of other going-nowhere cars or pay obscene rent and step on the Metro a block from her home. She chose the latter. From one spot she could watch sunset river cruises along the Potomac, and through another window she could imagine she saw the lights of Capitol Hill. In truth she was a little too far away, but the illusion didn't hurt anyone.

As she drove from Arlington along the George Washington Parkway and through Old Town, she was filled with churning emotions. What had she set in motion today by meeting with Mitch McDermott? She couldn't tell from his words as they parted whether she should be hopeful or expect to be disappointed. Maybe disappointment was safest.

She shifted her gaze and noted a few hardy boats cruising the Potomac. Probably romantic dinner cruises, the kind she would never take. Romance was for people who had needs she'd already put to death. A need to be seen. A need to be admired. A need to be cherished.

Jaime's needs were different. She needed to prove she was as good if not better than every man she worked with. To prove to herself she could stand on her own two feet, independent and strong. To prove she could affect the world around her in ways big or small.

These needs left her standing a bit outside the world of her friends. A lone star amid the constellation of friendship.

"Snap out of it, Nichols," she said under her breath. Jaime meant the words to be brusque, but they came out in a whisper in the small space inside her car. The longing for more always surfaced in the moments before she joined her law school friends for their monthly dinners.

Was it too late to create an excuse to stay home? A nice migraine would be perfect about now. Let the medicine knock it out after she un-RSVPed. Was that even a word? It should be. She sighed and parked her car. It was time to step into the lion's den of friendship with the women who could see beneath her mask.

As she walked into Il Porto at its prime spot along King Street in Old Town Alexandria, the sound of Caroline Bragg's laughter told her exactly where her friends had gathered. The cozy table in the corner would be their spot as long as they wanted to linger, since the waitstaff were used to the group's periodic binges on great Italian food and friendship. The women had made the restaurant their own while in law school, so walking in this door should feel like coming home.

It didn't.

Though the Italian restaurant was a favorite of the others, Jaime had never bothered to tell them she'd rather eat anything else. The story of her life. It wasn't their fault she'd be eating bad sandwiches for a week to compensate for the high-priced meal and still make her rent.

She gave a nod to the hostess and headed to the corner, passing tables covered in red-checked or green-checked tablecloths in the white stucco-and-brick-walled room. Her heels echoed against the red tile floor.

She heard Caroline laugh again. The woman carried a certain light everywhere she went. It was maddening. Caroline worked so hard, yet never seemed to get down from the briefs she read day after day in her job at the court.

It only took a glance to spot Hayden McCarthy and Emilie Wesley seated at the table. It was unusual for Hayden to be early—Emilie must have put some pressure on her roommate. Three empty chairs at the table telegraphed that two more would join them besides Jaime—likely their law school mentor, Savannah Daniels, and her new sidekick, Angela Thrasher.

Caroline spotted her and leapt to her feet.

"Girl! You're here. You know, each time I wonder if you'll really show up." She tugged Jaime into a reluctant hug. "Happy birthday!"

"Thanks." Jaime was relieved to see presents were absent, then paused to note the tight lines around Caroline's eyes. "You okay?"

"Okay enough."

Before she could follow up, Emilie stood and pulled out a chair for Jaime. "I already ordered your water with lemon. Happy birthday." She leaned closer. "I told them no presents this year."

"Thank you." It was hard to explain how uncomfortable gifts made her, even gifts from friends.

Hayden smiled a welcome as Jaime sank onto the empty chair. "You well?"

Jaime nodded. What else could she say? Blurt out how the last criminal trial had left her wanting to take a continuous shower? That the constant defense of men and women who had done terrible things weighed on her even as she believed in the importance of what she did? Mention that she'd finally taken the step to hold her uncle accountable? That would raise too many questions. "I'm good." Obfuscation was easier than the truth.

Jaime loved these women. They had carried her through classes that didn't make sense and provided a community when she hadn't been sure she could endure. Her goal had been twofold: persevere and find the voice her uncle had robbed from her when she was a child. It was only because of the women at the table that she had survived law school. Finding her voice in the way that mattered most was still to be realized.

"Earth to Jaime." Hayden's words pulled her from her circling thoughts.

"Yes?"

"Your body is here, but you haven't heard anything we've said."

"Sorry." Jaime forced her thoughts to return. "I'm here." But she looked up to see three concerned sets of eyes studying her. "Really."

"Okay." Hayden glanced at Caroline, who gave the smallest shrug.

The waiter approached with a tray of drinks, and a few minutes later Savannah and Angela bustled in.

"We are finally here, ladies." Savannah tugged Angela after her to the table, and the conversation paused as the waiter took their orders. When he left with the menus, Savannah started a story about her rescue kitten's latest antics. "Getting that little thing was the best thing I've done in a long time. It's so nice to have something eager to see me when I arrive at home." She glanced around the table, her dark, shoulder-length hair arranged in a perfect bob. "I'm surprised y'all don't have one. The relaxation I get from her is so worth the cost of cat food and vet visits."

Caroline jumped in with a story about a cat she'd had as a child, and in no time the conversation moved on to other childhood memories. Jaime stayed silent, smiling and nodding at appropriate times. She didn't share that she also had a cat, a beautiful orange-striped tabby named Simba. It seemed too personal, which only demonstrated how truly broken she was inside. Her friends knew her well enough not to ask her for stories. They gave her the grace to speak only when she wanted to share.

Her phone buzzed in her pocket, and she started. "Sorry." She pulled it out and glanced at the screen.

Need to see you ASAP. Come straight to my office in a.m.

It was from her boss, Grant Joshua. She frowned as she reread the message, then slid her phone back into her pocket.

"Everything okay?" Emilie's eyes creased with concern.

"Yeah. Just a meeting in the morning." Jaime pushed it from her mind. She could worry about it tomorrow.

The hostess walked past, followed by two thirtysomething men, whom she seated several tables away.

"So, Jaime, what do you think?"

Jaime pulled her gaze back to the table. Savannah turned to Hayden and elbowed her colleague. "I think we need to order Jaime something a little stronger than water."

Caroline piped up. "One sickeningly sweet tea, coming up."

"No, really." Jaime's protest was cut short by Caroline's laugh. "I know you, girlfriend."

Emilie shook her head as Caroline headed to the bar. "The rest of us would flag down the waiter, but Caroline has to fix it herself."

"She'd mother us to death if we let her." Hayden's concerned gaze followed Caroline. "That's why we have to help her."

"Help her with what?" Jaime asked.

"I told you she wasn't listening." Emilie tapped Hayden's arm with a triumphant smile.

"She was distracted by the guy who walked past a minute ago—the one who looks like Hawkeye." Savannah winked.

Jaime had to laugh. "Just because I like the Marvel movies . . ."

"Ah, but if Hawkeye ever gets his own movie, you'll be first in line."

"There is something about a superhero who's all about justice and freedom . . ."

Hayden nodded, but her fingers beat a staccato rhythm against the red-and-white-checked tablecloth. "We still have to create a solution for Caroline."

"She can have the couch in the basement." Emilie shrugged. "I can make room."

"She won't go for that," Hayden said. "She won't want to be an 'inconvenience.'"

Caroline came back to the table carrying a slightly sweaty glass of watered-down tea. She set it in front of Jaime. "Here you go."

Jaime picked it up and took a hesitant sip, then smiled. "An Arnold Palmer."

"I told you I know you." Caroline's calm words settled over Jaime like a comforting mantle.

"Thanks. So what is it you need help with?" Each time they gathered, somebody needed something. In law school it had been answers to legal theories. Jaime used to think those were complicated issues—now she wished that was as difficult as life got.

"Caroline needs a place to stay for a week." Emilie's direct gaze dared Caroline to contradict her.

"I'll be fine. How bad can it be?"

"Have you ever lived somewhere while the floors are being refinished?" Hayden raised an eyebrow.

"And it's not only the dust and then the fumes. Projects like this never go on schedule." Emilie looked like a sage as she made the declaration. "My family had our entire first floor refinished once. Next time we left town for a month."

Just then Jaime heard the sound of laughter coming from the entrance. She glanced in that direction and felt the blood drain from her head. She'd read that expression in books and always thought it was such a lame description, but now it was real as she went from fine to woozy in a matter of seconds.

Savannah scooted her chair back, the screech penetrating the growing fog. "Jaime."

Savannah snapped the word again.

Jaime couldn't answer. Her words froze in her throat at the sound she would recognize anywhere—her uncle's laughter echoing through the room.

In one moment she was back at his apartment.

She was paralyzed as he came closer.

And there was nothing she could do.

CHAPTER 3

Excuse me." Jaime scooted back her chair and dashed for the restroom. She waited as long as she dared, using every deep-breathing technique various therapists had given her. Still her tremors continued.

"Jaime?" Caroline's voice edged into the small room. "You okay?"

What would Dane do if charges were filed?

Jaime's heart pounded and her lungs tightened until she was sipping air through a straw. She leaned her forehead against the stall's metal door. Caroline was waiting for her, so she couldn't fall apart now. She had to hold it together until she was in the safety of her apartment. She pushed out a breath and then tugged another in. Her hands fumbled with her purse. Where was her lavender?

"Jaime?" Concern grew in Caroline's voice.

"I'm fine."

"Okay?" Her friend drew the word out until it sounded like a multisyllable question. There was no way she'd fooled Caroline. "I almost believe you, except you tore away from the table like your worst nightmare had come to life."

Jaime opened the door to find Caroline leaning against the counter. "In a way."

"Those military guys that just came in?"

"One of them."

16

Caroline watched Jaime as if expecting her to bolt. "They're gone now. Apparently they didn't have a reservation and didn't want to wait."

"You sure?"

"Watched them go out the door on my way in here."

"Okay."

"So you know, you don't have to do what the girls are suggesting. I'll be fine."

"What do you mean?"

"Emilie's decided you should let me stay with you." Caroline shrugged as if it didn't matter, but Jaime could read the uncertainty in her stance.

"For how long?"

"It's supposed to be a week. Emilie says that means at least three." She winced. "That's too long to impose on anyone. Besides, the management firm assures me I'll be back in a week."

The thought of opening her haven to someone else shook Jaime, but this was Caroline, the friend who saw her in a way few others did. "Plan on a week, then we'll play it by ear."

"You sure?"

"Would I offer if I didn't mean it?"

Caroline squealed and threw her arms around Jaime. "Thank you. You can send me away the minute I get on your nerves. Not that it would ever happen."

Jaime couldn't fight a smile at the warmth her friend's exuberance expressed. "Let's go tell the others."

As she exited the restroom, she pushed Uncle Dane far from her mind. She'd deal with him when she knew what the Commonwealth's Attorney had decided. Until then the odds of their crossing paths in the DC area a second time were small.

Chandler Bolton juggled a gallon of milk and two bags of groceries in one hand, a cup of coffee and keys in the other. The day had been unending, packed with appointments and intensity. He was ready to be home and forget the stress of his job helping returning servicemen and servicewomen with their transition back from tours of duty. He shifted his condo keys for a better angle on the door, and an envelope slipped from the pile of mail squeezed beneath his armpit.

Maybe he should have made two trips.

There, the key finally caught in the door, and he twisted the knob while trying to keep his mug upright. He sloshed lukewarm brew across his hand as he pushed the door open, the plastic grocery bags twisting to cut off the circulation in his left hand. He gave the door behind him a nudge and hustled across the small foyer to the galley kitchen.

He set the bags and milk on the small granite countertop and flexed his wrist and fingers. Then he looked around. Where was Aslan?

Usually the golden retriever was at the door the moment he entered, eager to go out and get some attention. Chandler turned and groaned when he saw the open door.

Where had his crazy dog gone now?

For a dog well trained enough to become a licensed therapy dog and hopefully a comfort dog in court, Aslan liked to disappear the moment he could sneak from the second-floor apartment. His usual good temper and obedience were overruled by the need to say hi to as many neighbors as he could find in the complex.

Chandler stepped into the hallway and whistled, but Aslan didn't reappear. Well, a shake of doggie biscuits, and the escapee would trot back with a happy grin. Chandler stepped back inside to collect his keys, phone, and the can of treats he kept by the door.

He whistled a long, piercing note. Still no response.

The elevator doors clanged open. What if Aslan had trotted

onto an elevator? There would be no way to know which floor the animal had exited onto unless someone took pity on Chandler and read the dog's tag.

He checked his phone. No messages yet. He'd start by going up, stopping on each floor to look around the hallway. He didn't want to consider how hard it would be to find Aslan if the dog had made it to the lobby and walked through the doors. With the Potomac River walking trails outside the main entrance, Aslan could literally go anywhere—including for a swim.

Chandler got out on the third floor. The lobby outside the elevators looked like a generic but nice hotel. He glanced both directions but didn't see the dog or anyone to ask if they'd seen an errant golden. He turned back to the elevator, then paused as his phone buzzed.

"Hello?"

"Is this the owner of a wild dog?"

"Um, I own a golden retriever."

"I don't care what breed it is. I have the dog. Or rather, your dog has my cat. I would suggest you collect him immediately before I contact animal control."

"Aslan has your cat?"

"Please come get him at once." The feminine voice vibrated.

"Where are you?"

"Fifth floor. In the hallway."

The elevator doors had closed, so Chandler headed to the stairs. "I'll be there in a minute."

"Sooner would be better." There was an edge to the woman's voice. An edge that warned him she wasn't a dog lover and had experienced a rough day.

He clomped up the stairs while she kept talking, and a minute later he banged through the stairwell door to the fifth floor. At the other end of the hallway he saw a woman gesticulating wildly while holding a phone to her ear. She was tall, dressed in a work pantsuit, with long, dark hair spilling over her shoulders. At her feet Aslan stood at attention, focused on something Chandler couldn't see but would bet was a cat. He hurried toward them and let out a short whistle.

The dog's head turned but he didn't move. "Aslan." When the dog ignored him, staying on point toward something in the ficus tree in the corner, Chandler raised his voice and inserted authority. "Release."

Aslan gave a clipped bark.

"Now."

The dog's head sank as he slunk back a step. Then another.

The woman backed away as if afraid of being grazed by his fur.

"You all right, ma'am?"

"Not yet." She glanced at him from the corner of her eye. "Your mongrel is still here."

He bristled at her words, yet as he took a second look he wondered why he hadn't noticed her before. The complex was large, but he would surely remember someone as striking as this woman, especially with the sparks flying from her. He bit back a smile. "Aslan wouldn't hurt a fly."

"Tell that to Simba." She pointed at a marmalade cat standing at the base of the ficus tree, gaze locked on Aslan. The ridge of fur on its back stood at attention.

"They look like they belong together."

"What?" She turned incredulous eyes on him.

"The colors. They match." He shrugged, realizing the ice queen didn't appreciate his comment. "Come, Aslan. Time to get you home." Aslan edged back with one more reluctant yip.

Chandler turned to the woman, who seemed to be studying him with the intensity of one assessing danger. "I apologize, ma'am. But really, he wouldn't hurt anything."

Her gaze softened a little, yet there was still an edge to her voice. "You might want to continue his training." She scooped down and picked up the cat, who didn't appear to relish the contact.

Did the creature reflect the emotions of its owner? Or had she picked a cat because it wouldn't require her to get too close?

He grabbed Aslan's collar, thinking it was the only way the woman would relax. "I'll get Aslan back home. I'm Chandler Bolton, by the way."

"Jaime." She nodded at him, and it was clear he'd been dismissed.

All right. "Come on, Aslan."

He headed toward the elevator, only releasing the dog when the doors opened and they could enter. When he turned around, with a firm hand command demanding obedience, he found the woman, cat in her arms, still standing as though planted, her gaze locked on him.

CHAPTER 4

Jaime waited until the elevator doors closed, then hurried down the hall to her apartment. She didn't want the Captain America look-alike knowing which apartment was hers. It was bad enough he knew the floor. And what was that beast of a dog doing up here anyway?

No one on her floor owned dogs, not even small, yippy ones. Just one more reason she loved the still-new-to-her sanctuary atop the apartment complex. The view and the trails edging it added to the appeal.

"Come on, Simba. Let's get inside where it's safe." Simba didn't squirm to get away, as if the cat knew Jaime needed a few moments of petting his silky fur to reorient herself. After she closed the apartment door, she refilled his bowl of dry cat food and set him in front of it. Then she stood at the refrigerator, even though she'd just returned from dinner with friends. There was no need to open the door. She knew exactly what she'd find: a bag of salad mix that had seen better days, a couple tubs of carryout, a small carton of eggs, and three containers of Greek yogurt.

Living alone used to be a balm to her weary heart. Now it seemed to spotlight how distant she'd become from everyone.

She shouldn't feel this weary at twenty-nine. She had her whole life in front of her—but if this was all there was, it promised to be depressing.

Taking the step to press charges against her uncle was supposed

22

to take away the sense of being restrained by her past, but she was no closer to resolving the ugliness of his abuse. His evil actions when she was eight years old had colored every moment of the years that followed.

She took the lid off her diffuser and filled it with water, then added several drops of lavender oil. It only took a minute for the soothing scent to begin to fill the space and edge back the darkness.

White.

She desperately longed for the color of newness and purity.

Her walls were white. Her futon was white. Her curtains an equally blank slate. The only colors were the gray-and-black throw pillows and the variegated black to gray to white blanket tossed artfully over the back of the futon. Her wardrobe was black, her car black, and her cat an annoying shade of yellowish orange that showed up on everything—just like the stain of her uncle's abuse.

Okay, she had to stop this runaway train of thought.

She inhaled slowly, willing the lavender to calm her harried thoughts. Maybe exercise would distract her.

After changing into workout clothes, she descended to the first floor where the workout room overlooked the Potomac. It didn't matter that she'd already invested an hour earlier in the day. She leaned over the handlebars of the stationary bike, closed her eyes, and pedaled as if Uncle Dane were pursuing her. If she pedaled long enough, she could leave his touch and scent far behind her. She could feel her body becoming more powerful . . . If he ever tried to hurt her again, she'd be equipped to escape.

WEDNESDAY, OCTOBER 3

The next morning the haze was fighting off the lingering night when Jaime reached the Alexandria Public Defender's office off the main road in Old Town. She loved the idea that she worked in the historic area where George Washington had worshiped and shopped.

She made a mug of peppermint tea and then settled at her desk to work. The lights in the hallway outside her office flicked on, but Jaime kept her gaze locked on the monitor. The behemoth filling her desk wasn't some slick flat-screen. You didn't get top-of-the-line new equipment when you worked for the public defender. The computer ran slow as a mouse through snow, but most days it let her do the research she needed. When it didn't, she grabbed her personal laptop and headed somewhere with faster internet. It wasn't ideal, but she did what she could to prepare the best defense for her court appointments.

People assumed when they landed a public defender they'd receive a halfhearted defense, but she lived to prove them wrong. To the extent it was in her control, she gave her best. Getting the Commonwealth to offer a plea bargain on occasion counted as success. But as she reviewed the file for her trial in two weeks, she didn't think that would happen.

Alexander Parron had been caught red-handed with enough drugs that no jury would believe they were for personal use. The amount was one evidentiary issue she'd dispute. The police officer alleged there had been over five hundred pills, but less than half of that was in evidence. So where had the rest gone, if it had existed? Alexander, of course, denied there had been that much, but the jury would expect that testimony.

She had to peel back this case until she identified the simplest story that was the truth. The Virginia code was clear. If someone was arrested for manufacturing, selling, giving, distributing, or possessing controlled substances with the intent to do any of those, the jail time and fines were steep. Unfortunately for Alexander, the state argued this was his third such offense, even though the other convictions were out-of-state misdemeanors. Based on the underlying charges, the judge could decide to treat those as if they had occurred in Virginia, where they'd be felonies.

If convicted, he could go away for essentially the rest of his life. What should be between five and ten years, based on her experience with other clients, would automatically bump to life imprisonment, with the possibility of less if the judge decided to be lenient.

She had to prove the drugs weren't in his possession, and, failing that, that he had no intent to manufacture, sell, give, distribute, or possess the OxyContin. It was enough to make her head swim, and she practiced in this space.

She picked up her mug, but when she raised it to her lips, it was empty. She'd reached the office at five to take advantage of the quiet hours to prepare before her nine o'clock appointment with Parron and the meeting with her boss. She'd reload her cup with the nasty coffee brewed in the small office kitchenette.

She grabbed her *You Got This* mug and walked to the kitchen. Her lower back was tight, telegraphing that she'd been hunched too long over her keyboard. She needed the hook for this case before the meeting, which meant she couldn't be distracted by whatever it was her boss needed to discuss.

Speaking of . . . Grant stood at the coffeepot, watching the black liquid drizzle down as though mesmerized by the process. She noticed a new box of Constant Comment by the pot and smiled. Someone had bought another box of the tea only she drank. Forget the coffee. She stopped next to Grant and filled her mug with hot water.

He startled and his attention shifted to her. "Morning. Need to talk to you."

"I got your text."

"How's your load?"

"Average." There was rarely a healthy balance. This job required mountains of time, and the office was routinely short one attorney and often two.

He stroked his trim, dark beard as he studied her. "I'm concerned about you."

"No need." She kept her head down and did her job.

"I've had a couple complaints."

"Not unusual." After all, if they didn't get off, the clients weren't pleased.

"These are different. Do I need to pull you off a few cases?" His gaze speared her.

"No."

"Then get your act together." His jaw was tense. "I need your best work, or I'll find someone else."

Was this their "meeting"? A threat by the coffeemaker in the break room?

"Message received."

"Good."

She sighed, wanting to defuse the tension that threatened to explode in the small space. "Is there anything else you wanted to discuss?" Maybe something productive?

He slid the coffeepot out and maneuvered his mug in place to get the coffee faster. As soon as it filled, he reversed the process and lifted the mug toward her. "We have a new attorney starting next week. I'll need you to orient him. He'll focus on misdemeanors. Get his feet wet before we throw felonies at him."

"If Grace can send me his first cases, I'll review them over the weekend, but I'll spend most of my time on trial prep."

"Watch your cases and let me know what you need."

While he meant the words, his hands were tied, given their tight budget. The office required creativity in making do. But throwing money at the Parron case wouldn't do much to turn it around anyway. That required good old-fashioned creative thinking.

An hour later Jaime led her client to a small conference room that had a one-way mirror, Grant's words still echoing in her mind. Who had complained now, and should she be concerned?

She settled in a chair and eyed her client. The one-way mirror provided some accountability, as anyone could walk by anytime and check her safety. While Alexander Parron was not a physical threat to her, that wasn't true of all her clients. Alexander was forty-four, thin as a sapling, and held himself stiff against the back pain that never relented, the result of a car accident. As he eased onto the edge of a chair, his tattoo sleeves caught her attention. He'd tried to tell her their significance the first time they met, but she'd delayed his erratic telling when he kept repeating himself in a cycle of confusion.

Could there be a seed there to build the story she needed to persuade the jury? There was something about his unfocused behavior that indicated it was possible he would fail a court-ordered drug test. Had he started adding heroin or another uncontrolled substance to his cocktail of pain meds? If so, could he even remember the reason behind his sleeves?

"Alex, I need you to focus."

He turned to her and groaned. "The pain is real bad today."

"That may be, but you are headed to trial. You'll sit in a courtroom for at least two days, maybe longer."

"I can't do that."

"You'll have to. It's that or plea bargain."

"But I didn't do what they say." His claim never changed.

"The amount of OxyContin you had far exceeded the prescription. That gives the state evidence you intended to distribute."

"There ain't no one I can give or sell it to when I need every pill."

"I understand. But the Commonwealth doesn't. At twenty-five dollars a pill on the street, you've got a good reason to distribute them. Remember, the Commonwealth's Attorney must prove two things. First, that you committed the illegal act, and then that you intended to break the law. One isn't enough."

"I was headed home."

"With five hundred pills?"

"Yes." The word exploded from him, and there was a fire in his eyes that made Jaime glad the solid table provided a barrier between them. "Sorry. I should have taken another pill."

"That's what got you into this trouble."

"It was that doctor. I wish he'd never given me the prescription."

"The state didn't charge him. You're the one on trial."

"Can't you make it go away?"

"Sure, but that requires you to accept the plea bargain."

"Ain't doing that."

"I know." She glanced at his arms and neck. Maybe talking about the tattoos would distract him. "Would you tell me about your sleeves?"

"Why? You weren't interested before."

"I am now." She met his gaze. "Please."

"I don't see how this will help with the trial. I can't go back to jail." He glanced down to where his hands trembled on the table. "Ain't no way I can defend myself in prison when I move like a ninety-year-old."

"Let me decide what will help. Tell me your story, Alexander."

So he did. He talked about the accident that wrecked a back already weak from high school football. The doctor prescribed the narcotic, and his life spiraled out of control. Each sleeve told a piece of his pain. It was exhausting listening, but then he mentioned charges in West Virginia.

"Wait a minute. Run that by me again." Jaime had the cause numbers from the court filings and had found everything she could online. The subpoenas requesting copies were out, but she'd had no response. "What were you charged with?"

He told her, and she grabbed a file from his folder. "That doesn't match what the state listed. Maybe that's why I don't have the files yet." She made a note to call and talk to someone. "I need everything you have on those."

"Didn't I bring those in already?"

"I requested them, but you've forgotten." More proof of how much the drug had messed with his mind. "If you get me that information, I might prove the prosecution made a mistake. What you've described sounds like a misdemeanor here. That wouldn't allow the state to compound the jail time it's seeking, and we could land a better plea bargain."

He started to sputter, but she held up a hand. "We need a stronger position. You want a convincing argument for why you had those pills, but knocking the other convictions down to misdemeanor equivalents helps."

"I don't see how."

"You don't have to. That's why you have me. For this to work, I need that information today. The moment you leave, I want you to find it and bring it to me."

"All right." He edged back on the chair, then froze. "Can I mail it?"

She reached for her pocket, but her roller bottle of lavender wasn't there. "No, you cannot mail it. Your trial is in eleven days."

She took a deep breath as a flash of pain swept his face. Time to refocus on his testimony.

Jaime looked through her notes. This wasn't going to be a straightforward matter of building a case that proved the drugs were only for him. The quantity was incriminating. But she could poke holes in the idea that he had intent to distribute. The prosecution didn't have evidence on that if he stuck to what he'd told her today.

She'd decided early in her career her job wasn't to build the prosecution's case. Instead, she would hold it accountable for every charge filed and every piece of evidence presented.

Today had solidified the direction her thoughts were headed about the proof. Now to pull together the law that would support her position. She walked Alexander to the front with a reminder to get her the information on his West Virginia charges. Then she settled in her office and opened the case database. The search for relevant cases was slow going, but eventually she'd find what she needed. The law demanded persistence, a trait Jaime Nichols had in abundance.

CHAPTER 5

Sunlight streamed through a crack in Chandler's curtains, knocking his eyeballs with the message it was time to get up, but his brain refused to cooperate. It felt like a razor blade sliced through his skull. His alarm went off, and he groped along his nightstand trying to find it. He cracked open his eyelids and groaned. 8:10? How had he slept through not one, not two, but three alarms? Had his nightmares of a convoy of exploding armored vehicles turning to shrapnel been so exhausting that his subconscious had clicked his phone off while he slept?

He used to wake up before his alarm, some sixth sense letting him know it was time.

Now each day he struggled.

He waited for things to change, but some days the depression from losing his marriage slammed against him in a way that demanded he stay in bed. He'd have to race to reach work in time for his nine o'clock.

Aslan nudged his hand to get him out of bed.

"Okay, boy. Starting tomorrow, you and me, outside for a run."

Aslan turned hopeful black eyes on him, that pesky word R-U-N raising false hopes.

"I need to teach you the concept *tomorrow*." Chandler rubbed the dog's ears and then launched to his feet. Another glance at the time on his phone sent him racing through a quick shower and a quicker walk with the golden retriever to the Potomac and back.

31

Even if it slowed Chandler down, Aslan needed to water the lawn at every post he passed before their drive to Clarendon. Aslan couldn't join him at the office every day, but Chandler found that people relaxed in a way when the dog was there that they didn't without him. That ability had gotten him thinking about how the dog could help more people.

He filled a cup with Lucky Charms to eat on the way and set out. He loved the reverse commute of his location as well as the energy of the neighborhood. Add in the walking trails he planned to start using with more intentionality, and it was a great fit, especially since, thanks to the Metro, his truck could sit in the garage on days he needed to commute to the Pentagon for training or meetings. Better yet, there were no memories of Rianna, his ex, in the apartment.

The Vet Center where he worked was located a couple blocks off the main strip of Clarendon. George Mason University School of Law sat to the west, while to the east was Arlington National Cemetery, and across the Potomac, Georgetown. It was one of those hidden gems of a neighborhood. While it was too expensive for most active duty military to live in, the location made it easy for them to access critical services.

The Department of Veterans Affairs had centers to help soldiers readjust to life at home after a tour of duty. Chandler had used his time on tours to complete the credits for a counseling degree and then a master's. The combination of active duty service and education had made him a perfect fit for a family counseling job with the Vet Centers. His accumulated vacation time showed just how much the services were needed. In fact, he'd gotten the lecture that he'd have to use some of the time in the next month or lose it.

The challenge was finding a good reason to take it. Sitting around made it too easy for his thoughts to wander to areas that could cause his outlook to spiral down. If he could save a few of his fellow soldiers from the pain of shattered families on reentry, then pouring out his life through counseling was well spent. Add in helping soldiers process what they'd seen and experienced, and he found purpose in his work.

His main job was listening and asking key questions before connecting services and families. Each family had unique challenges. If service members had children, sometimes they needed counseling as they became reacquainted. If a child was born while the parent served, they accessed different services. Some families reintegrated successfully on their own, but others wanted—or needed—assistance.

Aslan panted from the passenger seat, his doggie breath filling the truck.

Chandler had spent the last year developing connections with agencies, service providers, and others that brought the skills these families needed. He refused to dwell on what might have happened if he and Rianna had taken advantage of the help he now offered others. Instead, he set his face to the future and those he could help.

He drove through the rush hour traffic as he considered his next goal: providing more assistance to families prior to deployment. Coping skills and strategies could make the difference in keeping families together during long separations. Would such assistance have saved his marriage?

He didn't know.

But there had to be something he could do to help other families avoid that pain. People might say divorce wasn't a big deal, but it had rent his world in two pieces that could never be stitched back together, especially now that Rianna had remarried. No one had warned him how draining the work of recovering from a divorce would be.

The office was unlocked when they arrived. A two-story storefront, the inside had been made as welcoming as possible in a generic building. It didn't have the personality of a converted bungalow, but it wasn't as sterile as industrial furniture, either. The upstairs offices were what his colleague called 1920s Hollywood glam. It was a suite he wouldn't be caught dead in, with its hot-pink flashes opposite gray walls and gold accessories. Way too girlie. But the designer had tucked a clever kids' corner into the space, so that when women were receiving assistance or counsel, their kids could be right there yet not underfoot.

Too bad there wasn't a man cave equivalent.

Chandler's office was on the main floor down a narrow hallway, because his supervisory role required some closed-door meetings. Aslan followed him down the back hallway past the small kitchenette and conference room with a smaller counseling space on one side of the hallway. On the other sat a line of four offices, his being the first. The rest were reserved for counseling, a small round table with two or three comfortable chairs in each. His office wasn't much: a desk, a few chairs, a couple short bookcases, and a series of locking file cabinets. Someday he'd add art to the walls, but it wasn't a priority. Let the ladies have the froufrou decorations upstairs. Rianna had taken what little art they'd acquired, and he hadn't replaced it.

Each night he tried to clear his desk, but as he walked into his office this morning, he frowned at the piles on it. He walked right back out and headed toward the open cubicle space at the front of the building. In front of that sat a small receiving area, but his team liked the collaboration that the cube space allowed. It also allowed for maximum flexibility to have multiple meetings occurring without interrupting the work of the others. He glanced around the cubicles for Beth, the only woman who would pile stacks on his desk. "Beth?"

A middle-aged woman glanced up from her cube, wearing her fall uniform of jeans and sweater. "Yes?"

"What's with the piles?"

"Wanted to make sure you started your day right. You keep that desk too clean."

He shook his head and tried to hide a smile. "You know I can't work with a mess."

"That's all you do. If you haven't noticed, the people who come through that front door are a mess." She placed her hands on her ample hips and stared him down, her office manager persona in full effect. "You've got a string of appointments starting at ten."

"What happened to my nine o'clock?"

"Canceled. Take time in the next hour to research, because once ten hits, I don't think you'll have time to breathe until four."

"What happened?" His days were rarely that stacked with appointments, though as he looked around the workspace it was surprisingly vacant for the start of the day. "Where is everyone?"

"Rumbles of a sex scandal. We're getting calls from victims. Maybe even a few of the perpetrators." She shook her head, then sighed. "When are people going to wise up and realize you can't post that stuff? The team is working the phones to learn what they can."

That meant they'd be in the small counseling rooms to work without background chatter. "All right. Email me what you've got."

"Already in your in-box. It ain't pretty. This one is just as bad as the scandal last year with the marines that involved the private Facebook groups." She shook her head, and her eyes filled with sadness. "The world needs more men like you."

"That's not what my ex thinks." Chandler had returned from his last tour with a mild case of PTSD only to find his wife in the arms of another guy. It wasn't the homecoming he'd anticipated.

"Don't let her define you for the rest of your days. That woman didn't care what she walked away from, and I bet she regrets it to this day." Beth patted his arm, actually patted him, like he needed to be comforted. "You're much more than she thinks."

Chandler tried to accept her words, but he'd been there when his wife wouldn't even look at him. When the words weren't civil because he couldn't be whatever it was she needed. "Maybe."

"There are a lot of women out there looking for a man like you."

"I might be ready to find one."

"I know the perfect woman."

Chandler held up his hand. While he might be ready to push back the loneliness, he didn't want to rush into something with a stranger, no matter how wonderful his colleague thought the woman might be. "I can manage on my own."

"Sure." The woman gave him an mm-hmm look. "When you're ready, let me know. Until then, dig into that email. I expect half your appointments today will be tied to this new scandal."

"I can't counsel women, Beth."

"I know. But there will be a lot of husbands and boyfriends who need to process as well, since their women were victimized." She considered him. "It might take them a few more days to reach out, but they will come."

Chandler nodded, feeling unsettled and sick. The things people would say and do when they didn't think they were account-able. He'd watched good marines lose their careers last year be-cause they were stupid. He didn't want his fellow soldiers to do the same things. "Thanks for the heads-up. I'll dig into what you sent."

Beth nodded and Chandler returned to his office. As he opened his email, he didn't want to read what she'd collected. He didn't need further proof that the world was a broken place or that her research was stellar.

As he read the news accounts he wondered what his role was. He pushed back from his desk. Time to get some coffee and clear his head before the first appointment. He should pray too. This was a mess he couldn't enter without being impacted, and he wanted to make sure he entered in a way that helped those who were hurt rather than adding to their injury.

An unintentional or thoughtless word could be as damaging as not getting involved.

CHAPTER 6

J aime shifted against the hard chair in the reception area of the Commonwealth's Attorney's office. While not as battered as the chairs in the public defender's reception, it wasn't plush and soft. She glanced at her watch and noted she'd already wasted twenty minutes she couldn't afford. Her foot tapped against the carpet that wasn't covered with coffee stains.

She tried to type a memo on her phone, but she couldn't focus her thoughts. All she could think about was whether Mitch had called her in to let her down lightly or with the equally scary announcement that charges were forthcoming. When she misspelled the third word in a row, she gave up and closed the app.

Corny elevator music was piped in from somewhere, loud enough to be annoying as it cycled back to a song she'd already heard twice. How did the receptionist stand it? Maybe she wore earplugs, which would also explain why she'd ignored Jaime since acknowledging her arrival.

Jaime should have worn a sign that indicated she was a victim rather than the enemy.

The receptionist picked up her phone, spoke a few words, then glanced at her. "Mr. McDermott will be out in a minute."

The woman looked as though she spent every lunch hour sweating at some trendy hot yoga studio. She wore one of those oversized, flowy solid-color dresses over wacky leggings, the kind of

38

ensemble that emphasized how thin someone was without making you instantly hate her. But if she admitted it, Jaime was in a frame of mind in which it was easier to find reasons *not* to like people than to pull them close. She'd leave that to women like Caroline, who brimmed with Southern charm and sweetness.

The door between the lobby and productive regions of the office opened, and Mitch McDermott waved her back. "Sorry to keep you waiting." His grin was a bit lopsided, almost charming. "You know how it goes with emergencies."

She stood and thought of those he'd created in the cases they'd shared. "I do."

"This won't take long."

Yeah, because he didn't bill by the hour. She hoped Dane would pay an exorbitant fee each time he consulted an attorney . . . if charges were filed. She followed Mitch down the hallway to the third door on the left. He stepped aside to let her enter.

He closed the door behind him, leaving them alone in the room. She felt every inch of space, and it wasn't enough. While she knew Mitch, it didn't mean she trusted him. Not the way she needed to, to be comfortable with him in such a small space.

He sat and got straight to the point. "We're moving forward with charges. Lacy is interested to see what happens."

Lacy Collins, the Commonwealth's Attorney, was a focused advocate for victims, trying hundreds if not thousands of cases in her career. She was a formidable foe, one who had pushed Jaime to prepare diligently the time they'd been opponents.

Jaime sank to a chair as the weight of his words landed. "I don't want this to be a pro forma attempt." Thanks to double jeopardy, they got one opportunity to try, and then she was limited to civil remedies, which wouldn't carry the same weight or satisfaction.

Mitch leaned forward, focus etched in the lines across his forehead. "That's not how I operate. This will receive my best work."

She met his gaze and measured his commitment. When he didn't look away, she nodded. "What can I do?"

"It's what you should know. The moment we serve these charges, your life will change." He studied her across the small conference table and pushed a document her direction. "There's no turning back."

"I know." Jaime tugged the stapled pages nearer as a wisp of fear curled through her mind. What would Dane do when he learned what she had done? She tried to review the words that swam in front of her eyes. This was the most important legal paper she'd ever read, yet her mind couldn't hold the words.

Mitch must have noticed her challenge because he spent the next hour reviewing the preliminary charging document. She followed on her copy carefully, considering every legal argument she'd used against similar charges. This . . . everything she was reading and evaluating . . . this was why she'd become a public defender. When she pursued charges against Dane, she needed them to stick. Some technicality couldn't be sufficient to free him from responsibility.

Still, as she read the paragraphs, it reinforced in her mind how risky this was.

It was what she had wanted.

But now that she had to say yes, she was terrified.

On or about the month of July 1996, Dane Nichols sexually assaulted Jaime Nichols, an eight-year-old minor.

The words continued. Stark. Black and white. No ambiguity.

Somehow Mitch had captured her tragedy in stark, factual sentences. Each sentence held a subject and a verb. Very little color was added. A list of facts.

Yet each represented a raw wound that festered.

On or about the month of August 1996, Dane Nichols sexually assaulted Jaime Nichols, an eight-year-old minor.

The evidence was scant.

If she were the prosecutor, she would have demanded more, yet they had agreed to proceed on her word and her journal.

The moment Mitch filed these words with the circuit court, there was no turning back. Some enterprising reporter would notice the charges in a routine docket search. The genie would escape the bag, and she would be firmly committed.

It's what she wanted. Right?

Her breath locked in her chest.

She felt more than saw the pinpricks of black cloud the edges of her vision.

"Still with me?" Mitch's deep voice dragged her back, and she blinked.

"Yes." She slid the complaint back. "Let's do this."

"All right. I'll file it. How do you want to serve it?"

"Part of me wants to be the one who serves him."

Mitch frowned. "Not possible."

She stared at him. She wanted to do this. Needed to.

He shook his head. "You know as well as I do that if we don't follow the process precisely, we're giving your uncle's defense team appealable issues."

Jaime looked away and gave a small dip of her chin. She'd have her day to confront her uncle face-to-face. It would just have to wait.

The ringing sound jarred Chandler from the file review. He was ready to yank the landline from the wall and then bury his work cell someplace where he'd never hear it. It was impossible to accomplish anything with the constant interruptions. This week had seen more than usual with the emergency sessions happening just as Beth had predicted. Hopefully those would eventually slow, or there was no way he'd get to take time off.

"Chandler Bolton."

"Hello?"

Chandler heard the hesitation in the man's voice. "Hello, this is Chandler," he said again. "Who am I speaking with?"

"A fellow soldier. One who remembers too much."

That described most who served overseas. A tour without scars either physical or mental was rare. "Then we have something in common."

"More than you know." The voice was low, not one he recognized, but there was something about it that put him on alert.

"How can I help?"

"Exorcise the demons in my mind."

"When did you tour?"

"Three years ago, and then this year."

"Afghanistan?"

"And Iraq. The things I've seen."

"I understand, brother."

"You aren't my brother." The words were crisp, cutting.

Chandler took a breath. "What do you need?"

"An acknowledgment that you ruined my life."

The words were so bizarre, out of left field. "Can't do that." Translation: *I have no idea what you're talking about, crazy man.*

"Then you're in deeper denial than I am." There was a pause, one long enough to become even more uncomfortable than the conversation. "You're at the Clarendon office." A statement.

Chandler shifted, feeling the weight of his gun in the holster at his waistband. Most days he didn't notice it, the weapon was such a part of him, but in the middle of this conversation, it felt reassuring.

"If you'd like to set up an appointment, I can meet with you. Usually we start with thirty minutes and expand as needed. If you believe I contributed to your pain, you should come in so we can talk."

"You'll see me." The man hung up, and Chandler found himself holding a silent phone to his ear.

After he hung up, he stood and walked to the doorway. From there it was a stone's throw to the bank of cubicles that held his colleagues. Only two of the six spaces currently held people. He strode toward them, and Allison Ramsey looked up from her monitor. "Did you happen to patch a call to me a few minutes ago?"

Her green eyes held a dazed look, as though he'd interrupted a deep thought and she was trying to hear his words. "Ummm." She blinked a couple times, and it was like watching cobwebs clear. "No. Didn't answer the phone." She pointed at the earbuds he hadn't noticed through her dark hair. "Kind of in the zone."

"Sorry to interrupt." His attention shifted to Jake Robertson, the other caseworker. The former college basketball star had turned a tour with the military into a counseling career. The man was amazing with kids who adored him despite his large frame.

Jake shook his head. "Didn't take the call. We're the only ones here today. Three of the team are at all-day training at the Pentagon, and Beth called in sick."

Chandler nodded at the reminder the agency was running low on staff. "Then he must have my direct number."

"Or used the directory. If he knew your name, it's easy to reach you without going through us."

"Good point." He steered the conversation toward what was on each of their agendas that day even as he did a quick security audit of the facility. While it was attached to the Department of Defense, there weren't military police or marines stationed outside. Chandler acted as the de facto supervisor, since the man who oversaw the office worked from a second location. Moments like this, he worried their little office was the overlooked stepchild. A little bit of bulletproof glass wouldn't do much to prevent someone from harming the facility if he wanted to. The challenge with making a threat assessment was that Chandler was missing key information—like who the man was.

He felt the weight of silence and realized Allison and Jake were watching him, waiting. "All right." He clapped his hands together. "I'll just, uh, get back to my office. Let me know if you need anything."

Jake turned back to his computer without a word, but Chandler felt Allison's gaze as he returned to his office.

Chandler's tours had heightened his awareness of how danger could rest along the next bend in the road. He'd been attached to a quartermaster unit and focused on moving supplies, which should have been safe. But nothing was safe or easy in a part of the world where the next person could wear a suicide vest, or an IED could be planted in a dirt stretch. It would be easy to start living as if everyone were the enemy. Over the months he'd been stationed in Iraq, he'd developed a sixth sense for danger, but it hadn't saved his team. Even logistics couldn't protect them.

Was the phone call somehow related to that tragedy?

He'd risen to sergeant and felt cocky about it, if he was honest. There were never any guarantees one could rise in the ranks, and he had. That sense of self-assurance might have carried over to the supply convoy. He'd been prepared to join the convoy when he'd been called back to deal with a fresh-off-the-plane bigwig. He'd sent his team down the road, fully expecting them to return. They shouldn't have been in danger, since they were the ones who ensured the servicemen and servicewomen had what they needed.

It was a routine operation, until the lead vehicle hit an IED. Chandler's nightmares reinforced the realization that everyone was one instant from eternity, and most didn't anticipate their encounters. They happened when least expected.

He'd hardly had time to grieve his fallen brother and take care of those who were injured before his unit rotated out, and then he'd been transferred to the Vet Center. While the centers provided over a million counseling sessions a year, he couldn't tell from the truncated conversation whether this guy needed reentry or bereavement counseling or why he wanted to talk to Chandler in particular.

Aslan nosed his knee and Chandler froze, having forgotten his companion was there. "Sorry, boy."

The dog had an uncanny ability to detect his distress, making him a great barometer for Chandler's mental state. If Aslan felt the need to intervene, then he needed to step away.

"Need some air?" The dog looked at him, and Chandler grabbed his leash. "You might not, but a quick walk around the block would help me." And could be explained as a quick stroll to take care of the dog's needs, but Allison and Jake would understand. Five minutes was all he needed.

Aslan's dark eyes studied him as if to say, *Of course it would*. It was amazing how many conversations they had when only one of them formed words.

Aslan stayed relaxed as they walked out the back door, which Chandler tried to tell himself meant all was well. But he couldn't scratch the feeling of high alert. It was a leftover from his tours and helped him understand what the real heroes had experienced and what they brought back with them.

His phone buzzed, and he slid it from its holder as he reentered the center. "Chandler."

"This is John Walters with Fairfax County. Got your dog?" The man's tone was abrupt, pulling Chandler's attention.

"Aslan's right here." The dog's ears perked up.

"If you're still interested, we're ready to give him a try. We have a little girl coming in who could use a comfort dog." John's voice held an urgency that pulled Chandler taller.

"When do you want us?"

"The child is on her way in now."

Chandler grimaced as he glanced at his watch. "I'll need at least an hour."

"That should work. This is a delicate situation. Little girl needs a careful touch."

"Aslan is ready."

"I hope you're right, because we can't get this one wrong."

It must be serious if John was this uptight. The man had been a detective with the Fairfax County police before focusing on providing a safe environment for children to be interviewed. He attended the same church Chandler did, and he'd been intrigued when Chandler mentioned what he was trying to do with Aslan.

"I want that dog of yours to do well today."

"Me too." After a few more words, Chandler hung up, then reached down to rub Aslan's ears, the heaviness of the request pressing against him. "You're going to get your chance, boy, but first I have to clear it with my boss."

It only took a phone call to organize a half day off. He'd feel better about being out if there were a couple more people in the office, but he might be doing them all a favor by leaving. Especially if whoever had called meant to do something or come in.

Chandler prayed for the child even as he grabbed his jacket and hurried Aslan to the car. If a child's world had been upended, then he would like to be a part of putting it back together. With Aslan's help he might be able to do exactly that.

CHAPTER 7

A little over an hour later, Chandler stood behind the counter at the Fairfax County's child interview home, Aslan seated next to him. A small two-story bungalow on a mostly residential street, from the outside it looked nothing like a police or investigative facility. That was the point. The facility was designed to make traumatized children feel as safe and comfortable as possible from the moment they arrived, allowing trained investigators to piece together events through carefully worded and conducted interviews.

Brandon Lancaster, his friend who ran a foster care agency called Almost Home, had also told him about this agency and its need for comfort dogs. Some children couldn't tell their story to an adult, but they opened up to animals.

The idea had captured Chandler's attention, and he'd tracked down information on a training program. He knew Aslan understood emotions, and the dog's eyes contained wells of sympathy. Today was Aslan's first assignment, and the culmination of untold hours of work—Chandler had quit tallying the time after they'd reached one hundred hours of logged training over the last year. He'd taken Aslan to nursing homes, day cares, elementary schools, even to Vet Center events, looking to acclimate the dog to people in multiple settings. His supervisor had seen the value of what Aslan could do with some of their clients and supported the training as long as it was on Chandler's own time. They'd agreed to discuss how Chandler could leave when Aslan got calls but hadn't done it yet. Guess the issue'd been pushed up in priority now.

The way Chandler saw it, he could stick his head in the sand and deny that children were abused each day, or he could be part of the solution. Denial had never gotten him far, so he'd opted for action. Now all that action would either propel them forward or let him know he'd wasted all those hours.

When Aslan stood peacefully during the picnic and fireworks for the vets and their families on the Fourth of July, Chandler knew the dog was ready. If he could handle that level of chaos, he was ready to sit quietly with a child who needed a friend.

Now Aslan waited as patiently as his namesake from *The Lion, the Witch and the Wardrobe*, unfazed by the new setting. Chandler had led him behind the counter that hid a computer and files, feeling it right to be as unobtrusive as possible while maintaining a position where he could see through a one-way mirror into the room where the dog would go to work as soon as the team was ready.

A young girl, maybe eight, with blond curls rioting around her head, waited in a room that was supposed to look and feel like a playroom. He could barely see her, tucked in a corner, her arms braced against her sweater.

A woman who looked a little like Mrs. Potts of *Beauty and the Beast* fame stepped next to Chandler. "That little girl has experienced things no child should, but until she talks there's little we can do." She turned and eyed Chandler and then the dog. "Is he up to the task?"

Chandler nodded. "He's as ready as I can get him."

She nodded. "I'm Detective Jane Thomas."

"Chandler Bolton. And this boy is Aslan."

"Nice to meet you. Elaine has her hands full keeping the mom under control." Jane leaned down and let Aslan nose her hand before rubbing his head for a minute. "Two bad there aren't two of you, one for Ms. Ange and one for her daughter. Are you ready to help Tiffany, Aslan? That little girl needs to know you'll hear her."

Aslan panted, then licked her hand.

She laughed and wiped the doggie slobber on her pants. "I'll take that as a yes."

"You'll need a couple hand signals." Chandler quickly taught them to her, while keeping an eye on the girl's mother, who stood across the room from him, a hysterical mess, with a counselor trying to calm her.

"Ms. Ange, it doesn't help if Tiffany hears you going on like this."

The young woman shook her head and rubbed her hands up and down her arms. "The things he did to my baby." Her voice trailed off in a broken wail, and Chandler quickly turned his attention back to the playroom and away from the mother's pain.

The therapy room where the girl waited was wired, and every word and movement could be recorded. Jane opened the door. The fact that she was a decorated detective was cloaked by her warm demeanor and lack of uniform. Chandler released Aslan, who followed Jane into the room, then sat at the hand command as she sank to a chair beside a child-sized table.

The woman didn't speak. Didn't move toward the child.

Aslan waited.

The little girl ignored them both. She rocked, tucked against a bookshelf, tears leaking down her cheeks.

Aslan waited.

It felt like thirty minutes passed, but when Chandler glanced at his watch, he saw it had only been a few, when Aslan eased to his feet. He approached the girl, then sank to the carpet next to her. He watched her, then gently placed his head in her lap.

Through it all Jane waited, still and silent, letting the act of empathy unlock some hidden door inside the girl.

Tiffany sobbed as she wound her hands through Aslan's thick fur. Then, with the dog's gentle eyes locked on her face, she began whispering. Her story got louder as the words rolled in a flood. Words so sad, yet necessary. Through each one Aslan listened, not even twitching.

The girl's mother wept in the corner away from the one-way window, where Elaine had taken her. "I didn't have any idea. Not until yesterday." She nibbled at a cuticle. "What if he won't stay away?"

A weariness sloped Elaine's shoulders, as if a boulder pressed against them as she listened. "A lot will depend on what Tiffany tells us."

"But she hasn't been talking."

"Let's see what the comfort dog can do. I've seen them work wonders with other traumatized children." Elaine placed a hand on the mother's shoulder. "Tiffany will need help and lots of time. These kinds of events are world altering."

"I'll do anything I have to. Anything she needs. How can I keep her safe if I didn't see this happening?"

Chandler shuddered at the pain in Ms. Ange's voice. It was stark and real and deep. The kind that sliced through normal and left shredded dreams behind. The kind no mother should carry.

The counselor watched the woman from the corner of her eye, as if trying to discern the veracity of her emotional upheaval. "Ms. Ange, how well did you know the accused?"

"He was a new boyfriend. I'd known him a few weeks." She took a deep breath, and her voice was stronger when she continued. "I want him to pay. What do I need to do?"

"A lot of that depends on Tiffany. Her testimony will be critical to press charges. The final decision rests with the Commonwealth's Attorney's office."

Chandler returned his attention to the room on the other side of the mirror. Aslan suddenly popped to his feet, and Chandler stepped closer to the one-way glass. Before he could whistle a command, Detective Thomas gave a hand command, and Aslan sank back on his haunches. The detective extended her hand to the little girl, and a minute later the two exited the room. The girl hung back from her mother. Interesting. Her face was set in a mask that did not resemble the expressiveness she'd had minutes earlier when sobbing into Aslan's fur or talking with the investigator. Now Tiffany held herself rigid as if waiting for the next blow.

Then Ms. Ange knelt in front of her and opened her arms slowly, as if unsure her daughter would come.

It was only then that Aslan eased through the door as if to slip into freedom. He nudged his nose into Tiffany's thigh. After another nudge, she hurried into her mother's arms. Their embrace must have squeezed all the air from the girl, and Chandler sensed the hug would be repeated frequently in the coming days.

Aslan came and sat in front of him, expectation in the tilt of his head and quirked ears.

"Come on, boy." He eased around the mother and child but stopped when the woman spoke to him.

"Do you own this dog?" After he nodded, she continued. "Can I buy him from you?"

Chandler startled, then shook his head. "No, ma'am. He's not for sale."

She studied him a second, one hand playing with her daughter's golden curls. "Thank you for bringing him."

"I'm glad we could help." He reached into his pocket and pulled out a card. "In case you need anything else."

"I don't even know what we need." She took the card but said nothing more as he clipped on his dog's leash.

Chandler turned to Elaine and Detective Thomas. "Tell John Walters he can call if he needs anything else."

Detective Thomas nodded. "I will. Thanks for responding so quickly."

"Glad it worked."

He walked away, knowing he hadn't done anything other than chauffeur his animal, but that was reality in his life. The needs were always bigger than his capability to meet them, so he needed God in big ways. As he let Aslan have a minute to sniff the bushes and water the grass, his phone rang. He pulled it from his pocket. "Bolton."

"Aslan's owner?" The woman's voice was hesitant.

"Yes, ma'am." No mistaking Ms. Ange's broken voice.

"Tiffany would like to say good-bye."

"We're still in the yard. We'll wait until you come out."

A moment later the little girl ran outside and flung her arms around Aslan. Her mother walked out more slowly. She was too young to have a burden like this, Chandler thought. She couldn't be much more than twenty-five, and she seemed even more frail out here than she had inside.

"Is she going to be okay?" The woman watched her daughter pet Aslan as the animal smiled at the attention.

Chandler turned toward her. "With help and prayer, she will."

"When you said you would help, did you mean it?"

Chandler hesitated. "If it's in my power."

She bit her lower lip, and her gaze slid to the ground. "The investigator stressed that the police and Commonwealth's Attorney might not feel there was enough evidence to proceed. Do you know anyone who could help?"

"You mean an attorney?"

"Yes." Her hands fisted at her sides. "I'm over my head, but I have to make sure Tiffany knows I did everything I could."

Chandler didn't want to get involved, not that deeply. It seemed too much like what he did at work—but this Tiffany, the one playing with Aslan, was so different from the broken girl inside the interview room. "Have you talked to a victim's advocate? The county should have one for you."

"Not yet." She shrugged her thin shoulders. "Not sure that will be enough. I'd like someone who cares about us. I don't want to be just one of the two hundred people she's helping."

"When do you want to meet with someone?"

"Now. Before I lose my courage. This is too important."

A name came to mind. A woman he'd known as a kid, a couple years younger than him, who'd gone to law school. "Let me make a couple calls, see if I can get an appointment for you."

"Thank you." The words were quiet, spoken away from him as Ms. Ange watched her daughter.

"I'll need your first name if I get an appointment."

"Madeline. Madeline Ange."

"Let me see what I can do." Twenty minutes later he had a meeting scheduled for Monday and had promised to meet Madeline there if he could get the time off—though as he examined her older model Toyota he wondered if he should pick her up instead. Was this whole thing a good idea? Or was he going to find himself embedded in another situation he couldn't fix?

As he drove toward Old Town, Chandler wondered if he'd regret taking his involvement deeper.

CHAPTER 8

Jaime had barely had time to kick off her shoes and rub her feet to work the knots out from a day in heels when her phone buzzed. It had been a long, emotional day, and she was ready to ignore the world—but her phone rang so rarely that it must represent an emergency of some sort. She glanced at the screen before clicking on the call. "Caroline?"

"Hey, Jaime. It's still all right to come over, right?"

"Sure." What else could she say? Her friend needed help, and Jaime would not have survived Con Law second semester without Caroline's careful and meticulous prodding and outlining.

"Great! I just need to know where to park."

"What?"

"I'm here with my suitcases, and I've circled the block a couple times. Y'all don't have much in the way of parking around here."

"That's why I paid for a slot I don't really need." Not with the Metro a block away. There were a few visitor slots, but she'd need to plan for a longer-term solution. "How long are you planning on staying again?"

"A week. No longer than two."

Jaime bit back a groan.

"So where can I park?"

"That's a great question. Pull into one of the slots up front while I run down and check with the desk."

A few minutes later she stood in front of the security/concierge desk. The place didn't really need security because of its slightly out-of-the-way location, but someone important had moved in earlier in the year, and the security had appeared. Based on the level of upgrades, she did not want to know her new neighbor. Definitely a situation of ignorance being bliss.

After twenty minutes of wrangling and about that many calls from Caroline—which she ignored—Jaime was the proud owner of one very expensive bonus parking space paid for by the week.

She met Caroline at the drive and climbed into the classic Mustang. She hooked the tag on the rearview mirror. "The moment you leave I need this back so the charges quit accruing."

"You mean you're paying by the day for my parking?"

"No, you are."

"Right. I'll give my apartment manager the bill and tell them to get those floors stripped and refinished stat."

After Caroline slid her car into the pricey slot, Jaime helped her lug her suitcases to the elevator and then into the apartment. The moment the bags were stacked next to the door, the space that had always been adequate shrank to ridiculously small. Caroline blinked as she looked around.

"This is nice, Jaime. Is that where I'll sleep?" She pointed to the small futon Jaime had had since college.

Jaime cringed at the acknowledgment that she'd never had the girls over.

"I've been meaning to get a real couch." Every time she about had the money saved, something else demanded it, like new tires for the car she tried not to drive. Why did life have to cost so much?

"I'm grateful you're giving me a place to rest my weary head." While she could tell Caroline meant the comment to be light, there was an underlying stress vibrating her words.

"Everything okay?"

"Sure."

Definitely not. Well, Jaime was a queen of pressing an issue if it meant she could avoid her own. "You've got to be thirsty. I know I am after hauling your stuff up here. Have a seat on that old thing, and I'll get us some sweet tea."

"I don't want to be a bother."

Jaime could lie and say Caroline wouldn't be, but it had been a long time since her friend had shared. If Caroline were in her shoes, she'd press until Jaime finally came clean. This was her turn to be the friend she often needed.

"We all need to drink."

Caroline laughed. "When you put it that way, how can I say no?"

It only took a few steps to reach the tiny galley kitchen. The subway tile backsplash with small stainless appliances and granite countertop made her kitchen feel modern. There might not be much to it, but she didn't need more. She only had silverware, plates, and glasses for four—enough to host Hayden, Emilie, and Caroline, if such an occasion ever arrived.

She poured two tall glasses of tea and handed one to Caroline.

"Thanks."

"My pleasure." Jaime took a sip, unsure how to start the questions. "So you're sure everything is okay?"

"Of course."

There was a long pause, and Jaime let the silence stretch as though Caroline were a reluctant witness.

"No. I don't know."

"That sounds about right."

"I'm not like you, Jaime. I don't have a clear line for my future."

"I don't know that mine is a direct path."

"Oh, it is. You've had opportunities to leave criminal defense work, but you never do."

"It's my calling."

"But why? We took the same criminal law and criminal procedure classes, but you don't see me on the defense side."

"No, you carry their futures with appeals."

"How did you know that this is where you're supposed to be?"

Jaime could only stare at her friend. Caroline was the one who always wore a smile and a carefree tone in her words. Sure, she was deep, but she carefully schooled that for work. Everywhere else she was the friend who brought an occasionally quirky sense of humor and a real sense of caring. "I drank the Kool-Aid in class. You were gone that day."

"No, really. And you know I never skipped class."

That was true; Caroline had been that responsible. It'd been kind of sickening to watch her walk around the law school perpetually carrying a can of Dr Pepper in one hand and a textbook in the other.

Jaime took a breath. "This isn't anything you haven't heard before." Though tonight the words didn't pour out as easily as other times. "I believe in our system. Enough that I want to protect it. Without effective advocates, even for the guilty, the system collapses and government gets too strong. To protect the innocent, I have to also fight for the guilty."

"You still believe that?"

"The criminal process isn't perfect." She knew how far from that it was. "So I do what I can." She took another breath. "I went to the Commonwealth's Attorney today."

Caroline startled. "For what? Are you changing jobs?"

Jaime snorted. "No. I'm working with Mitch McDermott to file charges against Dane."

"Really? Wow." Silence settled and stretched as Caroline took a sip of her tea, all the while keeping her gaze locked on Jaime. "I admire you, you know."

"Why?"

"You're righting a wrong that is twenty years old. That takes real courage." Caroline was one of a handful who knew Jaime's story, and she held it in highest trust.

"Maybe."

"It does."

Jaime wished she felt brave. She sat next to Caroline, wishing her life sparkled like her kitchen. In truth, she was more worn and abused than this futon she'd dragged through her adult life. And some things couldn't be fixed with a simple swipe of a credit card.

"There is no statute of limitations on sexual abuse."

His attorney's words echoed through Dane's mind, and he knew he would have to take severe actions to halt his niece in her tracks.

His thoughts raced and then suddenly stilled. It was so simple he should have done it years ago. His brother, the perfect one, the one who would never see his next promotion because he followed the book to the letter, needed to be informed of what had transpired.

He would tell his brother that his most precious thing, his daughter, had gone crazy and filed criminal charges against him, her uncle. It would only take a moment to throw that family into chaos.

He grinned.

Jaime wouldn't expect the offensive move.

It was ideal.

It had been so easy to appear to be the perfect, helpful brother-in-law. The one poised to fill every gap left by his brother's deployment. He'd snapped when Bill became a hero all over again, settling his plane on a postage stamp of a strip without loss of life in the middle of a sandstorm. The dramatic landing had been caught on someone's camera. Next thing Dane knew, he was seeing the stupid sequence over and over and over again on all the newscasts.

Each time he'd gritted his teeth hard against the reality that his brother was lauded while he was left to babysit.

He picked up his phone.

Selected Bill's number.

Waited as it rang. Again and again. Over and over.

Then his brother picked up.

Dane smiled. This would be fun.

CHAPTER 9

The night's hand pressed Jaime as she huddled in her bed. She hadn't wanted to come. Had begged to stay home. Promised she would stay out of her mother's way.

She wasn't home.

She was here.

In the place where shadows smothered her.

It felt like the time she'd jumped in a lake without her life jacket. She'd been pulled under, and no matter how she struggled and twisted, she couldn't find the surface. She'd been so afraid. Then Daddy had come. He'd saved her. Tugged her back into the boat. She'd lain on her side and thrown up so much water.

Daddy wasn't here to save her.

And the shadow knew.

The shadow would overwhelm her, and she was too weak to stay in the light.

The door creaked open.

She held her breath. Squeezed her eyes tight. Maybe if she prayed, the shadow would go away.

God, help me. She wanted to speak the words, but her throat had clamped shut. She could barely breathe. The words repeated in her head. Over and over. Like a sad song on repeat. The kind that would drive Mommy crazy.

Maybe if she clung to the prayer, she would be safe.

Jaime clutched her teddy bear. Thought her prayer. Again and *again. Then the mattress heaved as the bed squeaked. The shadow was here. He was real . . .*

Jaime launched up in bed, gasping for air. She looked frantically around the room, the light she always kept on next to her bed insufficient to push back the darkness of the night.

She heard feet padding toward her door.

God, help me. The panicked prayer rose from her thoughts even as she knew how fruitless it was. God hadn't helped her when she was eight. He certainly wouldn't bother now.

"Jaime?" Caroline's voice edged through Jaime's panic. "You okay?"

"I'm fine." The words escaped in a yell, and Jaime wished she could recall and quiet them.

"It doesn't sound like you're fine." There was a pause. "Can I come in?"

"No."

The doorknob twisted and the door creaked open. "I brought you a glass of water."

"I don't need a drink."

"Let me come in, Jaime."

Jaime wanted to argue but couldn't. The sheets were wrapped around her feet like twisting barnacles. The diffuser had turned off and only the faintest scent of lavender hung in the air, so she must have slept for a while. Her gaze landed on the teddy bear next to her, and she batted it off the bed before turning back to the door, but Caroline had already stepped inside the room.

"Come on in, since you already are."

"This isn't the first night you've had a nightmare." It wasn't a question.

"I thought he was here."

Who lingered between them, the unspoken name known to both.

"What can I do?"

"I want to forget, but my mind won't let me. Can you help with that?"

"I can listen."

The thought terrified Jaime because Caroline meant it. She would crawl into the pain with Jaime, and Jaime couldn't let her. It was too dark there; a tarry substance would saturate Caroline's light, overwhelming it until it was extinguished. Ruining another life . . . she couldn't do that. "I'm fine."

"You aren't." Caroline handed her the glass of water, then sank to the floor next to the bed, her gaze tethering Jaime to this moment. "You have a story. There are chapters to your life, and some of them are horrible, but they are all chapters. It's up to you how much weight you give them and how long they last."

"It's not that simple." Fatigue pressed against Jaime. Another night of disrupted sleep. "I don't want to argue with you, Caroline." She glanced at the clock on her nightstand. "It's after three. If you want to get any sleep, you need to start counting sheep."

Caroline frowned at her and crossed her arms. "Maybe this is why I'm here. To help you through confronting your uncle."

"I don't need help." The idea made her want to spring from the bed and punch something harder than she'd flung her poor teddy bear.

"We all do. If I can be that for you, I'd count it a privilege."

She didn't want Caroline to know every sentence of her story. It was too gothic and tragic for Caroline's Pollyanna view of the world. "Some chapters are too personal."

"And some only lead to freedom when shared."

Her friend's words pierced Jaime.

That was exactly what Jaime had promised she'd never do. As she stared at her feet, tangled in layers of sheet and blanket, she heard a soft murmuring next to her. While she'd denied needing help, she couldn't stop listening as Caroline prayed for her and her heart.

SATURDAY, OCTOBER 6

Morning dawned well before Jaime was ready. Her nightmare shadowed her waking and the start of her day. She had to find a way to remove Dane's hold on her life. If the nightmares were already this disruptive, what would they be like after he was served with the charges from the Commonwealth's Attorney? The clanking of cupboard doors opening and shutting filtered through the bedroom door. Jaime groaned and pulled a pillow over her head.

Then the shower started, and when it turned off fifteen minutes later, Jaime's brain had switched on. She threw back the covers and pulled her robe from the foot of the bed. Good thing she'd placed it there last night, or she would have headed into her living area in her nightgown glory. Maybe she could pretend Caroline hadn't seen it in the wee hours of the morning when she was huddled under her white comforter.

Caroline grinned at her, a towel wrapped around her head like a turban. "Good morning. If I were my grandma I'd add 'Merry Sunshine,' but I'm not."

"That's a good thing." Jaime tried not to growl as she headed toward the Keurig parked on the countertop.

"I thought we could get coffee at Ebenezer's before heading to church."

Jaime froze with her hand curled around a pod of French roast. "I don't go to church." Besides, didn't Caroline know it was Saturday?

"Maybe you could today. There's a service project I think you'd enjoy. It's for kids." Caroline smiled sweetly at her. "I'll throw in a scone or muffin. Your choice. I notice you don't have much in the way of food."

"I said, I don't do church." The hardness in her voice reflected the rock-hardness of her certainty. If this untouchable God wouldn't be bothered when she'd been a child who needed His protection, then she wouldn't bother with Him now. Not even if Caroline turned on the puppy dog eyes. "No."

"Oh, fine. Then join me for coffee. I'll still buy the scone."

Maybe she could do that. "We'll drive separately."

"Or walk to the place around the corner." Her eyes twinkled at Jaime in a disturbingly happy way. "I haven't given up on you joining me at church, but it doesn't need to be today."

Jaime nudged Caroline's shoulder. It was practically a hip check considering how petite her friend was next to her. "Don't press your luck. But I desperately need that coffee."

Fifteen minutes later she was sitting at a table in the hole-in-the-wall, artsy coffee shop around the corner, a steaming café latte spiked with peppermint syrup in front of her, next to a plate holding a decadent carrot cake muffin with cream cheese frosting. She'd need to log an hour on the stationary bike if she wanted to eat each luscious calorie without worrying about where it landed, but it would be worth it.

Caroline was talking animatedly about something, but Jaime's attention kept drifting. The nightmare's tentacles weren't releasing. What would Uncle Dane do? She was sure he'd get a summons that didn't require actual jail time—at least not yet. Even so, his reaction wouldn't be good. But she had to move forward.

"You're not listening to me," Caroline pouted as she played with her maple scone.

"I am."

"Really?" Her friend arched an eyebrow in that precise way of all truly Southern women. "Then tell me what I was saying."

"How worried you are about your apartment."

She huffed. "Good guess."

Jaime laughed, then leaned back against the overstuffed chair. "You're easy to read."

"Here I thought it was that beautiful man that had your attention."

"What?" Jaime startled and looked around. "I wasn't looking at a guy."

"Too bad, because he's staring at you. If I were his girlfriend I'd be jealous."

"Then he certainly wasn't looking at me. That doesn't happen."

"Happens all the time, but you choose not to see." Caroline shook her head. "Don't look now, but he's coming our way."

Jaime froze as her gaze connected with her neighbor with the out-of-control dog. What was his name? Yeah, like she'd forget the name of a man who looked like a modern Steve Rogers. She found herself drawn into Chandler's slightly questioning gaze.

"Don't even pretend to tell me you don't know him," Caroline murmured.

"Let's, um . . ." Jaime licked her suddenly dry lips and wished she could guzzle her coffee to knock the dryness from her parched throat. "Don't be ridiculous, Caroline."

"Whatever." She all but rolled her eyes and stuck out her tongue. So juvenile, and yet somehow so perfect.

Jaime tried to glance away from Chandler, but he had arrested her attention. Maybe she'd been too frustrated at their first encounter to notice the way he didn't threaten her like most tall, powerful men with a military bearing. Instead, there was something friendly in the air as he ambled her way. Not good. She needed to take control from the start.

"Where's your lion?" she snapped.

Confusion flashed across his face and tightened the skin around those perfect blue eyes. "You mean my dog? As I recall, you were the one with the wimpy lion."

She shook her head as Caroline looked between them with her mouth hanging open. Jaime gave her friend a look. "You might want to be careful or you'll catch flies."

"Whatever." Caroline smiled her dazzling perfect smile and extended her hand. "I'm Caroline Bragg. You are?"

"Chandler Bolton." He shook her hand.

"It's a pleasure."

A barista called his name, but he lingered.

"You'd better get that before your coffee gets cold," Jaime said.

He smiled at her. "How's Simba? That's his name, right?"

She wasn't going to . . . She was too mature to roll her eyes . . . But oh, he brought that out in her. "Fine."

Caroline stood. "I'll grab the coffee while y'all spar."

"You don't need to do that." Chandler's words were quick, but Caroline was already off to the counter. Chandler watched her sashay away, then shook his head as he turned back to Jaime. "Is she always so—"

"Sassy?"

"I would have said spunky."

"Yes."

"Hmm."

"Here's your drink." Caroline offered the to-go cup to him.

"Thanks." Chandler took the cup and turned to Jaime. "See you around. I'll try to keep Aslan from Simba. He's taken a liking to that cat."

The quirk at the corner of his mouth made Jaime wonder if he might feel the same.

As he walked toward the door, Caroline fanned herself with a napkin. "Whoo. You didn't tell me there was a man in your life."

"He is not 'in my life.' We've spent exactly ten minutes together—and they weren't ten good minutes."

"Well, I'd try another ten. That man is into you."

As he exited the building without a backward glance, Jaime told herself Caroline was wrong. But as she watched, Chandler stopped to dig out his keys and looked in her direction. Their gazes collided through the window, and she felt a jolt. Maybe her friend wasn't as crazy as Jaime wanted to believe.

CHAPTER 10

The afternoon rays of sun were shifting through the gauzy curtains at the window when Jaime walked back into her apartment. Caroline had tried one more time this morning to talk her into church. Even if Caroline had had a great time serving kids the day before, Jaime wasn't interested.

Her friend had left a copy of the *Washington Post* on the island, open to a page in the Metro section, and Jaime was trying hard to ignore the headline: *Congress Moves Forward with Confirmation Hearings for Army Generals.* A row of stale headshots was lined beneath. Dane's dark gaze stared at her from the middle, and a roar of anger built inside her. There wasn't enough peppermint tea or quiet music in the world to soothe her. She grabbed a Sharpie from the junk drawer and scribbled all over his image until he disappeared.

She turned her back on the island and moved to the small couch. Why did her home feel so empty and crowded at the same time?

It was empty of people and full of dark memories. It hadn't bothered her before Caroline arrived.

Simba strolled out of the bedroom with a meow. He walked between her legs and chirped to be picked up.

"All right, birdie." She scooped him up and rubbed his belly as he purred. Her phone vibrated off the edge of the couch, and she bent down to pick it up, Simba lounging over her arm like an unconcerned trapeze artist hanging upside down from a bar.

We'll be there in thirty minutes. We need to talk.

What? Why were her parents coming over? Their relationship worked best at a distance. It was . . . challenging . . . nothing like *Leave It to Beaver.*

Should she call or wait to see if they showed up?

She typed in one word and hit Enter. Why?

Your father got a call from your uncle.

Bile churned into overdrive in her stomach. This was a conversation she did not want to have, yet she had known her parents would hear about the criminal case. She should have let them hear it from her instead of from Dane.

I'll be here.

Jaime hurried into the kitchen and pulled a brownie mix from the cupboard. At least she could try to distract her father with warm, chocolaty goodness. It would probably be as effective as drinking a Coke in front of a dentist, but she had to try.

Her thoughts churned as she stirred the gooey treat. How had Dane heard already? Surely he hadn't been served in the forty-eight hours since she'd talked to Mitch. Did his network spread into the Commonwealth's Attorney's office? She shuddered at the thought, flipping brownie goo onto the countertop.

The front door opened, and Jaime froze. They couldn't be here already.

"Hey, Jaime. I stopped and got us salads." Caroline set a bag on the island.

The woman didn't have to feed her every day, but it was nice that she did.

"Thanks. I'm . . . um . . . going to have company in a bit."

"Oh? Do you need me to leave for a while?"

Caroline didn't need to hear the conversation, but how could Jaime kick her out? "If you have some errand to run that might be good."

"Can I eat first?"

"Sure." Jaime finished stirring the mix, poured it into a pan, and slid it into the warm oven before grabbing the salad Caroline had brought her. Her friend didn't press and instead told her about the church service—something Jaime could ignore while she listened for footsteps.

As the oven's timer buzzed, a heavy knock shook the door.

Caroline started and almost fell off her stool. "What on earth?"

"Guess my parents are here."

"Oh, good. I've never met them. Well, that once at graduation."

No, not good at all. Jaime slid on oven mitts and pulled the brownies out, then dropped the oven mitts next to the pan. Caroline looked at her like she was crazy, so she hurried around the island to the door.

She opened the door with a fake smile that faltered the moment she saw her father's mottled neck and face.

"I got a call from Dane last night." Her father stood marine straight and would have intimidated her if she hadn't seen him like this before . . . when he was around.

"Hello to you too." She failed to keep the bite out of her voice. Could he ever come simply to see her? Did there always have to be a mission?

"Bill, why don't we sit first." Her mother meant the words to calm, but instead they stirred up familiar anxiety. If only she would decisively stand up for Jaime. "What's that great smell?"

"We need answers, Joann."

"We do, but we'll hear them better if we're comfortable." Her mother brushed past her father.

Joann Nichols was nearly as tall as her daughter, and she wasn't a pushover. She gave Caroline a curious look. "Hello there. Who's this?"

"I'm Caroline. Jaime's letting me stay with her for a few days. I'll get out of your way." She turned to grab her purse and mouthed the words *You okay?* At Jaime's nod she slipped out the door.

"I . . ." Jaime's voice caught in her throat. The look on her father's tight face froze the words in her throat, trapping all her carefully planned thoughts.

He powered past her without a hug, and she felt bereft, years of longing for a father's comforting and safe embrace welling up in a moisture she couldn't release.

She wanted to believe twenty years would make the telling easier. Instead, as she considered her mother's concerned eyes, she felt the words rooted inside, deep and stubborn. Her mom hadn't heard her as a scared eight-year-old. Her father hadn't heard her jumbled pleas for help as a relieved father returning from another tour.

Why would they believe her now?

The voice she'd worked so hard to gain turned mute.

Caroline blew back in the front door. "I got outside and realized that church wore me out. I think I'll rest for a bit in your bedroom, Jaime, if that's okay."

Jaime almost sagged with relief. Maybe Caroline's presence would corral her father's response. As the bedroom door clicked behind her roommate, Jaime slid into the kitchen.

"Can I get you something to drink, or a brownie? I just pulled them out."

Her father sat, and the futon sagged. "Nothing here stiff enough to help."

Jaime wanted to explain there was a reason for that. She couldn't trust herself with anything potentially addictive. She'd learned the hard way in college that it was too easy to self-medicate in destructive ways. That's when she'd turned to things like essential oils. Smelling the right scent was now enough to remind her to take a few breaths.

Mom sank next to him. "Honey, what is going on?"

Jaime cleared her throat and then rubbed her slick palms down her jeans. She tugged at a snag where she'd caught the left leg on something. Funny how jeans could be slashed, ripped, and torn and still look fashionable, while a snag made them imperfect rejects. She swallowed and fought back the panic. She needed to speak the truth. She needed to spit it out and know they heard her voice, her story.

"Honey?" Her mother leaned forward again. "Are you okay?"

"Can you explain why Dane called me with the crazy story that my daughter has pressed criminal charges against him?" The skin around her father's eyes tightened, the clue he was barely restraining his anger.

"I . . ." The words blocked her throat.

"Whatever it is, we're here for you." Mom patted her father's knee, and he took a slow breath.

"But you weren't." Jaime felt a tear release, and she fought to keep her breaths even. The dam breaking after so many years. Could she hold it back? Keep a torrent from being released?

Her mother edged closer. "Let me get you something to drink."

"No, Mom." Her words were sharp, and her mother flinched. "I don't need a drink. What I need is for you to listen."

CHAPTER 11

Her father leaned back against the couch as if the few extra inches would keep him out of her orbit of crazy. "That's why we're here."

Oh, Daddy. If he only understood how much she'd needed him.

Her mother sank against the couch's back, then exchanged a worried look with her father. Jaime could feel the tug to surrender to the silence. To let her thoughts slip to a safe place where she didn't have to tell her parents they'd been betrayed by someone who should have protected her and honored the family relationship.

That his evil still filled her dreams twenty years later. That she was destined for a life alone because the thought of intimacy with a man made her throw up. That she was marked as damaged goods in a way that predators sensed and that sent good men running.

That she'd learned all of this in college when she was desperate to fill the holes in her soul. When alcohol had about taken her under when the boys couldn't. That she had fought her way to the surface the hard and long way. That she determined isolation was better than submitting to the call of darkness that yawned within her.

Jaime didn't even know she'd started rocking on her feet until Caroline slipped up next to her and pulled her into a hug. How had her friend known to come out of the bedroom?

"I can't do this." Her words were muffled as she sank her forehead onto Caroline's bony shoulder. Her friend rubbed her back and shushed her like she was a child who needed comforting.

How very true that was.

She'd needed comforting.

But she'd needed protection more.

If her parents had defended her, the comfort wouldn't be needed. And maybe her voice wouldn't be trapped so deep inside all she could hear was the echoing scream. If she opened her mouth, would the scream escape? And if it did, could she silence it?

"I'm making tea."

Jaime sensed her mother standing and then moving toward the sink. Caroline continued to rub her back, and Jaime wished she could succumb to numbness, pretend this disastrous conversation could be avoided. Through it all, her father never moved. Frozen in place.

Before Jaime could collect her courage, her mother returned. Somehow she had found a tray and four mugs.

"I didn't even know I had those." Jaime wiped a tear from the corner of her eye.

Caroline gave her another quick squeeze. "I'll sneak out of the way, but I'll be praying." She looked deep into Jaime's eyes, her gaze sober and focused. "You can do this."

Jaime nodded, then accepted a mug from her mom. The warmth didn't seep into her fingers. She tugged a stool from the island and sank onto it and clutched the mug. Maybe her counselor had been right all those years ago. It would take supreme courage to confront her parents and let them into her pain.

She studied the green tea as if somewhere in the depths of the hot beverage she would find the words. "Uncle Dane molested me while Dad was in Iraq." She pushed the words out as fast as she could. "I went to the Commonwealth's Attorney this week, and they are pursuing criminal charges."

The words gushed from her to fall in the space with a thud.

Her father set his mug down and stared at her the way he

probably stared at the soldiers under his command. It was the same glare he'd turned on any young man who dared to ask her out while she lived at home. If only he'd understood then how unnecessary that had been—she'd been too scared to let any guy close in high school.

"Explain yourself." Daddy's words fell like weights, clanking against the laminate floor.

"It should be enough that I'm telling you."

"I don't understand." The color had blanched from Mom's face.

"There's not much to explain. Every time you sent me to Dane's, I dreaded bedtime and what happened in the dark."

"She knows about this?" Dad launched to his feet, his volume escalating with each word as he pointed toward the bedroom door. "Your friend knows, but your parents are just finding out?"

"Caroline knows the edges. I've talked to the Commonwealth's Attorney. Charges are filed, and Dane will be exposed."

"Exposed?" The words thundered into the space. "What do you mean, Jaime?"

Jaime pressed her fingers against her closed eyes. "I refuse to let the truth hide in the shadows one moment more. People need to know what he did to me before he harms someone else. I've wondered for years if I was the only one or if there are more, but I didn't know how to find out. I still don't, but I know I've remained silent too long."

"But why didn't you tell me?" Mom clenched her hands as if that would hold her together.

"I tried the best way I knew."

"This is the first time I've heard these words. After twenty years?" The words were heavy and sad. "I'm sorry, Jaime, but I don't understand."

"He groomed me like I was some special pet." The next words rushed out of her on a flood of tears. "And you didn't stop him."

Her mother looked devastated by the words, but Jaime couldn't take them back because they were true.

Two hours later her dad looked like he was ready to go hunt down his brother and take revenge. Minimal color had returned to her mother's cheeks.

"I don't know what Dane will do." Her father's words sounded lost in the void of her pain. "You have to be careful, Jaime. There's a lot at stake for him right now. Did you know he is up for a promotion?"

"I didn't know when I made my decision and went to the CA." Jaime rubbed her eyes. "I saw it in today's paper."

"What can we do, honey?"

"Nothing, Mom." That would be the hardest for her mother, truly realizing that today there was nothing she could do to remove the pain.

Her mother shook her head. "There is always something."

"Not this time." Jaime wanted to lie down and put this horrible afternoon behind her.

"Yes." Her mother stood and started collecting the empty mugs. "I can love you well in ways I didn't before." She hurried to the kitchen sink, and her shoulders slumped as she looked away. "I'm so sorry."

Her whispered words barely reached Jaime, but she clutched them to herself like a bouquet of wilted flowers. They might be late, but they sat in the space between mother and daughter, waiting to be accepted. "I know."

Her father stood and moved toward the front door. "I need to think about this."

"I understand." Jaime watched her parents leave, feeling the space between them that her confession had enlarged.

The door closed, and she felt drained. Emptied of caring. She wanted to sink onto her bed, pull the covers over her head, and never come out. She wasn't an eight-year-old anymore. She didn't have to ask for permission to speak and just pray someone would hear.

She was speaking. She would be heard.

Her gaze landed on the pan of brownies, untouched. An offering ignored.

CHAPTER 12

Monday morning Jaime arrived at work later than usual. Her sleep had been interrupted by her parents' doubts and disbelief, making her ignore her alarm. Then Caroline had jumped in front of her for the bathroom, and Jaime had let her.

Shouldn't she feel better after the long conversation with her parents, that the barrier between them had been exposed? She had tried hard not to blame her mother in her retelling, but the woman had left the apartment looking like she'd been gutted.

The work was piled up on her desk, another three cases added over the weekend and more coming. Looked like the police had been busy.

Her intercom buzzed, and she jerked from the file she was reviewing. "Yes?"

"The boss wants to see you. I'd hurry." The urgency in Gina the receptionist's voice caught her attention.

"All right. I'll be there as soon as I'm done with this file."

"He said immediately." Gina's voice lowered. "I think he's serious, Jaime."

"Okay. On my way." She clicked the intercom off and collected a notepad and pen. A minute later she rapped on Grant Joshua's door. "You wanted to see me?"

He looked up from a document he was holding. "We have a problem. Take a seat."

"All right." In her job a problem could be any of a dozen things. "What happened?"

"Read for yourself." He handed her the papers.

She took them and scanned the letter on top, and her hands began to tremble as she absorbed the heading. "An ethics complaint? Really?"

Why would the Virginia State Bar threaten to steal what mattered most to her, what she had worked so hard to create? She could sense her legal career teetering on the brink.

Grant spoke. "This leaves me no choice."

She jerked her gaze from the form to her boss. "What do you mean?"

He leaned back, hands clasped over his trim middle. The man managed to run mini-marathons while operating the Alexandria County Public Defender's office on a shoestring budget. The caseload alone should have him reaching for a Krispy Kreme every chance he got, but he directed all his energy into his work and his running.

"This ethics complaint forces me to put you on leave. It'll be paid for two weeks while we wait to see what direction it goes."

"Two weeks? That's not even time for them to decide what kind of investigation this will get."

"It's that or resign."

Jaime opened and closed her mouth, but no sound escaped. She swallowed and forced back the fog gathering in her mind. She had worked too hard to get where she was. She wasn't walking away without a fight. "I have a trial next week. In fact, I should be preparing for it right now." She thrust the paper back at him, but Grant stayed infuriatingly distant behind his desk.

"I'll give the trial to Evan Reagan. He can get a continuance."

"But it's my case. I've spent six months wrangling with the prosecutor and preparing witnesses."

"Give your notes to Evan. He'll be fine."

Evan was so wet behind the ears; she didn't know how he afforded this job with the years of student loans he must have. "But . . ." She sputtered to a stop as Grant raised a hand.

"Grab what you need for two weeks. Consider it a paid vacation. Get a good attorney, fight the disciplinary action, and we'll talk when it's settled."

"That'll take more than two weeks." Her shoulders slumped as she read the hard determination along his jaw. He wasn't budging.

"We'll reevaluate later." He finally leaned forward, as if engaged in the conversation for the first time. "Jaime, you're one of my best defenders. The fire you have is something I wish I could give all my attorneys, but you can't do your job while you're distracted by this. Take care of the charge, then come back ready to protect the innocent and provide a fair trial for the guilty."

She studied him another minute, then pushed to her feet. Nothing she said would matter, so she might as well get started with a plan to salvage her career. "Yes, sir."

She turned toward the door. If she was really going on this "sabbatical," then she needed to get the Parron file ready to hand to Evan. All six banker boxes of it.

"Jaime?"

She sighed and turned back. "Yes, sir."

"Better take this with you." He fluttered the stupid packet in his fingers.

She snatched it from him, trying to hide the darkness that wanted to snarl out of her. Why had he seen it before her anyway? It had been addressed to her and should have landed on her desk.

"Jaime." There was warning in his tone.

"This wasn't addressed to you."

"Take a break." The words were a hard order.

"Yes, sir."

Whipping around before he could see the moisture edging into her eyes, she gritted her teeth and strode toward her office, refusing to make eye contact with anyone. When she reached the safety of her office, she slammed the door behind her. Let them hear.

She leaned against the closed door, all the fight leaching away. Her battered desk was ancient gray metal of some sort that had surely seen service during World War II, but it was hers. Or had been. She sank into her chair, fingers stroking the arms where the fake leather had rubbed away to soft nubs.

Her mind felt as blank as her computer monitor, dark in sleep mode. She should pull up her trial notes on the Parron matter for Evan, but she didn't want to. This was her case. She reread the letter from the Virginia State Bar. Disciplinary proceedings? Her?

She was careful, meticulous, committed to giving her clients the best defense possible. She stared at the figurine of Michelangelo's *David* where it sat next to her phone. Few people realized that the seemingly perfect statue came from an unfinished, marred block of Carrara marble. Even fewer realized there was a fault in one of David's feet that could cause the entire statue to crumble, one reason he had been placed precisely in position at the Academia in Florence—to minimize vibrations.

That's how her life felt: one fault line away from fracturing into a million pieces that could never be recreated into a shadow of who she'd become.

A rap at her door pulled her head from her study of the replica.

Evan Reagan stood there, looking lanky and untried in his off-the-rack suit that hung on his frame. "Grant told me to see you about Parron."

She gave him the first of the boxes and promised to email him anything else he might need. As he walked away, her gaze landed on the ethics letter again. She needed help, so she called the person she could rely on. "Savannah, do you have a minute?"

"I was getting ready to call you. I need your perspective on a potential client."

"You've already got a team of good attorneys there." Some of the best Jaime knew.

"Yes, but if what I've heard is correct, this case needs you. Can you get away?"

There was the tone that communicated Savannah needed her and knew she'd respond. What else could she do for the woman who had helped her survive law school and find a practice she enjoyed?

"This client is one you won't want to miss. We meet in twenty minutes."

Jaime sighed, but it was worthless to argue. And besides, she suddenly had a completely free schedule. "Actually, I can come, but I don't know about twenty minutes."

But Savannah had already hung up in that abrupt yet endearing way of hers.

She knew Jaime would come because Jaime understood Savannah wouldn't ask if she didn't mean it. Savannah didn't waste anyone's time, least of all her own.

The heavy box Jaime carried as she left the office was filled with the things she thought she might need, but its weight was nothing compared to the heaviness of heart. The elevator took her down to the lobby. She needed to step out, carry the box to her car, and drive away from the only job that mattered to her. Despite assurances, she knew the paid leave wouldn't last. Her days at the public defender's office could end if the ethics charge stuck.

The elevator doors began to slide shut, but she didn't move.

Why not ride back up?

Then down.

She had no reason to stay.

No reason to leave.

The doors opened again and a man in a suit, someone she vaguely recognized from some meet and greet, entered. "Which floor?"

"First." She refused to make eye contact. This wasn't a day in which she could hoist her shield and keep people from seeing how shattered she was. A stranger could take one look at her and read her soul.

And today that would not be a pretty sight.

Then she inhaled, and her breath froze as the man's cologne tickled her nose. That scent. She was instantly back in her uncle's apartment and felt the pressure of blackness. She tried to tell herself that the man in the elevator wasn't her uncle, even if he wore the same cologne.

The doors opened, and she couldn't move.

"Are you okay?"

She nodded because she couldn't find a drop of saliva in her throat to lubricate words.

The man held the door for her, and Jaime reluctantly exited. She placed one foot in front of the other, her heels clicking against the fake marble as she made her way across the lobby, through the door that led to the parking garage, and then down the second elevator to where her old sedan was parked. She opened the trunk and set the box inside. Then she scurried to the driver's side, climbed in, and locked the door. Her breath gushed in and out, and she tried to slow down.

This wasn't the way her life was going to play out. In a broken-down car leaving a broken-down career. She had a vision and purpose.

It didn't matter that the ethics claim was fabricated. Her boss had no tolerance for anything that might undercut his authority in the courtroom. Today that "anything" was her. Tomorrow it could be some other unsuspecting attorney who was faithfully doing the job.

She tossed her purse into the passenger seat and then lowered her head until it hit the steering wheel.

The scent of the stranger's cologne still lingered in her nose.

She wanted to be brave, to pretend her world wasn't crashing around her head, but she couldn't. She stayed where she was, wishing she could cry. Instead, she gulped huge lungfuls of air and tried to calm her thoughts and pretend she was in control.

The problem was she wasn't.

She hadn't been this out of control since she was eight years old.

She'd vowed to never place herself in a vulnerable position again. Well, she wouldn't. Her jaw tightened and her fingers clenched. There had to be a way to make this whole mess disappear.

CHAPTER 13

Traffic was stop-and-go along the Jefferson Davis highway, but eventually she pulled into the small parking lot behind Savannah's storefront office. What was Caroline's car doing there? Jaime double-checked her phone for the time. It was barely after noon, so Caroline should be slogging through a pile of motions and briefs for at least four more hours.

A sneaking suspicion made Jaime sit in the car a minute.

This wouldn't be another one of Savannah's interventions, would it?

That woman could be worse than a den mother at times. The last thing Jaime needed or wanted was a bunch of her friends holding her hand and asking questions, especially under the guise of helping a client.

She. Was. Fine.

She turned the car back on but couldn't put it in reverse. What if it wasn't what she expected and Savannah really needed her help? She moaned and collapsed against the steering wheel.

Could she do it?

Could she walk in there and pretend she didn't understand what was happening?

Could she give that to her friends?

She wanted to, oh, how she wanted to. They'd given her so much. But all she felt was the churning and the warning that if she let them past her wall, they'd decide she was too much work.

She kept a safe distance, so no one saw the depth of her pain and the ugliness of her scars. They thought they knew, but they didn't understand a shadow.

Something knocked at her window, and she yelped.

"You okay, ma'am?" The words were muffled through the closed window, but she barely noticed as she looked up into the bluest eyes she'd seen . . . in several days. They were the kind of eyes that begged you to sink into their depths, something she would never do. A small quirk to the man's lips communicated he recognized her too.

Jaime pressed the button to lower the car window inches to answer without letting the cold air in. "Can I help you?" She tried to insert the right note of *back off buddy* into her words.

He held up his hands. "Just making sure you're okay. I'll take the snark as a yes."

What was he doing here? Chandler Bolton had been a nonentity in her life until his dog chased her cat a week ago. Now she saw him everywhere? Really?

Maybe he wasn't human. Maybe he'd been sent to keep her safe in some twisted *It's a Wonderful Life* remake. Each time she saw him, a piece of her was drawn to the dream. Yeah, more like an illusion. The reality was he'd turn into a toad that only gave you warts when you kissed him.

"I'm fine. Thanks." She rolled up the window and gathered her things. After she turned off the car, she slid from it.

He was still watching her, and she was tempted to say, "Nothing to see here." Instead, she lifted her chin and walked by without a word.

———

What was she doing here?

The princess tipped her chin and closed her eyes as if walling herself off. He couldn't figure her out. She refused to look at him in such a determined way he wanted to laugh. He shrugged. Whatever made her life better. Yet he caught an edge of a cloak of sadness. Maybe she was intimidated by him. It wouldn't be the first time his height did that, though she was taller than most women . . . with the look of an Amazon warrior princess. Would she be a perfect fit under his chin?

He knew better than to give more than someone was willing to take. When Rianna left, she'd taken his heart with her. It had taken a while to repair it, and he didn't need to hand it over to another dark-haired beauty to mangle what remained.

He'd slipped outside the law offices of Daniels, McCarthy & Associates to grab his tablet from his car and check on Aslan. The law firm's interior was too perfect for a big mutt like Aslan, no matter how well the dog was trained.

He wasn't convinced he should even be here, but his childhood friend Angela Thrasher had promised that her colleagues could help Madeline Ange navigate the legal environment she found herself in.

When the woman had followed him out of the interview at the county building, he hadn't wanted to get involved, but he couldn't abandon a child who needed help. He'd had too many experiences where he couldn't help.

He blinked back the image of convoys that didn't make it back. Of innocents harmed in explosions.

Today would be different even if it made him uncomfortable.

He slipped back into the building and paused in the reception area. The TV playing in the background displayed some news program focused on Capitol Hill. Looked like another hearing. Those were a dime a dozen unless Congress was recessed, and even then the agencies kept busy. The next recess would be the week of Thanksgiving. A little over a month until the members left town.

The headline indicated that the talking heads were focused on new military appointments. There'd been a time he would have cared, but with his position at the Vet Center, other decisions had more bearing on his day-to-day than who gave the orders to troops on the ground.

Madeline's daughter, Tiffany, sat at a small table under the watchful eye of the receptionist. The lady was prepared; she'd pulled out a tub of crayons and coloring books, followed by a bucket of Legos and a stack of books for kids of all ages.

Angela entered the reception area and spoke to him. "Thanks for referring Ms. Ange."

"She needs an advocate."

"This is the right place." Angela glanced at the receptionist, who smiled warmly at her, then pointed her chin at Tiffany, as if in warning. Angela nodded, then gestured to the door. "Chandler, I'd like your take on something, if you have a minute."

Tiffany was absorbed in building some sort of colorful eclectic structure with the Duplos, her tongue between her teeth. Chandler felt protective of her in a way he hadn't since the little girl in Afghanistan, the one he'd sheltered with his body.

"Shouldn't I stay with her?" He didn't know who had hurt the child, but it wouldn't happen again while he stood watch.

"She'll be fine." The receptionist gave him a calm look. "I won't leave her. We'll have a good time, won't we, Tiffany?"

The little girl nodded, then added a bright green block to her tower. "I have to make a castle for Winnie-the-Pooh." She held up a smallish character that stood on a Duplo.

"He'll like that very much." The woman shooed Chandler toward the door. "It's not a good idea to leave those women waiting. No telling what they'll generate in their whirlwind."

Angela waited for him to open the door, then led him down the hallway. While not as public a space as the lobby, it still had professional warmth. The walls were painted a light shade of gray, and colorful modern paintings were spaced along one wall at shoulder level. On the opposite wall, framed images of the attorneys with a list of their accomplishments felt like invitations to know them rather than braggy bios, but Angela's pace didn't allow more than a glance.

She paused in front of a door, then squared her shoulders and opened it.

Madeline sat at one end of a long wooden table with two women on the other side, an older woman and—"Jaime?" He sank onto a chair opposite.

She nodded, but it felt like a regal acknowledgment rather than an admission that they'd met before—and just had a conversation in the parking lot.

The older woman glanced between them, and Jaime gave a reluctant sigh. "Savannah, this is Chandler Bolton, my neighbor. Chandler, Savannah Daniels is one of the best civil attorneys in the state. Ms. Ange will be well served."

"And your role?" He didn't mean for the words to sound hard, but he didn't like her tone.

"Consultant." She returned her attention to Madeline. Her face softened as she tapped her pen against her notepad. "Your friend was telling us what happened."

Madeline looked at him in alarm. "Is Tiffany all right?"

"Building a tall Duplo tower under the watchful eye of the receptionist." He settled against the chair. "What do you need from me?"

"Tell us about your dog." Savannah, who could only be ten or so years older than his ancient-feeling thirty-one, leaned forward, elbows resting on the table as she focused on him.

"He's been trained as a comfort dog."

"Meaning . . ." The word lingered as pens hovered above legal pads.

Chandler filled them in on Aslan's training and preparation

to be available for the traumatized. "He helped unlock Tiffany's words during her interview."

"Hmmm." Jaime settled back and eyed him. "How exactly did he do that?"

"By being there." Madeline's voice was small. "He sat next to my baby and loved on her until she broke down. He made her feel safe." Tears slid down her cheeks.

He tried to keep his focus on the conversation, but as the crying continued he felt more uncomfortable with each second. Chandler wanted to find the guy and make him pay before he could inflict this pain on anyone else.

CHAPTER 14

MONDAY, OCTOBER 8

The office had emptied now that the mother and child had left, taking Chandler with them. Savannah stayed in her chair, and Jaime did the same.

"Thanks for coming, Jaime." Savannah considered her with that caring scrutiny she had.

"I'm glad you called. Is Caroline here?"

"No, she left her car here while she ran an errand." Savannah waved the question aside as she continued to study Jaime. "You sure you can handle helping with Tiffany's case?"

Jaime nodded. "As it happens, I have plenty of time. I need to talk to you about why." Jaime pulled the bar charges from her purse and handed the letter to Savannah. "I need your professional opinion."

Savannah took the letter. "An ethics charge?"

"Yes."

"Give me a second to read it."

Jaime tried to still the energy bouncing through her legs as she watched Savannah read the letter. It felt like each second stretched to an hour. Why hadn't her mentor already evaluated it? Savannah excelled at executive function, processing information and decisions before most people could scan a document. The silence stretched till Jaime felt the need to speak.

"Do you think this is serious?"

Savannah peered over the papers at her. "Really, Jaime. Give me a minute to finish."

"You're the fastest reader I know. The fact you aren't already telling me what to do means this is serious."

"Then don't ask my opinion," Savannah drawled. Not a pronounced Southern accent, just enough to let people know she was a transplant. She settled back against her leather executive chair, and Jaime was surprised she didn't kick her feet on top of the desk.

Jaime resorted to counting the ceiling tiles. She could be patient. When she had to. And this seemed like the perfect, terrible definition. She'd started counting the rows of colors in the carpet when Savannah finally leaned forward.

"We can fight this, but it's going to take time."

"Savannah, I need to work."

"It's a paid leave, right?"

Jaime frowned. "For two weeks."

"Then think of this as a sabbatical."

"But I don't want to take time off like this."

"You get to."

"Argh." Jaime tried to stare a hole through the stupid paper as if destroying it with X-ray vision would somehow erase the words and right her world. No one understood how much she needed her job to know her life had purpose and meaning.

Savannah leaned forward with the same sympathy she'd used when talking Jaime off the ledge during the brutal days of legal research and writing. "You'll get through this."

"Thank you." The words fell flat. Things didn't go right for her. Life was a struggle for survival. Had been since she was eight. She closed her eyes. Pushed back the images and reminded herself, "I have a voice."

"Of course you do." Savannah quirked an eyebrow as she studied Jaime.

"Sorry. Whom should I hire to help me?"

"Don't want to use your own voice on this?"

"No."

"Good. You know the old joke . . . An attorney who hires herself . . ."

". . . has a fool for a client."

"Exactly." Savannah handed the letter to Jaime. "Photocopy this for me in the other room. I'll get to work on your response. I just need some details from you."

Before long Jaime was explaining the entire trial. "It was one of those times when I knew my client was guilty."

"Did it give you any pause?"

"What do you mean?"

"Did you do less than your best? Not pursue witnesses, investigate less rigorously?"

"Absolutely not." Jaime crossed her arms and stared at Savannah. "You know me better than that."

"This panel doesn't." Savannah leaned forward and stared intently at Jaime. "You have to convince them you didn't shirk your ethical obligations."

Jaime thrust back her shoulders. "I exceed them because I believe the hope that people are innocent until proven guilty."

"Why do you call it a hope?"

"For every innocent person I defend, I know four or five clients did what they were charged with. It's just a question of whether they did what the Commonwealth's Attorney claims. Our system doesn't work without someone like me making sure all accused, regardless of whether they are innocent or guilty, have a fair opportunity to defend themselves."

"Why you?"

"Because someone has to give the innocent a voice and hold the system accountable for the guilty." The words erupted from her in a volcano of passion. "If the prosecution could act without restraint, our system would fail and no one would find justice."

"Good." Savannah's lips tipped up at the edges. "Remember that as we fight through this. It won't be easy."

"Thank you." Jaime cleared her throat. "What do you need from me right now?"

"A list of what happened at the trial. Everything you did. Why you did or didn't do it. Remember, the people on this review board are a mix of two attorneys and one non-attorney. We have to show you did exactly what every reasonable defense attorney would do at the investigation stage."

That was all. It sounded simple, but Jaime knew it was anything but. The reality was each trial required its own strategy and approach. It was too easy to armchair quarterback and see things that shoulda, coulda, woulda been done differently. This complaint could end the career she'd carefully built case by case. "Would you be worried in my position?"

"I'd find the best attorney I could and leave it to him or her to make something happen." Savannah settled against her chair. "The question is what do you want?"

"I want my career back."

"Then we proceed." She reached toward her computer keyboard and hit a few keys. "I'll be in touch."

"One more thing. The Commonwealth's Attorney has pressed charges against my uncle. I think he's been served, because he called my dad on Saturday." The words slipped out, and Jaime wanted them back.

Savannah paused. "What do you mean?"

"Now was the time to see if charges were even possible."

"You've known since law school there is no statute of limitations."

"I had to get strong enough." Jaime glanced at her fingers that trembled in her lap. "What if Dane's somehow involved in these charges?"

"I don't see how that's possible. Not if the charges were just served."

Jaime nodded, any words of explanation stuck in her throat. "Thank you."

And Jaime left, because that was all she could do.

When Chandler returned to work after the appointment at the law firm, Beth waved him down. "Perfect timing. There's a call for you on line two."

"Thanks." Really, he wasn't thankful. He needed a couple hours to tackle the piles of work waiting on his desk before he could put this Monday behind him.

"I can take a message if it helps. It's been one of those months." Beth's gaze speared him in place.

"It's okay, I've got it." A minute later he was in his office where he grabbed his phone and clicked it on as he walked around his desk. "This is Bolton."

"It's me again." The voice was vaguely familiar but indistinct.

Chandler pulled the phone from his ear and then put it back. "I'm sorry, but who is this?"

"We talked Friday."

Chandler settled onto his chair and pulled a scrap of paper in front of him for notes. "What can I do for you? Are you ready to set up an appointment?"

"Talking doesn't solve anything."

"You might be surprised. I've watched relief spread across the faces of men as they talked."

The man snorted. "I thought you were military."

"I am." Always would be. You couldn't give years to the country and not have it change you permanently.

"How do you sleep at night?"

"On a bed with pillows." That answer was more flippant than he'd intended. "I'll admit there are still nightmares, but they're easing." And he had to believe that would continue.

"Must be nice." A click followed by silence telegraphed that the man was done talking.

Chandler set the phone down and took a couple quick notes.

He couldn't do anything with what the man had said. There were too many questions, but the man had called twice, on back-to-back business days. He was reaching out for something but didn't seem to know what. That would make helping him difficult but not unusual. The military didn't foster an environment that encouraged discussing weakness. If it did, maybe it would be easier for those returning to the States to articulate the events they'd experienced. Leaving an experience buried deep only increased its hold.

He slipped the note into a folder he labeled *Pending Matters*. He then set that file on top of another new one, this one filled with research on the new military scandal. The calls were continuing to come in, not just in this office but in the three hundred Vet Centers across the country. The needs were deep and raw, predominantly women who had learned someone they trusted had betrayed them in an intimate way. Chandler funneled those calls to the skilled women on his team. They had the heart and words to connect at the deep levels. It would be inappropriate for him to try. And even if he felt qualified, many of the women who were calling wouldn't easily trust a man.

The sexual abuse scandals filling the headlines were new and old at the same time. Words and investigations wouldn't end the activity. The deviants would simply find another place to hide.

All he could do was the next thing.

The challenge was understanding what that was and how to best serve those in pain.

CHAPTER 15

The apartment felt small, the walls closing in on her as Jaime lay in bed with no reason to get up. It had been years since she'd lacked a reason to launch from bed on a weekday morning.

Yet now, nothing.

And if she were honest, her reaction inside the elevator yesterday had freaked her out.

Would she sense Dane everywhere with something as simple as a scent serving as a trigger?

She might not be strong enough to handle that.

Just thinking those words made anger boil inside her.

She didn't want her world to shrink to the space of her apartment while she waited to see what would happen with the ethics charges.

She threw back the covers and slid her feet into slippers before heading into the living space. She grabbed the remote on her way past the TV and turned it on as she took the fifteen steps to the galley kitchen.

Simba stretched from his perch on the tiny shabby chic table and then moved to the edge and stuck out a paw toward her as if he wanted to bat her nose.

"Hey, buddy." She grabbed his paw and pulled him next to her. Her hand ran along his soft spine, and he nuzzled her fingers.

"Wish you could keep me company while I work out." Having Caroline as a roommate, even temporarily, highlighted how isolated she'd become. A run on a treadmill in the building's fitness center would help her manage her stress and boredom.

Jaime was fifteen minutes into a workout when the door opened and Captain America walked in. She stumbled on the belt and then steadied herself on the arms of the machine, praying he hadn't noticed.

He headed toward the weights, then caught her gaze in the floor-to-ceiling mirrors. "I haven't seen you here before."

She tried to keep her voice steady and her posture erect as he changed course and stepped onto the treadmill next to hers. "I thought when your dog attacked my cat, you'd figure out I live here."

"It wasn't an attack, Jaime." He turned on the machine and got it moving at a quick clip.

He grinned at her as his legs ate up the treadmill's speed. He wasn't that much taller than her five foot nine—probably just over six feet—but he sure made it look easier than it felt to her. There had been a time exercise outdoors had been her salvation. She blew a strand of hair that had slipped from her headband. Of course, he had to come in when she was unshowered and on the verge of doing more than glistening.

Not that she cared.

She pushed the speed up a few ticks. Now she was at a fast walk but not quite a jog, as he loped along. She glanced at his reflection in the mirror. He looked comfortable and ready to settle in for a long run.

Guess she might as well make conversation. "How often are you here?"

"I run at least five times a week. Do it here if it's not nice enough to run outside."

That explained the Captain America physique.

"Mind if I turn on the TV?" he asked, not sounding at all out of breath.

"Sure." She wouldn't stay much longer, not when his presence pushed her off balance. He didn't need to know how short her time had been. Next time she'd bring a magazine to cover the control panel. And monstrous headphones so she could slip them on and look unavailable. Just in case.

He clicked to a news station, and she tried to ignore it. The last thing she needed was talking heads yapping about nothing.

This was ridiculous.

No man, in person or on the screen, was going to deter her from her plan.

She bumped the pace up.

She might be on hiatus, but her life was far from over. And she was not going to let her concerns about this man whom she barely knew change what little she could accomplish for the day. She could use this leave to focus on her fitness and help Savannah with Tiffany's case. In fact, she should knock out the material Savannah had asked for. She smiled. That would give her day needed purpose.

The treadmill belt picked up speed, and she jogged to keep up. She glanced at Chandler's readout. How could he go so much faster than she was and make it look easy? Long legs were unfair. That's all there was to it.

She glanced at the TV, where two men in suits relaxed while ogling a pretty blonde in a too-short skirt reading some prepared script for a local morning show. Video of several men in military uniforms rolled, and Jaime's steps hitched. She flailed for the handles and double-timed her pace.

"Turn it up." She didn't want to know, but then she saw her uncle's face. Or was it just someone who looked like him? She shuddered but wanted to know what they were saying.

"What?" Chandler clicked a few buttons, and words popped up on the screen.

"I need to hear what they're saying."

He clicked a few more buttons, but the story had ended by the time she could understand what they were talking about.

"That what you need?"

"Never mind. You can turn it down now." It wasn't his fault the story was over. But as her hands trembled on the treadmill's handlebars, she wished she could deep breathe her way out of the building tension.

"Anyone ever tell you you're bossy?"

"All the time." Yet few knew that being tightly in control was what held her life together. Because as appealing as Chandler Bolton might be from a distance, she knew that up close he would find her lacking.

What was happening between her ears? He really wanted to know, because the signals she sent were crazy. A mix of come-hither and stay-thee-far-away.

As he watched, she hit the stop button on the treadmill and slowed down before hopping to the side.

He hadn't seen her in the workout room before; she seemed unfamiliar with the equipment. And why was she leaving so soon . . . Did she want to get away from him that much?

It wasn't Aslan, since the dog was upstairs in the apartment. And Chandler knew he wasn't misreading her cautious interest. He wanted to know what was behind that hesitation, because he didn't think it was directed at him. Their interactions had been insufficient for her to decide he wasn't worth the effort.

His phone vibrated, and he glanced at the screen. Rianna? Why was his ex contacting him? He hadn't spoken with her since the divorce was finalized a year ago.

He shrugged. His gaze drifted back to Jaime, who had stepped off the treadmill on the side farthest from him.

"Answer your phone," she said. "I'm leaving anyway."

"No need." Not when he had someone more interesting standing in front of him. Rianna represented his past. Could Jaime be his future?

The thought ricocheted through him with the force of an IED. He felt exposed in a way he didn't like.

He frowned, then leaned forward to play with his phone, anything to break the direction of his thoughts. He upped the speed on the treadmill until his legs were pumping at about his capacity. This was what he needed. A pounding so intense it forced his focus to stay on the treadmill.

"You okay?" There was something like concern on her face as Jaime watched him.

"It's not every day you get a call from your ex-wife."

Her expression turned to confusion. "You're married?"

"*Ex*-wife. Not anymore." The words hurt, but not like they used to. "Let's just say while I was stationed overseas my wife decided she was too lonely to wait."

"I'm . . . sorry that happened."

"Not your fault." He tried to keep the words light.

"But I can hate you came home to that."

There was something healing in her words and the way she acknowledged the pain of his experience. "Thank you."

This time it was her phone that buzzed. She glanced at it, and the color drained from her face.

"My turn to ask if you're okay."

"I will be, but I need to get to court. Enjoy your workout." She pivoted and hurried toward the door with a quick look over her shoulder.

He shouldn't have mentioned his divorce, not now. That would always be part of his story, but maybe it wasn't wise to lead with it. Oh well, he couldn't unsay it.

He upped his intensity level to the crazy level and then kept it there for fifteen more minutes . . . as if he could sweat her from his system.

CHAPTER 16

Jaime walked across the parking lot to the courthouse, butter-flies flying in anything but formation. Dane was waiting within for the first hearing related to her charges. Mitch's text had thrown her into an adrenaline-laced rush. Somehow the email he'd sent her with details on the hearing had gotten hung up in his out-box.

The thought of seeing Dane made her feel like an eight-year-old girl begging her mother not to take her to his home. If she could live those days over again, there were so many things she'd do differently. She'd tell her mom why she didn't want to go. If that didn't work, she'd tell her teacher. Someone would have understood what she struggled to put into words and helped her escape.

Today would be different. She'd be in the safety of a court-room. This was her world, not his. And she'd have someone on her side this time, someone who knew the full story.

She forced a bravery she didn't feel into her steps. If she was supposed to fake it until she made it, she'd be faking a very long time. Maybe into the next century.

You've got this, Jaime.

Only she didn't.

At moments like this she wished she could believe in God like her friends did. Hayden's faith was this natural extension of her life. Caroline's flowed from her in bubbly streams. Emilie's might be quieter, but it was a bedrock when life shifted—as it had done significantly last year when her friend was being stalked. But anytime

Jaime dared to consider it, she couldn't escape the reality that God had not bothered to intervene for her when she was an innocent girl.

She wasn't doing badly on her own.

If she ignored the nightmares.

She'd known a recurrence was a risk when she moved forward in her plan to bring Dane to justice, but she hadn't expected to relive the abuse every night. It was like her mind had reverted to being that child who felt out of control, alone, and so scared.

Was it better to yank the Band-Aid off all at once or let it slowly peel back?

Neither felt good.

She lifted her face to the sun and let it warm her even as a chill breeze blew across her shoulders and down her neck. If she wanted to arrive in time, she needed to pick up her pace.

The white stone building towered above the cityscape in the bustling area squeezed between Rosslyn and Clarendon. The courthouse area continued to evolve and pulse with the energy of a hipster locale crammed into a few square blocks. Unlike Old Town Alexandria, this part of Arlington was relatively new, with the courthouse opening in 1994 and many of the buildings around it cropping up after 2000. A slight detour across the paved courtyard led to the movie theater. Turn a little farther and one could slip into the Metro system and be whisked to any corner of the larger DC area. Hayden and Emilie could have Old Town. Jaime liked the energy of these more urban spaces.

And right now she needed that energy to propel her through the metal detector and to the courtroom. This preliminary hearing should be routine, with the CA presenting evidence to establish probable cause for the charges to proceed. Then it would be a grand jury. She'd likely testify at both, since she was the only evidence other than her journal.

The thought had her stomach churning. If it had been so hard to talk to her parents, what would it be like to share her blackest moments with strangers?

She walked down the hallway and took the elevator to the courtroom floor, striding past other attorneys without really noticing them. The civil attorneys wouldn't recognize her unless they'd had reason to appear in criminal court. Most wouldn't dirty their hands.

When she entered the courtroom it was empty, not even a bailiff or clerk lurking in a corner. Then her eyes adjusted to the light and she noticed a man. From across the room, she knew it was Dane. Even seated, the way he held himself reinforced his confidence that he was in control.

She turned to leave. She'd check the hallway for Mitch, then poke her head into the judge's office.

"I wouldn't leave." His voice echoed with authority in the vacant space.

"Why?" She forced the tremble from her voice.

"Because I arranged this time to talk to you."

"Really?" He couldn't do that. Not when a preliminary hearing was required by law.

"The judge is one of my golf buddies."

"Of course. Thanks for the information. I'll be sure to request a change of judge."

His gray gaze bored into her. He gestured to the courtroom. "This isn't going to accomplish a thing."

"Other than seek justice for what you did to me."

"You think this will resolve whatever your twisted mind thinks happened?"

"I do."

"Then you are more delusional than I thought." He eased to his feet in a catlike move, unnerving in its smoothness. Shouldn't he be getting creaky in his advanced years? "No one will believe your allegations."

"The Commonwealth's Attorney already does." She wanted to glance around but kept her eyes locked on Dane. Where was Mitch?

"Everyone knows that cases like this are Lacy's mission in life. It would be easy enough to sway her your direction."

"No swaying needed." Jaime felt the blackness pinpricking the light. No, she wouldn't let him see her weakness. She forced words from her parched throat. "They sensed the truth."

"Then you'll start a war." His eyes were lit with a fire that would consume her if she didn't get away. "There are things you don't comprehend."

"You're right." Her lungs threatened to stop working, her breath coming in the barest sips. "I'll never understand how you could molest an innocent child."

"I didn't do anything to you." His gaze was unflinching.

"I'm leaving." She turned and walked deliberately toward the door, when what she wanted to do was sprint. Put as much distance between them as she could. She felt the light-headed sensation that signaled a panic attack.

"One last thing." His voice commanded her to stop with so much authority he might as well have shouted.

"Yes?" She didn't turn around, couldn't turn around.

"If you continue, I will destroy you."

"I'm not your soldier. I don't follow your orders and won't be cowed by your threats."

"That makes you easier to break."

Jaime tipped her chin, squared her shoulders, and pushed the door open. She had worked too hard to now allow this man to reenter her mind and psyche, but she felt his presence as if tendrils had latched into her soul. She kept moving. Where was Mitch?

He wasn't in the hallway, so she quickly entered the office for circuit court and waited for the judge's assistant, Marlene, to finish a phone call.

The woman looked at her and did a double take. "You okay, Jaime? You look like you've seen a ghost, hon."

A ghost. That was a good way to describe Dane. A man who was a part of her terrible, dark night of the soul, but not a being who could hurt her now. She wasn't a little girl anymore.

"Is the judge ready for the hearing?"

Marlene shook her head, dangly earrings jangling. "No. I called your office to let you know it had to be postponed. An emergency hearing cropped up." She glanced at her desk and tugged a file free from the pile, then slid it toward Jaime. "Are you sure about this?"

"Yes."

"The defendant was in here asking questions. Guess he doesn't plan to hire an attorney. Seems to think he can snap his fingers and make it go away."

"He has that ability at his job."

"Last time I checked, he wasn't the judge." Marlene crossed her arms over her chest and leaned back with attitude. "Anyway, thought you'd want to know he's unrepresented."

"Does he know the judge personally?"

"Not that I'm aware of. Why?"

"He said they were golf buddies."

"Then he doesn't know this judge. She hates golf."

"Good. I didn't want to change judges anyway."

"Um-hum." The phone rang, and Marlene glanced at it. "This thing has been ringing all day. Mitch will let you know when we reschedule, probably tomorrow."

"Thanks, Marlene."

She knew Marlene was right. She had to count the cost of this lawsuit. She wanted to finally hold Dane accountable for what he'd done to her. She wanted him to acknowledge the ways she had paid for that violation through high school and college, and still did today with her fear of relationships.

Family was supposed to love and protect you. Yet he hadn't. How could she risk love with anyone else?

Ignoring the elevator, Jaime slipped down the stairs and stopped in an alcove on the first floor to pull up her work calendar on her phone. There were meetings and hearings coming up, some related to the Alexander Parron case. It wouldn't hurt to stop by the PD's office to check on things and make sure Evan didn't have any questions. Maybe her boss would realize how much he needed her and be ready to lift this ridiculous leave. A woman could hope. And it was better than risking seeing Dane on his way out of the court.

CHAPTER 17

Chandler poured over another intake form. It was lunchtime, and his stomach was grumbling, but one of his clients no longer needed services, so he had a slot to fill. For each person who graduated from one of the vet center programs, four more waited to enter. How was he supposed to divine which one to move from the waiting list?

Each application represented a real need.

A rap at the door pulled him from his thoughts. Allison stood in the doorway, a stack of files balanced on her laptop.

"Ready for me?"

"Grateful for your help." It would take hours to wade through the pending files, and he trusted Allison's intuition. The no-nonsense woman had a way of seeing through the paper version to the real person as if she could sniff out a brewing crisis even the client couldn't identify.

She settled onto the chair in front of his desk, and he winced as she sat with a back so straight it looked painful. "Our list is growing."

"There's not much we can do about it." Without more resources, he couldn't get the authorization to hire more staff to help soldiers and airmen and airwomen. That was the harsh reality.

"I think we should revisit holding more group sessions. Those become critical when the need outstrips services."

"How would that work?"

She laid out a developed plan, and he nodded at key points.

"I can tell you've thought hard about this."

She tapped the stack of files. "It's getting more difficult to know who is critical."

"They all feel that way."

"Yes." She flipped along the tabs on the files without opening any. "Each of these individuals has seen things on tours that no one should experience. In a group they can support each other, since they've experienced similar situations and stresses."

"We can try it." Group sessions went against the macho military environment. "How will you create a setting where they can share?"

They talked about logistics, and then Chandler pulled her back to the immediate issue. "So who gets the open slot?" He glanced over the files he still needed to review. "I'll finish these and give you my vote by five."

She nodded, then pushed to her feet and left him to the files. The men and women represented had achieved heroic things in their tours. They had not all received medals or recognition, but he sensed their losses, their fears. Their reentry issues were unrelenting, but they could be managed. Often it just took knowing they had the freedom to talk. Admitting there was an issue and asking for help.

He leaned back in his chair and gazed at the map he'd hung on the wall reflecting his own tours.

Each person had a map like that, if not physical then seared on their consciousness. Superimposed on top of that were the comrades who hadn't returned home.

Chandler's thoughts turned to the mysterious phone calls. What was the caller's story?

The fact that he would call and threaten Chandler indicated that he had serious need of the exact services the Vet Center provided.

How many military members just like that man were in this pile? He couldn't be part of their slipping through the cracks. Maybe trying Allison's groups was the best way to reach more. It was surely a better option than receiving no services while lingering on the waiting list.

His stomach growled loudly enough to break his concentration. Chandler reached for the file cabinet beside the desk and tugged on the drawer that held a stash of soft drinks and sparkling water. He felt around in the drawer and frowned. Empty. Guess he'd have to go out.

He walked past empty offices and then into the open area where a couple work stations were located. Allison looked up from her desk.

"I'm headed to grab a bite. Need anything?"

Allison glanced at her desk, then at the empty reception desk. "I'd join you, but I'm the last man standing during lunch."

"I could bring back something."

"Thanks, I'm good." She patted a container on her desk. "I think the first flood of callers related to the latest sex scandal is slowing."

"That's good news. I'll be back in time for my next appointment." Chandler strode out the front door and walked the couple blocks to one of the restaurants lining the square around the Metro stop. He felt like some tandoori chicken from the Delhi Club. Inside, the butter-colored walls alternated with slices of red to give the small restaurant an exotic feel. Black chairs and tables stood against the colorful backdrop, creating a weight for the space. The line was unexpectedly short, and it didn't take long to enjoy the feast of the lunch buffet. He was pacing himself through some spicy curry when he felt a presence behind him and to his right.

Chandler glanced over his shoulder. At the two-topper nearby sat a man with a Washington Nationals hat pulled low over his face. He was slouched inside an oversized hoodie, making it difficult to determine his actual size.

Then the man reached for a napkin, his chair scraping against the brick floor, and Chandler saw he carried a weapon.

In an instant the dynamic changed.

While military installations were scattered in this area, thanks to the proximity to DC and the Pentagon, that didn't stop many in civilian clothing from telegraphing that they carried.

Casually, Chandler stood to get another plate of food, giving him an opportunity to eyeball the man more directly and assess the risk.

He'd gladly laugh if he were overthinking the matter, but the phone calls on top of his military experience made him cautious. He kept an eye on the man as he started down the buffet line, but when he returned to his seat, the man had disappeared and a note rested on his chair.

Chandler set down the food and picked up the note.

Maybe I'll do to you what you did to me.
Watch your back. You might see me coming.
Then again, maybe you won't.

Chandler frowned. What kind of delusional gobbledygook was this?

He tucked the paper into his jacket pocket and then turned back to his food. The *gulab jamun* he'd put on his plate didn't look like a welcome dessert anymore. He pushed it away and settled his check.

As he walked back to work, he considered the note. He'd only touched it by the edges in case it became evidence. Of what he wasn't sure, but it didn't feel right.

He squared his shoulders and pulled open the door to the office suite. The furnishings were mismatched and looked as though they'd been pulled from a sixties or seventies sitcom set. He marched to the receptionist's desk. She barely glanced at him, so he cleared his throat and glared.

She rolled her eyes but didn't look at him. "What can I do for you?"

"Tell Grant Joshua I need to see him."

Grant Joshua, the public defender, wouldn't be thrilled by his impromptu visit, but he wasn't thrilled it was required. Senator Langdon's ultimatum had left him little choice. He had to apply effective pressure immediately. The promotion was his. Anything else was unacceptable.

"You think that's enough to get him out here?" The woman's sarcasm was thicker than Nutella on a slice of bread. "Unless you have a court order, you can get in line."

"Just pick up the phone and tell him Dane Nichols is here."

CHAPTER 18

It was early afternoon when Jaime reached the Alexandria Public Defender's office. When she walked in, she was surprised to see a stranger at the receptionist's desk. A temp? But the woman was busy on the phone, so Jaime went on back without introducing herself and knocked on Evan Reagan's door.

He glanced up. "Hey, Jaime. What are you doing here?"

"I was in the area. Stopped to see if you needed any help with the Alex Parron defense. Have you had time to go over it?"

He sat back, then gestured to a chair. "It's not your problem anymore. I can handle it."

"I'm sure you can. Still, if there's a way I can help, I'd like to. Alex needs all the friends he can get."

"I've got it, Jaime. It's a straightforward case."

She frowned. While Evan was only a couple years younger, he didn't seem to have the fire in his belly necessary for a case as tricky as Alex's. "Is this job a calling for you?"

He frowned at her, his dark hair flopping in his face. "What do you mean?"

"Do you believe people need a defense when charged, or is this job just a paycheck?"

"Can't it be both?" He spread his hands wide as if placating her. "I promise I'll give him a good defense. He could be guilty, you know."

"Maybe, but the Constitution doesn't say only the innocent deserve its protections."

Evan shrugged. "It's better when I know they're innocent."

"When you figure out how to 'know,' fill me in." Jaime studied him and then took a breath. "Sorry, but I just need to know you're taking care of Parron." She sighed. "He doesn't believe in himself, so you have to."

"Sure. Don't worry about him."

She glanced at his desk and saw the Parron file on top. "Here's what you have to remember about this case. Alex is a man in immense pain. He can't manage that pain without help. You must find a way the jury can relate to him. We all know someone who struggles with chronic pain. That's what the OxyContin was for."

"So he says."

"Yes." She bit back a rebuke. "Right now that's what you focus on. Not whether you believe him. What matters is what the jury believes."

"This isn't my first trial, Jaime."

"Then act like it." The words were strong, but she didn't care.

"If you were so good at this, you would be defending him. Instead, you're defending yourself. At least I'm not under bar scrutiny about my job." He sneered at her, then seemed to catch himself. "I've got this. Focus on your problems, and I'll run his trial."

Jaime stepped back. "Just remember, a stint in prison would kill him." She left the room without another glance.

As she walked past Grant's closed door, she heard heated voices within.

"Jaime is a key employee." Grant's words halted her forward movement. Why would he be talking about her? She glanced both directions in the hallway but saw no one, so she stepped closer to the door.

"Find a way." The deep voice froze Jaime in place. Who was talking to Grant about her?

"If we give it time, this will go away." The placating tone was not the one she was used to from her boss, who represented the worst sort of criminals with firmness. "Don't make this more than it is."

"I'll make sure those photos reach the right audience. I've given you a vehicle to fire her. Do it."

Why would this man pressure her boss to get rid of her? She was excellent at her job and Grant knew it, ethics charges notwithstanding.

Jaime leaned closer.

"But you appreciate your position. People always regret when their younger selves' mistakes resurface." The voice, male, was low and intense.

"This is wrong," Grant said.

"You'll do it."

There was a scraping noise of a chair moving. "I don't like threats."

"This isn't a threat. Do it or the photos will be emailed Thursday." There was another noise. "Don't worry, I'll see myself out."

Jaime scrambled around the corner and then into the lobby. She lingered for a moment, holding the door to the hallway open so she could see who might come out of Grant's office, but the receptionist gave her an irritated glare.

Jaime let the door close, her heart in her throat, and headed out to her car.

Who had the clout to insist she be fired? And would her boss actually do it?

———

Jaime drove toward the law offices of Daniels, McCarthy & Associates and purposefully parked a few blocks away. Maybe the walk and fresh air would clear her head and change her perspective.

Savannah had somehow purchased the brick storefront in the prime real estate market of the historic neighborhood as a solo practitioner. The space had been much too large, but she was filling it with her law student protégés. So far Jaime had dodged suggestions that she join the firm too, but maybe she should consider it.

As she opened the door, she was grateful to see Bella Stoller's welcoming face. The middle-aged receptionist wore her trademark dark suit, a uniform that had always struck Jaime as though the woman were prepared at a moment's notice for a funeral. Guess it was the twisted way Jaime looked at the world. For all she knew, Bella just liked a simple wardrobe with a slimming color.

"Hi Bella. Is Savannah available?"

"She just ran out. Some kind of emergency."

"Any idea when she'll get back?"

"None, but you should grab one of the girls for a coffee break. They could all use it."

"I'm sure they're busy."

"Who's busy?" Hayden entered the reception area with a file, which she set on Bella's desk. She stepped around the desk and hugged Jaime. "What brings you here?"

"Needed to ask Savannah for advice, and I was in the neighborhood."

"That is not what her face was saying a minute ago, when I told her Savannah had hightailed it out of here a bit ago." Bella gave Jaime a look.

"It's nothing terribly pressing." Just the collision of her past and future in an unsettled now.

"Want to grab a cup of coffee?" Hayden turned as if to head back to her office.

Bouncing everything off Hayden would work as well as talking with Savannah. "I could use a mug of tea."

"Come on back. Leigh brought in some homemade muffins. They're super-healthy, and somehow still yummy."

Jaime had to laugh at the way Hayden's nose crinkled. "You say that like muffins can't be healthy."

"Have you seen the calorie counts on those things at coffee shops? But Leigh assures me these can taste good and be nutritious."

Hayden led Jaime down the hallway to the small kitchen at the very end. A table and four chairs filled one wall, and a small refrigerator, stove, and sink the other.

Hayden reached into a cabinet above the dishwasher and pulled out two mugs. She filled one with hot water and pointed to a container. "Help yourself to a tea bag." After filling her own mug with coffee, she took a seat. "What did you want to ask Savannah about?"

Jaime repeatedly dunked her tea bag until it became an obvious stalling tactic. Hayden waited.

Now that she was here, Jaime was almost desperate to avoid the topic that had brought her. But that was the coward's way out, and Jaime was not a coward. "I've pressed charges against my uncle."

CHAPTER 19

Hayden stared at her like she couldn't have heard correctly. "I'm sorry, but you did what?"

"I went to the Commonwealth's Attorney last week."

"Your birthday present to yourself?"

"Yes. She agreed to press charges against Dane. He's been served. And now someone is pressuring the PD to fire me, though I don't know that there's any connection between the two." She blew on the steaming tea, and her hands trembled as she thought of Dane. "He showed up at court this morning. Somehow he knew about the hearing before me and that it had been canceled, and he tried to intimidate me."

"Did it work?"

"I don't want it to. I've been building to this my whole life, and the Commonwealth is taking the case seriously."

"Oh, Jaime. Why now?" Hayden's hands clutched the coffee mug so tightly Jaime hoped it didn't crack.

"I want Dane to admit what happened. He's an overconfident man who believes he can get away with anything."

"Well, he has."

"What if he's hurt others? The thought haunts me at night." She felt the wash of goose bumps. "If he continued and I didn't say or do anything . . ."

"You were eight years old."

"When it started." Jaime sighed, feeling the stretch of the words against old scars. "I could have spoken up since, and I haven't."

"You had to get healthy."

"I'm not sure that's possible anymore. When he was in that courtroom, I froze. Me, Jaime Nichols, the woman who always knows what to say in every situation. I was a little girl again, fighting to prove I'm bigger than he is." She shuddered. "I'll always be that little girl. He did this to me." She blinked rapidly against the moisture that wanted to overflow, then startled as she felt an arm slip around her shoulders.

Emilie leaned into her. "I am so sorry, Jaime."

"Where did you come from?" Jaime cleared her voice and tried to act like she hadn't just alluded to terribly intimate parts of her life.

"I thought I heard your voice and came to investigate. Everything okay?"

"No." Hayden's word punctuated the small room. "Jaime has decided to right the wrongs of the world, and it's coincided with her uncle's possible promotion."

Jaime heard the words from a distance. "That's not why."

"I just saw the headline." Hayden pulled out her cell phone and punched a few buttons. Then she turned the screen toward Jaime. "Your uncle has been nominated for one-star general."

Jaime scanned the article, glad she'd already heard the nomination was viable as she stared at the black words on the small screen. "I need more time for my case to progress."

Emilie sat next to Jaime and rubbed her arm. "What can we do to help?"

"Get a brown bag before I hyperventilate?" She couldn't breathe deeply and felt her old companion panic rising inside her.

Emilie kept rubbing her arm and leaned closer. "Look at me. In the eyes. You're with us and safe."

Jaime tried to nod but could only rock as the tightness squeezed her chest. "I. Can't. Breathe." How could she have been so foolish as to poke the bear that was her uncle?

"We'll get you through this. I promise you won't be alone." Hayden's voice reached her as if through a cave.

"I'm sure Savannah can help."

Jaime wanted to latch on to Emilie's words for dear life.

"You're sure I can help with what?" Savannah stepped into the room, a tailored squall jacket belted over her suit. "What's the convention for?"

Jaime looked up at the woman who'd had such a calming presence on her throughout law school. "I'm an idiot." She forced the words through the narrow opening in her throat.

"I know that's not true." She sank onto the chair opposite Jaime. "All right, ladies, I know you have work to do. Leave me with Jaime." She loosened her belt. "Sorry I wasn't here when you arrived."

Hayden crossed her arms and looked ready to argue, but a look from Emilie stopped her. "We're here for you, Jaime. Maybe I can talk to Senator Wesley."

"Why?" What would that accomplish?

"He's on the Armed Services Committee."

"Oh." The word eased from her. "I'm not sure I can talk to someone like him."

"You might not have a choice."

That's what Jaime was afraid of. That by filing this case, something she needed to do, she had lost control of her choices. Even surrounded by her friends, she felt so alone, like she'd been marooned on an island since childhood.

The moment the two left, Savannah stood and closed the door. "I have about ten minutes before a prospective client arrives."

"I thought I was ready." Jaime sucked in a breath and then blew it out, then sucked in another. The terror was easing, only to be replaced by a boulder-sized knot of worry.

"Thought you were ready for what?"

"To hold my uncle accountable."

Savannah nodded thoughtfully. "That's good. You are ready."

"I thought I was, too, but I didn't realize he was up for promotion when I went to the Commonwealth's Attorney."

"Does that really change anything?" Savannah's calm words penetrated the lifting fog.

Jaime closed her eyes tightly, then eased them open. "No. I need to pursue this for me."

"All right." Savannah sank back and kept a close eye on her. "What's your plan?"

That's right. Time to turn on her left brain and logic this problem out as she would any client's lawsuit. "Hope the Commonwealth's Attorney will keep moving forward with the case."

"Interesting strategy."

"It seems to work." She rubbed her temples because she knew she needed to do something other than wait. "I'll dig through my journals for every line that documents what he did and the subsequent harm."

"Good. Hayden's right that we may need to call the senator for assistance." Savannah leaned forward, and her gaze intensified. "You shouldn't have launched this without calling in your support team."

Jaime nodded, and Savannah's presence touched her with a sweet concern that helped ease the heaviness filling her.

"Now, the Commonwealth's Attorney team is good. If there's a way to get him, they will. And you won't be alone in this fight. I can promise that."

Jaime cleared her throat. "Thank you."

"So what did you want to see me about?"

Jaime blew out a breath. "I overheard someone pressuring the public defender to fire me."

Savannah straightened and reached for her phone, which she used like a tablet to take notes. "What do you mean?"

Jaime related what she had overheard of the conversation.

"And you don't know who it was?"

"No. It was too muffled through the door." Should she mention it might be Dane? "I really couldn't hear, but what if it was Dane?"

Savannah made a notation. "Let's be careful to avoid jumping to conclusions, since you're not sure. And you didn't know Dane was up for promotion?"

"Not when I approached the Commonwealth."

"Okay. But this isn't why you came by. What did you need?"

"I don't remember." Jaime rubbed her forehead, fear and anger warring against her desire to run away. Savannah gave her the space of silence, and she covered her eyes and tried to focus her thoughts. Why *had* she called? She glanced up.

"I wanted to see if you knew anything about the ethics complaint. Any progress or movement? I want to get back to work."

Even if it forced the PD's hand. Would he choose her or who-ever had threatened him?

"I've got a call in and will follow up. These can take months, especially when logged by a criminal defendant proceeding on his own, but I'll move it along as quickly as possible. I'm calling in a couple favors. Next time let us know before you're over your head."

"I'll try."

"Do more than try." She softened her words by leaning forward and brushing Jaime's arm. "You need to let us in. This burden is too much to carry alone."

Ouch. She hated to admit Savannah's point. "Maybe I didn't tell you all because I didn't want to be talked out of it."

"Maybe you should have been."

Sometimes Jaime didn't like her mentor much. "As I said. This is why I didn't tell you."

"It's done now. I can ask some questions about who lodged the ethics charge, since you have a right to know your accuser. I can't promise how quickly I'll have an answer."

"Thank you." If only it didn't feel like she was already on the defensive. Could Dane be behind it? The timeline didn't work, even though she knew her uncle was well placed with friends across government. If he was, what else would he attempt to stop cooperating with the criminal charges? The stakes were so high. She didn't want to consider what he'd risk to silence her.

Her phone beeped, and she glanced at the screen. Mitch? She swiped the screen and scanned the message, and felt the blood drain from her face.

"What's wrong?" Savannah asked.

"The probable cause hearing for the criminal charges against Dane is scheduled for tomorrow morning at eight."

Ready or not, she'd get to confront her uncle again. She didn't feel strong enough. She typed a quick message to her mom.

Probable cause hearing tomorrow. Can you come?

A moment later a reply popped up. Tell me when and where. You are not alone.

If only words could make it true.

CHAPTER 20

The news played from the small television as Jaime worked in the kitchen. The space felt empty, since Caroline hadn't returned from work. The silence made the background noise of two journalists arguing over the latest celebrity sighting a necessity.

Jaime was determined to try to cook, since Caroline, in spite of claiming she had no ability in the kitchen, had made several meals since moving in. Simba prowled beneath Jaime's feet, looking for one of the little bowls of scrambled eggs Caroline slipped him when she thought Jaime wasn't looking.

Then the reporting shifted back to local political news. "Today the Armed Forces subcommittee began hearings for the candidates for one-star general."

Jaime glanced up at the words and froze as an image of her uncle in his dress uniform appeared over the anchor's shoulder along with several other candidates. Then the next story appeared, and Jaime took a breath.

Dane was cropping up everywhere.

She brushed at a spot on the granite countertop as her thoughts raced. The criminal charges would take too long. They still had the grand jury and then trial to proceed through. Even with a speedy trial, it could take months before she had an opportunity to tell her story to a jury and see whether her uncle would be held accountable for his abuse. And that was if the charges survived each stage. Maybe she'd delayed too long to bring him to justice, although he might be dishonorably discharged if found guilty.

Her pulse began to pound a painful rhythm in her head, and she fought to think clearly. There had to be a way to let the world know what the man was really like before he'd be elevated to a higher position.

Maybe Hayden was right and Jaime should meet with Senator Wesley. She pulled over her phone and opened up a web browser. A few clicks later she was looking at the list of members of the Senate Armed Services Committee.

She nibbled at her lip while she considered.

Was she desperate enough to pull one of her best friends that tightly into the fray? Would Dane go after Hayden if he learned Jaime had asked for her help? Because she knew Hayden would do it with the intense focus of someone who loved fighting for the underdog and holding Goliath accountable.

Maybe there was another way.

But ten minutes later Jaime was still staring at the list without generating fresh ideas. Her phone rang, and she leapt at the excuse to derail her dead-end thoughts.

"Hello?"

"Aslan wonders if Simba would like to play." Chandler's teasing voice made a warm feeling spread through her.

But she couldn't allow it. No man would be interested in her without focusing on the wrong things once he knew her history. Chandler would be no different. Yet her heart wanted to believe. The words that slipped from her mouth weren't the ones she'd intended.

"I'd like that, but I think I'll leave Simba at home."

Chandler laughed. "Aslan will be disappointed, but I'll prepare him."

"I need a few minutes. Wait for me in the lobby. I'll be down in fifteen." Jaime filled a glass with water and drank it quickly. Maybe that would convince her stomach she was full, since her dinner plans had stalled with the story on her uncle. Then she hurried into her bathroom to freshen up. As she looked in the mirror, she noticed the purple circles under her eyes from lack of sleep. It was a miracle no one had mentioned them, because they looked like bruises.

After brushing her teeth and swiping on some tinted lip balm, she grabbed a down vest and a hat and headed to the elevator.

When he spotted her, Chandler jerked to attention. "Hey. You look great."

She frowned, biting back a protest. Why would he think that when she hadn't tried . . . much? She knelt in front of Aslan and rubbed his neck. "Hey, boy."

"What? You talk to the dog and ignore me?" Chandler mock pouted, and it only made him more appealing. How did he do that?

"A woman has to have her priorities." She stood and looked at him, chin tipped slightly so she could meet his gaze. Bad idea. Those blue eyes bored into her.

"I hope one of those priorities is to get some coffee."

"Coffee?" *I didn't agree to that.*

"Promise I don't bite." He smirked. "At least not on Tuesdays."

"Nice." She shook her head and shoved her hands into her vest pockets. "Lead on."

They strolled the path that curved along the Potomac and then away toward a small neighborhood, periodic streetlamps casting halos of light along the wide sidewalk. An occasional jogger or brisk walker passed them, but for the most part they had the space to themselves, and she found she wasn't nervous being alone with him.

"You've gone quiet." His deep voice broke into her thoughts.

"Guess I was focused."

"On what?"

"Nothing important." No way would she tell him he'd been the subject. She could imagine how his chest would puff.

"Hmm." He let the silence settle again, the clip of Aslan's nails against the concrete creating a beat for their steps. "Let's go up those steps." He guided her toward a small collection of shops. A sign in the shape of a coffee cup, the words *Savor the Sip* blazoned on it, hung above a door. "You know this place?"

Jaime shook her head.

"I think you'll like it."

She doubted it. How could it be good and this close to her apartment without her hearing about it? Yet when he opened the door for her and the aroma of freshly roasted coffee beans assailed her, she rethought her opinion. She took in the heavy wood counter with a display case of desserts and the tables and chairs scattered among couches. "How did you discover this place?"

"It opened a month ago. One of the ongoing efforts to revitalize the area. That's why some of the other storefronts are still empty."

He commanded Aslan to lie down by the door and then led Jaime to the menu board. He ordered a decaf Americano, and she settled on a latte.

"Sure you don't want something sweet?"

"I'm a basic kind of gal." Keep expectations low and it was hard to be disappointed.

He must have seen a flash of that sentiment in her face, because after he paid, he stepped closer. "Jaime, you can want more."

The words ricocheted through her. Want more?

Not an option.

Chandler hadn't expected his short sentence to bounce across her face in a cascade of distrust to disdain to dismay.

"You wouldn't understand."

The words felt like a punch to his solar plexus.

"Really?" At least give him a chance.

"There are some things only the person who experienced them can understand."

"And that negates any desire on the part of another person to understand the first?"

"Yes."

The word cracked through the space between them. She looked ready for battle, fists on her hips, shoulders squared.

He took a step back and slid his hands into his back pockets. "Every person who's lived more than a few years has experienced some trials and tragedies. I've seen more than I care to share. I'm military, remember?"

"Can't forget." Her tone suggested she wished she could.

"You don't strike me as a peace activist."

"You know me well enough to judge?"

"Maybe I want to."

"Don't hold your breath." She sank onto the couch and glanced around. "We need to lower our voices."

She was right. He wanted to ease onto the couch next to her, but it didn't take a psychologist to warn him that wasn't his best idea. Instead, he glanced toward the counter where the barista was setting their drinks. "I'll get those."

When he returned a moment later, she had curled into the corner. He handed her the mug of steamed milk and coffee, then hesitated.

"You can sit."

She patted the cushion next to her, but he didn't quite buy the turnaround in attitude. "You're an interesting woman, Jaime Nichols."

She watched him over her mug, her dark eyes intoxicating in their intensity. "Is that your way of saying I'm difficult?"

He grinned at her, the grin that usually had women swooning just a bit. No reaction. "Maybe a bit."

Her gaze dropped as she took a sip of the latte. "I know I am." She held the mug tightly with both hands as if trying to capture all the heat leaching from its sides. "I don't want to be." Her eyes implored him, like Aslan's when he was repentant over something. "It escapes against my better judgment at times." She quirked an eyebrow as if inviting him to decide her meaning.

Chandler settled against the brushed eggplant suede. There wasn't much room to kick his long legs in front of him, but he tried. "Do you want help?"

"From you?" Her nostrils flared just a bit. ". . . Maybe."

The word was hesitant, as was the twitch of her lips that accompanied it. It took all his willpower to drag his gaze back to her eyes. While they were mesmerizing, her lips begged him to lean in. But move too fast, and he was doomed. This woman would bolt in the other direction at the first misstep faster than her cat could skitter away.

She glanced at her watch. "I need to get back. I've got an early morning."

"You sure?" He glanced at her coffee. "That's not decaf."

She met his gaze with the slightest bit of challenge. "Yes. Gotta be at court at eight."

"That's early for a client."

"Not really, but I wish the client wasn't me."

"Where do you need to go? Maybe I can give you a ride." Just to be a helpful neighbor. Not to have the excuse to spend more time with her. Not at all.

"It's only Arlington. I'll hop on the Metro."

"All right." As he followed her to the door, he was more intrigued than ever. Why did she have to go to court? Good thing he knew how to dig for info. But he knew he'd have to tread carefully.

He set his mug in the collection tub next to hers.

Pursuing this multilayered woman would take a carefully constructed plan.

And if there was one thing the military had taught him, it was how to execute on a deliberate approach to victory.

CHAPTER 21

Caroline knocked on her door early with a steaming mug of coffee laced with caramel creamer. "Ready for your big day?"

"No." The word slipped out in a groan. She'd seen every hour on the clock as she tossed and turned through a long and restless night. That full-caff coffee with Chandler had been a bad idea on many levels, not the least of which was the way he'd filled her thoughts.

"This is what you've wanted. A chance to tell your story. I wish I could be there."

"I'm glad you can't." As Caroline's face fell, Jaime raced to explain. "It'll be easier to tell the story without people I love there." Except if her mom and dad showed, that excuse was exposed.

"Then know I'll be praying. You might want to too."

"Why? God doesn't care."

"Take this as a chance to test your theory. Maybe He does but you haven't asked for anything in so long you haven't let Him show you."

"I'd have to be pretty desperate."

"Aren't you?"

Jaime froze at her friend's piercing gaze, and then Caroline handed the coffee over. "I made this for you." She turned to leave but then stopped. "Let them see your hurt. No one can walk away from the reality of your wound. I love you, Jaime."

"I know." The words came out in a whisper as Jaime clutched the mug as tightly as she wanted to control her emotions.

An hour later she was sitting behind the prosecutor's table, waiting for the judge to call the hearing to order. She kept her eyes forward, ignoring Dane sitting at the defense table with a high-priced attorney out of DC. Guess he hadn't decided to represent himself after all. She pulled her gaze back to Mitch. His three-piece suit was a bit over the top even if the tie was GQ perfect.

She glanced back over her shoulder, and her heart stalled when her parents walked in—with Chandler Bolton right behind them.

What on earth was he doing here?

She hadn't given him enough information last night to find her, had she?

She wasn't prepared for him to hear the sordid details.

Judge Anna Thatcher whacked her gavel against the bench. "The probable cause hearing in State v. Nichols is now in session." She glanced at the court reporter. "Everything ready?"

The young man nodded at the judge, who pulled a file in front of her. "We are here for the matter of the probable cause hearing." She rattled off the docket number. "The State may proceed."

Mitch stood and unbuttoned his jacket. "Thank you, Your Honor. The state calls Jaime Nichols."

Sweat slicked her palms as Jaime stood and approached the witness stand. She couldn't ignore the weight of her uncle's gaze. She had known when she approached the Commonwealth's Attorney that the only option was to testify. To do it at this stage meant the prosecutor felt unsure they could survive the probable cause stage without her testimony. But while she understood, it left her feeling vulnerable. Anything she said gave her uncle and his defense team ammunition and insight if this survived to trial.

She was grateful that her parents were there supporting her, but the weight of their questions only added to the heaviness that threatened to overwhelm her.

What if she blew it?

She felt the vise lock her lungs as spots dotted the edges of her vision. Quickly she slipped her wrist to her nose and inhaled the lavender oil she'd dabbed there that morning; she felt calm begin to slide into place.

Mitch's look communicated his concern, and she gave him a small nod as steel stiffened her spine. She had to do this. The costs were too high to allow Dane to continue to appear as someone cloaked in light and goodness when such evil filled his soul.

She walked to the witness box.

The judge looked down over the rim of her reading glasses. "Do you swear the testimony you are about to give is the truth and nothing but the truth, so help you God?"

"I do."

"Then you may be seated." The judged turned her attention to Mitch. "You may ask your questions. However, keep in mind this is only the probable cause hearing. I will not grant wide latitude with your questions, as the scope of this hearing is whether these charges will proceed to grand jury."

"Understood, Your Honor." Mitch stood as Jaime settled into the large chair behind the witness stand. The microphone poised on the edge of the stand hadn't intimidated her all the times she'd been an attorney, but from this side it loomed large.

She shifted against the fake leather and then reminded herself to freeze like a rock. This was about looking resolute and not letting them see her fear. She tipped her chin and met Mitch's gaze.

"Ms. Nichols, there is a fundamental question I need to ask. Why wait this long to approach the Commonwealth's Attorney with your allegations?"

Even though she'd known he'd start with this question, it hit her in the chest. *Give the answer you rehearsed in front of the bathroom mirror.* "I needed to know I could be taken seriously."

"Why should you be taken more seriously now?"

"I went to law school in part to learn if there was anything I could do about the violations and abuse I received at Dane Nichols's hands." She lifted her chin in hopes of stemming the tears that wanted release.

"So you've spent the last ten years preparing?"

"Not preparing as much as learning. I knew this would be painful and disruptive." The words felt so rigid and tight. What had Caroline told her? Let them see the hurt she'd buried all these years . . . Could she relinquish her control like that?

"Is this a trap to ruin your uncle's career?"

She blinked. Where had that question come from? It wasn't one they had discussed. "No. I didn't know until I started digging that there was no statute of limitations on sexual assault crimes. I was afraid I'd waited too long, but at eighteen I wasn't strong enough to fight for myself."

"But now you are?"

"Yes. And I can't live with myself if I don't do everything I can to make sure he isn't hurting other children."

From there Mitch went back on script with questions about when the abuse had occurred and why nothing was done at the time of the crimes.

"I didn't know how to tell my mother, and my father was deployed outside the country. After that tour, if my father and his brother were deployed, it was at the same time, and I never went to Dane's apartment or home without my parents. Once I was an adult, I made sure our paths did not cross." She felt the tremor in her hands and wished the court allowed a comfort animal like Aslan to rest at her feet. If she felt this upset and unsettled, how much more threatening this situation would be for a child like Tiffany.

"I have no further questions." Mitch sat, and as much as Jaime wanted to dash for the prosecution's table, she forced herself to wait.

The judge turned to the defense table. "Roger?"

"I have a few questions." As the man stood and buttoned his suit coat, Jaime braced for the barrage that was sure to come. "Ms. Nichols, you tell a nice tale, but why should the court believe any of this happened? Aren't you out to humiliate your uncle?"

"No. I want to make sure he can't hurt anyone else."

"Can you prove any of this alleged abuse happened? Did you go to a hospital?"

"No."

"Was any sort of rape assessment conducted?"

"No. I was eight and not talking."

"Was child protective services called?"

"No." She felt anger pressing up but forced herself to remain outwardly calm. She knew exactly what he was attempting since she'd used the same technique with witnesses herself. Badger, and eventually they would lose their cool and authority.

"How about any law enforcement organization?"

"No."

"You want the judge to believe your testimony alone—because there is no physical evidence?"

"Yes." She gritted her teeth to keep from exploding. Mitch caught her gaze and barely shook his head. She had to control her emotions. But then she caught Chandler's eyes, and the pain she saw there speared her. He shouldn't be here, shouldn't hear this in such a casual way.

"Is there any corroborating evidence?"

"That is up to the Commonwealth's Attorney." She wasn't sure if Mitch planned to admit her journal but didn't want to tip off the defense if she could avoid it.

The defense attorney paused and looked at her, then pulled his reading glasses off his nose and twirled them in his hand. "You don't know?"

"No."

"You're an attorney. A public defender. And you want us to believe you don't know?"

"Yes. I'm not prosecuting this matter."

He smirked at her, and she wanted to knock the expression off his overweight face.

"You want this court to allow the criminal charges to proceed without any evidence to support your allegations?"

"Yes. I want my uncle to be held accountable for the great evil he did to me."

"I see. It's all about revenge."

She bit her tongue so hard she tasted copper. She would not give the man the satisfaction of talking without a question. She was too disciplined for that.

The man glanced at her uncle, but she did not follow his gaze. Instead, she wished she could glance at Chandler again, longing for his steadying gaze.

Her edges were fraying. What was it Caroline had asked her to do? Pray? She still didn't believe God would listen, but she needed help to hold it together. *God, if You care, I need to know You're real. Right now.* The words landed with a thud in her mind.

The defense counsel asked additional questions, forcing her to walk through part of the horror, and she wished her parents hadn't come. She'd wanted to spare them as much of the reality as she could, but as she gave her answers, they heard every word. So did Chandler. This would be the last time she saw him . . . unless all that interested him was a physical relationship.

The man finally looked down at his list of questions and decided he was done. "No more questions."

"You may step down."

Such relief coursed through Jaime at the judge's words, she could barely stand. However, she forced her legs to cooperate and wobbled to the prosecution's table, grateful she'd worn sensible flats. She caught her father's grim look and her mother's shattered one.

They needed to know she didn't blame them anymore. They hadn't known back then, and now that they understood, the brokenness was etched into the lines on their faces.

She sank into the chair, and Mitch slid her a note.

Now it's up to the judge.

Either the judge would allow the case to proceed to grand jury, or she wouldn't.

The woman stared at her notes in silence for a minute, then pulled her glasses off and looked at Mitch. "I find that sufficient testimony was presented to reach the standard of probable cause. This case can proceed to grand jury."

"Thank you, Your Honor."

Jaime exhaled, then froze as Mitch tapped her arm.

"The grand jury hearing will take place on Friday. I'll need you there at nine."

"I'll be there." She didn't look at her uncle. She didn't want to see his reaction, not when he'd been so smug that his expensive lawyer would make it all go away.

The stakes were high for him. Depending on how the case proceeded, it could affect his security clearance and his promotion, might even lead to a dishonorable discharge. Would he let Lady Justice take her course?

And what would he do to her?

What could be worse than what he'd done twenty years ago? But he was a man with power . . . which would only expand if he survived the senate subcommittee hearings.

CHAPTER 22

The words and images of the last hour rolled over Chandler in a kaleidoscope of pain and anger. Now he understood the odd vibe he'd felt from Jaime—and why Daniels, McCarthy & Associates had asked her to consult in Tiffany's case. He sat bolted in place as Dane Nichols exchanged angry words with his attorney and then strode from the room. The man was clearly upset, but not as volcanic as Chandler felt. What he wouldn't give to have ten minutes alone with the general wannabe.

That man represented everything that was wrong with the current military. *If* what Jaime said was true. As he'd watched her testify, he couldn't doubt the horror was real.

How hard had it been for her to sit and listen to Tiffany's story Monday?

He studied this woman he was beginning to care about and acknowledged a deep-seated need to do something to help. The question was what. The image of Tiffany with Aslan flashed through his mind. If his dog has been such a help to the little girl, could he play a similar role with Jaime? Seemed reasonable, except she seemed determined to push the animal away.

His phone buzzed in his pocket, and he tugged it out.

Can Aslan come over?

139

The number was Madeline Ange's, but the accompanying emoji made him suspect Tiffany had grabbed her mom's phone. He'd confirm as soon as he left the court . . . but shouldn't the girl be in school? Maybe he'd need to use a few vacation days to help her. It would make HR happy to have them used.

Jaime eased toward him, looking tentative, and he schooled his features to the neutral expression he would use with a client. A strand of hair had fallen in her face, begging for him to reach out and move it. One glance at her father, who looked ready to break someone in two with his bare fists, was enough to squelch that instinct.

"What are you doing here?" Her words sounded hurt—not what he'd expected.

"I didn't want you to be alone, whatever it was you were facing."

"I wasn't." She gestured toward her parents, who were looking between them.

The mother, an older version of Jaime, stepped forward. "I'm Joann, and this is my husband, Bill. You are?"

"Chandler Bolton." He opened his mouth to say more, but Jaime spoke over him.

"His dog tried to kill Simba."

"Oh." A frown spread across the woman's face. "Why did you come today?"

"Because he doesn't know when he's not wanted." There was so much hurt in Jaime's voice he regretted his ill-conceived idea to attend.

"I didn't know exactly what this was for. I just knew Jaime was stressed and shouldn't be alone." He swallowed. "No one should be alone at a time like this."

The bailiff approached them with a frown. "Y'all will have to leave. There's another hearing scheduled."

"Thank you." Jaime led the way into the hallway. She looked as though she had more to say, but Chandler pulled out his phone.

"If you'll excuse me a minute, I received a text while in there that I need to follow up."

That would give them a moment to collect themselves. There was so much tension in Jaime's parents; the guilt rolled off them in waves.

Maybe she needed a distraction. Maybe helping Tiffany would give Jaime a sense of empowerment and purpose that she needed after such a gut-wrenching experience as the hearing. When he'd finished texting a quick message back to Madeline and Tiffany about needing to check his schedule before committing, Jaime was still talking with her parents.

He tapped her shoulder, and she jumped. "Sorry about that. Tiffany wants to see Aslan, and I wondered if you'd like to come."

"Why?"

"Because Tiffany needs someone who understands."

Chandler's words from the courthouse rang in Jaime's ears as she parked her car where he had suggested.

Oh, she hated that he thought he knew her story. There was so much she hadn't said on the stand. And why had he asked for her help? Did he think she didn't know exactly what he was doing? She wasn't one of his clients.

The sun broke through the clouds and added a hint of warmth to the afternoon as Jaime walked toward the park. She wanted to turn her face to the sky and let it warm her to her core, but nothing could do that.

In the distance she spotted Aslan waiting next to a bench. She blew out a breath. *God, if You're real, I could use some help so I can reach this little girl. I don't want her to feel alone like I did.* Like she still did.

The quick prayer froze her.

She could not believe in a God who had allowed such evil to happen to a child.

She could not.

She closed her eyes as if to block the thoughts, and when she opened them she saw Tiffany curled up next to Aslan. Madeline huddled a short distance away, observing everything. Chandler was nowhere in sight.

"Thanks for coming." Madeline's teeth chattered.

"Today was a good day for it." Jaime kept her gaze on Tiffany and Aslan. The dog stood patiently, leaning slightly into the girl's leg.

"It is a great day to be at the park." Madeline nodded toward her daughter. "Aslan works magic on Tiffany. I'd buy him if I could, but Chandler won't let me."

"I'm sure Chandler doesn't want to sell his friend." The two had a relationship that seemed even tighter than the one she shared with Simba.

"You can't blame a desperate mother for asking." Madeline brushed her blond hair behind her ears. "It's hard to be everything Tiffany needs. I'll have to get back to work soon, and that's not possible when she remains this worked up."

"She has reason." Jaime remembered all too well the fear that had followed her each time her mother left the room, let alone dropped her somewhere. "Has the prosecutor located her abuser?"

Madeline grunted. "Nothing about this process has been what I would have expected. The police and prosecutors are kind, but there is so little they can do. My former boyfriend is walking around somewhere, and I can't promise Tiffany she's safe." She wiped her eyes. "If I'd never met the man, she'd still be innocent. This has confirmed the terrible instincts I have regarding men."

"You have to focus on doing exactly what she needs to find wholeness." Jaime edged forward, and Aslan turned his ears as if listening to her progress. He was attuned to her as she inched nearer. "Hi, Tiffany. I'm Jaime Nichols, a friend of your mom's and Aslan's."

The young girl turned to her with a solemn expression and old eyes. "Hello, Ms. Jaime."

"What are you and Aslan doing?"

"Sitting."

"Does he like it?"

"He likes me, so he does what I want to do."

Jaime eased onto the ground next to the girl, leaves crunching beneath her as she sank to the cold earth. "It must be nice to have someone who likes you because you're you."

"Do you?" The question was matched with the gaze of a girl who'd seen too much.

"Yes." Jaime clasped her hands on her knees. "I know how important that is. When I was your age, a man wasn't nice to me either. He did things he shouldn't have, and I wished for a friend like Aslan who would listen to everything I said until I ran out of words."

"And then he stays." The words were a whisper.

"Exactly." Jaime forced a small smile. "I wish I'd had that."

"He helps me feel safe." A grin burbled to the surface. "He doesn't interrupt me with questions."

Jaime laughed. "I'm sure he doesn't. Where's Mr. Chandler?"

"On his phone. It's okay as long as he lets Aslan come." There was such quiet confidence in the sentence.

Jaime bit back a flush of emotion. She was glad Tiffany was getting the help she needed. Chandler seemed to have a knight-in-shining-armor side—rearranging his life to show up at court hearings and parks. Just because no one should be alone. He'd said his job wanted him to use up his vacation time, but still . . . It took a special person to spend it getting involved in other people's messes.

It didn't matter how wonderful he appeared. She had to remember he was perfect for someone else, not for her.

Wasn't that the lesson she'd learned in high school and college? That she was death to any relationship? That the part of her that was supposed to welcome companionship and love was broken? She either demanded too much or not enough, so she'd decided to look for neither. "Is it okay if I talk to your mommy a minute?"

Tiffany shrugged and went back to petting the very patient dog.

Jaime stood and brushed off her jeans before turning her attention to Madeline, who sat on the bench a few feet behind her daughter. "How is her counseling going?"

Madeline shrugged. "It's barely had time to start. She's seeing two counselors though. With the play therapist, it's almost impossible to tell what's accomplished. Tiffany is eight. It seems like they should be talking or something."

"I don't know much about play therapy." Jaime wanted to be careful not to say too much about something she didn't understand. "What about her other counselor?"

"Tiffany gets so upset every time, it takes several hours to calm her down. This is not my girl. She's always been so sweet, and I don't know what to do."

Tiffany chose that moment to swivel around and look at her mother—who quickly wiped the tears from her cheeks and forced a smile.

Jaime wasn't the girl's mother, but she knew she couldn't walk away without helping the child, even if it meant more time with the intriguing Chandler Bolton. She'd have to find a way to guard her heart while making sure Tiffany found justice. Just as she was seeking with Dane.

CHAPTER 23

Chandler turned back toward the park. Returning calls had been a good way to maintain a professional distance and give Tiffany and Madeline space until Jaime arrived. He was happy to loan them Aslan from time to time, but he had to maintain his responsibilities at work too.

He slowed as he crested a slight rise. Tiffany was crouched on the ground talking with Aslan. Madeline and Jaime stood a few feet from them, a study in contrasts. Delicate, blond Madeline, awkwardly chewing a fingernail while her shoulders were bowed, and tall, authoritative Jaime, who stood like she'd defend Tiffany from anyone who would hurt her.

There was something about Jaime's brooding intensity that drew him like gravity tugged at the leaves. He was certain if he gave in to the attraction it wouldn't be a delicate dance of wind and petals, but a collision of fire and ice.

Could he risk it?

He'd lived through the painful destruction of his marriage and finally found himself on the other side, scarred but ready to move on. A relationship with someone like Jaime would take a strong man. One willing to risk everything for a possibility.

After what he'd learned in court, and Jaime's reaction to his knowing . . . he must be crazy.

Still, gravity and the hill drew him toward her. Aslan's ears swiveled to follow his movement, but the dog stayed firmly in place beside Tiffany. Chandler saw Madeline swipe at her cheeks, and he frowned. He didn't tolerate tears well. At all, really.

What had made her cry?

Jaime was intense, but he'd never seen one unkind act on her part, nothing thoughtless or cruel. In fact, as he walked toward them she moved closer to Madeline.

Her gaze locked on him. "Chandler."

"Hi, Jaime, Madeline. How's Tiffany doing?"

Madeline sniffed but kept her gaze on her daughter. "She's better. The visit with Aslan helps." She turned and looked at him with weepy eyes. "Thank you."

"I'm just the driver."

"Of a very well-trained dog who is saving my girl." Madeline sighed, but a soft smile touched her face. "Thank you for taking the time off."

He shrugged. "Today worked." He nudged Jaime. "What do you think? You heard what she called Aslan?"

"You might want to reconsider 'well-trained.'" Jaime crossed her arms.

It didn't take an EQ specialist to know she'd taken his bait. "That was a onetime lapse in judgment."

She didn't match his lighthearted jest. Instead, she met his gaze steadily, and he felt as though she were assessing him and finding him lacking. "It only takes one moment to destroy a life."

They were no longer talking about Simba. He glanced back at Tiffany. "You're right."

Jaime walked to the nearby picnic table and, ignoring the benches, sat on the table instead. He could sympathize with the awkwardness of folding long legs into a small space.

He followed and sat next to her, leaving Madeline to focus on her daughter. "You okay?"

Jaime kept her back perfectly straight. "I learned a long time ago it wasn't about me. Life is about how we serve others. That's why I'm here right now."

"It's never about you?"

She looked at him. "When you experience the things I have, there are two options. You can be swallowed by the events or you can decide to move beyond them. For a long time, the only way I could survive was to pretend they didn't happen. Now I try to right wrongs for others. I don't want Tiffany to wait a lifetime. I will do everything I can to give her a voice against her abuser, and if that means using your mangy dog, then I will."

"Jaime, would you trust me with your whole story?"

She snorted, an unladylike noise. "No."

"Why not?"

"Because you've done nothing to earn it."

"I'm here helping Tiffany."

"Actually, I'm pretty sure your dog is helping her. You're just annoying me."

He placed his hands over his heart and leaned back. "You wound me."

"Whatever." A movement flickered at the corner of her lips.

He dragged his gaze back to her eyes. "I'm safe, Jaime."

This time she turned to face him completely. "No man is safe. And to quote one of my favorite movies, 'You couldn't handle the truth.'"

He wanted to argue that she should let him decide. But as her gaze returned to the duo on the edge of the playground, he realized she might be right.

Maybe the demons plaguing Jaime were best left unknown.

———

A few minutes later Jaime made her good-byes and drove off, desperate to get away from Chandler. His rock-solid calm would wear her down if she spent too much time near him. It didn't help that she felt a flicker of peace when he was around, as though she knew he would never intentionally hurt her.

As she switched lanes, she noticed a vehicle a couple cars behind do the same. No big deal. In the growing traffic, it was hard to see many details. But she continued to glance in the rearview mirror and keep an eye on the large SUV. It wasn't a Hummer, but nearly that size. Maybe she should pay attention.

The Golden Arches were illuminated about a block ahead. A burger and fries would work for dinner. And she could see whether that car was following her or her imagination was working overtime.

Without turning on her blinker, she drove the car between traffic and into the restaurant's parking lot. The vehicle whizzed past. Jaime sat in her car trying to talk her heart out of racing. *You scared yourself over nothing.*

After Hayden and Emilie's experiences, she was predisposed to think that someone trailed her. It hadn't been a year since Hayden's world had been upended when a case she took ended up having ties to a Mexican drug lord who hadn't wanted her digging deeply into his son's death. And only a month ago a stalker had terrorized Emilie. With those cautionary tales, Jaime tried to be aware of her surroundings, but maybe she was letting her fears run away with her.

Except for Dane. He wasn't imaginary.

She leaned over to collect her purse from the back seat. She'd go ahead and grab something to eat. A little sweet tea with a side of fries and a burger sounded better than anything at home. Jaime slid from the car and then paused to wait for a gap in the cars lined up for the drive-through.

As she saw a break and moved ahead, a dark SUV suddenly turned on its lights and barreled toward her. Jaime froze, then forced her limbs to move. The rush of a breeze brushed her as the vehicle lurched past. The driver wore a ball cap pulled low, shrouding his features in shadow.

She tried to read the license plate number, but her thoughts were a jumble of adrenaline and fear that kept her from focusing before the vehicle tore around the corner and out of view.

"You all right, ma'am? That driver was crazy." A teen in a McDonald's uniform, his kind, dark face full of concern, offered her a hand. "Let me help you. You look like you've seen a ghost."

As her stomach tightened, the only thing Jaime was sure of was that food suddenly didn't sound so good. Curling up in bed with the covers pulled over her head sounded like a better option, but she let the boy lead her into the restaurant. "Thank you. I'm fine."

"Can I get you anything?"

"No, I'm okay. I'll just get a drink. Thank you again." She walked to the counter and ordered a large sweet tea. She'd sit for a minute and give her nerves time to settle before she headed home.

She rested at a table with the tea and dug out her lavender oil. She inhaled deeply and tried to force her body to calm, but it didn't work like usual. Her phone buzzed, and with shaking hands she pulled it out and saw a text from Caroline.

You okay? I started thinking about you and wanted you to know. I'm praying for you. Need anything?

Jaime wiped a tear from the corner of her eye. I'm fine. Thanks for checking. Did you stop by your apartment? How are the floors?

Ha! Never ending. Wishful thinking on my part that they'd be done.

You can stay as long as you need. As she typed the words, Jaime realized how much she meant them. Life was fuller with her friend filling the space with words and laughter.

Are you sure? Feels like I've crashed long enough.

I'm sure. Her thumbs hovered over her phone. Should she tell Caroline what had happened?

No. She'd just worry. But there was someone she might reach out to.

CHAPTER 24

The night felt heavy and oppressive as Chandler sat at his desk in the office and made up the time he'd taken to help Tiffany. He couldn't fall behind on the cases and veterans assigned to him. That wasn't fair to them, so he'd burn the midnight oil to catch up. He grabbed the next file from the leaning tower perched on the corner and opened it.

Seaman First Class Jordan Otley. He'd gotten involved in some drugs while on a tour and needed help to break free. It hadn't led to a court martial yet, but it would if the young man didn't act quickly. Chandler jotted a few notes on a Post-it note and closed the file. He'd set up a time for the sailor to come in and get him connected with resources. Help him see he wasn't the first and wouldn't be the last seaman to succumb while away from home. Depending on how that conversation went, Chandler might get his commanding officer involved, but he hoped to avoid that or to help the young man initiate that conversation on his own. What Seaman Otley chose to do now would determine his future.

The next file contained a story of a mom struggling to reconnect with her kids. There were ways to help facilitate reattachment. She might need a few services, but he could fix this.

It felt good to tick through a list of challenges and know he had solutions.

These files were different from Tiffany's. No matter what he did, he could not make her abuse go way. That was something that could be addressed but not removed. He prayed God would touch her heart at the most painful levels and that he'd have wisdom to know how to provide the support the child needed without usurping her mother's important role. Over time she was the one who would have to help Tiffany the most.

He leaned back and rubbed his face. How could he navigate this space? *Father, I need You to show me what to do. Would You restrain me from doing too much? Help me to obey Your prompting without overstepping my position and pretending I can do what only You can do.*

That was the rub.

It was easy to focus on the fix rather than on Who did the fixing.

His work cell phone buzzed on the desk and he glanced at it. A text from an unidentified number? This would be good. He rolled his eyes as he flicked a finger on the screen and pulled up the message.

Did you enjoy your tandoori chicken? It might be your last.

What kind of message was that? He took a screenshot to preserve the information, then tried to figure out a way around the blocked number. Nothing. He'd have to leave that to the techie geniuses.

His phone rang and he glanced at the screen. Jaime? Why was she calling?

"This is Bolton."

"Every time you say that I think of Michael Bolton." Jaime's voice had a hoarse edge to it that grabbed his attention like a hand to the throat.

"You're dating yourself."

"Not me. My mom listened to his music."

"Sure she did." He leaned back and glanced at the ceiling. "What's up?"

"I'm hiding in a McDonald's, too scared to go to my car."

He popped out of his chair. "What? Why?"

"I may have been followed, but I'm probably imagining it." She took a breath.

"Which McDonald's?" He was already reaching for his jacket and keys.

"I'm not even sure. I was driving home when I saw this vehicle following me." She laughed, but it was a hollowed-out sound. "You must think I'm nuts."

"No." Never that. She was too strong to let an unfounded fear take over. "Turn on your phone's map app and drop a pin of your location; then send it to me. I'm headed to my car now." He glanced at the remaining files. They'd be there in the morning.

Chandler hung up and headed to his truck. As he unlocked the door, his phone vibrated, and he looked at the screen and frowned.

His phone rang again, and the moment he answered, Jaime asked, "Did you get my location?"

"Looks like you're past Falls Church."

"I guess I got rattled."

"Must have." She'd traveled the opposite direction of their apartment complex. He slid into the car and turned the key in the ignition. "I'll be there in thirty minutes." If traffic cooperated. "Don't move, and if you get concerned, call the police."

"Yes sir." There was a bite to her words that made him wonder if she'd mock saluted him. Good, that meant her spunk was back.

"See you soon."

When he pulled into the well-lit parking lot, he could see Jaime sitting by a table near the front door, hunched over a large Styrofoam cup as if it was holding her together. This was not the strong woman she had presented in court that morning. Instead, this was the scared, broken woman he'd seen in the law firm's parking lot.

He went to the counter first, then slid into the booth and pushed a tray with a large order of fries across the table to her.

"How did you know I haven't eaten?"

"I took a wild guess." He purposefully relaxed his shoulders as he sank onto the booth. "Besides, there's always room for fries."

She nodded and took one but didn't eat it. "I think I blacked out."

"What do you mean?"

"I don't remember how I drove here."

"Like I've-driven-the-route-so-often-I'm-not-sure-which-way-I-came?"

"The kind a grown-up who was abused as a kid experiences."

He felt the world shift beneath his feet. "Do you usually lead with that?" He kept his words light and, he hoped, unthreatening.

"No, only with the people who don't know what they're getting into." Her eyes were hooded and her shoulders squared as if she expected him to leave her sitting there. "But then you do, since you were at court this morning."

He settled more firmly into the booth. There was no way he was leaving, not when he sensed others had. "I wanted to be there. It was important."

"Why?"

"Because we're friends."

"Even now?"

Her question pinged through him, an echo of times the answer had been *no* reverberating between them. "Yes, even now." He swallowed hard, then took a swig of Coke.

Her jaw squared and she leaned forward. "Ground rule. You can't fix this. It simply is, so turn off your male, fix-the-world mentality."

"I can try, but . . ." He ran his hands in front of his chest. "I'm all guy."

A faint color climbed her throat. Interesting. Maybe she wasn't quite the ice queen she liked to portray.

"Yeah."

Silence fell, the tension-filled kind, but he forced himself to stay quiet. If she wanted to lead this conversation, he'd let her. Maybe it made her feel safer. He could understand that.

"As you saw this morning, I'm going after my abuser in a public way, and he'll fight back. But not always in an obvious way. But maybe I'm paranoid."

"I doubt that."

"All I know for sure is that the stress of finally trying to expose who he is has pulled everything back to the top of my mind."

"And the blackouts?"

"They're becoming more frequent." She swallowed hard as her fingers clutched the cup so hard she might crush it. "I'm scared."

He could see what that admission cost her, and chose his words carefully. "What would you like me to do?"

"Drive me home. Have a buddy help you get my car to the apartment. I'll take tomorrow to recuperate and then see what happens."

He nodded. "I can do that." Her shoulders relaxed, and he felt her exhale. "We've all got pain, Jaime."

"Your pain and mine aren't the same."

"Agreed. But my divorce rocked my world. A key difference is I was an adult when it happened. But I believe that even on the darkest days there is hope. Sometimes I have to look harder. I have a favor to ask . . ." She started to close, and he held up a hand. "I want you to call me immediately the next time you feel threatened. No matter the time of day or night, I'll come."

"You can't promise that."

"I can." As far as he was concerned, she'd acquired a shadow— the friendly kind. "I have something to wrap up tomorrow at work, then I'll take some vacation time until you feel safe again."

"I can't let you do that, Chandler. You barely know me, and I can take care of myself. I've done it for years."

And he could see in the shadows haunting her eyes how it had worn her down. He couldn't do anything about the past, but he would do all he could to protect her from future harm.

The more she revealed, the more he knew he wanted to learn as much of her story as she'd share, and see what made her the strong woman he saw even now.

CHAPTER 25

Chandler felt the cool air press against him as his feet pounded the pavement. His sleep had been deep but not deep enough. He kept moving, dragging a worn-out Aslan with him, trying to outpace the memories that haunted him. The nightmares weren't his reality, he reminded himself. They were the remnants of his past.

The ghosts of his failures.

A swirling image of Rianna overlapped by the man who had died at the end of his tour, then the little girl he'd tried so hard to protect in Afghanistan.

He huffed out a breath, forgetting everything he'd learned in basic training: breathe in through his nose and out through his mouth. Instead, he gulped air as fast as his arms pumped.

He'd outrun his nightmare for the moment. But if he closed his eyes? There was no guarantee it wouldn't barrel back to his subconscious. Good counseling helped, but it took more for him to clear the trauma of what he'd seen and heard on tour.

He wanted to believe it would get better, but there were no guarantees.

The sidewalk came to an end, and Aslan skidded to a stop and leaned into Chandler's leg.

A minute later they were in the building, and he opened the apartment door and then stepped out of the way as Aslan bounded straight to his water bowl. Chandler bent over and rubbed the dog's ears, eliciting a doggie grin of epic proportions. Then he sank to the floor, and Aslan plopped next to him and placed his head in Chandler's lap, gazing at him with concern.

Chandler glanced at his watch: 5:00 a.m. No point in going back to bed; by the time he could pretend to sleep his alarm would buzz. He took his Bible and a Tervis tumbler of coffee out to the small patio table.

He could tell it was going to be one of those days when the caffeine wouldn't be enough to keep him going. But would his faith? He wanted to believe God would provide what he needed, but he already felt off. God had been faithful throughout the divorce, meeting him time and again as he battled to heal from Rianna's abrupt decision to leave. She'd taken his heart along with the furniture, leaving him to find a new place and furnish it with whatever he could find on the cheap. That about summed up their short marriage.

God had been with him through that, and God had been there every moment of his tour. He may never know why God allowed some things to happen, but he was convinced that He would turn everything to good. He'd seen it time and again.

So what was setting this day up to be an off one? Was it the nightmare? Or could it be Jaime?

His phone rang and he grabbed it. A little early for a call, so it must be important.

"This is Bolton."

"Did I disturb your dreams?" The voice was low, guttural. Almost as if the person were trying to disguise it.

"Nope. I'm an early riser."

"Not usually this early."

Chandler stiffened. How would the caller know his patterns? Or maybe it was a lucky guess. "I'm assuming you have a reason to call."

"Just wanted you to know I'm watching."

Chandler snorted. "That doesn't frighten me."

"I didn't think it would. But when you figure out who I am and what I can do, it will."

The call ended abruptly, and Chandler set the phone down. What had he done to make this vet fixate on him? The caller wasn't the first disgruntled vet to focus on the wrong person. It was almost a hazard of the job. Chandler had known that when he took it.

He took five minutes to capture the conversation, then time for more exercise. He had no hope of shaking the effects of the call unless he did it with old-fashioned sweat. He looked at Aslan. "You get to stay home this time."

———

The workout room was empty when Jaime arrived. Her sleep had been short, and rather than bother Caroline, she'd slipped on yoga pants and a running shirt and headed to the workout facility. She'd warmed up with a quick walk on the treadmill, then headed to the weights.

At one time she would have done her exercise outside where she could breathe, but after what happened last night, she'd decided to play it safe. If her uncle really was seeking revenge, it could escalate quickly. The best way to fight back was to be in top shape. She needed to outrun the shadows. She'd just moved on to the stationary bike when a movement caught her attention.

She froze, then relaxed when she saw Chandler's face. "Morning." He looked worn out, like he hadn't slept.

"Hi." His camo tee was like a slap, reminding her how much she didn't like or trust military men. They were all like her uncle . . .

even if she knew they weren't. So why did her two-timing heart want her to stop and stare at this guy? "You're up early."

He nodded, then went over to the water machine and filled a plastic cup, which he quickly drained. "It was one of those nights."

While some might consider his words evasive, she understood what it meant to be a survivor. "Nightmares?"

"Nothing a good long run couldn't take care of."

Part of her wanted to probe, but he'd been kind enough to let her control the pace of sharing. She'd give him the same gift.

He hopped on the bike next to her and pushed a few buttons. She wrinkled her nose. "Guess it was a long run."

"Aslan thought so. You should have seen him flopped over his water bowl. I must have pushed harder than I thought."

"I'll bet he liked the exercise. A big dog like that must need lots."

"Yeah. He does." A small smile tipped his lips.

She slowed her pace since there was no sense puffing next to him. He'd beat her in any competition with that physique. She winced at the direction her thoughts had taken. He wasn't supposed to do this to her.

He glanced at her and arched a brow in a look that would make Clark Gable proud. "This is early for you too."

"Not really. I haven't been in my regular routine since you've known me. When it's nice out, I prefer the trails." She arched an eyebrow in return, curious where this fire between them could lead. That settled it. She was crazy. She forced her attention back to his military background and how that represented nothing but pain to her. The military had stolen her father and created the context where Dane could perform his evil.

Could she ignore this man's military experience? Could she allow herself to explore what could develop between them? She blew out the spark of hope before it could ignite, because she knew herself too well. She couldn't be trusted.

It took effort for Chandler to peel himself away from the workout room; the interaction with Jaime was so intriguing and different. She didn't react like so many women. She was prickly on the edges, but he could see more beneath the surface, a depth waiting to be explored. But he had to get to work no matter how tired he was from his fitful night. As he showered and dressed, his thoughts traveled back to his caller. He'd tried dialing the number the call originated from, but all he heard was a mechanical voice saying the number was out of service.

There was nothing else he could do until he figured out who the man was. Meanwhile, the next thing in front of him was his job. He'd perform each task to the best of his ability and push the man to the area of "nuisance to be ignored" until there was something he could do.

He kept that in mind as he walked through meetings, counseling sessions, and paperwork. He'd be vigilant and alert, but that's all he could do until this threat either materialized or disappeared.

His work cell rang, and he glanced at the caller ID. Madeline Ange.

"This is Chandler."

"Tiffany is really struggling today." The mother didn't bother with niceties. "Is Aslan free?"

Chandler glanced at the dog bed in the corner of his office, then to the pile of paperwork and reports. "He can be after work. Tiffany's at school, isn't she?"

"I had to pull her out. She won't say anything, and if anyone talks to her, she curls into the fetal position." Madeline pushed out a shuddering breath. "She seems most comfortable when Aslan is around. Yesterday seemed to help."

Chandler glanced at his desk calendar and noted a few critical appointments he couldn't skip. Those would only add to the time it took to get caught up. "I'm sorry, Ms. Ange, but I can't today."

"How about tomorrow?" She was persistent.

"How about Sunday?" Chandler rubbed his forehead, trying to ease the tension that coiled there. "I could meet you somewhere early afternoon." There was a required military ball Friday night, and he wanted to keep Saturday free to get Jaime used to the idea he'd be her shadow as much as time allowed.

"You're sure you can't today?"

"I'm sure." Time to solidify boundaries.

"Then Sunday will do. I don't know what I'll tell Tiffany though."

"You'll tell her Aslan looks forward to a playdate then." His dog's ears perked up at his name. "I'll text you Saturday for a location."

She sighed, but he remained resolute. He'd help as he could, but he had a job and responsibilities. Madeline had to learn how to cope with what had happened as much as Tiffany did. That wouldn't happen if he dropped everything to respond the moment she called. It was a hard but necessary truth.

CHAPTER 26

The morning workout hadn't removed the feeling of her blackout, and Jaime hurried through her front door. Maybe she just needed to relax a bit. Curl up with the novel she'd been reading in fits and starts. But when she walked through the apartment she couldn't find it. She frowned, but she'd probably misplaced it, or Caroline had put it somewhere in one of her bursts of cleaning.

Without the book's plot to distract her, the walls of her apartment pressed against her. It felt so empty and small that she toyed with asking Caroline to take a vacation day or two. Would that help press back the trapped feeling? She wasn't really sure, but she couldn't ask her friend to use precious vacation time to babysit her.

She felt the energy bottled up inside.

After pacing like a caged cat, no insult to Simba, Jaime decided enough was enough. It had been four days. She wanted that to be long enough for everyone to decide she was ethically sound. After all, attorneys had a lower professional responsibility standard than most would find acceptable. It had been a surprise to learn in law school that her personal standards for ethics were higher than those required by the bar.

Left to her thoughts she'd go crazy. The questions were endless.

What if the criminal charges didn't stick? What if Dane decided to make her pay anyway? What if she lost her job?

She got dressed and headed to Old Town via the Metro. She'd

forgotten to ask Chandler if he'd had time to reclaim her car, but it would be a while before she was jumping to drive anyway.

When she reached the King Street offices of Daniels, McCarthy & Associates, she was ready to argue long and hard for her dream. Bella had barely nodded her back to Savannah's office before Jaime launched into her argument.

"It's been long enough, Savannah. The bar must have had the allegations for at least a couple weeks before they sent me the letter, so surely they've made their decision." Jaime met her mentor's gaze.

Savannah was shaking her head. "These things take more than a couple days to handle."

"What if I don't have more time? I've got to get back to work or I won't have a job." Especially if someone was maneuvering to get her fired.

"You know that's not true. You've always got a job." Savannah spread her arms wide, indicating the office.

"But maybe that's not what I want." Jaime ignored the flare of emotion on Savannah's face. "I am a criminal defense attorney. That's who I am. I give a voice to the innocent who need an advocate they can't afford, something I can't do while I'm sidelined."

"These things take time, Jaime."

"I don't have time." Grant had been clear that he could only hold her job for a couple weeks—she'd overheard the pressure he was under. Was it only three days ago? Every hour away made it easier for him to talk himself into taking away her job. The injustice of the situation made her so mad—she wanted, no *needed*, to fight back. If only she knew how. "I don't know who I am without my work."

Savannah leaned forward. To Jaime, her black suitcoat fitted against her black sheath suggested she was dressed to attend the funeral for Jaime's career. "You hired me to talk you out of craziness, so listen to me."

"I didn't hire you. You won't let me pay you."

"Then pay me a dollar."

"I can afford to really pay you. I've got a little saved." If she ate ramen noodles for the rest of the year.

"And I'm here to save you from yourself." Savannah picked up a pen from her desk and put it dancing across her fingers. "If you rush this process, you'll lose more than a few weeks at the PD's office. You have to trust me."

Trust.

It was easy to say but so hard to do.

Jaime met Savannah's gaze and thought of all the times the woman had been there for her. Bile rose in her throat at the thought that her career was on the line. She swallowed against it. "I can't lose my career."

"I know." But Savannah's gaze hardened as she studied Jaime. "This is about so much more than a job. You must let go of control. You hold on to it so tightly, but you must trust me and ultimately God."

"You're easier to trust than He is."

"Right now. But what if all of this is about pushing your future beyond your ability to mold and control? What if you have to lose it to see how unimportant it really is?"

"Unimportant? How can you say that when you know how hard I had to fight to get into law school and then get through it?" Jaime's voice shook. "I can't depend on anyone else to take care of me."

"Even me?"

The quiet words fell with the force of a thunderclap between them. Jaime got up and paced in front of Savannah's desk, feeling as if there was a battle going on, one she couldn't understand other than that the tight knot in her stomach told her she wasn't all right. "That's not fair."

"Of course it is. You can't make statements like that without expecting a reaction." Savannah relaxed and placed her hands on the desk. "Jaime, there is more to you than this job."

"It involves my reputation. No one will hire me if these charges follow me."

"They won't. But you have to be patient."

"I can't. I have to get back into court."

"Why?"

"Because that is what I spent my adult life working toward."

"Why?"

"Because I want to give a voice to the innocent and protect the rights of the guilty."

"That's noble, but why?"

"Because without help they will be wrongly imprisoned."

"Wouldn't that be easier to do from a firm like this?"

"No."

"Why?"

"Because many lack the funds to pay for good representation."

"And that's your duty?" Savannah studied her with an unrelenting gaze.

"Yes."

"Why?"

"When did you become a two-year-old?"

Savannah just studied her.

"Because I know the pain of not being believed. I needed an advocate, and no one came. I want to ensure that doesn't happen here."

"So help Tiffany."

Pain shot through Jaime with such an intensity she almost wished Savannah had sliced her open with a knife. At least then she could be put back together. Instead, she felt herself slipping into a memory. Into a well of pain she kept locked up. With three words, Savannah had thrown up the door to expose it to the light.

"I can't." The words barely qualified as a whisper, but she felt them vibrate from her soul.

"You can." Savannah stood and came around to Jaime. "Sometimes the only way we are made whole is when we take our pain and use it to help others. You can do more for Tiffany than I ever could, because despite my best intentions and efforts, I have not walked her road. I do not know the unique pain she has experienced. You do."

The words reverberated through her, a pulsing call to arms.

Jaime wanted to run from it, pretend she hadn't heard. But she couldn't. Savannah's words echoed the call of her heart to be that voice for the innocent. What was more innocent than a violated child?

"Isn't the fact she was abused further evidence that your God is one I should run the other direction to avoid? What kind of God would allow this pain for a child? And abusers rarely have one victim. They leave behind a string of ruined lives."

"I can't help all of them, Jaime. But I can help Tiffany. You can help Tiffany. She's the child who's been placed in front of us with a sign that says Help Needed. The only question is whether you'll be part of her healing."

"Where were people when I needed healing?" The words were too loud for the space.

"God is always there. Even when we can't see Him. When He seems most hidden, He is most present. I've found in those moments He is closer than my breath. I have to choose whether to see Him, but He's there." Savannah reached for her hand, but Jaime tugged free of the touch.

The words rolled off Jaime. They didn't connect with her reality, with her experience.

"Don't forget He brought you to us." Savannah let the words settle. "Will you help?"

"No." Then, before she could walk away, "Yes."

"Good." Savannah opened a desk drawer and pulled out a slim red folder. "Here's a list of questions we need to answer."

Jaime felt numb as she took the folder. She didn't want to look at the questions and see what Savannah thought was important. She already knew. What was important was getting Tiffany as far as possible from her abuser so he couldn't molest her again. Until that happened, all efforts were wasted.

"Bella will show you an empty office. It's the last one we have, but I have the feeling we'll need more."

"Are you attracting strays?" Savannah had given Hayden and Emilie space when they'd had to leave their jobs.

"No. This is about bringing together strong women who know how to use the law to help people."

"Angela doesn't fit."

"Angela needed an escape to a meaningful practice."

"I don't want to be another charity case for you."

"You aren't, Jaime. By helping Tiffany, you're freeing me to keep your case moving. Between your uncle and the bar, you create enough work for a couple clients."

Jaime glanced around the office, took in the framed licenses, the graduation certificates, the Harvey prints. There was a dignified air to the space, with the colorful Persian rug and the real ficus tree in the corner. African violets bloomed on the wide windowsill. But it was clear that Savannah invested in people rather than things.

"What if I say yes to pay you back for helping me?"

"I want you to say yes because you want to help Tiffany."

"I do, but I need to know I'm compensating you for your time."

"Then do this, and I'll consider the debt paid."

Jaime heard her, but the words slammed around her soul. Could she do this? Could she really go deeper into Tiffany's pain without losing herself? As she thought of the child's shy smile and shadowed eyes, she knew she didn't have a choice.

Savannah had found her Achilles heel and was using it forcefully.

"All right." For better or worse, she was in.

CHAPTER 27

Friday morning a knock at her apartment door startled Jaime where she sat drinking a cup of coffee and scanning headlines on her phone.

Caroline glanced at her sheepishly as she collected her trench coat and briefcase. "Don't hate me, okay?"

"Why would I hate you?"

"Because I might have set this in motion." She nodded toward the door, then blew her a kiss and scurried away at a pace that would have left Jaime breaking an ankle had she tried it in those stilettos.

As Caroline went through the door, Jaime's mother stepped inside. Her tunic sweater and skinny jeans paired with boots made her look like she was only a few years older than Jaime. "Hi, honey."

"Was I expecting you today?" Jaime flipped over to her texts to make sure she hadn't missed something.

"No, Caroline texted me. She said you needed a reason to get out of the apartment, and I have the perfect one."

"I'm going to kill her." This was how she repaid Jaime for taking her in when she didn't have a place to stay?

"Your father and I have decided to take you to the military ball tonight. You and I are going to have a girls' day shopping for a gown and then going to the ball."

"You think I'll find Prince Charming there?"

"Maybe not, but it will be fun all the same." Her mother looked around the apartment, and her nose crinkled. "Aren't you about to go crazy?"

Jaime wanted to argue, but she could tell by the set of her mother's shoulders and determined look that was a no-win proposition. "What if Dane's there?"

"There will be so many people it would be hard to see him if we wanted to. Besides I've rarely seen him at these sorts of events. I've always believed he deliberately scheduled exercises with his team to avoid them."

Jaime sighed and knew she had to give in to her mother's attempt to bridge the space between them. "All right."

"Thatta girl."

Seven hours later, as their nail polish dried under LED lights, Jaime felt more pampered than she had before prom. Still, a thread of uneasiness tugged tight around her middle. She wasn't sure she had the courage to wade into a ballroom full of military uniforms. "You're sure Dane won't be there?"

"As sure as I can be. I wish I could promise he won't, but . . ." She shrugged.

There was no way to know. Jaime would assume he'd be there and brace for what that could mean. Anything else would be foolhardy. And while the thought of seeing him made her want to avoid the ball, she also wanted to step fully into a place of freedom where the thought of him didn't terrify her. Maybe going to the ball was a step.

"Remember, you won't be alone. Your dad would like nothing more than an excuse to deck him."

"If he's there, I'll try to avoid him." The ball could be fun, and her mom had gone to a lot of effort to create a special day for her.

She couldn't let her fears of what might happen if Dane showed up hold her captive. Instead, she'd focus on the excitement of attending an event like this. "All those years you and Daddy have gone to the military balls, I never have."

"I know. We always have such a good time." Her mother's light clicked off, and she slid her fingers free to examine her nails. Then she reached for Jaime's arm. "I want tonight to be a special Cinderella moment for you. Who knows, maybe you will meet a prince! Now let's get dressed and collect your father."

Her parents had gotten a room at the Renaissance Washington, the location for the ball. It was a nice but expensive touch that matched everything else her mother had done today. In return Jaime determined to give her mom the gift of joining in and pretending to have a good time. Surely it wouldn't be that hard in a ballroom surrounded by men and women in dress uniforms, their dates arrayed in a kaleidoscope of colors.

She'd chosen the gown, a royal-blue halter dress, because it reminded her of the one Diana wore at the ball in *Wonder Woman*. Tonight she needed that same fortitude, determination, and grit. A military ball might be safe terrain for her uncle, but for her it felt risky.

She lifted her chin and examined her image in the mirror. She'd spent twenty years trembling at the thought of him. This evening she would walk into the ballroom knowing it was possible he'd be there. In court she'd cowered in his presence; tonight would be different.

Her phone chimed with a text from its place on the bathroom counter. She glanced at the screen, then smiled as she read the message.

You sure you want to do this? I didn't know this was what your mom had in mind!

Caroline, her worrywart friend.
It pinged again.

I'm here if you change your mind. Well, I'm here if you don't.
What I'm trying to say is you're the bravest woman I know,
regardless of how tonight goes.

I'm fine. Thanks for checking. See you on the other side.

She should type a smiley face. It was something Emilie would
do, but Jaime couldn't. Her life wasn't the kind that had an abundance of emoticons.

But tonight would be one more step in taking back her life on
her terms.

She set her phone back on the counter, then braced herself
against the counter and studied her expression. Her hair was swept
into a fancy updo, with loose strands curling in tendrils around
her face. *You can do this. If you don't now, you never will.*

Her self-talk did nothing to ease the tightness around her eyes.
No amount of makeup could hide it even if her mom had spent a
small fortune pampering her into beauty. *You've got this.*

She blew her bangs from her face, then fingered them back in
place.

"You look beautiful, honey." Her mother was standing in the
bathroom doorway. She squeezed Jaime's arm, a look of love and
pride filling the curves of her smile. "Let's go before your father
wears a path in the carpet."

Her father whistled as they glided toward him. "I am the luck-
iest man in this city tonight." He offered each of them an arm and
then escorted them out of the room, down the elevator, and to the
ballroom level.

Dark military blue carpet lined the hallway, with chandeliers soaring two stories overhead. Her father had timed their arrival so there was precisely half an hour left in the cocktail reception. He was nothing if not punctual. They followed other elegantly dressed women and men from the elevator into the expansive space outside the ballroom. The service member attendees like her father were in their best Dress A uniforms. Many of the spouses and dates like her mother wore floor-length gowns. Some wore tea length, but she saw nothing above the knee. The non-military men wore suits with bow ties and the occasional tuxedo. Taken together it created the illusion they had stepped into a fairy tale world strung with miles of tulle and white lights.

Jaime smoothed a hand down the silky fabric of her gown. Mother's rose-colored, floor-length gown added blush to her cheeks, and she looked incredible with ringlets from her chignon falling around her face. It only took one look at her dad to note from his swelled chest to his cocky grin that he believed he escorted the most beautiful woman in the room.

At a roped off area, Dad handed their tickets to a young woman in dress blues.

"The cocktail hour ends in thirty minutes, Captain."

"Thank you." He guided her mother inside the roped cocktail space, then waited for Jaime to join them.

Jaime held her head high, trying to feel as confident as Wonder Woman had appeared as she entered the nest of Germans, then turned to her mom. "I never asked you, what is the ball for?"

"To raise awareness and support for the returning heroes and their families."

"In many ways it will have the formality of a branch birthday ball." Her father shrugged as he placed his hand over his wife's. "Then when the brass leave, it'll be time to let loose and dance till dawn."

"You sound positively romantic." Jaime smiled at her father. "I'm sure it will be fun."

If nothing else, for a few hours she could pretend there was nothing more than this moment. Feeling like a princess, and no one knowing any different.

She followed her father and mother through the crush.

"What can I get you ladies?" Her father gave a gallant bow.

"A ginger ale for both of us, sir." As her father headed toward the line snaking from the bar, Mom took Jaime's hand and squeezed it. "How are you feeling?"

Jaime considered for a moment. "Good."

"You sound surprised."

"Uniforms can sometimes have a negative connotation."

"Well, not tonight." Mom smiled so brightly any clouds would be forced to part. "Tonight we're going to enjoy each other's company while supporting a good cause."

Jaime nodded, but her gaze skimmed the room. It wasn't just Dane on her mind. Would a certain other officer make his way to the ball? She shoved the thought aside.

The doors leading to the ballroom opened, and the sounds of a string quartet warming up filtered out. In the lobby, wait staff circulated bearing trays laden with tiny hors d'oeuvres. She wasn't sure she'd know what she was eating if she tasted some of the delicacies. Her mom had been a mac and cheese and frozen pizza kind of cook.

Her gaze scanned the crowd as she followed her mother between groups. Then she froze.

Dane was here. The man's military bearing remained unchanged, the image seared in her memory like a twisted brand that coiled too tightly. She might never understand what had made him the man he was. Why had he looked at her one day and decided she was his?

She tore her gaze from him, determined he wouldn't ruin her evening, but when she looked away she still sensed his presence. The thought was eerie, uncomfortable, like a second skin that didn't fit.

She could still escape before he saw her, but she fought the instinct. Today she was done being the scared little girl who begged not to go to her uncle's house. The girl who turned to stone at his touch. The teen who panicked when she thought of him. Those chapters of her life were finished.

She leaned into her mother's shoulder. "I'm going to circulate."

Her mother's gaze zipped to hers, concern laced through it, as her father stepped near. "Want us to come?"

"No. This is something I need to do. Go say hi to all your friends. I'll be fine." She let the flow of people swirl her away from her parents and closer to Dane. She knew her parents were watching, and her father would come in an instant if she needed him. She wasn't going to live in fear. Maybe Dane had sent someone to track her last night, maybe he hadn't, but today she would do the tracking. She would be the one who controlled their encounter.

She was not a little girl anymore.

He turned as she neared, and the smile he graced her with was almost warm, close enough to fool anyone who might observe them. "Jaime. I didn't expect to see you here."

He was so precise. Controlled. Only the faintest tightening at the corner of his eyes gave an indication he felt . . . anything. Discomfort? Annoyance? The difference was one of degree.

"Dane." She refused to grace him with the title uncle. He had forfeited it and any honor.

"I see you're here to congratulate me." He tipped his chin until he looked down at her.

"Congratulate you?"

"You're looking at the next one-star." He shrugged, the movement revealing the ripple of tight muscles that hadn't sagged with time. "I've been told it's done."

"It won't happen."

"Your little game will fail, Jaime."

"That's where you're wrong. The light will expose the truth." She stared at him for another minute until he knew she wasn't afraid, even if she felt a tremor inside. "Enjoy the ball," she said. "It may be your last." She eased away from him, in control.

Then his hand clamped on her arm, and he tugged her back until his mouth was almost on her ear. "You will not succeed, little girl."

She shrugged from his grasp and returned her gaze to his. "You don't scare me anymore. I'm not the child you took advantage of. I am strong enough to fight back, and I will."

"Everything all right?" Her father was suddenly there at her elbow, and his words had a hard edge. She fought the desire to sag.

"We're fine, aren't we?" She reached for his arm as she shook free of Dane's hold. "Dad, would you dance with me?"

"It would be my pleasure." He walked her toward the floor. "Sure you're fine?"

"I am." She settled into her father's arms and felt a comfort and security she'd longed for as a child. As the string quartet's music swirled around her, she relaxed in the moment.

As Dad swirled her closer to the door, she noticed two men, one in uniform and one in a tux, leaning casually against the wall. Something about the military guy arrested her attention.

Chandler. He had the build of a warrior, confident, sure of himself. But there was more to him than that.

Did he see her?

She stayed firmly in the protective circle of her father's arms. Would Chandler come to her?

Did she want him to?

Oh, yes. Yes, she did. In a way that she hadn't let herself feel before.

CHAPTER 28

The last place he wanted to be was in a crowded ballroom with a bunch of military and their dates. If it weren't such a good cause, he would have stayed at home, but while he might not be full-time military anymore, he still carried a reserve commission, and with it came an expectation of supporting the branch. How long did he need to stay at one of these events anyway?

It was all about staying long enough to be seen by the higher-ups and then leaving the moment they exited the event.

Frankly, he'd have more fun Sunday with Tiffany at the Franklin Delano Roosevelt Memorial than he anticipated now, wearing his dress blues uniform that he'd had to pull from the back of his closet.

Brandon Lancaster stood beside him, dressed in a tux that did nothing to hide his size as the two guys held up the wall. As a favor to a friend, Chandler had helped the former NFL linebacker find some resources as he recovered from a career-ending injury. Then, as Brandon had shared his vision for Almost Home, Chandler had found himself intrigued and wanting to help. Foster placements were an unfortunate reality for some deployed service members' children. Knowing this man of integrity ran the home from a faith perspective and accepted sibling groups clinched the deal. Their friendship had grown to encompass more than the shared passion to help others.

Chandler shot his cuffs from beneath his jacket as he shifted his feet.

Then a woman caught his eye. She had the exotic look of a movie star with dark, loose curls and high cheekbones, but she also—

Jaime?

"You might want to stop drooling." Brandon's voice was droll as he stepped away from the wall. "I think she's looking at me."

"You wish." There was no way he'd let his friend have an instant with his girl. *His girl?* What was he thinking? He couldn't feel anything more than friendship between them. Not until he knew the state of her heart, something he'd have to move up the priority list ASAP, because in that moment he admitted it: his heart wanted nothing more than to dive into the abyss that was Jaime Nichols.

"I think you mean fine, as she is mighty fine." Brandon took a tiny cracker with something unidentifiable topping it from a passing tray and tossed it into his mouth.

"Any good?" Best to ignore his friend's statement about Jaime until Brandon was distracted and Chandler could chase her down. Who was she stopping to talk to now?

"Passable."

"I'm surprised you had time to taste anything."

"It's a superpower of mine, taste every molecule as I gulp. Remind me why we're here?"

"My boss said this was a good place to schmooze." And had given him the tickets with strict orders to enjoy himself.

"That's right." Brandon brushed a hand across his mouth. "Well, don't see we're doing much of that standing here."

The man was right. The last place Chandler really wanted to be was in this place at this moment. Getting his wisdom teeth pulled without Novocain sounded like a better experience . . . unless he could get time with Jaime. One dance with her . . .

He and Brandon placed a few bids on silent auction items along the edge of the room while he tried to keep tabs on Jaime. His name on the lists would serve as evidence he'd been to the event, in case his boss took the time to look that closely. It would be nice to erase monkey duty from his job description, but his boss insisted that civilians liked to see the dress uniforms. It helped open their pocketbooks to provide the extra finances the Veterans Administration relied on to help returning servicemen and servicewomen reintegrate with their families and life after a tour of duty.

But right now he needed to see if Jaime was okay.

It was only two nights earlier she'd been terrorized.

It wouldn't be hard for someone to do something similar here in such a mass of people.

There she was, still dancing with her dad. He smacked Brandon's shoulder. "See you later, big guy. I have something to tend to." He headed into the fray.

Jaime's dress was a startlingly rich blue, like a sapphire, making it easy to follow in the sea of more muted colors. He caught up with them after they'd spun around the dance floor a few times. "Mr. Nichols, may I have this dance with your daughter?"

Her startled gaze collided with his, and he noted the strength there. She looked like she belonged in this place with all these people. A reminder of all that was beautiful in the world and what the soldiers fought for.

"Jaime?" Her father matched her intensity and then notched it up a few levels. The man was flat-out intimidating, so Chandler stood a little taller, a hint of "at ease" in his stance.

Jaime's gaze bounced between the men. A slow smile grew across her face, making her even more lovely, something Chandler would have sworn wasn't possible until he watched the transformation occur.

"I think I'd like that very much."

He whisked her from her father's side before the man could state an opinion. A moment later her mother joined him, and Mr. Nichols led her onto the floor.

"Should I be worried?"

"About what?" Jaime looked around and spotted the couple. "I'm glad he's taking Mom out. She loves to dance, but he insists he has two left feet."

"I don't." He spun her in a tight circle, and she laughed.

"No, you don't." She sighed and leaned against him as the music slid into a slow song. She fit . . . in a way that felt divinely unfair and perfect.

"Miss Jaime Nichols, you are incredible." He side-stepped around another couple and kept them moving in smooth steps that put his academy education on display.

She leaned back. "You can say that knowing what you do about me?"

The question felt important, like so much depended on how he answered. "Everyone has a past."

"Not all are as bleak as mine."

He stopped in the middle of the floor, the string quartet continuing the song while he tipped her chin up so his eyes connected with hers. "It does not define you."

"It always will." The words whispered across his heart.

"God can redeem anything."

She stiffened and her eyes widened as she glanced past his shoulder. She refocused slowly, and when she did it felt abrupt, like something broke between them.

"Not you too." She slid from his arms and started looking at the couples swirling around them. "You can't bring God into every conversation. Where are they?"

"Where are who?" How had a perfect moment so quickly degraded?

"My parents. I'm ready to leave." And she walked away, leaving him alone in a sea of uniforms, wondering what had happened.

CHAPTER 29

That feeling that spiders were walking over his skin pulled Chandler from a nap in front of the TV, where a college football skirmish between Purdue and Nebraska played in the background.

He scrubbed his hands across his face.

He'd sworn he was done with that feeling when he left the Middle East and returned stateside for the final time. There was something about knowing anyone watching could be a hostile that put one on edge. He'd lived it during his deployments and tried to resolutely shove it aside back home, but it lingered like the memory of the friend left in a body bag after a routine supply run gone bad.

He'd worked hard, as he encouraged his clients to do, to thrust the guilt behind him. He'd also worked hard to invite God into the process. He didn't want the process short-circuited and incomplete, but it wasn't moving quickly.

There was no logical reason for this creepy-crawly sensation.

He glanced around.

He was right where he was supposed to be. His apartment, on a Saturday afternoon. Aslan at his side. The big oaf wouldn't let anyone near him. He knew who provided his food. The dog's training was excellent, unless a steak was involved.

Chandler stood and paced. Blood flow would help. He shook his head as he felt Aslan lean into his side, a firm force anchoring him in the here and now.

His work cell rang and Aslan's ears perked. Chandler pulled it from his pocket and answered. "Bolton."

"Hey." It was a soft, feminine voice, but not the one he wanted to hear.

"Hi Madeline."

"Are you free?"

He frowned at the words. "What do you need?"

"Tiffany is asking for Aslan.

"We're getting together tomorrow," he reminded her.

She sighed. "I know. But Tiffany's had a hard day, and I thought time with Aslan might help. I rented a movie."

The press of responsibility lowered his shoulders, and he relented. "What are you watching?"

"*Moana.*" Madeline chuckled, but it felt forced rather than joy-filled. "You'll be saying 'You're welcome' nonstop once you see it."

"Huh?"

"It's one of the songs." She hesitated. "It would really help if you came."

He heard Tiffany in the background. "Can Aslan come, Mom?"

Aslan's ears perked up as if he'd heard his name, but Chandler hesitated. Aslan's training hadn't covered what to do when a client asked for more services. Was he creating a codependent relationship? The image of Tiffany curled into the corner of the interview room floated into his mind, and the internal conflict intensified. "Anyone else coming?"

"I've asked Jaime. She had said she wants to see Tiffany 'in her natural environment.' She's not a lab animal, ya know?"

The thought of Jaime also being there made the idea more palatable. "I'll see what I can do."

"Thirty minutes, soldier."

Madeline clicked off, and he called Jaime. "I heard you need a ride."

"Hello to you too?" Her voice was clouded with confusion. "A ride where?"

"You got an invitation to spend time with Tiffany. So did Aslan, and there's no need for both of us to drive."

"It would be more efficient."

"Yep." It'd also allow him to ensure she wasn't followed.

"All right. I told her I'd be there in twenty minutes."

"Make it thirty, and we can stop for ice cream on the way."

"Sold, as long as it has peanuts and chocolate sauce."

Chandler would gladly pay for those items if it meant more time with Jaime. "Be at your door in five." He hung up and looked at Aslan. "Looks like you get a car ride."

An idea flashed in his mind. Maybe he could do something for Jaime at the same time she did something for Tiffany. He went to his bookshelf and grabbed a copy of one of his favorite books. It might help her, and it certainly couldn't hurt.

He clipped a lead on Aslan and then grabbed his keys and headed out the door. Aslan trotted beside him, tail high as if to celebrate the outing. Chandler popped open the door to the stairwell and dropped the lead, letting Aslan gallop ahead of him up the stairs. Chandler was huffing when he reached the top floor. "Hold up, boy."

Aslan turned and looked at him while Chandler gulped a lung-ful of air. As he stepped into the hallway, Jaime jolted from her position next to her apartment door.

"You didn't need to wait out here." She must know he'd have knocked. "What if whoever followed you was waiting?"

"We do have security in this building, Chandler. Besides, I didn't want to waste time." A faint flush of color climbed her neck. Interesting. Aslan nosed up to her side, and she patted his ears. "Shall we go?"

"Absolutely." There were so many layers to the mystery of Jaime Nichols, he wasn't certain where to start. He'd thought that after their dance the night before, she might lower her guard. He hadn't done anything that should put her on alert, but she was. All the time.

When they reached the garage, she scurried around his truck and hopped in the seat before he could open the door for her. An independent woman. He liked that she didn't fawn over him, but he really wished she'd indicate some level of interest. But then . . . what was with that flush of color?

———

Jaime's phone buzzed in her pocket before Chandler could start the truck, and she tugged the phone free. Tiffany collapsed into sleep. No need to come.

"Looks like we don't need to go to Tiffany's after all." She typed a quick reply, letting Madeline know the message was received.

"Really?" The look on Chandler's face caught her. It was a mix of concern, maybe fear, a little relief, and a strong dose of something she might call pleasure, but there was something magical about letting it remain unnamed. "I'd already planned to take Aslan over tomorrow, so Tiffany will still get her time with him. Would you like to join us? Madeline mentioned you need to spend time with Tiffany."

"Where are you going?"

"The FDR Memorial, assuming the weather cooperates."

She considered a moment. "I think I'd like that."

"Great, I can drive. But here, I have something for you." He didn't start the truck, but instead pulled something from his jacket pocket and held it behind his back.

She bit back a smile at his antics and pivoted so her back was against the truck's door and she could see him better. "Should I be worried?" She carved her features into a frown. "Surprises are too far out of my control."

"This is one you'll like."

"Really?"

His grin took on an impish character. "I know you like to read."

"How do you know?"

"Instinct. Things you've said." He pulled a slim book from behind his back and held it toward her.

"*The Lion, the Witch and the Wardrobe*?" She looked at the cover, then flipped it over. "I've seen the movie."

"Really? That's great. What did you think?"

"I don't remember much of it. We watched it during law school when some friends decided we needed a study break."

"It's one of my favorites. I promise the story will capture your imagination."

"Huh." She flipped it back over. "Isn't this a kids' book?"

"Give it a try." He gave her some puppy dog eyes that would make Aslan proud. "For me?"

She laughed. "All right. Is this where Aslan got his name?"

"Maybe." Then he sobered, and the change was dramatic. "Read it with an open heart, okay?"

"Why?"

"We all have questions about life. Big questions. Yours are hard ones. This little book might help."

He was so sincere, she couldn't have told him no, no matter how much she didn't want to consider the big questions. Like where was God when she was eight.

"Have you been talking to Caroline?"

A small smile quirked his lips, but he shook his head. "Nope. We aren't ganging up on you." He held up three fingers. "Boy Scout promise."

She looked from him to the book and back. "If it's important to you, I'll read it."

"Thank you. No essay required."

"That's good." She slipped the book in her purse. How much effort could a kids' book be? She'd read it in a night or two, honor his request, and then forget about it. She smiled at him. "Since we're not headed to Tiffany's, does that mean no ice cream?"

As he smirked at her in that breath-capturing, Captain America way, she knew she was falling hard. Time to back away, as fast as possible.

CHAPTER 30

J aime had caught up with Caroline over supper, read the first chapters of *The Lion, the Witch and the Wardrobe*, and sunk into a sleep filled with dreams of what could be instead of nightmares from the past.

When he brought her home after their ice cream yesterday, Chandler reminded her of his invitation to join him today as he took Tiffany and Madeline to the Memorial. She hadn't committed, but as she lay in her bed, comforter snuggled to her chin, she realized how much she wanted to go.

Maybe if she spent enough time with Chandler he'd prove he wasn't who he appeared. That might be the best way to protect her heart. But even as the thought surfaced, she knew it wasn't valid. He *was* who he appeared.

While he seemed to be hero material, she shouldn't ignore he was military and let him draw her too easily to his side, longing for something she couldn't have.

Still, she'd say yes today.

When should I be ready? She hit Send, and while she waited for a reply she heard the shower turn on.

Caroline must be getting ready for church. Her friend hadn't asked her to go this week, and Jaime was glad and annoyed at the same time—she'd looked forward to telling Caroline no. Further proof of how broken she was inside.

She rolled onto her side and grabbed the book that rested on her nightstand. The thin volume felt weighty in her hands, filled with Chandler's expectations of what she would find as she read. He wanted her to come to faith—just like Caroline and Hayden, probably Emilie too. He didn't understand how impossible that hope was even if he thought he knew her story.

Her scars were too deep to be wiped away by an encounter with a novel.

She flipped the book over and scanned the back cover. She knew the gist of the story from a middle school English class and the movie. If she started reading again, she'd finish in a couple hours and could tell him she'd done what he wished.

She held the unopened book like she clutched the quiet desperation that wouldn't release her. Was it possible God could love her when He had ignored her pain? How could a God who allowed the horrible abuse truly see her and care?

These were questions she couldn't reconcile, but she wanted to believe there were answers.

Her phone lit up and she grabbed it with one hand.

Pick you up at noon.

Okay. See you in a few hours.

She set her phone aside and as the shower turned off, turned her focus to what she'd wear for their excursion. It was supposed to be a perfect fall day.

Jaime opened the door at noon to find Aslan prancing beside Chandler.

"Hey."

She loved the way one word from his lips could fill her with warmth. "Hey yourself. Let me grab my phone and keys." She shoved the items into the pockets of her hooded vest and zipped it up, then nudged Simba back inside. "All ready."

Chandler's gaze slid down her with a smile, but it felt different from when so many men did it—like he really saw her. They made quiet conversation as they took the elevator to the garage.

"Have you noticed anyone around since Wednesday night?"

She shuddered at the memory of the blackout and fear. "No. But I was with my mom all day Friday and at the ball Friday night. And yesterday I didn't leave the apartment except to go for ice cream with you." She felt the warmth climb her neck at his knowing grin.

"That was a good reason to leave."

She met his gaze and nodded. "So's this."

"Yeah." The doors to the elevator slid open and Chandler stepped out, first holding the doors open while he scanned the space. "All good."

A minute later they were in his truck and headed toward 395, the interstate spur that crossed the Potomac into the heart of Washington, DC. Instead of heading north into the city, Chandler drove south to Arlington and then through Seven Corners toward Madeline's town house.

The ride was quiet but comfortable. Jaime didn't feel the need to fill the space with words, and she liked that as they drove to the out-of-the-way section of the suburb where Tiffany and her mother lived. A row of small town houses folded into another row as one community street melded into another. Trees of a size that indicated they'd been planted thirty or forty years ago pushed the sidewalk up in uneven waves, and the townhomes appeared maintained if not in tip-top shape. The schools would be decent, though not up to the standards of those in some of the suburbs. It looked like a pleasant enough place for a young girl to grow up.

It was a safe if slightly depressed area similar to the neighborhoods Jaime had lived in at Tiffany's age.

Jaime blew out a breath as Chandler pulled up to the curb and Aslan bounced against her seat. She laughed even as she brushed the golden fur from her sweater. "Too bad we had to bring Aslan along."

"Really?" Chandler looked, and the small dimple in his chin appeared and she felt herself melt.

"I was just kidding." Her thoughts turned toward Tiffany. "Aslan is so good for Tiffany, I just wonder if we're doing the right thing."

"What do you mean? Helping her is good."

"Maybe, but we don't know her story well enough."

Aslan tried to climb out of the back seat, but Chandler nudged him back. "What do you mean?"

"We don't know where her abuser took her or how he groomed her. You wouldn't believe the places I refused to go to after my uncle was done with me." She still had a hard time looking at arcades, let alone stepping inside one. "I guess I'm encouraging flexibility. We'll have to watch for her subtle cues."

Chandler took the words in and then nodded. "I see what you mean. It's why I'm glad you're here. You can keep me from doing or saying something that will harm her."

As she waited for Chandler to open her car door, Jaime struggled to imagine him hurting anyone. While he had a steel core, there was such gentleness to the man. He was a study in contradictions.

After stepping from the truck, she walked with Chandler up the short sidewalk to the door, a shiver brushing her spine as their arms swung next to each other. It was the whisper that he was near and she was safe. Chandler knocked on the door, then knocked again when no one came.

There was a sound of footsteps within, and Jaime pasted on a smile. The door opened, and her smile disappeared. Madeline stood there, one eye almost swollen shut and an angry set of welts lacing her neck. "What happened to you?"

"Corey Bowman happened." Madeline's voice rasped as if she had a bad cold.

"Who?" Jaime glanced from Madeline to Chandler, who looked like he wanted to punch someone.

Chandler cleared his throat as he closed the door. "He's the one who abused Tiffany."

Madeline nodded, her hand creeping to her throat as if she could hide the welts.

"Isn't he in jail?" Jaime's thoughts spun as she took in the bruises. "Wait. Where's Tiffany?"

"In her room watching a movie on my tablet. I knew we'd need to talk first." Madeline's eyes filled with tears that leaked down her cheeks. "He heard we'd gone to the police. Thought I'd back down, and when I didn't he hit me."

"Looks like he tried to kill you." Jaime turned in a quick circle in the narrow hallway. "Ice. You need ice."

"I've done all that. This happened last night."

Chandler frowned. "Did you call the police again?"

"Yes. They're looking for Corey, but I don't know when they'll find him." The *or if* hung in the air.

Jaime rubbed her temples as thoughts pinged through her mind so quickly she wasn't sure she could capture them. "Please tell me Tiffany didn't witness this." The trauma of watching her mother beaten or the police investigate might be too much for the poor child.

"She was asleep when he arrived." Madeline started shaking, and Jaime led her to a chair at the tiny kitchen table. "I don't know what to do. Until the police find Corey and put him in jail, he could show up again. And he'll be angrier."

CHAPTER 31

Madeline stood frozen, looking shaken and confused. "What can I do?"

Jaime put a hand on the woman's shoulder. "Madeline, go upstairs, grab enough clothes and toiletries for a few days, and then we'll get you to safety."

"Doesn't Tiffany need to stay in her safe place?"

"We'll tell her it's a vacation of sorts."

"But where can we go? I'm not taking my child to a shelter. And all of our things are here." Madeline glanced around.

"I know the perfect place. Pack a bag for yourself and another for Tiffany. Make sure you include any stuffed animals or books that are special to her. Anything that will comfort her." She stepped toward the front door.

"Where are you going?" Madeline asked.

"To make a call. We can leave as soon as you're ready."

Tiffany appeared at the top of the stairs, her nose crinkled and shoulders hunched. "Mommy?"

"We're going on a little trip, baby. Let's get your bag packed so we can leave with Mr. Chandler and Aslan."

As Madeline headed up the stairs, Chandler followed Jaime out the door. "What's your plan?"

Jaime pulled out her phone. "I'm calling my mother."

She sank onto the front step, ignoring the cold that had worked its way through her jeans and vest, and tapped her mother's number.

The call went to voice mail, so she sent a text. You home and up for company? I need a favor.

Then she tapped her phone against her chin and tried to think of anyone else who might be willing to take the small family in for a few days. Emilie and Hayden didn't have extra space, and Caroline was staying with her. Maybe Savannah? She sent a text to her with a quick update.

> We need to talk. Developments with Tiffany. She needs a place to stay.

While she waited for a reply, she couldn't help wondering how her mom would react. Would she take this opportunity as a chance at redemption?

Her phone rang. Mom.

"Jaime, is everything all right?"

Ouch. Was she such a distant daughter that her mother assumed any call contained bad news? "Are you home?"

"Yes." The word was drawn out.

"I have a favor to ask."

"So you said. You know I'll do it if I can." The desperate edge to her mother's voice broke Jaime. She wanted to end the distance between them but wasn't sure how.

"I have a single mom and her daughter who need a place to stay for a few days." She gave her mother the quick summary.

"This little girl is you? And I get a chance to do things right this time?" The quiet words knifed through Jaime.

"Yes." Her whisper matched her mother's. "I know it's a lot to ask. Tiffany was already in pain, and now this. They can't stay in their home, not when her abuser came back and attacked Madeline. Tiffany didn't witness it, but she may be fully aware of what happened. If she is, then staying here could add to her trauma."

"We can help her?"

"Maybe her mother too. Madeline is a single mom and so overwhelmed. Hearing your story might help her hold on, and she needs her own place to heal."

"But I failed."

"And that can warn her, while all the things you did right can help her."

There was silence until her mother sighed. "I failed you completely, Jaime. I will be sorry until my last breath."

"Then help make things right for Tiffany. We can make a difference for her, take the lessons we learned the hard way and shield her from the same mistakes." She heard the door opening behind her and stood to walk away. "The woman needs our help, Mom. She simply doesn't have the coping skills."

"Bring them here. They can have your old room, and we'll play it by ear. They can stay through the end of the month at least." Mom paused. "How long until you arrive?"

"Thirty minutes if traffic cooperates."

"Enough time to put fresh sheets on the bed and clean the bathroom. Do they have a car, or will they need help getting around?"

"Madeline has a car."

"Good. See you in thirty minutes."

Jaime turned back to the house and saw Madeline waiting on the top stair, arms crossed over her stomach.

"Do you have a place?"

"Yes. You can stay with my parents." And Jaime prayed that her mom could do for them everything she hadn't known to do for Jaime.

Chandler followed the GPS to her parents' home, while Madeline followed with Tiffany and Aslan. They drove in silence, and Jaime felt the urge to pray that somehow this moment, this bringing of

Tiffany to her mother, would begin the healing for everyone. But she didn't know what to do with that urge. Chandler and Caroline must be rubbing off on her . . .

She wanted the hope she saw in Caroline. The peace Emilie held. The determination of Hayden and the protectiveness of Chandler. Her friends all seemed to know who they were in a way she didn't. And she knew their acceptance came from a source she'd ignored for good reason.

How was she supposed to match her reality to the God they talked about?

She glanced in the side mirror to make sure Madeline was still there as Chandler executed a series of turns that took them from the main road and into the older neighborhood that sat on the line between town and suburb. In the northern Virginia area, it was easy to slip in and out of those, but her parents had found a pocket that created the perfect oasis. The fact they found it before housing prices skyrocketed only made it sweeter. The full basement had been a haven for Jaime when she needed a place to land during summers in college. That same space might cocoon Tiffany and Madeline now.

Chandler pulled his truck to the curb in front of the Cape Cod–style home. "I'll get Aslan and take him for a walk somewhere as a reward for his patience. We'll be back in an hour or so to pick you up."

"Are you sure you don't want to come in?"

"Yeah. We don't need to add to the chaos."

Jaime bit her lower lip. He was right. Best to get Tiffany settled and comfortable. That was her job. Besides, her parents' dog would be a Scooby snack for Aslan. "All right."

"Call me the moment you need me. We won't be far."

Jaime nodded, determined not to let him see that she wanted him to stay, to be her rock while she was Tiffany's.

The bright teal front door opened before Jaime could even unbuckle her seat belt. *Please don't let her overwhelm Tiffany.* The young girl needed a safe place, not a woman who was so intent on righting the wrongs of the past that she went overboard.

Madeline seemed frozen in her seat. At some point the woman would crash from the sustained pressure. Jaime hoped her mother could provide a safe place to weep.

Jaime walked back to Madeline's car and leaned down to the window.

"I don't think I could find my way back here without GPS, but that's good. Means *Corey*"—she mouthed the name—"can't find us either. Is there a neighborhood park?"

"I think so. I'm sure Mom will show you around. Although you'll need to stay cautious until we know where he is."

Her mother had stepped onto the front porch, a nervous smile on her face. She brushed a highlighted strand of hair behind her ear and came down the sidewalk. "You must be Madeline." Her smile wavered a moment at the corners before firming. "I'm so glad Jaime asked if you could stay. We have plenty of space."

Madeline edged around her old sedan. "Thank you. I wasn't sure what to do."

"Well, we're glad to give you a place to regroup." Mom turned toward the back seat where Tiffany lingered. "Is this your angel?"

Madeline gave Jaime a panicked look as Mom opened the door and cooed at the girl. Amazingly, Aslan let her mother slide Tiffany out.

Jaime shrugged and had to keep from laughing. This was why she had brought them here. Her mom would force them out of their shells and love them fiercely. It was something she did very well, and something Jaime was only now beginning to appreciate. For so long she'd allowed the past to control their future. No more. Today she changed that pattern.

CHAPTER 32

An hour later, Tiffany was running around the fenced backyard in pursuit of the Nichols family's Maltese, Happy. Jaime tried to relax but kept a vigilant eye on the little girl. Happy yipped, and Tiffany belly-laughed. Where usually the dog drove Jaime crazy with his barky happiness, she could appreciate the joy he elicited in the child.

Tiffany's squeals filled the space amid the crunch of leaves that needed to be raked. Her buzzing phone pulled Jaime from watching the chase. "Hello?"

"Hey." Chandler's slow enunciation tickled her ear. "You got them safely tucked away?"

"Yes." Jaime turned back to the yard as more squeals made her wince. "I don't know if you can hear that, but I think Tiffany's in love with my parents' dog."

"I'll try to shield Aslan from that knowledge."

"Good idea. He could eat Happy in one gulp if he wanted."

"One of those lap dogs?"

"Yep." She leaned her forearms on the deck's railing. "Are you ready to collect me?"

"Wondered if you were ready for pizza delivery."

Jaime turned to look inside the kitchen where her mother was a cooking whirlwind while Madeline sat at the table nursing a cold can of Pepsi. "I think my mom's cooking enough for a small army. Come join us."

He hesitated, and she tried not to read anything into her impromptu question and his delayed response.

"I can kill more time if you need it."

"I don't. My mom's philosophy has long been the more the merrier, which is why me as an only must have been a disappointment. She's one of those women who needed a brood."

"You haven't disappointed them."

"No way you can know that without really meeting them."

"Touché." There was a sweet silence where she knew she had him.

"It's a home-cooked meal." She straightened and walked to the door. "Mom, you have enough for one more?"

"Sure. Probably enough for a basketball team."

"That's what I thought. Thanks." She closed the door. "Hear that?"

"I did. We'll be there in five minutes."

"See you soon." A silly sappiness spread through her at the thought of Chandler meeting her Special Forces dad. Quick interactions at court and the military ball weren't enough to see what her dad would think of this man. Her father was a hard judge of men, and she needed to know if he had the same read on Chandler's character that she did.

Officially meeting Jaime's family rather than sitting near them in court shouldn't mean anything. Not really. But it felt like the next step. Problem was she wasn't ready.

And the critical separation of faith remained between them. That was something he couldn't waver on, but he needed to see for himself that Tiffany was all right. At least that's what he was telling himself. He might even believe it.

He pulled to the curb in front of Madeline's sedan.

A minute later he paused as he strode up the sidewalk with Aslan. Was that laughter? It sounded like a young girl's, and it was musical. Aslan pulled him to a stop to sniff a tree and then led the way around the small home to the side yard. Chandler peeked over the small fence and smiled at the sight of Tiffany running around, braids flapping in the breeze as a small, white dog yipped at her heels. Aslan's ears perked and he woofed, barely gaining the attention of the small dog before it raced after Tiffany.

"I think you have competition, buddy."

Aslan ignored him, attention locked on the activity within the yard. His tail wagged and he pulled against the leash before woofing again. Chandler glanced around and then walked to the gate. "Let's join the fun."

As soon as the gate opened, Aslan tugged the leash from his hand.

"Great." So much for introducing the animals with supervision. The yipper didn't seem to care as he redirected toward Aslan, who raced for Tiffany. The moment he reached her, Aslan stood and put his paws on her shoulders as the girl laughed and hugged the large golden.

"Aslan?" Jaime's voice reached him about the time he heard someone clomping down stairs. "Where's your owner, since I know you didn't drive?"

He woofed at her and Chandler imagined a happy doggy smile on his face. His dog was as smitten with Jaime as he was.

Chandler closed the gate and walked toward the action. "Sorry about letting ourselves in. Aslan was pretty intent on joining the fun."

Jaime grinned at him, her hands stuffed in the back pockets of skinny jeans that fit just right. He hadn't noticed before that the coat she wore was the color of her eyes, making them startlingly bright. He swallowed hard. She stole his breath in a way no one had since Rianna. As he stood in front of Jaime, reality hit him. He was a goner where she was concerned.

Did she feel the same way about him? And what would he do if she did?

"You okay?" Her grin slipped.

"Yeah. The question is how's our girl?"

Jaime turned toward Tiffany. "I've never seen her like this. She's practically carefree."

"Yeah. Even with Aslan she hasn't been this free."

"Aslan is a safe place for her, but there's something about my dad's pipsqueak, Happy. He pulls people out in a way little else can." The dog in question jumped as if to grow Aslan-sized.

"He's got heart."

Jaime nodded. "That he does."

Chandler took in the carefully groomed yard. "Is this your dad's hobby? It looks better than most golf courses."

"Actually, it's my mom's. You should see it in the spring when her bulbs burst from the ground. Then in the summer it's her roses and peonies. There are also a few crepe myrtles by the alley." Jaime smiled as her shoulder brushed his. "The yard is her canvas."

"Well, she's a master artist."

"You should tell her."

Chandler nodded, but all he wanted to do at this moment was pull this woman, the one in front of him, into his arms—the exact thing he couldn't do.

"Jaime, reintroduce me to your friend." Her mother came off the deck. The family resemblance was striking. So this was Jaime's future. It was a nice vision of what could be.

"Chandler Bolton." He extended his hand and she took it for a firm handshake.

Her mother gave him the once-over, and he stood straight, wanting to meet with her approval.

"I'm Joann Nichols. Bill will join us for dinner." She smiled, but it was tight. "I've lived long enough to presume everyone's as bad at remembering names as I am." She studied Chandler, and he tried not to shift his feet. "You're the one keeping Jaime out of trouble."

"Mother." Jaime rolled her eyes like a teenager.

"Nothing to it, ma'am."

Joann gave a nod. "I like you. Now come on in. All of you. It's time to get our guests settled and then have some dinner." She glanced at Chandler. "I imagine there are some bags you can help with."

Madeline frowned as her fingers brushed against the bruises around her neck. "Tiffany and I brought everything in with us."

"That's all you brought?" Joann turned to Jaime. "I thought you said they'd be staying for at least a week."

Jaime shrugged. "I can always take Madeline back for more if needed."

Her mother clucked over Madeline and then cooed as Tiffany came in, her cheeks chapped from the cold and a smile gracing her face. "I think the time outside was good for you." She hollered down the hallway for her husband. "Time to eat, Bill."

"Coming." A deep, resolute voice came from somewhere down a short hallway. A minute later a man in his early fifties walked into the kitchen, bearing erect and firm. This was a man who knew who he was and wouldn't be blown about by the winds of challenges. He extended his hand while studying Chandler. "Bill Nichols. We met at the hearing and briefly at the ball."

Chandler stood even taller and allowed the man to study him, glad for every moment in the gym. He didn't want to be measured lacking by this man's man.

Through dinner Bill Nichols kept a careful eye on him but allowed the conversation to flow without interrogating him about his intentions.

As he watched the family's careful, almost stilted, conversation with their daughter, Chandler knew that restoring the relationship would still take some work, but he sensed they were trying. The abuse Jaime had experienced impacted her whole family. Maybe he could help find a way to ease the strain.

CHAPTER 33

On Monday morning at eight o'clock, Caroline knocked on Jaime's bedroom door. "I've decided today's a good day for a mental health break."

"A what?"

"I'm playing hooky." Caroline straightened the asymmetrical hem of the tunic she wore over workout leggings. "You need a break from everything, and the only way that will happen is if I'm your babysitter."

"What?" Jaime pushed against the edge of the bed as her mind struggled to wake up.

Caroline smirked at her. "You know exactly what I mean." She picked up the pad of paper on the nightstand that contained a list of things to do regarding Tiffany. "I see your ethics issue is no longer top priority."

"For the moment. I only asked Savannah to push on it last Thursday. It seems reasonable to wait until tomorrow to nudge again."

"Sure. Let's grab coffee and then watch a total chick flick."

"I don't own any."

"So I've noticed, and it's a crime." Caroline made a face. "Isn't that ironic for the defense attorney? Lucky for you I grabbed a couple from my collection when I went home yesterday."

"Any progress on the floors?"

"Not enough. I have a bad feeling, but what can I do?" Caroline shrugged. "This is one thing that is so firmly out of my control, there's no point worrying."

"That works as long as you keep staying here."

"And paying that ridiculous parking fee. Talk about gouging." She shook her head. "The Keurig's ready to brew whatever magic you want, and the DVD player is ready to plug in the movie of your choice. You have five minutes to get dressed."

"Make it ten." Jaime hurried through a shower, then came to the small living room and sank onto the futon with a towel wrapped around her head. "What are my choices?"

"Get your coffee first."

Jaime pushed from the futon and obeyed, then settled in.

A couple hours later the credits to *Spider-Man: Homecoming* played across the screen, and Jaime shifted as though to get up.

"You have to wait for the bonus scene."

"There won't be one."

"This is a Marvel movie." Caroline plopped her feet on the coffee table. "There will be at least one."

"I'm still not sure how you call this a romance."

"Well, Iron Man and Pepper are back on." Caroline opened her mouth to say something else, then shut it.

Jaime sighed as she reached for Simba and pulled him onto her lap. "You might as well say whatever's on your mind."

"All right. Just remember you asked." Caroline took a breath and her fingers twirled a piece of hair. "I've noticed something. Living here will do that, you know."

"It can't be that bad." Simba began to purr and nuzzle her fingers.

"Why don't you have any pictures of your family? I realize

things have been hard, but you're their only child, so I guess I expected more contact between you."

"Our relationship is complicated."

"You know they love you. I could see that when they were here."

That was the thing. Jaime was never certain. A part of her mind screamed that her mom should have protected her and her father should have done something the moment he returned. Why hadn't he noticed she had changed? The should-haves could kill her. Yet she wanted to know her dad approved of Chandler, and she'd gone to her mother for help with Tiffany and Madeline. "It's complicated."

"Jaime." Caroline's clear voice grabbed Jaime's attention. "They love you. It's the way of parents."

"Not all families are wonderful and pristine like yours. Some are just messy and mixed up."

"I don't buy that for a second. And don't presume you understand my family." There was a sad note to the words, but Jaime didn't probe.

"Caroline, your childhood was nothing like mine."

"True. And be grateful."

"Grateful that I'm messed up."

"You are not. You are this amazing woman who has risen above a terror that could have branded you for life. Instead, look at you doing crazy good things to help those who can't do that for themselves."

"Don't make me a saint."

Caroline snorted. "I know you too well for that. I also know there's a reason you don't have photos celebrating your parents." She bit her lower lip as if weighing whether to continue. "Do you blame them?"

"Yes. No. Of course. I was eight years old. I needed someone to protect me." She plunged forward. "Your God didn't do that either."

If Jaime expected the words to silence Caroline, she was surprised.

"You're right. He didn't stop the abuse." Caroline's jaw firmed and her fists clenched. "I don't understand why He sometimes allows horrible things. But I've wrestled with it until I can trust He's God. I know He's good. And I believe the Bible when it says vengeance is His. There are days I'd like a mighty dose of vengeance right now. It'd sure feel good, but that doesn't mean it's mine to dole out. And I also don't want His vengeance extended to me."

"Does that qualify as a sermon?"

Caroline laughed. "Maybe it does. Did you listen?"

"I heard. I'm not sure I can trust like that."

"Have you ever seen a mustard seed?"

"Sure. Those tiny things are crazy."

"That's all the faith I need. Faith the size of a mustard seed. Then I can believe God is who He says He is and He will do what He says."

Jaime let Caroline's words settle between them. Her friend was such a mystery, spending her days in the relative safety of a career clerk role. Jaime had always wondered why. Before she could ask, Caroline changed the topic.

"I'm surprised you didn't become a crusader like Emilie." Caroline brushed at her shirt. "Why not be the voice for the voiceless?"

"In some ways I am."

"Sure, criminal defendants need an advocate, but that's not what I mean."

Jaime blew out a breath and shifted against the futon. "It's too close to what I lived. I can't relive it through others' pain every day." It was bad enough hearing the little bits Emilie shared. And now Tiffany was ripping the veil off her delusion that she'd moved on. "But I did take Tiffany to my mom, and I'm helping where Savannah needs it. That's a start."

"All right."

"Really? That's all you're going to say?"

"Jaime, someday you must come to terms with your past and your family."

"I know." Jaime tugged a throw blanket under her chin as if it could shield her from Caroline's concern. Just in time the bonus scene flicked by, and she prayed for a moment to escape to her room. She could close the door and stop Caroline from saying anything else. But that wouldn't still the words echoing through her mind that her friend was right.

That afternoon, after Caroline's "mental health day" was disrupted by an emergency call from the judge, Jaime grabbed *The Lion, the Witch and the Wardrobe* and headed downstairs to the exercise bike. Maybe the book would distract her while she logged some miles.

She sank onto the saddle of a bike and started to read, flipping pages as she pedaled.

The story was simple. Four children discovered a wardrobe in an empty room when they were evacuated from war-torn London to the country during World War II. The back of the wardrobe led to a magical world filled with fantastical creatures who were ruled by a witch. These animals believed the children fulfilled a prophecy and would free them from the witch's control. The challenge was, one of the siblings was under the spell of the witch and the other three couldn't quite believe they were there to fulfill anything other than saving him and getting back to England.

Jaime had reached the point in the story where Edmund, the deceived younger brother, was freed. The words swept over her, and she could see herself in the scene with the great lion Aslan and the young boy. Maybe the scene was so powerful because of what *wasn't* said. What a moment of accountability and grace. Aslan had done absolutely nothing wrong, yet the golden lion was willing to bear the penalty for what Edmund had done. The message reverberated through Jaime.

It would be easy to say she was merely the victim. As a child those words were true. She had done nothing to deserve the evil acts her uncle had inflicted on her.

She would forever bear those scars.

But maybe she didn't have to walk with a pronounced limp of brokenness the rest of her life. She felt a flicker of hope . . . Could she fan that into a flame?

She reached for her phone and texted Caroline. You on your way back?

Soon. Almost done here. What's up?

I had a question.

There was silence then she saw the flashing that indicated Caroline was typing.

Okay. Be there in an hour or so.

As she waited, Jaime felt the burbles of nervousness. How could she ask her questions without Caroline going all Christian cheerleader fan-girl on her?

She needed thoughtful answers to her questions. Maybe she should ask Chandler, but their friendship had already borne a lot of weight for an acquaintance all of two weeks old. This felt like something she should share with a friend who had walked life with her as Caroline had the last eight years. She'd better get cleaned up from the biking, or Caroline would turn around the moment she entered the apartment.

Jaime went back to her apartment, but when she reached the bathroom she paused.

Something was out of place.

Caroline was more meticulous than Jaime, but in the bathroom Jaime had a system. She didn't want to waste precious time looking for toiletries. She ran a hand over the bottles, and it hit her. Her moisturizer was out of order and backward.

She frowned and slowly walked through the apartment again. Nothing else seemed out of place, but she couldn't shake the feeling that someone was watching.

Half an hour later Caroline breezed into the apartment without knocking. "I like having keys. I really should try TP-ing your bedroom."

Jaime chuckled but didn't move from the couch. She hadn't been able to shake the violated feeling. "Did you use some of my moisturizer this morning?" She hurried on as Caroline quirked her head. "It's okay if you did. I was just curious."

"I wouldn't use your things, Jaime." She folded her arms over the chest. "Is that why you called me to come here?"

"No. Something was out of place, but it was a crazy question. Sorry." She felt pressed against, as if the decision in front of her was a stone restricting her movement.

Caroline came around in front of her. "You okay?"

"I'm not sure." She pointed at the book she'd set next to her. "I finished it."

"Oh." Caroline glanced at the book, then at Jaime. "That's a good one. Why read it?"

"Chandler asked me to."

Caroline's lips formed an O, but she stayed silent.

Jaime twisted the blanket around her fingers. "Am I Edmund or Susan?"

"Wow, that's quite a question. Why not Lucy or Peter?" Caroline sank onto the edge of the futon and turned toward Jaime.

"I don't want to be Edmund."

"Edmund's ultimately a hero in the book, Jaime."

"He isn't for most of it though."

"Sure, but how many of us can be heroic for long periods of time, let alone our entire lives?" Caroline kicked off her shoes, then pulled her feet onto the couch. "Don't we hope for a moment of walking in brilliant truth amid a lifetime of slogging through our days?"

Jaime looked at her friend. "Are you all right?"

"Oh, I'm fine." But the shadows under her eyes warned Jaime that wasn't a fully truthful answer. "I'm here for you, remember?" She brushed a strand of hair out of her face. "Don't fall into the trap of believing you have to be one or the other. I like to think I'm Lucy with an optimistic outlook on life. I don't want to be so meek and gentle I fade into the background like Susan."

"Maybe I want to be Peter the Magnificent. Blazing into battles and slaying my foes."

Caroline laughed. "Jaime, you are that every time you step into a courtroom. You leave your foes decimated by the power of your voice."

"Then why do I feel voiceless?"

"Because you are, until the real 'Aslan' takes your voice and directs it." Caroline leaned closer, and there was a fire in her gaze. "It's only through Him that questions make sense. Even in our hardest times He is there. Sometimes we just have to look hard to find Him."

"I shouldn't have to."

"Why? Do you think you get a special pass?" Caroline paused as if considering her words with care. "Jaime, as much as you want to be healed, God wants it for you more. He will deal with you as gently and directly as Aslan did with Edmund. He will give you the tools you need to raise a battle cry as He did with Susan. He can give you the perfect elixir for healing like He gave Lucy. And He'll do it so you can turn around and extend healing to others the way you are doing with Tiffany."

What would it be like to walk like that? To walk whole, without the deep, seeping scars? To be able to extend hope and healing to others who'd been hurt as she had?

"Wishing it doesn't mean it will happen."

"But it could. What if it did?" Caroline clutched the blanket to her. "It's what you want. It's what we all want." The words whispered between them yet ricocheted through Jaime.

It was exactly what she wanted.

"What about all my questions? There are so many, and they aren't going away."

"It's okay. God's got big shoulders and can handle your questions. Even the dark ones. The ones you don't think you can ask anyone else. He's there and wants to listen."

"That sounds so good." But could she believe it?

"He's good. You can trust Him."

She'd never feel safe, no matter how secure the building she lived in or how high the apartment. The reality was her uncle had stolen much from her . . . but maybe God could restore it. Maybe He could remove the winter from her soul and replace it with the breath of spring. And maybe then she'd know what it meant to walk without fear.

CHAPTER 34

Despite his best efforts in arranging vacation days, Chandler had needed to go to work for an emergency with a vet. When he'd arrived at the office, the man had never shown. That wasn't necessarily unusual, but it was odd when the impromptu appointment was set so quickly after the call. It made him antsy, even though Beth insisted the man had sounded legitimate. Something was going on that didn't make sense, so maybe a break from work would help ease that tension.

Now if he could help Jaime. Her friend Caroline had assured him she'd keep Jaime home, and he'd had to trust she would. Now as he drove back home, he kept an eye on the rearview mirror.

Was that midnight-blue Mustang following him?

He'd considered the idea that Tiffany's molester might be the one harassing him, but it didn't fit. The man didn't have a military record and had seemingly disappeared since attacking Madeline. He didn't like the fact the man was still out there, but at least Jaime had found a safe place for Madeline and Tiffany.

Still, without more to go on, he was stymied about who might be calling and following him, and he didn't like it. He wanted to find the man who'd been at New Delhi, see if he was the one who'd made the calls.

Meanwhile, he could honor the promise he'd made last week to keep an eye on Jaime. He picked up his phone and touched her number. "Quick question."

"I might have an answer for you." She seemed subdued yet spunky.

"I made a promise to watch a certain movie with Tiffany last Friday. Any chance your parents would be up for company?"

"It would give us a good excuse to check on her."

He frowned. "You need an excuse? They're your parents."

"It's complicated."

"Doesn't need to be."

"Thank you, Captain Blunt." She sighed. "I'll ask Mom if we can bring over a movie and snacks. What are we seeing?"

"*Moana.* So you'll come too?"

"You weren't really thinking you'd go without me."

He could hear the teasing smile in her voice.

"Besides, I haven't seen that movie, but I've been told I should."

"Right. We'll have to stop and rent it somewhere."

"Don't do that. I'm pretty sure Caroline owns it."

"We can grab snacks on the way."

"I'll let Mom know. Meet you in the lobby in ten?"

"Sure." That's what he said, but no way he was going to do that again; his mama had raised him better. He'd meet her at her door and then hold the truck door for her as well.

Aslan pranced at his feet as if he'd understood the conversation. "Yes, you're coming too."

When Jaime opened the door to her apartment, she stole his breath. Her jeans and chunky maroon sweater with a down vest looked like something she should wear on a runway. All casual elegance and gaze capturing.

"You didn't need to come up here."

"It's what we do." He let out a low whistle. "You look great."

A soft rose tinged her cheeks. "Thanks." She cleared her throat and patted her oversized bag. "I've got the movie and bags of microwave popcorn. Mom said the distraction would be a great idea."

Aslan bumped her leg with his nose, so she rubbed his head. "Aslan is coming, of course."

"Of course."

When they reached her parents' house, Jaime clambered out of the truck almost before he had it parked. Women usually struggled a bit with climbing from the vehicle, but Jaime's height made it easy for her. She took off without waiting for him to catch up, and Aslan whined to be released.

"I've got the same feeling, buddy." He slid his seat forward, and the dog jumped to the ground.

As they caught up with Jaime, her mom opened the door. "Hi, Jaime, Chandler. Do y'all mind if I run to the grocery store while you're here? I didn't want to leave them alone." She grimaced. "Madeline's gotten some texts today that have her locking down. Maybe you can find out what's really going on."

"Sure, Mom. We've got everything we need, so take your time."

Jaime seemed relaxed, but Chandler noted her clenched jaw and the way her stance hardened.

"We'll get to the bottom of this, Mrs. Nichols."

The woman studied him. "I believe you will. More important, I know they'll be safe as long as you're here." She hiked her purse strap higher on her shoulder. "I'll be as fast as I can."

The little white dog came tearing around the corner and only skidded to a stop when he was nose to nose with Aslan. The dogs romped, but Chandler looked past them to the couch, where Tiffany was curled up next to Madeline, blue light from a muted TV coloring her face.

Madeline stood and approached them.

"Thanks for bringing us here," she said, directing her gaze to Jaime. "Your parents are great, but Tiffany's in a funk. She won't even talk to me."

"She's entitled." Jaime watched the girl a moment, then her gaze met Chandler's. "There are many ways to recover from trauma. Silence is one."

"Not for this long." Madeline took a deep breath and exhaled. "I don't know how to help her, and counseling is slow. If anything, it seems to make things worse."

"Remember, Tiffany doesn't have the language to understand or describe what's happened to her. Counseling will help her peel back what happened, but it will be painful. Silence feels like a safe option." Jaime's words had a tinge of knowledge and experience.

Chandler returned his gaze to Tiffany and saw that Aslan had jumped onto the navy couch next to her. "Will your mom mind Aslan sitting there, Jaime?"

"Happy's up there all the time. I'll gladly vacuum the couch later. The fact that Tiffany looks content is what matters. Let's make the popcorn, and then we can run the movie." Jaime led him down the short hallway to the kitchen.

Madeline followed in step with him. "It's easier to clean a couch than salvage my daughter's soul." She stepped into the kitchen. "Can I get you anything to drink?"

"Water's fine." Jaime took the bottle Madeline offered, then studied the woman. "My mom mentioned you'd gotten some texts."

Madeline shuddered and wrapped her arms around her middle, looking cold and frail. "Corey. He says he'll find us and take Tiffany."

Chandler felt a slow burn start, but Jaime placed a hand on his arm, and he actually felt the anger tame.

"How would he know where you are?" Jaime's words were soft. "I don't know."

"Unless he followed you here, he doesn't. Maybe we should check your car for a tracker."

"If he'd done that, he'd already have shown up." Chandler turned toward the hallway. "I'll check to be sure though."

It didn't take long to examine the underbody of the car to

confirm there was nothing that looked like an add-on or tracking device. The man was probably making idle threats in an effort to intimidate Madeline.

Chandler headed back inside the house and paused in the doorway of the living room. Jaime had settled next to Tiffany, allowing space between them as if inviting the girl to choose whether to trust her. As he watched, the girl shifted closer without taking her eyes from the screen. Just like that she was sandwiched between Jaime and Aslan.

Madeline cleared her throat from the kitchen and he went into the room. She held an empty glass. "Want anything?"

"Water is fine."

She handed him a bottle. He thanked her, then glanced toward the living room. "So tell me about Tiffany's counseling."

"It's a waste of time and money." She gave him a summary, and he could sense her frustration. "They're the experts, yet your dog does more to calm her."

"Trust the process."

"Easy to say when you aren't the one calming her nightmares. She's practically sleepwalking through the days." Madeline brushed under her eyes. "But I know you're right. It's just hard to watch and know there's nothing I can do right now other than be here for her."

"That might be what she needs most." He set the glass down and then headed toward the couch.

Tiffany lay curled into Jaime's side, Jaime rhythmically brushing the little girl's blond hair from her face as Jaime spoke softly. It didn't seem to matter what she said, just that she spoke in a soothing voice, as the girl's eyes drifted shut, then fluttered open. Jaime shook her head slightly at him, and he stepped behind the couch, out of Tiffany's line of sight. It was magical watching Jaime soothe the girl.

Twenty minutes later, Jaime carried Tiffany to the basement, staggering slightly under the girl's weight. Once Tiffany was settled in bed, with the light on, Jaime headed back, and Chandler noted the fatigue in her stance. She still seemed to carry the weight of the girl, even though she'd tucked her into bed.

"Maybe we should head out."

She nodded. "Mom texted that she's on her way back, so they won't be alone."

After they said good-bye and climbed into the truck with Aslan, he reached for her hand. He was surprised when she didn't resist, though he hid his reaction from her. "You did a great job with Tiffany."

"I didn't do much. She just needed a safe place to fall. Aslan and I provided that for her today." She reached back, and the traitor dog leaned into her hand as she scratched behind his ears. "We're a good duo, aren't we?"

Aslan rested his muzzle on the seat back and grinned.

"It's getting close to suppertime. Let me take you to dinner."

She looked at him in surprise. "You don't need to do that."

"I'm sure you thought your mom would cook for you. As I see it, you did the hard work with Tiffany."

He considered some options. "What about dinner at Busboys and Poets down in Shirlington? I'm hungry for their blackened salmon."

Her eyes widened. "That's too much." She glanced down at her jeans and blouse.

"You look amazing," he said. "Every man in the place will be jealous because you're with me. But if it would make you feel better, I'll take you back to your place first and you can change. We have to drop Aslan off anyway."

She studied him, then nodded, a slow smile spreading on her face. "If you're sure. I'd like that."

Not nearly as much as he would.

CHAPTER 35

J aime's phone pinged, and she picked it up. What was this? A photo of her walking to the truck with Chandler, followed by another showing them in her parents' backyard the day before, and a third showing her in the lobby at her apartment complex. The fact that someone was watching her this closely was terrifying. It had to be her uncle's doing.

She stared into the bedroom mirror, her thoughts swirling into fear.

Chandler would be at her door any minute, and her heart wouldn't stop somersaulting.

"Do you want the questions to plague your life? Do you want a relationship with Chandler more than you want to cling to fear?"

She whispered the questions into the emptiness of her small apartment. She'd spent so much time fighting what she wanted or desired, she didn't know if she could risk wanting more. Or if she even should.

What was that verse Caroline had told her? God doesn't give us a spirit of fear?

The thought that it was coming to her mind in this moment made her laugh even as she wanted to cling to the promise. Could there really be a promise of no fear? A way to trade her longtime companion for one of love and a sound mind? It was such an odd way to think, but she found comfort in it.

Maybe without the fear she could wrestle her questions about God and His absence to the ground.

"While it's a nice thought, it won't get me ready before that man knocks on my door."

Jaime never talked to herself. Maybe she should warn him that in the short time Caroline had stayed with her, she had lost her mind. Instead of feeling like a place of safety, her apartment carried the weight of solitude with a side of depressing and lonely.

Jaime stepped from the mirror and pulled on a pair of olive-green skinny jeans and a loose-weave silver sweater that she threw over a cami. With a pair of boots that would bring her to Chandler's height and a chunky necklace she could use as a weapon if needed, she felt ready. She could hold her own and stand her ground. She pulled her hair into a loose bun on top of her head and teased a few strands from the edges. A stroke or two of makeup and a swipe of mascara, and she stopped. Anything more would look like she was trying. She paused long enough to inhale a whiff of lavender oil, begging it to calm her nerves.

A knock at the door as she stood brushing her teeth made her freeze. She spit and then wiped a towel across her lips as he knocked again.

She closed her eyes and drew in a long breath that she blew out slowly.

Time to go.

Had Jaime changed her mind?

If she didn't open the door quickly, he might slink away so neither of them was embarrassed by her change of heart. He rapped on the door again, then stepped back, swinging his arms as if the motion would release his nervous energy.

How could one woman unnerve him like this? Even trying to narrow down the soldier who was harassing him was nothing compared to the knot in his gut about what she would say and do. He heard steps and froze his arms at his side. A moment later the door eased open. If he hadn't already been locked in place, he would have been rendered incapacitated. As it was, his voice abandoned him.

Those boots brought her almost nose to nose with him. She carried herself with the regal bearing of an Amazon, and she wore her casual outfit like armor, any softness counterbalanced by the guarded look in her eyes. Words whooshed from him. "You look great."

A slow flush of color climbed her neck, and he resisted the urge to fist pump. She might be a standoffish woman, but she still wanted to be told she was a princess warrior worth his time and attention.

"Thank you." The words were a breath that had him leaning closer.

He didn't want to miss a word, but as she flinched slightly, he eased back. There was still a piece to her past he needed to understand. If he didn't know better, he'd say she was the classic domestic violence victim, only the violence had occurred when she was a child, and made a deeper imprint. He struggled to reconcile that with the hard-as-nails woman he'd seen in the legal arena.

"Ready to go? Busboys and Poets has a poetry show starting in a little over an hour."

She met his gaze with a directness that left him feeling he could read her mind.

"I don't really like poetry."

"You'll like this."

She frowned, then smoothed her face back to neutral. "I'll let you convince me." She visibly relaxed her shoulders and turned toward a table he could barely see from his vantage point in the hall. A moment later she held her purse and keys. "I'm ready."

"Isn't it customary to invite someone in for a moment before you depart?'

"Not for me." She smiled, but there was distance coloring it. As if she wanted to test how he'd react to her attitude.

That was all right. He could skirt the fight. "I'm ready for a good steak and some entertaining poetry."

The walk to the elevator and ride down was quiet, but he decided to feel comfortable in it. She could set the tone for the conversation and evening. He'd provide the food and the diversion as needed.

Thirty minutes later they'd parked at one of the Shirlington lots and walked toward the restaurant. "You know, we can see a movie if you'd rather."

"I'm willing to try poetry. If you like it, I'll try to find value in it." There. The touch of sass was back in her voice as she slid her hands into her jeans' back pockets and sauntered nonchalantly down the sidewalk. Next to him. She seemed oblivious to the admiring gazes from the men they encountered, but he noted each one. Why was she so impervious to her own beauty? She was proving to be someone who made the chase interesting, and that made him more determined than ever to figure out what made Jaime the intriguing woman she was.

———

Jaime loved the neighborhood vibe Shirlington cultivated. She really should visit more often than the one evening a year she usually spent there.

As they walked down the sidewalk, Chandler stayed on the outside nearest the road. Who had taught him such a level of courtesy? He never talked about himself other than the mention of his divorce. It was almost like he'd been on ice for thirty years and lacked a history, but that wasn't possible.

Jaime glanced at him again, noting how his hair curled around the edges of his ears. It frustrated her when men took such pains with her. In some ways it made her feel like they thought she wasn't capable—but with him it ignited a cherished feeling. Not even her dad had treated her with such care. She glanced at Chandler. What did he see in her?

Somehow, he seemed immune to the blot that stained her life. She wasn't sure whether to call him a fool or cry in relief that her deepest secrets hadn't caused him to flee. She swallowed against sudden tears that threatened to spill over.

"Hey, you've gotten quiet." He nudged her with his elbow, a light, playful touch. "Everything all right? We could walk the trails if you'd rather."

She glanced down at her boots and chuckled. "Not in these." He guided her around a lamppost. "Why do you do that?"

He stopped and looked at her, his gaze boring into her. "Do what?"

"Why do you make sure I'm safe?"

"My mama taught me to treat women well."

"Hmmm."

"The restaurant's right there." He checked for traffic, then led her across the street to a brick building painted a soft butter and past a small section of outside seating with green and mustard-yellow umbrellas. She shivered and glanced around.

Chandler stilled beside her. "Everything okay?"

"It is." But as she said the words she glanced around. Why did it feel like a presence lurked? She froze.

Over there.

A shadow.

Was it simply the light from the setting sun casting long fingers of darkness? Or was someone really lurking there?

"Jaime?"

"Is there a shadow over there?" She pointed, and the shadow shifted.

"Stay right here." Chandler eased her toward the pool of light from a storefront window and then leaned close. "Pretend you're enjoying this." He ran his fingers along a strand of her hair before tucking it behind her ear.

A traitorous tickle snaked up her spine, and she looked down.

"I'm going to check it out." He raised his voice. "I left my wallet in the car. I'll be right back."

Then he spun and hurried toward the shadow. Before he got there, the shadow bolted. Chandler started after him, and Jaime shivered. What had started as a nice evening now had a sinister tinge. Had it been Dane? He'd been quiet since the ball, but she knew it couldn't last, not if he wanted the appointment. He had to know she wouldn't simply walk away.

A stiff wind tossed a few leaves down the sidewalk, and Jaime wanted to go inside and hide from the shadows and the wind.

Chandler hustled back, barely breathing hard. "Whoever it was took off."

"What was he driving?"

"An SUV of some sort. Dark. I wasn't expecting him to bolt that direction."

"I'm ready to eat." And push the last five minutes aside. She would physically shove the thoughts aside.

Chandler held the door for her. "Are you sure you still want to do this?"

"Yes."

When Chandler held the door, she stepped inside, curious to see the restaurant. Wooden tables were mixed with a few red high-backed armchairs, resting on tile and then carpet. Behind that were floor-to-ceiling wooden bookshelves loaded with an assortment of books.

She loved everything, from the bright paint to the eclectic paintings hanging behind the bar. "What a fun environment."

Chandler placed a hand at the small of her back as he led Jaime to the hostess stand. "It is."

She pointed to the bookshelves. "Is that really a bookstore? What a perfect place to wait." She'd take the opportunity to recover among the books. There weren't many—it was just a nook—but she loved the look of the dark wood bookshelves interspersed with beautiful book spines and covers. The floor-to-ceiling red curtains grabbed her attention. "Is that a table perched on a stage?"

"That's where the poetry reading will be." He gave the hostess his name, then led Jaime to the bookshelves. "We'll have a few minutes before a table opens up."

She ran a hand over one of the sliding ladders attached to the bookshelves. "Every time I see one of these, I want to pretend I'm Belle and sing my way across the shelves."

"Belle?" Chandler's eyebrows knit together as he frowned in confusion.

"From *Beauty and the Beast*. Did your mama forget to let you watch Disney classics?"

"Guess my dad was too busy taking me to Star Wars movies."

She grimaced and stepped closer to the books. The shelves were filled with an eclectic mix of authors, with modern art filling the space between bookshelves. "Your education was clearly incomplete."

"You can help me rectify that."

She turned and looked at him, lifting her chin to meet his gaze head on. "You realize that would involve cartoons. About princesses. And singing teapots and candlesticks."

He shrugged. "How bad can it be?"

He had no idea. "All right. Then when we're done here, come to my place, and we'll watch it." She wanted to bite back the words the moment they escaped, but she'd gotten caught up in their banter and he nodded before she could, almost as if he sensed she might revoke her invitation.

"Some really good salmon, then movies at your place."

"Instead of poetry?"

"Only if you're sure." He winked at her, and part of her heart melted.

"The chance to see you watching not just any movie but a classic princess cartoon? I'm completely in." She couldn't wait to see his Marvel loving reaction to such culture.

The conversation over the meal flowed easily. She even got him to open up some about his family and childhood. After a meal that left her groaning she was so full, Chandler insisted on getting dessert for later during the movie.

She looked from him to the waiter. "The only way I'll have room for that is if we walk home."

"Don't worry, by the time we watch your movie, you'll be begging to eat the key lime pie." He grinned and held up two fingers. "We'll take two slices."

And funny thing, two hours later she was. Chandler had been a gentleman, and she'd slowly relaxed as they went from Belle singing about the small town she lived in to the snowball fight. He looked . . . right . . . in her small space. Where she should feel threatened and on guard, she knew he would honor her in all his actions. He'd certainly demonstrated that as he stayed on his side of the futon, only once stretching an arm along the back. She couldn't blame him since he was too big for any of her furniture . . . but he may have slid a bit over so his fingers brushed her hair.

The last song played over the closing credits, and she turned to him. "What did you think?"

"It's not Star Wars."

"No, but there's a plot."

"I would have never pegged you as a happily-ever-after girl."

She snorted, though with him here, she had whispers that it might be more than a storyteller's lie. "I wouldn't hold my breath."

"I can do that for three minutes."

"Of course you can." She rolled her eyes. She didn't want him to leave. After all, Aslan and Simba were curled next to each other on the floor. So much for dogs and cats hating each other. Maybe she didn't have to pretend she disliked him either. She held up another DVD. "Want to watch another movie?"

"*The Lion, the Witch and the Wardrobe*? Did you read the book?"

"Finished it this morning, and I'd love to watch the movie again. It's been years."

"I'd like that." He leaned toward her until she could feel his breath warm on her face. "You are an amazing woman, Jaime Nichols."

What couldn't this specimen of male perfection do? As he nudged toward her, her breath caught on the hope he would kiss her. Was she ready to risk her heart to him?

But then he eased back and stood to clear their dessert dishes from the small coffee table and carry them the fifteen steps to the kitchen. And she knew. She wanted to plunge in and see just how perfect Chandler Bolton was.

As she watched him, their gazes collided. Was it possible he felt the same?

CHAPTER 36

Chandler fought the desire to pull Jaime into his arms. There was something in her eyes as she watched him that telegraphed he needed to leave, fast, or he'd get swept up into a dream that his failed marriage had told him was as much a fairy tale as the idea that Belle could kiss a beast and unleash a prince. Those story lines were best left in fairy tales and not where they collided with reality.

But when Jaime looked at him like that, with the mixture of hope tugging him toward her and fear reminding him to take his time, it was hard not to tug her close and see how well she fit inside his arms.

Besides, Aslan must need to step out. He edged back, latching onto the excuse. "Thanks for the movie. I need to be a responsible dog owner." The animal's ears flicked, but the traitor didn't budge. Instead, he leaned down and nosed Simba.

A flicker of something like disappointment flashed across Jaime's face. "Are you taking him out?"

"Probably. Last walk before bed."

Simba stood and sauntered away as if he'd been disturbed by their voices. The only way a cat was better than a dog was he didn't need walks. But one look at Aslan's intelligent mug and warm eyes was all it took to know that dogs were far superior.

"Can I join you? Walk off the dessert?"

He should probably say no. It seemed too much like extending the date if she came with him. At the same time, it interested him that she wanted to do exactly that. Where were they headed, and was she willing to go there?

Wherever it was, he couldn't say no to the light in her eyes. It would be worth whatever tangling of hearts happened to know that he was the reason it was there.

"Let me grab a jacket." A moment later Jaime popped back out of her bedroom, and his heart expanded when she reached down and rubbed Aslan's ears. "Ready for some exercise, boy?"

The crazy cat jumped on the back of the futon and settled on the blanket spread across its back, as if to say they could have their walk while he stayed right there. Chandler knew he was getting the better experience.

TUESDAY, OCTOBER 16

Jaime's dreams had been filled with images of lions, wickedly white witches, and four siblings colliding with a beautiful girl and her beast. It was as if her subconscious couldn't release the questions that filled her after reading Chandler's book or seeing the movie. Maybe she should invite him over for dinner to talk about the book since she'd chickened out last night. After the quick walk around the complex, she'd wanted to settle into the peace of the moment rather than disturb it with her questions.

Could she trust him with her thoughts?

He'd cared enough to give her a book he valued. Then he'd watched the movie with her, even though it was more a family movie than a grand adventure. He was giving her space.

She tapped a quick question into a text. Come for dinner tonight?

He'd been sticking close, almost as if to keep her safe. She wanted to deny she needed it, but last night's scare in Shirlington made her grateful he'd decided to be her self-appointed knight in shining armor.

She tapped her phone against her chin as she waited for a reply. Maybe it had been a bad idea, too spontaneous. She knew better than to risk her heart becoming invested.

Sure. What time?

Her fingers trembled as she typed a simple word. Six?
See you then **After a moment:** Aslan or no Aslan?
She glanced around her small apartment and noted Simba perched on the couch back. The cat had places to hide if he wanted, and he'd enjoyed the company last night. He would be fine, and so would she.

Bring him

She'd barely noted his smiley face emoji when a text came through from Savannah.

Need to see you ASAP. I have an opening at nine.

See you then

Time to fly if she wanted to arrive in Old Town on time. Maybe her mentor had good news for her. She definitely needed some. After the appointment, she could grab groceries for this impromptu dinner on her way back.

With a minute to spare, Jaime knocked on Savannah's door. The woman rarely closed it all the way, instead keeping an open-door policy for staff and friends. Still Jaime felt the uncertainty of why she'd been called holding her back from entering like she belonged.

"Come in, Jaime." Savannah smiled at her, her dark hair slicked behind her ears and a brightly colored scarf knotted at the throat of her dark sheath dress. "You made good time."

"Nothing much demanding my attention today."

"Let's see if we can't change that."

"Does that mean you heard back from the bar?"

"I did. Their investigation showed everything we expected. They aren't even calling a hearing. Instead, I expect the letter clearing you to be in my in-box today." She shifted and clicked a few buttons on her mouse. "I'll forward it to your boss at the PD's office and get you back to work tomorrow."

"That's great news. Thank you!" Jaime fought to keep her voice steady. She should be elated because her name was cleared, but would Grant call her back to work? "Do you think he'll let me?"

Savannah frowned, highlighting a web of wrinkles along the bridge of her nose. "This letter should take care of it." She clicked another button and then leaned closer to the monitor. After a moment she tilted and twisted it so that Jaime could read the letter. "See? It's a full clearing and closure of the case."

Jaime shook her head and then sank onto the edge of a chair. "It's more than that. Don't forget that last week when I was there, someone was pressuring Grant to fire me."

"Have you talked to Grant?" Savannah's question was sharp.

"No, I didn't know how to broach it. I wasn't supposed to be at the office, let alone lurking outside his door. Someone wants to squeeze me out." Jaime hadn't wanted to say the words, but she knew they were true. She just couldn't prove it definitively.

"I'll strongly encourage Grant to have you report to work tomorrow. This was just a hiccup in your career."

"What? No push to have me join you?" There were days the

idea appealed to Jaime, but she didn't want to be her own boss. She might be high on justice, but she had a little too much mercy in her to chase down a client for payment.

Savannah leaned back in her chair, steepled her fingers, and studied Jaime. "You know you have a safe place to land when you're ready. If you never are, that's fine too. I trust God will lead you in the right direction."

"Why would you say that?"

"Say what?"

"That you trust God with my career?"

Savannah's lips twitched as if she fought to remain stoic. "Because I do. I trust Him with everyone I care about."

The words wrapped around Jaime. Was God pursuing her through friends who brought Him into routine conversations? "It isn't that simple."

"It never is, yet it is." Savannah shrugged and then stood. "I'm always here if you have questions about God." Then she grinned. "Until you do, let's see what Grant does. Then we'll take the next step. Until then anything we say is just conjecture. The other reason I called you in is I have a message from Madeline. She has questions about Tiffany's testimony at the grand jury hearing. I'd like you to stay point for her, regardless of when you restart at the public defender's office. Y'all have a rapport and she trusts you. I'll clear it with Grant if needed."

"I would like to continue helping them." Tiffany needed her, and maybe Madeline did too. Jaime stood and waited for Savannah to sweep in for one of her warmth-transferring hugs. "Thanks for all your help." The words were muffled by Savannah's shoulder.

"It's what I do." Savannah stepped back. "Now go enjoy your last free day."

"Yes, ma'am." Jaime felt the warmth of freedom as she walked out of the office, and hesitated before turning toward Hayden's office. The door was cracked, and she heard Hayden's calm voice. Jaime waited until the conversation stopped and then knocked.

"Come in."

She pushed the door open and walked inside. Hayden met her gaze with a quirked eyebrow. "Savannah just gave me the letter clearing me from the ethics investigation."

"That's good, though I'm not surprised."

Jaime motioned to the chair. "Can I sit?"

"Sure."

Jaime did, and then took a breath. "Would you be willing to call Senator Wesley's office on my behalf? I need to know that I tried my best to hold Dane accountable. With my options as narrow as they are, I'd like to meet with the senator if he'll make time." Jaime looked around, noting the peaceful pastoral painting that was opposite the typical lawyerly bar admittance hangings. Oh, to be in a setting like that rather than embroiled in all the conflict that was her life right now.

Hayden crossed her arms and leaned back. "Um. I already did. The impression I got was he was going to have someone from his staff contact you."

"When did you talk to him?"

"Saturday night. Andrew and I had dinner with his parents, so it provided a great forum. I wouldn't be surprised if someone followed up today. With the hearings in motion, it'll be a priority or it won't happen at all."

Jaime's phone vibrated, and she glanced at the screen. "Senator Wesley's office?"

"As I was saying." Hayden stood and headed to the hallway. "I'll give you some privacy."

"Thanks." Jaime's fingers trembled as she swiped the screen. "Hello?"

Dane resented being called to meetings. He was the one who should do the calling. Hadn't he earned the right after his years of faithful service to his country?

The senator apparently didn't think so.

Instead, the man insisted that Dane show up on demand like some faithful knight of old called to serve the prince. Only the senator wasn't a prince, and Dane wasn't a knight of old. No, he was a man who would rise to an elite rank in a matter of weeks. It was a done deal.

Or so the man had assured him just two weeks ago. Yet something wasn't right.

Senator Micah Langdon swirled his brandy in a thick cut crystal glass. The trappings of wealth that he'd tugged close couldn't hide the fact he was still an uncouth rebel at heart. "We've got a mess on our hands, Nichols."

"I've got it handled." He barely resisted the urge to spit the words.

"I don't think you do. My intelligence says these charges could stick."

No question about whether he did what was alleged. Interesting that the senator didn't seem to care. Maybe that meant there were things in that man's past that could be useful to him today. He'd have to dig deeper.

"You have one week to fix this. Make the charges disappear before the media gets wind of them. The last thing they need is the illusion you're unfit for duty."

Dane's back straightened at the insinuation. "I shouldn't have to fix this. Innocent until proven guilty."

The man chuckled, but it grated. "Those are nice words, but words the media doesn't care to embrace."

"I know. I'll get it taken care of."

"See that you do, because I will not push your nomination

through to commission without the assurance that this will not erupt in my face."

"It won't." No need to tell the man that surveillance was well in hand. His niece was a fool. She might think there was security in her apartment, but she didn't know anything. It had taken two minutes to slip into the apartment. Small, dank place that it was.

Service entrances were such an easy access point, especially when one had the right credentials. So easy to manufacture with today's technology. She'd never know what happened or who was there, but she'd know someone was. He had a staff of men who would do his bidding to move up the ranks with him. It was a simple trade: their futures for hers.

Maybe in time she'd understand she'd messed with the wrong man, but he doubted it.

CHAPTER 37

"This is Andy Gomez, legislative aide for Senator Wesley."

Jaime frowned at her phone and held it away from her face before pulling it back to her ear. "Yes?"

"Senator Wesley would like to schedule your testimony for the subcommittee."

Hold up. She had not signed on for this. All she'd wanted was a chance to talk to the senator privately. "What do you mean?"

"The senator always prefers for witnesses to cooperate without a subpoena, but we can send one if necessary."

"I still don't understand. Testify for what?" Jaime leaned back against the chair, all the fight leaving her.

"The senator believes you may have important information on Dane Nichols, and he wants the subcommittee to hear it from you."

Jaime closed her eyes and pinched the bridge of her nose. "When would I testify?"

"You'll appear next Tuesday at noon in the Russell Senate Office Building."

In the quick pause, Jaime's legs began to shake. Her heart raced until she wondered if this was the beginnings of a cardiac event. "Testify about Dane?"

"Yes. Someone passed along your lawsuit. Said you wanted to talk to the senator."

Jaime tried to focus, to breathe, but she just couldn't. "A subcommittee is more than one senator."

"That is true." He chuckled. "You'll check in with me, and then I'll escort you to the hearing room. Because you're an attorney, think of this as testifying under oath in a court."

"That's it?" Her thoughts raced. She wasn't prepared. Not for this. "Will Dane be there?"

"Possibly, but not required."

"What if I don't want to? I can't do this."

"Ma'am, I hate to be this blunt, but you don't have a choice."

She slumped over her knees and reminded herself this was what she wanted. The moment she mentioned the lawsuit to Hayden, this was a real risk. In fact, she'd asked Hayden to start this in motion. She should be thrilled. *Shoulds* didn't make it real though. "Will media be present?"

"Possibly. It depends on how interested they are in what's happening. Right now there hasn't been much because the hearings have been routine. Anything could happen though."

What could she do? A congressional subpoena had great authority she couldn't ignore. "I'll meet you then." She repeated the information and then hung up.

Hayden slipped back into her office. "Everything okay?"

"Yes. No. I don't know. Your future father-in-law is subpoenaing my testimony for my uncle's hearing."

"Really? That's great." Hayden walked behind her desk and sat. "This means those making the decision will hear your side of the story. Know more of who he is."

Jaime put her head in her hands as she leaned over. "Now the entire world will know what he did to me. Then they'll choose who they believe." She felt deflated and ready to crawl into bed, but that wasn't who she was becoming.

"They could also hear your story and realize this man does not have the character we expect in our generals."

"What if I black out during my testimony?"

Hayden studied her. "Then it further reinforces that this is not a minor issue. Only harsh trauma causes that kind of ongoing reaction."

Jaime looked at her fisted hands. She'd opened the door for all of this when she filed the criminal charges. She knew that. Now she must live with the results, but she didn't have to live through them alone. "Then you're my attorney."

"Absolutely. Let's get you a few minutes with the senator." She winked at Jaime. "He owes me one."

That afternoon Jaime followed Hayden through the Capitol Visitors Center. There was something about her heels clicking on the white marble that founding fathers had trod upon that made her knees tremble. She lived in the nation's capital. Some days she could pretend it was just another city. One moment in these halls of power brought the reality crashing over her. Decisions that impacted the course of her country happened here.

"We'll take the tunnel to Russell." Hayden led her beneath the senate chambers to the bowels of the Capitol, where they boarded a monorail. "This is a fun way to get between buildings. Normally you'd have a staffer with you, but I've got a pass."

"Thanks." Jaime didn't even try to grin as her stomach clenched at the upcoming meeting and what it represented.

"You'll be fine. Senator Wesley is a nice guy underneath the suit. You're a friend of mine, so that should help."

Senator Wesley sat on the powerful Armed Services Committee, and his office location near the standing committee's room reflected that stature.

"Did you know that Russell is three stories on the side that faces the Capitol and Constitution Avenue, but from C Street there are five stories above ground?"

Jaime shook her head. "Hayden, Washington trivia isn't going to distract me from what this meeting means."

The car jerked to a halt, and Hayden squeezed her shoulder and then stood. "This is our stop."

The Russell Building was as impressive on the inside as it was from without. While the façade outside was Doric columns and marble overlays, inside a checkerboard pattern covered the floor, and carvings covered most surfaces around doorways and soaring to the ceiling. Even the knobs indicating which floor the elevators were at had an Old World elegance.

Hayden led her through the warren of halls and stairs toward the senator's offices. "You can text as soon as your meeting is finished, and I'll come lead you back out."

"Where are you going?"

"I'm meeting Andrew for coffee. He happened to be spending today with his dad."

Jaime nodded, but her thoughts were already back on the hearing. The Armed Services Committee considered fifty thousand nominations for armed services positions each year.

Could her voice make a difference in such a pressured environment?

The familiar cold sweat slicked her hands. She took a deep breath, held it a moment, then another moment, then hissed it out slowly. Then she repeated the action until she felt her heart rate slow. She could beat this panic . . . and eventually her uncle.

She'd left nothing to chance on this road, except for the timing.

Clean, simple, direct.

Now that she had launched the first volley, she felt as she had each time her mother had taken her to Uncle Dane's house. The marbles rolled freely through her stomach until nausea loomed strong enough that no amount of controlled breathing would send them away.

Hayden led her to a heavy wooden door that had a United States and a Virginia flag standing next to it. "This is it."

A minute later, Hayden introduced her to the receptionist, a solemn woman somewhere in her late forties. "Please have a seat. The senator will be with you shortly."

Jaime nodded and ran slick palms along her pants. Thank God she'd dressed for work when she met with Savannah that morning. "I can't breathe."

"You'll do great. Scott just wants to hear your story. Learn the truth."

"He may be Scott to you, but to me he's an intimidating US senator."

"He won't be after you meet him." Any further words of comfort Hayden might have shared were cut off when the door to the senator's private office opened.

Jaime's heart took off in a gallop, trying to outrace the dance in her gut.

The silver-haired senator looked every bit as noble as his pictures portrayed, the man Andrew Wesley would become evident in the strong posture and rugged Cary Grant look. Jaime tried to see the hints of teddy bear softness that Hayden promised lurked beneath his surface, but all she saw was the iron focus and will of a man who was sure of who he was and what he could accomplish. Somehow she must direct that focus to the issue of her uncle.

A studied but focused smile revealed his perfect teeth. He walked toward her, and she rose from the couch, forcing her legs to lock rather than wobble.

"Miss Nichols, it's a pleasure." He shook her hand with the firmness of someone who knew his place in the world, and it was making important things happen. Then he turned to Hayden. "Thanks for bringing her here and making me aware of her story."

"A pleasure, sir."

"Now Hayden, we've talked about this 'sir' business."

There was a genuineness to him that made Jaime trust him.

"Yes, sir, Scott. It's just you're a senator."

"And you're an important family friend."

"More than that, Dad." The younger Wesley exited his father's private office. He leaned in to kiss Hayden's cheek. "Ready for our coffee?"

"Especially if there's more of those included." Hayden winked at him.

Jaime smiled at the playful, flirtatious side Andrew brought out in her friend. "Thanks for the escort."

"My pleasure." Hayden turned to the senator. "Be nice to Jaime. She's one of my best friends."

The words warmed Jaime as she watched Andrew take Hayden's arm and guide her to the door. Then she let out a breath and turned back to the senator. "Sir?"

"Why don't you come into my office?" He motioned her to proceed him.

"Thank you for making the time to meet with me."

"Hayden told me you had some concerns about testifying. Your testimony will be important." Instead of moving behind his broad, dark wood desk that looked large enough to serve as a mission control station, he sat on an antique, uncomfortable-looking couch. "Please have a seat."

She sank onto one of the upholstered wingback chairs that sat across from the couch. A row of flags was posted behind the couch, providing a patriotic backdrop as if he felt the need to remind her of his role. Her gaze ran over the prints on the red walls, one an antique, detailed map of the counties in Virginia. Another had *Life* magazine WWII covers. The iconic cover images told the story of strength, resolve, and patriotism. She hoped they communicated something about the man.

"Now how can I ease your mind?" His gaze was steady, and he adjusted his cuffs beneath his suit coat, only revealing the edges of his watch, but Jaime got the message. His time was valuable, and she'd been given a gift she shouldn't waste.

"I was subpoenaed today for my uncle Dane Nichols's advice and consent hearings."

"Yes, he is scheduled for a week from now."

That didn't give her much time to make things happen in the court case. The wheels of justice turned too slowly for that to impact this hearing. Her uncle would be confirmed long before he spent a full day in court. "I've never been asked to testify before Congress. Why now? Have you met my uncle?"

"Once. He's hard to forget."

"So I've been told." She forced herself to look up and hoped he could see her heart. "I'm not here because I don't want him to be a general, though I'll admit the thought makes me nauseous. Will my testimony matter?"

"I believe it will."

"Is it possible to close the hearing to media?"

"I don't believe so. We have all these open meeting laws. Don't you want people to hear what he's done?"

"Yes, if it can protect even one person."

"Do you have reason to believe he's abused other girls?" The senator looked suitably concerned.

"No, sir. Only research that shows many times abusers attack more than one person." She sighed and glanced back down, his direct focus difficult to meet for long. "The military is having enough challenges in the sexual abuse area. You don't want to add my uncle to a position of authority."

They spoke for a few more minutes as he asked probing questions, and she answered as honestly as she could.

"Your testimony will be timely." He stood, and a moment later she was shaking his hand and then being ushered out of his inner sanctum so quickly she wasn't entirely sure what had just happened. After meeting with his assistant, she walked the hallway of the Senate Office Building, then around a corner where she sank on the first bench she found, her legs collapsing under her.

Had she just told a powerful stranger her darkest secrets? Her hands trembled as she opened her purse and dug through it for a mint or some gum.

Important people walked past in herds. A senator with support staff, followed by lobbyists and aides. The tourists were easy to spot as they moved through the hallowed halls with wonder and a look of bewilderment. This was where decisions were made that affected their daily lives.

And here she sat, with no driving direction other than to finish the path she had started.

She wanted to weep because she'd started the path convinced it was the only way to closure.

Instead, she'd created a trajectory laced with pain and fear. Nightmares chased her sleep, and she wanted to stuff this genie back in the bottle. Even if she could, she sensed her uncle would continue until she was pulverized. She'd taken on evil without tools to combat it.

Whatever her next step was, remaining on that bench was not it. Hayden had texted during the meeting an apology that she had to return to the office for an emergency, so Jaime would have to wind her way back via the Metro.

Her phone vibrated and she tugged it from her purse to find a text from Caroline.

RU done? Meet me at Ebenezer's? I can grab a late lunch

Jaime texted back. Be there in 30

Perfect

If anyone could ease her from this funk, Caroline could.

Jaime slipped her coat on and then walked to the eclectic Coffee with a Cause next to the Securities and Exchange Commission. As she waited inside the heavy brick interior, Caroline walked in.

"Thanks for meeting me." Caroline's honeyed words were a balm.

"I needed the break."

"I figured. That had to be intense."

Jaime nodded but kept her focus on the menu board. "Any recommendations?"

"Try the honey lavender latte. You won't be disappointed."

"Okay." Jaime lengthened the word because it didn't sound good, but a minute later when they sat in a nook with long windows warming the space, she took a sip and decided it was a good experiment. She filled Caroline in about the meeting. "I thought you were getting lunch."

"I'll grab something at my desk. It's an excuse to hear about the meeting. Spill."

"The senator was nice, but the thought of testifying scares me. It's my word against an almost general."

Caroline held on to her mug, a sky-blue scarf wrapped loosely around her neck and bringing color to her cheeks. "Maybe this is exactly how everything is supposed to unfold."

"What do you mean?"

"What if God wants to bring you to a place of healing with help from a senator?"

Jaime bit back a snort. "I don't know."

The hurts felt so raw, the questions still so deep. She wanted an outlet to ask them and be heard. The testimony didn't feel like that forum.

"He cares most where our hurts are deepest. This is a crater in your soul. What better way to prove His existence to you than to force the issue of healing?"

"Wait. I'm the one who filed the charges and got called to testify."

"By a senator who just happens to be the future father-in-law of one of your closest friends and happens to sit on the perfect sub-committee?" Caroline cocked an eyebrow and pointed a perfectly manicured finger at Jaime. "I don't believe in coincidences."

"And I struggle to believe in a God who allowed Dane to abuse me."

"Yet."

"What?" Jaime could feel a fire rising in her bones.

"You don't believe yet." Caroline shrugged. "I'm not giving up on you."

"Is that a threat?"

"Absolutely." Caroline took a sip and then smiled. "I wouldn't be much of a friend if I didn't fight for you."

CHAPTER 38

TUESDAY, OCTOBER 16

Simba waited by the door when Jaime opened it after the Metro ride back from the city. She'd opted to walk slowly from the station, trying to organize her thoughts and emotions. It had been a crazy day, and she'd invited Chandler over before she'd known how draining it would be.

She felt soul-level emptied.

Could this all be part of God's pursuit of her, as Caroline suggested?

Was He big enough to take her questions and love her anyway? Would He absorb her anger and release her to feel? She sensed His tug, but the next step felt massive.

She dropped her bag beside the catch-all table, kicked off her shoes, and then scooped up the cat. "What was I thinking, boy?" She walked to her bedroom. "I must have felt weak this morning when I promised Chandler supper."

She squeezed into her room and changed into a pair of jeans and blouse. Then it was back to the kitchen to work through food options since she'd skipped the grocery store due to lack of time. "Looks like it's pasta with homemade sauce and some kind of salad."

Jaime was dicing vegetables for the sauce when the front door-knob jiggled, and Caroline opened the door. She carried her things to the small closet and hung them up before turning around to greet Jaime.

"What are you working on?"

"Supper. I forgot to mention at coffee I invited Chandler over."

"No problem. I'll make myself scarce."

"You don't have to do that."

"Yes, I do. You're letting me stay here, not disrupt your life." Her smile didn't reach her eyes. "By the way, I stopped by the apartment again to get a couple things. It's looking like the people the management company hired haven't even started yet. I'll be the first to admit I don't understand home improvement projects, but I expected something to change."

"That's not a good sign."

"I've got a call into the company. I'm sure it'll be fine." But the way she twisted a strand of hair around her finger and then let go only to do it again conveyed Caroline's discomfort. She wasn't certain of anything.

"You're welcome to stay here as long as you need."

"You're sweet, but you weren't looking for a permanent roommate." She shook her head as if clearing the thought. "Oh, before I forget. Brandon's hosting a cookout at Fort Hunt Park in a few days. We want you to come."

Jaime wiped her eyes as the onion hit her. "Are you two becoming an item?"

A blush climbed Caroline's cheeks even as she shook her head. "He's way too busy with his kids, and I'm not interested."

"In an ex-football player who happens to be jaw-dropping?"

"Says the girl fascinated by the Captain America look-alike. Jaime, there's no way he's interested in me. It's a shame, because he's great with kids, but that wouldn't work anyway."

"So he needs a nudge."

"No!" Caroline stepped away from the doorjamb. "Don't even think about doing something like that. I'm content with my life."

"Do you want me to speak the truth?"

"Not even in love, girlfriend. What time is Chandler coming?"

"Nice try. Six. Why don't you want the truth?"

"Because. But save the date for the picnic. And bring Chandler. It'll give you something to look forward to." Caroline waggled her fingers at Jaime and collected her bag.

"Where are you going?"

"I'll grab dinner, maybe go back to the court. Brandon brought some girls in today that I used to know. Between that impromptu drop-in and coffee with you, I'm behind. Don't wait up."

Before Jaime could respond, her friend was out the door. She knew she didn't need someone as a buffer to make sure all stayed well. She knew she was safe with Chandler. He was a kind warrior. The sort who would give his life to protect the innocent. Her innocence had been stolen years earlier, and he still stayed.

She stirred the sauce and then walked to the bathroom, leaned into the sink, and studied her image in the mirror. "He's coming so you can ask him questions. You've eaten together before. You've watched movies together. This is no big leap forward."

The problem was her heart knew those words were lies, every one.

———

Chandler stepped from the elevator, then held it open for Caroline. "Am I chasing you out?"

"Not at all." She made a no-big-deal expression. "I'm headed to work. Have a nice time."

"Isn't it late to head in?" He released the door to let her descend.

She stuck her hand there to hold it open. "Not really. But listen. You do anything to hurt Jaime, and I have friends who can hurt you." The door started beeping a warning, but she continued to hold it. "That woman is precious to me and not to be toyed with."

"Promise. She's special to me too."

"Good. The flowers are a nice touch." Caroline released her hand on the door and let them slide closed.

Chandler glanced down at the bouquet he'd picked up at a local market. The sunflowers and mums had felt like fall and a pulse of color that he hoped would make Jaime smile every time she saw them. The way she engendered such protectiveness in Caroline was both endearing and a little terrifying. Jaime had an agenda for inviting him up, but he didn't know what. *Give me wisdom.*

The hallway started smelling of garlic and onion before he reached her door. His stomach rumbled as he knocked on the door and then stepped back. A minute later she opened it, and her studied casual elegance made him want to tell her she didn't need to try so hard. He loved everything about her. He needed to back away though. She couldn't be his, not yet.

"Thanks for inviting me over. Whatever you're cooking smells better than the microwave meal I'd have scorched." He held up the flowers. "I got these for you."

Jaime's mouth tipped open as her eyes misted. "Thank you. They're perfect." She took them and slid around the island. "I've got a vase here somewhere." She dug around, avoiding looking at him.

"Anything I can do to help?"

"No." She popped up from digging through a cabinet. "I found one."

"Jaime, I'm glad to be here, but not at the expense of your peace." She fidgeted with the flowers, so he reached across the island and stilled her hands. "You are important, and I wanted you to know you're seen."

A tear trickled down her cheek, and his heart squeezed. "Why?"

"Because you are valuable." He reached across and ran his thumb down her cheek. The skin soft as rose petals to the touch.

She stilled and he felt time freeze. A moment to capture. Just like he wanted to taste her mouth and let her know how much value he found in her. He held back, knowing it could be too much.

Time to get back to whatever purpose she had. He slid his thumb from her cheek and took a step back. "What are you making? Something Italian?"

She blinked as if coming back from a daze. "It's a bit of this and that. Hopefully it will be good."

They made small talk while she finished preparing the meal, then sat at the tiny table to eat the chicken and pasta with a nice salad. Jaime kept up her end of the conversation but seemed quiet and lost in her thoughts at times.

He wiped his mouth with a napkin and then leaned back. "That was excellent. Thanks for a home-cooked meal. Now can you tell me what's bugging you?"

She swirled her fork through the chunky vegetables left on her plate. "I finished the book you loaned me."

"You mentioned that last night. What did you think?"

"I can see why you like it."

"Oh?"

"It's a simple yet compelling story. You named your Aslan well."

"I've always liked that the lion Aslan isn't tame."

"Why? I'd be like Susan, afraid to meet him."

"If he were tame, we could control him. The magic of Aslan is that he's bigger and more than we are." Chandler took a sip of water. "I like the idea that God is wild and so much more than me, but He fights for me."

"I don't like the idea that following Him means being out of control."

"But He's a good king."

She shook her head and then shrugged. "Maybe He has been for you. I've had a different experience." She sighed. "I want so much what you and my friends have, but there's this insurmountable reality of my past."

Chandler heard the longing in her voice. There was so much hope, if she could just reach out and grab it. He prayed as he leaned toward her. "There's nothing in your past that scares God. I know to my core He was there with you, crying with you."

"But I never sensed Him."

"He was there. And He's with you now. So many would be devastated by your experience. Instead, you're this amazingly strong overcomer. And I know to the absolute core of my soul that He will use your past for good if you let Him."

"I want to believe that. But I'm struggling." Her voice was beautifully broken.

"That 'want to' is the first step, Jaime."

A blaze of emotions skated over her face, one followed by the other, until hope chased fear away.

CHAPTER 39

A man stood in the doorway. He crept closer, and Jaime tried to push farther into the shadows of her bed. If she pretended she was asleep, he would go away.

But he didn't. He paused as if sniffing the air, and then stepped closer.

Again.

And again.

Until he was so close, she felt his breath.

Jaime jerked awake. She fought against lungs locked in panic, her mouth open in a silent scream.

Caroline opened the door to Jaime's room and slipped inside, her face illuminated by the light cast by the bedside lamp. She eased onto the edge of the bed and slowly rubbed Jaime's arm. "You aren't alone, Jaime." The circular motion began to orient Jaime to the fact she was in her room. "Father, please make Your presence known to Jaime through Your peace that passes all understanding."

"I don't want to be afraid anymore." The words escaped in spurts and gasps.

"I know. You're the bravest women I know, but you can't walk this alone."

"I have you, right?" Jaime tried to laugh and break the tension still squeezing through her, but she couldn't. Pressure built to know the truth. To take the risk to trust this God as her friends did.

Maybe Chandler was right and He could use her life.

He didn't feel safe or tame.

She'd liked the idea of a tame lion she could control and mold in a way that didn't shatter her world. She wanted the powerful parts He offered without the sacrifice, yet it was both. She needed Him to touch and heal her. She couldn't do that, and this lawsuit attempt had reinforced how very much her efforts were doomed to fail.

Maybe He could be trusted. Maybe He was good, as the beaver in the book said. Maybe she didn't need Him to be safe as much as she needed Him to be good to her.

The thought chased her the way Simba chased a ball across a floor. Everywhere she went it dogged her. Hounding her as she made supper, following her as she jogged on the treadmill in the exercise room, following her as she watched a show with Simba curled against her side. No matter what she did, she felt the presence. What if He would be good to her?

It was almost worth any risk to find out.

So many had disappointed her, and yet she knew more was possible. She knew it to the core of her being.

It felt odd but so right to reach out to Him with the echo of her darkest moments fading like a mist in the morning light.

"What do I do?"

Caroline's smile rivaled the first light of dawn. "Ask Him to break through your walls. I'll lead."

And as Jaime repeated the simple prayer, she didn't feel a quake that shifted her foundations the way the Stone Table cracked with Aslan atop it. Instead, she felt the softest vibration, an echo that felt like love and peace combined, a sensation she wanted to clutch and memorize.

Caroline hugged her and then bounded off the bed, wiping her eyes. "I need to get ready for work." She started toward the door, then turned back. "Thank you for letting me be part of this."

Before Jaime could reply, her friend slipped into the living room, easing the door behind her. Jaime stayed propped in bed, tipping her face toward the ceiling. It felt like drops of grace washed over her in a gentle sprinkle. It was the gentlest scrubbing she'd ever experienced. A cleaning at the deepest levels.

The feeling stayed with her as she dressed in a suit that made her feel invincible and prepared to return to work. The only problem? Crickets were louder than what she'd heard from the public defender's office since Savannah had forwarded the letter from the ethics panel. Had that only been yesterday?

If she got back to work quickly, she could attempt to salvage the Parron trial. That would take a miracle, but maybe she needed to believe in one.

She'd march into the office as if her leave had expired and see what happened.

There was a knock at the door, and she frowned at Simba. "Were you expecting anyone, boy?"

She edged to the door and opened it. Chandler straightened and a grin spread across his face. "Hey, you."

"Good morning." She leaned against the door and tried to resist the magnetic pull to him. She didn't want to resist. She wanted to believe he was the perfect man for her, and it went far deeper than his Captain America persona. It would be hard to explain to someone how much his character tugged her to him as surely as Cupid's arrow.

"Ready for an escort to wherever you're going?"

She tipped her head and studied him. "Don't you have to get to work?"

"Not today. Took a vacation day to spend time with my girl."

The words settled over her. "I'd love that, but I need to see if I still have a job."

"Then your chariot awaits."

She bit her lip and then nodded. "Thank you."

He leaned toward her, his lips inching nearer. "You're welcome."

She held her breath, hoping, wishing, expecting . . . and then sighed as he edged back.

"Get your things, and we'll grab coffee on the way."

"All right." When they were settled in his truck, she glanced out the window. "This morning was a big one."

"Oh? Why's that?"

"Caroline prayed with me."

He slowed at a stoplight, then reached over to squeeze her hand. "That is fantastic news."

She bit her lip and nodded. "I think so too." She tried to ignore the warmth that spread up her arm. "I've never felt this . . . loved."

"It's a great feeling. Take a mental snapshot, because it won't always feel this perfect." His eyes met hers with quiet joy. "But you won't regret it."

She'd watched Hayden, Emilie, and Caroline for years. She'd observed them experience hard things and still hold to their faith. She might not ever understand why God had allowed certain horrors in her life, but she had a feeling He could handle her questions, and she'd decided to trust Him regardless.

"So, the public defender's office?" He pulled out of the coffee shop drive-thru.

"Yes." She needed to see what would happen. It was a gamble to arrive unannounced, but it was too easy to tell someone they weren't wanted or needed over the phone.

Fifteen minutes later Chandler slowed and pulled to the curb in front of the PD's office. It was one suite of offices in a skyscraper of a building a five-minute walk from the courthouse. He glanced at her, then at the building. "Want me to wait here?"

"It would probably be a good idea." She sighed. "I don't know if they'll welcome me back."

"I bet they will."

She knew better than to hope but had to take this step. Would Grant give in to whoever had told him to fire her? She wanted to know just who that man was.

Could she clutch the morning's earlier feeling of peace tight and hold on a little longer? As she looked out the truck's window and took in the stone behemoth in front of her, she didn't know. But she couldn't sit here and let some faceless man rob her voice. She would fight for her job the way she fought for her clients.

Chandler parked the vehicle and stepped from it. A moment later he was holding the door for her. "Whatever happens in there, you have a future, Jaime."

She wanted to believe that.

He offered her a hand and helped her from the truck. "I'll be waiting when you're ready."

Somehow she knew he would, even if she was there for hours. "I'll call as soon as I know how long I'll be."

Then she squared her shoulders and walked toward the double door that led to the lobby and the elevators that would whisk her to the PD's suite.

Time to get inside and see what her future held.

CHAPTER 40

Chandler returned to his seat behind the wheel and watched Jaime head into the building.

She was undoubtedly the bravest woman he knew, and the fact that she had prayed at all made him grateful. It was a conversation they needed to finish, but he felt a release to pursue her that he hadn't had before.

What would it be like to explore a future with the engaging and enigmatic Jaime Nichols? There would be challenges . . . there had to be, given her pain-filled past . . . but he had no doubt she was worth it.

His phone rang and he dug through the trash on the dash until he located it. "Bolton."

"Chandler, this is Allison. We need you here at the office immediately. There's an emergency."

"What kind?"

She sighed, but he heard a thread of fear. "A bird flew into the office, and he wants to hurt us."

He stiffened. That was the code phrase for *we need help immediately*, developed after such a situation had literally occurred. It had taken a butterfly net and some creativity to safely escort that bird back outside. Fortunately, they had a plan in place for two-legged "birds" as well.

"I'll be there as soon as I grab my net."

The moment the call disconnected, Chandler dialed the military police at the Pentagon and then 911. They would cycle up to help, but he needed to get there too. He quickly shot a text to Jaime. Called to work. Text when you need me. I'll be in Clarendon.

He hit Send and then pulled his truck from the curb and drove the mile to the office. Should he make his presence known or await reinforcements? They couldn't be far behind.

The curtains were drawn over the front windows. That was a terrible sign, and battle alertness coursed into his system. The curtains were always open when someone was in the building to allow line of sight even if the glass was bullet-proof.

He parked a block away and was hurrying toward the building when a police vehicle screeched to a halt on the other side of the street. The officer exited and waved him back. "Sir, you can't be here. We have an emergency situation."

"I'm the one who called 911."

"All right." The officer spoke into his radio. "What can you tell me?"

"Only that one of my staff called utilizing our emergency protocol. Also the curtains shouldn't be drawn. They're always left open."

Another police vehicle arrived, followed by one with the Pentagon's police logo on the door. A woman hopped out of the passenger door and hurried toward them. "What's the status?"

Chandler slipped into military mode. "Unknown. I got a call from a colleague inside. She used the emergency phrase to launch our emergency procedures. I was in the courthouse area, so I called you and 911 and then proceeded here. I arrived approximately five minutes ago. Long enough to park and meet this officer."

The woman turned to the uniformed police officer. "I'm Agent Michelle Weldon with the Pentagon Police."

"Chuck Nollan, Arlington Police."

"How do you want to handle this?"

"You can take point since it's your building."

She nodded and turned back to Chandler. "What's the layout?"

"Open floor plan in the entryway. Leads first to a cubicle space, then there's a hallway with a series of small offices and conference rooms. More on the second floor."

"Okay. Any security feeds?"

"Yes, should feed to your office."

She turned to the man who had come with her. "Check on that. We need to see what's happening inside."

Time ticked by with more police arriving but no answers. Chandler paced as the pressure built. Something was happening, but he didn't know if it was a hostage situation or something different. "Can I call Allison? See what's happening?"

Agent Weldon considered and then nodded. "Let's try."

He quickly pulled up the number and then waited while it dialed.

Finally she answered. "Hello?"

"Allison, you okay?"

"He wants you to come inside." Her voice shook.

"All right. Who is it?"

"He says you'll know."

He froze as he considered. "Must be my mystery caller."

"Maybe."

"All right. I'll come in the back door."

"That's a good idea. The front is bad." There was the sound like a slap, and she groaned.

"Hold on, I'm coming." He hung up and turned to the others. "Anyone have a bulletproof vest?"

"You're not going inside." Agent Weldon jutted her jaw, but it did little to change Chandler's mind.

"My team is there, getting slapped around for telling me not to use the front door. My guess is there's an explosive or something on it, so proceed with caution. I'll use the back." He took off his coat and slipped on the vest Officer Nollan handed him. Then he slid a comms unit into his ear, and chatter filled his head. "I'll let you know what's happening in there."

Before the feisty detective could say anything else, he took off for the back door. This team wouldn't be lost if he could help it.

———

When the elevators opened for the PD's floor, Jaime tried to march in like she belonged, but her key card didn't unlock the door. The floor dropped from her stomach. Had Grant revoked her access?

Maybe it was going to take more than a letter from the ethics commission to clear her indefinite leave.

She was standing at the door digging her cell phone from her purse when Evan Reagan walked up.

"Good morning, Evan."

"Hmm. Can't get in?"

"I must have done something to my keycard. I'll just follow you in and get it cleared up."

He looked at her, something like pity filling his eyes. "You don't understand what's happening."

"Then fill me in. Please."

"You're done. Someone's pressuring Grant and he can't budge. Keeps saying it's out of his hands."

"Who's doing this?" She didn't mention the conversation she'd overheard.

He grunted and slapped his card against the reader. "No one can figure it out. But we all know you should be back here."

"Thanks." She preceded him into the reception area and then walked to her small-as-a-closet office. It no longer felt like coming home.

Evan stopped when he reached her door. "Grant'll be a little late this morning. A breakfast meeting of some sort."

"I'm sure I've got plenty to do while I wait." Email had piled up while she was gone, and it took more than an hour to read and deal with each. She was turning to the stack of files on the corner of her desk when her phone intercom beeped to life.

"Miss Nichols, Grant wants to see you."

"When?"

"Right now."

Miss Nichols? Since when did Grant's paralegal call her that? She didn't like the signal that sent. "I'll be right there."

Her cell phone rang, and she glanced at the screen. Savannah? Really? She took the call.

Savannah didn't even wait for her to say anything. "The police need to interview Tiffany and prepare her for the grand jury testimony."

"She'll need Aslan for that."

"Exactly. I need you to spend more time with her so you can explain to the judge why Aslan is needed as a comfort dog. I'd also like you to sit in on the interview."

"I don't know that I can do all of that."

"Why not?"

"I'm at the PD's office and need to go meet with Grant."

"All right. Do that, but make Tiffany your next priority."

"I'll get something arranged."

"Good. Then come here around two, and we'll prepare for your testimony."

"Mine?"

"The congressional hearing."

Oh. That. "It's not until next Tuesday."

"True, but soon your presence will be required at work. We need to be ready when the PD office calls. Consider this getting ahead."

As she hung up, her office intercom buzzed again. "He's getting impatient."

"Coming." If only Jaime could shake the feeling she was walking toward the death of her career.

CHAPTER 41

There was a sense of waiting as Chandler approached the back door. Jaime slipped into his thoughts. Had she seen his text?

He pushed the thought firmly away. All he could do in this moment was focus on the problem in front of him. That meant making sure his team was okay.

He keyed the mic that was embedded in the vest. "It seems quiet."

"I hope you know what you're doing."

Agent Worrypants didn't know that for two tours he'd seen his share of death.

"Got it." He examined the doorframe. Nothing obvious, and Allison hadn't warned him away from that one. If whoever was inside wanted to talk to him, it made sense they'd leave a way for him to get there while protecting the integrity of the front by pulling blinds and possibly adding an explosive device. The police needed eyes in that area. Heat-seeking goggles wouldn't be enough to determine who was where.

He eased the door open and slipped into the back hallway. The light on the security camera blinked, a subtle nod they had eyes on him. Good. Now he could hope that meant they had eyes on his team and the rogue.

"I'm coming in." He held up his hands and inched down the hallway. He passed the last set of offices. The lights were turned off and the offices empty. It was quiet. Eerily so. What had happened while he waited for backup to arrive? His phone vibrated in his pocket, but he ignored it. Anything vital would go through the comms unit.

He eased down the hallway until he could see the entry to the reception area/work space. Beth and Allison huddled in chairs while Jake stared defiantly at a masked man pointing a gun at him.

"You're finally here, Mr. Bolton. Good." The man didn't even flinch as he pulled the trigger and Jake fell over, blood seeping from the hole in his chest.

The women screamed and his comms unit started firing with questions and demands. Chandler held his hands in front of him as he tried to evaluate the rapidly deteriorating situation. Had anything vital been hit? How much time did he have to get the situation resolved with any hope of Jake surviving?

"Let me get some help for Jake."

"Is that his name?"

"Yes, he has a wife and three kids."

"Then you'd better resolve this quickly." The man turned dead eyes toward him.

Resolve what? Chandler blinked as he studied the man. There was nothing familiar about him, his features hidden by the mask. Nothing gave him a clue about why here, now, and them. He felt the press of time ticking by, and his fingers twitched to hold his gun and end this, but he couldn't. "You served."

"Active duty for six years and three tours. How does my country thank me? Sends me on mission with an IED. Sends me to Germany to rot at Landstuhl."

"What does this have to do with me and my team?"

"Your team is collateral damage." His lifeless eyes flicked to where Jake lay bleeding. "I'd say that man has less than thirty minutes before he's critical."

Chandler couldn't argue with that assessment. "You saw enough of these injuries on your tours."

"And worse." He tapped his leg and the pant leg moved. Did the man wear a prosthesis? "It was supposed to be a routine supply run. You were assigned to come with us. You didn't."

Scenes from Chandler's nightmares flashed before his eyes overlaying on top of this moment. "You were in Iraq?"

"Yes."

"Injured on August 14?"

"Ah, now you remember." The man spread his arms wide as if in victory.

"But I don't know you."

"That's right. I was a new addition, replacing someone shipping home to watch his baby be born." The man snorted. "I was with your division two days." His nostrils flared and he whipped the gun toward Chandler. "In two days my life was destroyed. You sold us out."

Keep him talking. Ready to breach.

The quiet words in his ear were music to his soul.

Jake twitched, blood starting to pool beneath him, and Allison crouched next to him, pressing a jacket to the wound. "We've got to get Jake out of here. Please."

"I'm not done yet." The man gestured toward Jake. "Your choice is easy. Admit you were the traitor and die, or I'll make sure your friend dies."

Chandler's thoughts raced. He'd lived that day so many times, felt the crushing burden of guilt for the paperwork and VIP that required him to stay rather than head out with the supply convoy. Twenty minutes later the routine run erupted in flames and chaos. He should have been with his team. "I'm sorry. If I could change what happened, I would."

Chandler shifted from the hallway. Whatever was planned had to come through the back door. He eyed the explosives attached to the front door. "You have the trigger for the bomb."

"And motion sensors."

Chandler kept his face neutral as he heard the hissed intake of breath in the comms unit. *We've got a handheld trigger.*

The man's mouth moved as if in a smile beneath his ski mask. "Jar that door, and we all go boom."

Grant glanced up when Jaime rapped on his door. "Good, come in." He waited while she took a seat at the desk in front of him. "So the ethics board cleared you."

"Yes, as I anticipated." She kept her hands folded in her lap.

"Good." But instead of smiling, he sighed and fisted his hands together on the desk. "I still have to let you go."

"What? Why?" Even if she'd anticipated his words, they punched hard.

"Because you've compromised the integrity of this office."

"How? I was cleared." She felt pressure rising inside.

"You've had too many of these brushes with ethics."

"All of us have. It's part of being a public defender. Our clients fight back and sometimes they play dirty."

Grant met her frustration with stony silence. "Jaime, you are no longer employed here. You have an hour to pack your things. After that I'll have someone escort you out." He met her gaze with a hardness that surprised her. "Leave peacefully, and I'll give you a good reference."

Like that would be any help. "Who was the man?"

"What?"

"The one who told you to get rid of me? I overheard the conversation. If you're going to do this, you owe me that much."

"I don't owe you a thing." The man didn't even seem flustered by the path he was taking.

"Maybe not, but you owe our clients our best. That's me. I'm the best assistant defender you have." She leaned forward, her fists almost touching his on the blasted desk. "Clients like Alex don't stand a chance without me."

Grant harrumphed. "You're not the only one in this office who's passionate."

"Maybe, but there's something political going on here, and I will get to the bottom of it." She didn't bother to add he'd regret it because it would be wasted breath. "Was it my uncle?" The words escaped in an unexpected whoosh, and he jerked back with a frown, his shoulders pushed back. It was all the tell she needed to know she was right. Where else did her uncle lurk that she hadn't thought to look for him?

"You have one hour."

She stood and left his office without a word. Anything she said now would only get her in trouble.

An hour later she waited at the base of the building for a taxi, laden down with a box of her belongings, since Chandler hadn't responded to her text or call. *Please keep him safe.* Something inside whispered he needed every bit of help he could get, and she didn't know what to do with that other than copy what she'd seen her friends do.

A cab pulled to the curb, and she gave the driver the address for Daniels, McCarthy & Associates. When she juggled her box and purse and keys to open the door to the firm fifteen minutes later, it felt like déjà vu.

Bella looked up with concern. "What on earth do you have there?"

"I lost my job at the public defender's office." She set the box on a chair, worn by the emotion of her new reality. Even if she'd known it was coming, it remained the death of a dream.

Bella stood and came around the side of her desk with arms

opened. She tugged Jaime into a hug. "It'll be all right, sugar. I have a feeling God's got big plans for you."

"He's got a strange way of showing it." The thought that she'd started to trust Him and He'd allow this to happen so quickly was unsettling.

"That's His way. Sometimes He makes total sense in the moment. Other times it's only in the rearview mirror that we can see the why of the experience." She released Jaime and sniffed. "Now get back to the conference room. I'll let the girls know you're here."

"Where should I put my things?"

"You don't worry about that. Get on back to your friends."

When Jaime entered the conference room, she found it had been rearranged with a podium for her to stand behind while Savannah, Emilie, Hayden, and Caroline sat behind the table with stacks of legal pads and pens at the ready.

"What are y'all doing here?"

"Making sure you're ready for your testimony." Caroline winked at her. "I've always heard it takes ten thousand hours of practice to become truly proficient at anything."

"But we don't have that kind of time." Hayden tapped her pen on her legal pad. "We need to get started or we'll be here all night."

"You haven't filled those with questions already, have you?" Jaime eyed the legal pads with something akin to fear.

Emilie straightened her suit jacket and smiled. "We're prepared to get you ready for every eventuality we can think of."

Savannah nodded. "We'll throw questions at you every night for an hour or more."

"I won't have to stand at the hearing."

"No," Hayden assured her. "But you will feel more comfortable then if we make you as uncomfortable as possible now."

They launched into a mock session with Hayden acting as

Senator Wesley and Savannah acting as the chair of the subcommittee, Senator Langdon.

"It would probably be a good idea to research who else is on the committee."

"I agree." Hayden wagged her pen at Jaime. "Nice attempt to distract us. Now let's get to work."

They started by throwing softball questions her way. Then Caroline decided to act like the bad cop, which would have been funny if she wasn't so good at the role.

"How can you prove any of this happened? These alleged events occurred more than twenty years ago. Seems like a mighty long time to wait to me."

Jaime felt a spike of panic. This was the key question. She had no form of proof other than her testimony, the hidden scars she still bore, and her childish journal—that would not go into the hearing with her. She wasn't sure how much the journal would add anyway. It was a contemporaneous account of her experience, but it still might not be admitted.

Taylor, Emilie's assistant, slipped in and handed Hayden a piece of paper. Was this real, or was she playing the role of aide? Jaime tried not to be distracted, but avoiding Caroline's question would be welcome.

"Miss Nichols, I'm waiting."

So much for avoiding. "I have the counseling records, which show the long-term harm that was done. I also have the journal I wrote at the time of the abuse, as well as journals noting the impact over time."

"Couldn't your harm have been caused by any of several issues? Why him? Why now?"

"Because I'm finally strong enough to withstand grilling like this." Jaime kept her hands on the podium, but she wanted to make a face at Caroline. "My uncle destroyed my innocence, and I cannot allow him to do that to anyone else. As an eight-year-old, there was nothing I could do, but now I have a voice."

"How noble of you," Caroline sneered, her acting feeling too real. "I find your timing convenient. If you really cared about making your uncle pay, you'd have pursued justice years ago. Who's paying you to come forward now?"

"What? No one!" Jaime sputtered as she glanced at the others. Would no one jump in? While this was practice, she wasn't eager to reveal her deepest soul even to women who knew her like no one else. How on earth would she be able to respond in the hearing? Her mouth was as dry as when the dentist filled it with cotton. "I can't do this."

"You can and you will." Hayden met her gaze with directness. "If you don't do this voluntarily, the committee will enforce the subpoena. Congressional subpoenas have broad power. The optics are better if you willingly testify."

"You don't understand." Jaime could feel her breathing speed up until it felt like she'd start to pant. "I can't. I physically cannot do this."

Emilie was the agent of mercy as she stood and then walked around the table and escorted Jaime to a seat. "This is why we practice. We will help you do this." She crouched beside Jaime's chair and looked her in the eyes. "You will not be alone."

"Is this a good time to mention I'm moving out tonight? After all this time, the apartment manager decided only the main room had to be redone right now." Caroline made a face. "She assured me they're done in my unit. And my rent restarts today."

And just like that, Jaime was alone. Again.

CHAPTER 42

S weat slid down the hollow of Chandler's back as he searched for a solution.

There had to be one. It was impossible that Jake would pay with his life for a sin that wasn't Chandler's, let alone his friend's. Jake's wife and kids needed him to come home. Chandler had to keep the masked man talking while those outside the office formed an executable plan. Fast.

"What do you want to do? Tell me what you want me to know."

"That you and the military destroyed my life."

Chandler gritted his teeth to avoid arguing the point with a man who seemed on the brink of losing it all. "What could we have done differently?"

"You should have been on the delivery run." He stepped toward Chandler but halted still out of reach. Where was the trigger?

"There are many nights I feel like I am there."

"Nightmares aren't the same."

"I'm sorry for all that happened to you. Killing Jake won't solve it."

Jake groaned from his spot on the floor. The blood spilling everywhere could not be good. Chandler had seen enough even on his relatively straightforward tours to understand that much. Allison kept the jacket pressed down. "He needs an ambulance."

At her words, the man spun on his heel and shot above her head. The bullet might have parted her hair on its path, because she froze, features forged in a caricature of shock. Beth opened her mouth, and Chandler gave a slight shake of his head. She shut her mouth, but her eyes told of her displeasure. Now to keep Jake alive.

"Let them go. We've got to get Jake help or you'll have a murder charge waiting."

The man snorted. "You think I care? Fool. No one cared about me, so while I'm glad to hear you caring about your friend here, he gets to take care of himself."

"Then let the women go. They haven't done anything to you."

"I know exactly what will happen. They'll tell those outside where I'm standing and where you're standing. I'll take a sniper shot to the head, release my hold on the trigger, and blow you up with me."

The guy had to be bluffing.

"What was your job in the army?"

"Ordnance expert."

Of course it was. Talk him out was the best option then.

Keep him talking. We're working on a plan.

Sure they were.

Time was running out.

That knowledge accelerated with each frenzied step the man took.

Chandler had to end this now, whether or not those outside had a perfect plan.

The man took a step toward Jake, then three away.

He turned.

Looked at the women, gun still directed at Chandler.

Then he stopped, arms twitching.

An eerie calm settled on the man, and Chandler braced.

"Know what? I'm tired of waiting. I think I'll just blow the bomb now. Take you all with me." He raised his hand, as a voice in the comms unit told Chandler to duck.

How could a sniper crack the bulletproof glass?

Chandler lunged for the hooded soldier as he heard the ricochet of multiple shots.

The man jerked, and Chandler grabbed the trigger from his hand. He scrambled to ensure his fingers were locked on top.

"I've got it. Send in the bomb unit and EMTs."

"On their way. Should be in the back door in seconds."

Allison looked up from her position over Jake. "Come on, Jake. Stay with us. Your kids need you!"

A moment later Beth was there with a stack of paper towels. "Give me the jacket, and apply these to the wound."

Then the back door banged open and the area swarmed with EMTs and police.

As soon as EMTs dropped next to Jake, two officers escorted Beth and Allison to safety. Chandler didn't move as he clutched the device the man had wanted to detonate. The adrenaline ebbed from him and his arms began to shake.

"I need someone to take over the trigger."

A member of the bomb squad hurried over. Another approached the package left on the door.

EMTs positioned Jake on a gurney. Pushed him out the door.

Chandler followed a step behind.

Agent Weldon approached and led him into one of the small conference rooms, away from the action. Chandler tried to ignore the blood that soaked his clothes while he fought the crash of adrenaline.

"How did you penetrate the bulletproof glass?" It hadn't stood a chance against whatever they'd used.

"We have our ways. Secrets we don't share." Agent Weldon crossed her arms and studied him. "You did well in there. What can you tell me about Russ Goldman?"

"Is that his name? He's called several times and may have

followed me at the local Indian restaurant. There were other times when I saw a shadow, so he may have followed me." Or it could have been Dane focused on Jaime. Now they'd never know for sure.

"Why you?"

He frowned and looked at her. "What?"

"Why you and why now?"

"Misplaced frustration. He'd just been shipped in, filling in for a soldier headed home to be a father. Then he went on a supply run, and it didn't end well. We lost a man, and others were injured." Chandler's gut clenched. "I had to call their families. Letting them know their son was dead or critically injured. Russ Goldman must have slipped through the cracks in my system. It was a time I never want to repeat."

She made a couple notes in a slim notebook. "All right. Don't go anywhere yet." She walked away, leaving him to collapse on a chair in the corner while the room down the hall buzzed with activity.

It was late in the afternoon, really time for her to leave the law firm and head home, but Jaime couldn't. She glanced at her phone, growing more concerned with time. What had happened to Chandler? He'd been called to work hours ago. The fact he hadn't returned her calls or texts told her something terrible had happened.

She needed to get Aslan with Tiffany, but without Chandler that wouldn't be possible. She called her mom to check on Tiffany.

"She and her mom returned to their home today."

"What? Why?" What was Madeline up to? She'd seemed quite content to stay where Jaime's mom would take care of them.

"They were doing fine but ready to be back in their space." Her mother sighed. "I don't blame them, though Happy has been mopey since Tiffany left. He's going to miss her."

"Has Corey Bowman been arrested?" He must have been, or surely Madeline wouldn't return to a place he knew.

"She got a call from the police. Your father took Madeline over this morning to make sure it was okay before taking Tiffany."

"Oh."

"They'll be fine. Just call Madeline and touch base." There was a smile in her mother's voice. "I wouldn't have let them leave if they weren't ready and your father didn't think it was safe. Much as we enjoyed having them, Tiffany needs her room."

"I know, Mom. Thanks for helping them."

"Of course." There was a pause, and then her mom continued in a quavery voice. "Thank you for asking."

"I love you, Mom."

"I love you too."

Jaime swallowed back a sudden lump. "We're going to make it."

"Yes, we will."

Her phone beeped. "Mom, before I go, I've been subpoenaed to testify at Uncle Dane's congressional hearing Tuesday."

"Want us there?"

"I'm not sure, but I didn't want you to be surprised."

"Just let me know when and where. Your dad will want to be there."

"Be careful, okay?"

"Why?" Her mom's response was quick.

"Because I'm not sure what he'll do when he finds out I'll be testifying before the subcommittee. But it's something I have to do."

"Your father can take care of us. Should you come home until this is over?"

"I don't think so. Then he wins." She took a breath. "I'll let you know the details about the testimony." The phone beeped, a reminder of the holding call. "Love you, Mom. Gotta grab this call."

As she clicked over to take the other call, it hit her that it had been a long time since she'd said those words to her parents. "Hello?"

"Hey, beautiful."

She pulled the phone from her ear and glanced at the name on the screen. It sounded like Chandler, but the words couldn't be his. "You okay?"

"It's been a long day. I'd recommend ignoring the news for a bit."

She leaned over to click the computer to life. In a moment she was surfing. Horror bubbled inside her as she found a story about an attack at the Vet Center. "You were in the middle of that? No wonder you didn't return my calls."

"Yeah. The man was injured in a convoy explosion. I was supposed to be there, so he blamed me for his injuries."

"Are you okay?"

"I am. This guy must have suffered some horrible things on his last tour, because he didn't make sense." He blew out a breath. "He shot one of my team members, so I'll be here awhile and then at the hospital. I'd like to come by when I get home if that's okay."

"Sure, let me know when you're done."

"Will do." Exhaustion overshadowed his words.

"Will your colleague be okay?"

He sighed. "I don't know. I'm praying no news is good news."

"Then I'll believe that with you." She would until they could put this day behind them.

CHAPTER 43

The office of Daniels, McCarthy & Associates was dark when Jaime left. Bella had stashed her box in the last empty office, and Jaime had spent the afternoon drafting a preliminary report about Aslan's impact on Tiffany. As she researched comfort dogs, it was fascinating to quantify the effect these animals could have on stressed and traumatized children. She'd add specifics when she saw the two together again.

Somehow the women in the firm managed to work regular hours if they weren't preparing for trial or an oral argument. Jaime packed her bag, leaving the box where it sat. After saying good-bye to Savannah, she headed to the backdoor and her car, then remembered she'd had to take a cab.

She was ready to be home and forget about this day when she'd officially lost her job. It was also the day she'd said yes to God. That incongruence made her feel off balance—tired yet energized.

She'd need to take time to dream and decide what she wanted to do next. Other than not moving, she didn't have much in the way of direction. After pulling her phone from her purse, she paused to pull up a ride share app. As she waited for it to load, she stepped forward and the door closed behind her. The hair on her neck stood as if a breeze had just snaked down her shirt.

Someone was out here.

She knew it just like she knew the car that had almost hit her at McDonald's hadn't been an accident.

She fought a shudder and the desire to flee back into the building. Without the building key in hand, the safest route was around the building to the safety of the sidewalk and street lights. She clutched her phone as she hurried forward.

A rustle from somewhere near the row of trees at the edge of the parking lot made her stop.

She couldn't move forward. Not if someone waited by the edge of the lot.

Her gaze bounced around the parking lot, and then she decided to run for the front of the building. Light would pool on the sidewalk and there would be sufficient traffic on King Street to prevent anything from happening. As soon as she reached the edge of the building she tugged her phone free and called for the police. Then she called Savannah, and a moment later the front door opened.

"Jaime, you out here?" Savannah stood silhouetted in a pool of light from the building.

"Here." She hurried to the door. "I think someone was on the edge of the parking lot, but I can't be certain."

"You called 911?"

Jaime nodded.

"Then a patrol will come by here soon." Savannah reached for Jaime. "Grab your things and get back inside."

Twenty minutes later, an officer had confirmed that anyone who might have been lurking was long gone.

Jaime didn't want to return to her empty apartment. And she didn't want to call the girls, especially since they'd already spent so much time helping her.

Was this to be her life?

She felt the flicker of hope thinking of a certain Captain America look-alike . . . but they hadn't yet fully addressed her past and what it meant for them today. She knew the long-term consequences of abuse and how it could impact future intimacy, even when it was an intimacy she longed to have with someone she loved. But when even the thought left her out of breath with her vision swirling, she had to do something.

What?

She blinked and found she had walked to the end of King Street where a parking lot sat along the Potomac River.

How had she gotten here? Was it another blackout?

What now?

Find her way back to people.

It was something. With no clear direction in mind, she started walking. Old Town never really closed. As she walked by windows, she looked inside to see tables of people enjoying time together around food.

How many times had she watched from the outside? Even when the girls included her, she'd often felt she didn't quite fit or belong.

I'm tired of feeling like this.

The thought reverberated through her mind.

Look at the people she loved. Their lives were full, challenging, and rich.

Would she forever be marked with this disconnect?

She kept moving, weaving through the hardy souls who walked along the King Street sidewalk. When she reached the city building, she walked toward the winterized fountain. It wasn't unusual in warmer weather to see a romantic interlude, the kind she ran from.

She sank onto a bench, and the cold leached through her. "God, I'm beginning to believe You care about me, so You must know I can't keep living like this. My life feels stripped away. And the nothingness that I am is revealed."

She thought of the way Aslan confronted Edmund with direct kindness. Would God do the same with her?

"I'm not a saint. You know everything I've done, everything that's happened to me. I need to know You are real." She felt foolish, whispering the words into the air, but she also had this deep need to get the words out of her mind and into the world. Would God respond?

She sat there until her legs felt numb. Before she gave herself pneumonia waiting for a response, she stood and hailed a passing cab. The drive home went quickly, and she almost left her attaché case on the seat, she was so befuddled.

But maybe she'd spend tomorrow working on her résumé and looking for jobs. It might feel better than staring out the window wondering what to do with herself.

The elevator doors opened and she stilled. Down the hall by her door sat a man with a mountain of a dog.

Chandler? Aslan?

How long had they been waiting?

Aslan's ears perked and Chandler stumbled to his feet. "You're home."

"I am." She stared at him, taking in the slight five o'clock shadow that added to his rugged appeal. The stress etched in his face reflected his hard day. "You're here."

Wonder colored her voice, and her eyes held a light she couldn't hide. Maybe waiting until he couldn't feel his back end had been worth it. After his terrible day, he had to see her. A few words on the phone wouldn't be enough.

Aslan had scratched at the door a couple times, making him wonder if she'd snuck in before he'd arrived, but here she was now, nose and cheeks red from the cold. "Have you had dinner?"

"No."

"Then let's get you something to eat." He resisted reaching out to touch her. Over the last days he'd done research. As much as he wanted to hold her, he would wait. She'd have to make the first move, or he risked pushing her away. That wasn't something he would do.

She watched him another moment, then reached into her purse and snagged keys. She walked around him, letting her shoulder brush his arm. This was progress.

"Let's order a pizza." She jiggled the keys in the doorknob and then opened the door. "Will Aslan behave?"

Could there be a double meaning? "I can guarantee my dog will be a gentleman."

"Then come on in. I have a stack of takeout menus in a drawer."

"I'm already pulling up a website." After they agreed on toppings, he entered the order and paid. Aslan snuffled along the living area. "You won't find the cat that way, boy."

"You never know." Jaime kicked off her heels and headed toward the closed door. "I'll be back in a minute." When she opened the door the cat peered out, then pulled back with a hiss at the sight of Aslan.

Aslan ran at the door but not before Jaime shut it. He plopped at it with his nose down at the crack and whined.

"I know how you feel."

Chandler sank onto the futon and leaned his head against the back. He was starting to drift to sleep when the door opened. He resisted the urge to peek at her. Instead, he waited until she walked around and sat in the opposite corner of the couch.

"Pizza should be here soon." He kept the words casual. She'd have to lead the way on the discussion. He was here for her but not to crowd.

"Would you like some water or something else to drink? I don't have much."

"Water's fine." He finally looked her way as she stood and made her way to the small kitchen space. She'd changed into leggings and an oversized sweatshirt, and he had to fight the urge to get close to her and let her know how attractive she was. Was she testing him with that outfit? On her athletic form he doubted anything would make her less attractive, but he wouldn't let her in on that secret.

A minute later she handed him a glass filled with water and ice. He took a sip.

"Where are you?"

Her question jolted him. "What do you mean?"

She cocked her head as she studied him. "You just had a horrible day. I think I'd be past crashing in your shoes. Are you okay?"

He took a moment before he raced forward with an easy answer. "No." He closed his eyes. "Today brought back some of my darkest moments. On my last tour I lost a good man from my unit. I was supposed to be with them but stayed behind at the last minute. The man today was injured in that attack."

"I'm so sorry." A soft hand touched his shoulder.

Chandler cracked his eyes. "When he shot Jake . . . I thought we'd lose him."

"But you didn't."

"Not yet." He knew too well all that could go wrong in a situation like Jake's. "He has a long road in front of him."

"But he's alive. You did well."

Chandler rolled his head from side to side along the futon. "If I hadn't gone in, Jake might not have been shot." Just like if the convoy had delayed to wait for him, the explosion might not have happened.

"That *might* is everything."

"What do you mean?"

Jaime ran her fingers through her hair then swept it up like a ponytail only to let it fall lose and free. "When we live with mights, we live with regrets."

Aslan whined next to him, and Chandler turned to see why. He held back a laugh as he saw Simba walking out, legs stiff and tail high. The cat walked around the couch, keeping distance between himself and Aslan, then leapt onto the back by Jaime's head. She pulled him onto her lap and stroked his fur until the cat purred and Chandler was jealous. Simba looked at him with a self-satisfied expression.

Give him time. He'd displace the cat, and then guess who'd be satisfied.

Aslan rested his muzzle on the arm of the couch and grinned at him. So his dog liked the cat as much as he liked the owner.

"Help me forget about those hours. Tell me about your day."

She almost walked past the fact she'd been officially fired. "So I was only at the office long enough to pack a box and call a cab."

"Sorry I couldn't be there for you."

"You were where you needed to be."

He knew she was right, but . . . "I wanted to be there for you."

"So you can help me by being a friend as I figure out what I want to be when I grow up." She shrugged, but pain radiated from her eyes. "I thought I'd spend a career there, but that was unrealistic. There will be something else. I'm way too young to retire."

"There are so many people you can help."

"I just have to figure out how." She turned the attention to the report she was writing for a judge about Tiffany and Aslan. Did Jaime understand how much Tiffany's story tugged Jaime herself toward freedom? Was it in helping someone else climb out of their pain that she moved beyond hers?

He wasn't sure, but he wanted to find out. If ever anyone needed freedom, she did. The question was how to breach her walls so that she could sense the hope just beyond her castled heart.

She'd let him hold her hand, but he wanted to hold her heart. He felt the tug of knowing he could help her, and she could challenge him. There would be no easy answers in a relationship with Jaime, but he didn't want easy. He wanted a woman complex and rich. Desirable and just out of reach.

Jaime Nichols was all of those things and a thousand more.

He'd try to let things follow a path of their own choosing, a path that would let him woo her and entice her to come to the other side. The side of light and freedom, of challenge and joy. But with Jaime, a plan wouldn't work. The relationship would have to grow organically at its own pace.

———

The pizza arrived, and Chandler set it on the coffee table while Jaime collected plates and napkins. She couldn't believe how comfortable it felt to have Chandler in her space. Even Simba and Aslan had settled. Maybe it was time to see what was possible.

Chandler was always a gentleman, and she wasn't quite sure what to do with him. She could sense his interest, but he carefully restrained it.

She respected that about him.

But what did she want to do with him?

The conversation stalled while they ate, but that was okay after his insane day. Hers hadn't been so great either, so the silence was welcome.

Her phone vibrated, and she wanted to ignore it, but it continued. She glanced at the screen and grimaced. She should have left it alone.

"Need to take that?"

"No." It was the last thing she wanted to do.

"Sure?"

"It's my dad." She didn't know what to tell him. "Our relationship is tricky."

"Because they weren't there for you?"

"I didn't explain well what was happening."

"You were a child."

"But I could have told them before I decided to press charges against my uncle."

He considered her with a serious expression that let her know he was thinking rather than reacting. "Would it have changed anything?"

That was a question she didn't want to consider, because if it wouldn't have, she would feel even more alone. "I want to believe it would have."

He nodded, his eyes never leaving her as she held Simba. "Parents aren't perfect, Jaime."

"I know." She knew better than most. "I just wanted to know they'd support me. I guess the relationship is too complex to hope for something so simple."

"No. You're their child."

"Their only child."

"Should that make a difference?"

"I don't know. Maybe." She hugged Simba until he scrambled free of her hold. "I guess they weren't distracted by the needs of other children. We're making progress, but it doesn't change the fact Dane marked me for life."

Chandler frowned and set his plate down on the coffee table. "What do you mean *marked you*?"

"Everywhere I go, men seem to think I'm an easy mark." She held up a hand as he protested. "You're different, which is why I let you in here. But others brush against me, make insinuating comments, as if I'm marked for sexual ease. I've learned to keep a moat of distance between me and men. I've accepted I'm flawed by experience." She snorted and it was a harsh sound. "I cannot believe I'm talking about this."

Chandler carefully kept his body language open yet as physically distant as he could while they sat on the same couch. "So what do you do about it?"

"There's nothing I can do. It was done to me, and I'm surviving. Thousands of dollars on counselors suggests this is my future." She collected the empty pizza box and plates and headed for the kitchen.

He followed her into the kitchen, knowing he couldn't let her create distance between them. "I'm not going to work tomorrow. And you don't have a job, right?"

"Thanks for the reminder."

"Let's do something we can't do when we're working stiffs. Let's explore the Mall. Be tourists in our own backyard. Then Friday you can go back to being there for Tiffany, and I'll go back to my active duty and veterans." He could see the conflict on her face. "We'll forget the mess for a bit."

"Okay."

"See, that wasn't so hard."

As she let a smile grow on her face, he felt hope rising inside to press against his fatigue from the extraordinarily long day.

CHAPTER 44

The knock at her apartment door startled Jaime so that coffee sloshed out of her mug and onto her hand. "Ouch." She glanced at the clock, then turned toward the door. It must be Chandler. "Coming."

She grabbed the rag from the sink and wiped up the spill before heading to the door, trying to avoid Simba who seemed determined to wind around her legs and trip her. She scooped him up and opened the door. Her heart stuttered a moment as she took in Chandler standing there, Aslan at his side. The man looked like he'd stepped out of a Banana Republic ad in his khakis, sweater, and dark pea coat. How did he keep Aslan's long, golden fur off that coat?

Simba tensed, then struggled free of Jaime's hold and leapt to the tile. He poked his nose in the air and strutted back toward the couch. Aslan whined but looked at Chandler and didn't budge even though Jaime knew it must be killing him not to follow the cat. As if to emphasize his freedom, Simba leapt to the couch's back and stretched his front legs. The stinker was taunting Aslan.

She pulled her attention back to the man in front of her. "Good morning."

"Hey." The word lazed out of his mouth. Not a drawl, but a caress. "You going to let us in?"

"Of course." She fought a losing battle with the heat that crawled up her neck into her cheeks, until the scrutiny of his look had her blushing. "Let me grab a jacket. Help yourself to coffee. I've got travel mugs." Before she could say anything that might make her more flustered, she waved him into the apartment, noting again how the space shrank when he stepped inside. "I'll be right back."

The moment she escaped into her bedroom, she closed the door and leaned against it. The space of palest blue walls and white bedding did little to calm her. Instead, she breathed deeply and tried to force peace into her veins. Once her heart had returned to an almost normal rhythm, she pushed away and hurried to the mirror. Shoot, color heightened her neck and cheeks.

There was no way he could have missed her reaction to him. She was a mess, but this modern-day hero wanted to spend his off-duty hours with her. In fact, he'd finagled his vacation time to make time for her before the incident at his work created the space for today. The real danger was that the more time she spent with him, the harder she would fall.

There would be no halfway measures when it came to Chandler Bolton.

That should terrify her, but instead she was intrigued. Emilie would tell her to relax and enjoy it, but she couldn't. Not yet. Maybe though . . . maybe he was a man she could will herself to trust.

"Everything okay in there?"

She bit back a grin. Busted by his impatience. That had to be a good sign. "I'll be right out."

Jaime grabbed her clutch and a hooded squall coat. While she wasn't exactly sure what they were doing, the weather looked like it would maintain a decided chill in the air. She added a pair of gloves to the ensemble just in case. Now to convince him she was relaxed and eager to spend time with him, when in truth she felt as tightly strung as a cat in a room of rocking chairs. A scratching at the door warned her time was up, and she opened the door for Simba. He wound around her legs, tail high, a soft rumble coming from him.

She scooped up the cat and buried her face in his fur. "Keep the place safe while I'm gone, all right?"

Simba batted her chin with a paw and continued to purr.

She set him on the blanket at the end of the comforter and slipped her clutch around her wrist.

———

Chandler watched as Jaime came out of the bedroom, pulling her heavy dark waves of hair from her coat's collar. What would it feel like to bury his hands in that thick mane?

She scooped her keys off the counter and slid them into a pocket. "Did you find the coffee?"

He shook his head, unable to form words, and she pushed a button on the Keurig. "This is made from beans a friend brought back from the Dominican Republic. It's got a rich flavor I think you'll like."

When she handed him one of the cups, he bit back a laugh as he read the words scrolling across it. *Women who read are dangerous.* She glanced at the cup and colored again. He could get used to watching the way her cheeks turned into soft roses. "Sorry. You can have this one instead." She slid the other mug his way. *Too much Monday, not enough coffee.*

"I like them both."

"I do too." She added more than a splash of some fancy creamer to hers and tapped the lid in place. "Let's go adventure."

He let her open the door since he couldn't figure out where she stood on chivalry. His mom wouldn't be proud, but Jaime was a riddle he needed to crack. He put a hand at her back as they walked down the hallway to the elevator. She didn't step away, so he'd call it progress.

He helped her into his truck, and a comfortable silence fell as he steered through the late morning traffic toward the Mall. Favor was on his side, as he found parking large enough to accommodate the pickup along Constitution Avenue. Soon Aslan was reluctantly clipped to the lead, and they joined tourists strolling the Mall.

"Where would you like to start?"

Jaime flipped her hair away from her face. "Could we go to the World War II Memorial? I don't have to be at Madeline's until seven tonight."

"Absolutely." There was something sacred about the space, something that called to his soul with the reminder that some battles were worth any sacrifice. The war on terrorism felt so unrelenting and futile sometimes that he needed the reminders that the country had fought other, large wars on multiple fronts and won. We could do it again this time if the country maintained its will, though the unity of World War II couldn't be easily replicated.

They walked past the Washington Monument on their way to the Memorial. Aslan stayed close to his side as they waited for traffic to ease before crossing 17th Street and entering the large memorial.

She stiffened at one point, and he stopped her. "What's wrong?"

"I feel like I'm being watched, but that's crazy." Her eyes darted around. "Look at all the tourists here."

The place had its share for an October morning. He didn't want to think that someone was keyed into her, that the shadow at Busboys and Poets hadn't been his vet but someone else. "Where do you see them?"

"That's just it. I don't." She huffed out a sigh. "I'm imagining things. Maybe Tuesday after the hearing, I'll be able to laugh at myself. All stressed over nothing important."

He didn't want to tell her she was wrong, but as he scanned the crowd he didn't see anyone who seemed especially focused on her.

"Forget I mentioned it."

He turned his attention back to her and tipped her chin up

with a finger. "Don't ever apologize for being alert. I want to keep you safe too."

She leaned into his touch and nodded. "Thank you."

He had to consciously step back and turn to telling her the history of a monument that she probably knew as well as he did. All the while he kept his gaze moving behind his sunglasses. The placement had been controversial when the WWII Memorial was constructed, but Chandler couldn't imagine it anywhere else than nestled between the Lincoln Memorial and Washington Monument. The oval series of fountains in the pool would be winterized soon, but right now they added a peaceful note. Jaime walked down the shallow steps that led into the Memorial and then spun slowly. Her face wore a solemn expression as she walked to a stone bench built into a ramp and sat down.

He joined her, and Aslan crouched next to her, placing his head in her lap. She absently stroked his head.

"I never got to ask my great-grandpa what he did at the Pentagon during the war." There was a trace of sadness in the words.

"What would you have asked?"

"What he did. What it was like. Did he wish he got sent to a front?" She turned away so that all he saw was her shadowed profile. "So many questions I'd ask."

"We all have those." The past was a giant void that couldn't be filled, but he knew she was talking about more than just the questions she wanted to ask about the war.

"Chandler, how can you work with returning veterans every day?"

"How can you work with those accused of terrible crimes?"

"It's not the same." Her jaw firmed.

"It is. You are called to help people navigate the criminal system. I'm called to help people reintegrate to a new normal when they return from combat tours."

"*Called*? That's a strong term."

"It's the best word. I've seen you light up when you talk about what you do. It's more than a job."

She nodded but let the words die as if they reminded her she didn't have a job. After a few minutes she stood and wandered out of the memorial. They next waited in line at the Washington Monument, followed by a breathtaking view of the city's monuments from the top. Morning wore into afternoon, and they grabbed tacos from a food truck before heading back down the Mall to where the Lincoln waited at the other end. As twilight fell, he sensed her walls shift. Then he snapped a photo of her sitting on the steps of the Lincoln with her arm around Aslan as twilight painted bright colors across the sky, and he felt something shift inside him as well. She slipped into his heart, and he couldn't evict her if he wanted.

CHAPTER 45

The beige walls of the courthouse's hallway pressed against Jaime as she paced, the adrenaline of what was to come filling her with an energy she couldn't contain. Madeline should have arrived by now, but she had insisted she could drive Tiffany over without an escort. Jaime had spent an hour Thursday night at their home trying to explain to Tiffany what was coming. Then the conversation with Madeline had gone another hour. Today Jaime needed to guide Tiffany through the hearing and help her voice be heard.

The last week felt like it had been unending with a race from one pressure-filled scenario to the next. The first leg of that race culminated here with Tiffany's hearing, then it was on to her testimony at the Senate.

"Miss Jaime?" Tiffany's high voice pulled Jaime from her thoughts. She turned to find the girl waiting, wearing a sweet T-shirt and skirt over leggings. The ensemble only emphasized the innocence she should have to go with her youth.

"Hey, sweetie. Are you ready to talk to the judge?"

The little girl's upper teeth clamped down on her lower lip, and she shrugged.

Jaime looked at Madeline. "As Savannah and I explained yesterday, first I'll talk to the judge and explain why Tiffany needs Aslan with her. You two will wait in a room off the court while we have that conversation. I've asked the bailiff to have a TV and movie in there to distract her. After the judge decides, we'll proceed to her competency hearing and then to the grand jury testimony."

"That's a lot."

"It is, but Savannah and I will walk through each step with you."

"And if he won't allow Aslan?"

"Let's worry about that after we know his ruling." She forced a smile. "Let's get you through security."

Jaime guided the pair through the security process and then led them upstairs to where Savannah already waited. Savannah leaned down to talk to Tiffany and then led the girl and her mother around the courtroom, explaining who would sit in what chair.

"This chair"—she patted the witness box—"is where you'll sit, Tiffany." After she was sure the girl had no questions, Savannah led them to the anteroom. A minute later she returned. "Ready to get that dog into the court?"

Jaime nodded as she felt the weight of responsibility. She'd watched the video of the investigative interview. Tiffany had refused to talk until Aslan came in. The girl needed the support of the comfort animal. "There's a lot riding on him."

"Yes, and on us, but I know you're ready."

Jaime wished she felt as certain. After her time with Tiffany and Madeline, she'd spent the balance of the evening reviewing the law and formulating her arguments. Then she'd made them to the mirror until it felt natural and routine. "Let's get started."

The air in the courtroom felt heavy, somber, laced with all that is evil. Jaime had sat in courtrooms like this one so many times she'd lost track of when and where. But never had she felt the oppression quite like this.

This time it was an unknown, amorphous mass. She wanted to shield Tiffany from it, but the case could not proceed without the girl's testimony. The physical evidence tying Corey Bowman to the criminal abuse Tiffany had suffered was minimal.

As soon as the Commonwealth's Attorney, defense counsel, and defendant were in the courtroom, the judge entered. Judge William Thacker was something of an institution, having served on the bench for more than twenty years. He tended to be pro-victim but ultimately fair. His reading glasses would slide from his nose up into his white hair depending on whether he was reading or listening. With him on the bench, Tiffany would at least get a fair hearing.

Jaime wished in this case that the defendant wouldn't have a voice in this part of the process, but she knew it was necessary. While he wouldn't be allowed to participate in the grand jury hearing, he could be part of the process to determine whether Tiffany was competent to testify. Once they were all settled, the judge entered the courtroom.

Judge Winters peered at Savannah over the rim of his glasses. "Help me understand your role here today."

"The child's mother has hired us to help her navigate this process. Part of that includes making sure her testimony is minimally harmful to the child. We've filed a motion requesting a comfort animal to be with the child through today's proceeding and any in the future."

The judge turned to the Commonwealth's Attorney, Lacy Collins. Jaime was surprised the woman had shown up for such a foundational matter, but maybe she wanted to make a point with the judge about the importance of the case. "Ms. Collins, are you okay with their representing the child?"

"Yes, Your Honor." The middle-aged woman ran her hands along her navy pencil skirt and then straightened her tweed jacket. "As is so often the case in matters like this, the bulk of this matter relies on the victim's testimony. We agree that the comfort animal is necessary for today's proceedings."

"Thank you." The judge turned to the public defender, and

Jaime tried not to stare at her former boss. "Mr. Joshua? What is the public defender's position?"

"We are unconvinced that such a concession is necessary."

"So you oppose the motion?"

"Yes, sir."

The judge pinched the bridge of his nose, then turned to Savannah. "Then we must proceed. Please make your argument."

"Sir, my associate Jaime Nichols will present the argument."

Jaime felt her cheeks flare as Grant turned to her.

"Associate, huh?"

She didn't want to tell him it was the first she'd heard of it, so she let it go. The judge nodded to her. "Miss Nichols, please keep your remarks to less than ten minutes. Five would be better, since I've read your memo."

"Thank you." Jaime eased to her feet without a clear place at the table other than the need to protect a little girl who had experienced too much. "May it please the court." She took a breath, glanced at her notes, and then returned her gaze to the judge. "For centuries we have known that pets have a calming effect on people. Study after study, a few of which I included in the memo, document this. Few places are more stressful for people than court, especially when they are called upon to testify. The child witness in this case has been the victim of molesting. She needs the support provided by a trained comfort dog to help tell her story to this court."

Jaime looked down at her notes but didn't really see them. "Your Honor, this would not be the first court in Virginia to allow such a use of a dog. In Stafford a black Labrador retriever has served as a comfort dog for years, helping calm victims and witnesses. These animals are also allowed in other courts." She quickly summarized a few of the courts and how the dogs' presence had been demonstrated to help children. "Because comfort dogs have already been allowed in Virginia courts, we ask that you allow one to assist the child who will testify today so that she will have a voice to share her story. Thank you."

After she sat, Savannah squeezed her hand. "Nice work."

"We'll see."

Grant launched to his feet the moment the judge looked at him. "Your Honor, this is ridiculous. This dog does not qualify as a service animal, and the child does not qualify as disabled. As such, the animal should not be allowed. Either the girl can answer or she can't."

The judge tapped the edge of his pencil against his lips as he looked over their heads. "Because of the age of the child, I'm going to allow it. Your objection has been recorded, Mr. Joshua." He turned to Savannah. "How long will you need to get the dog here?"

Savannah glanced at Jaime who could only shrug. Chandler was supposed to be close, but she wasn't certain. "Twenty minutes should be sufficient."

"All right. Then we will reconvene in thirty minutes after my next hearing."

The attorneys stood as a unit and made their way into the hallway, where Jaime broke off and called Chandler. "We're ready for Aslan."

Chandler sounded a little out of breath. "I just found parking. Probably should have walked from the office."

"It's too cold for that." Jaime sighed. "Good luck getting Aslan through security."

"He's got his tag. Hopefully security here will accept it." Chandler grunted, and Jaime could imagine Aslan was tugging him toward a tree or door. "We'll be there as soon as we can. Which floor?"

Jaime told him, and when she turned around found herself nose to nose with Grant.

"What are you doing?" His words hissed into the narrow space between them.

"What do you mean?"

"Do you understand the hornets' nest you've kicked over?"

She frowned at him and thrust her hands on her hips. "What is this? Twenty questions?"

"I'm trying to warn you." He glanced around as if checking for anyone too close. Then he abruptly took a step back. "Be careful."

Jaime watched him stalk off, confused about what had just happened. Savannah found her there a minute later.

"Are you ready to tell our clients the good news?"

"Ummm. Right." Jaime shook her head as Savannah watched her closely.

"You all right?"

"I think Grant just warned me that Dane is getting anxious."

"You think or you know?"

"I'm not sure. It was a surreal conversation."

"Then let's focus on the thing in front of us: getting Tiffany through the hearing."

Ten minutes passed in the anteroom as Tiffany quietly ran colored pencils up and down a sheet of paper. Jaime tapped her phone against her teeth as she glanced at her watch. "I'm going to see if I can find Chandler. He should be here."

Madeline nodded from where she sat next to Tiffany. Her voice seemed locked in her throat as she tapped her fingers against her skirt-covered legs. "Tiffany needs Aslan."

Jaime nodded even as she thought that all of them could use the dog's steadying presence. She glanced again toward the judge's chambers, but the door was still shut, so she worked her way to the room's exit. When she reached the hallway, she looked up and down but didn't see Chandler or Aslan. The door opened behind her as she pulled up his number and hit Call. Tiffany slid up next to her and leaned into Jaime's side.

She led Tiffany to a bench lining the wall. "Aslan is on his way. You okay, kiddo?"

The little girl nodded, but Jaime could feel her tremble.

She breathed a prayer over her. *Please, God, be with her. She shouldn't have to go through this.*

At least Jaime could make sure she didn't get through it alone. The child had experienced too much through the abuse and the investigation. Now to have to testify at the grand jury proceedings . . . it was all too much.

CHAPTER 46

The northern Virginia area created a love-hate relationship for Chandler. Nothing reinforced that complex relationship as much as trying to find parking when time was of the essence. Walking would have made sense if he'd been at work, but the office would be closed for at least one more day before they could begin the process of reopening. Jake hung on to life, but in intensive care, his status a harsh reminder of everything that had happened Wednesday.

Chandler had to find a way to keep his angst and frustration from bleeding into Aslan.

Aslan had to do his job and bring presence and calm to Tiffany.

He led Aslan up the steps and into the courthouse's lobby. There was a layer of dark green marble or stone topped by a beige layer that ran to about his shoulder height, topped by beige paint to the high ceiling. The marble floor caused every sound to echo and be magnified. The security officer waved him to a stop.

"That animal can't go inside."

Chandler fished in his jacket pocket for the paperwork showing Aslan was a trained comfort animal. "He's here to support an eight-year-old who has to testify before a grand jury."

The man glanced at the papers. "I need more than this."

"All right." Chandler pulled out his phone and called Jaime, noticing he'd missed her call. "We're caught at security. Do you have anything from the judge that shows Aslan is needed in court?"

"It was an oral order." She paused. "Let me talk to the officer."

He handed his phone to the officer, who was looking more impatient by the moment. The man nodded and grunted acquiescence.

"Miss Nichols, I'll need you to meet them here and take responsibility for them." He handed the phone back to Chandler. "She's on her way. As soon as she arrives, I'll let you through."

Time seemed to drag as he waited for Jaime.

The elevator doors opened, and she burst out as if pushed. "I swear it stopped on each floor." She turned to the guard. "Arthur, they're with me. My client needs this dog before her competency hearing." Jaime glanced at her watch. "Which starts in five minutes."

"All right. Because they're with you, I'll let them through." Then he proceeded to tell her what paperwork she'd need for the next time, while Chandler read anxiety in Jaime's clenched fists.

She hurried them toward the elevator. "Tiffany's so fragile."

"We'll get there. She won't be alone."

"That's right. I won't let her be, which is why we have to get Aslan up there."

He shook his head. "No. I mean God will be with her. She won't be alone."

Jaime stilled and her eyes met his. "I'm trying to believe that."

"That's where we all start." The doors dinged open, and he held them for her. "Let's go take care of our girl."

———

His words echoed in Jaime's mind. Our girl. She liked the sound of that even as she wished that Tiffany had never needed their help. The elevator opened on the courtroom's floor, and Aslan stepped out, his nails clicking against the floor.

Savannah straightened from where she'd been leaning against the wall. "Thanks for coming."

Chandler nodded and leaned down to pet Aslan. "Where's Tiffany? He's ready to go to work."

Aslan tipped his head, ears flopping, almost as if he understood the words.

"We've had her waiting in a room with coloring books and a cartoon." Jaime gestured for him to follow her. "Come this way."

They walked around two corners, and then she rapped lightly on a door. When it opened, Madeline stood there, worry filling her gaze. Then she saw Aslan and her shoulders slumped. "He made it."

Jaime put an arm around the woman's shoulders. "Of course. Now where's our girl?"

Tiffany looked up, her tongue stuck between her teeth, the picture of concentration. Her face lit as if candles illuminated it from within when she saw the dog. She tossed her colored pencils down and sprang to her feet. "Aslan!"

The dog glanced at Chandler, then at Tiffany. "Release."

Aslan bounded to Tiffany's side and let her maul him in her excitement. Savannah stepped toward the door. "They'll be expecting us in court. Time to move this show."

In moments the hearing was called back to order. "This time we are here for the competency hearing for Tiffany Ange." The judge pulled his glasses from his round face and smiled at the little girl. "Tiffany, would you mind coming and sitting in this chair over here?" He gestured to the witness chair.

"Yes, sir." Her voice was small.

"Thank you. I understand you have a dog with you. He can go with you."

"Okay." Tiffany looked at Jaime, eyes round and big. "Do I have to go?"

Jaime knelt in front of the girl. "Yes, but Aslan and I will be here the whole time."

"Promise?"

"Yes, ma'am." Jaime squeezed her shoulders. "You'll be fine. I promise nothing bad will happen here."

Tiffany stared at her for another moment and then walked to the witness chair, Aslan half a step behind her after a single voice command from Chandler.

The judge waited until she was settled, her sneaker-clad feet kicking over Aslan's back. "How old are you?"

"Eight."

"Where do you live?"

"Arlington."

"Do you know what a lie is?"

"Not telling the truth."

"And what is the truth?"

"What really happened."

"Today we need to ask you some questions about something that happened to you. Can you tell me the truth?"

She looked at him. "Yes, sir."

"Why?"

"Because if I don't my mom will be upset, and Miss Jaime will be disappointed. I know it's important to tell the truth."

The judge nodded. "It's very important. Especially when you're in court." He considered the little girl. "Does either attorney have any questions?"

Grant stood. "I do, Your Honor." At the judge's nod, he turned to Tiffany and held up a sheet of paper. "What color is this, Tiffany?"

She looked at him with crinkled eyebrows and nose. "Green."

"If I told you this was blue, would I be telling the truth?"

"No, it's green."

"So calling it blue is a lie?"

"Yes. It can only be one color at a time."

"Do you know if it's wrong to tell the truth in a court like this?"

Jaime frowned as she realized what he was trying to do. *Stay focused, kiddo.*

Tiffany looked at Grant like he was crazy. "No, I can't tell a lie, but I can tell the truth."

He tried to get her to explain what a lie was (not the truth), and how it differed from the truth (one was true and the other wasn't), but after several minutes the judge called a halt to the badgering.

"I deem Tiffany Ange fit to take the oath because she understands the difference between the truth and a lie." The judge looked down at his court reporter. "Let's take a fifteen-minute break and these proceedings will transition to a probable cause hearing. If I find probable cause for the charges to proceed, it will then move to the grand jury." The judge turned to Tiffany. "Young lady, you may step down and take a break." He stood and left the courtroom, his black robes billowing around him.

Lacy Collins, the Commonwealth's Attorney, stood and turned to Savannah. "I need to see you in the hall now."

Madeline looked at Jaime as Tiffany made her way back to them, Aslan trailing at her side. "What's happening?"

Chandler leaned into Jaime's side. "I'm going to take Aslan for a quick lap."

She nodded, then focused on Madeline. "Tiffany did what she needed to convince the judge that she can tell the truth and understands the difference between that and a lie. Next she'll tell the judge what Corey did to her. After that will be the grand jury."

"When will that happen?"

"We'll see how Tiffany's holding up."

"Will the public defender ask her questions?"

"Possibly."

Madeline's nostrils flared and her shoulders stiffened, so Jaime hurried on. "But it's not guaranteed. I often wouldn't because I didn't want to tip my hand to the prosecution." Even a few days earlier she could have anticipated Grant's strategy. Now she had no idea.

The fact that Tiffany had survived the competency hearing was a win. Now the young girl just had to survive two more hearings.

CHAPTER 47

The judge called the hearing to order as Savannah leaned into Jaime. "Lacy is concerned about Madeline."

"Why?"

"She thinks we need to get the mother out of here."

"Okay." Jaime drew the word out as she tried to consider what the Commonwealth's Attorney was truly concerned about. "Is she afraid Madeline's going to coach Tiffany?"

Savannah shrugged. "I'll escort her out. Tell her the judge has cleared the room for purposes of the probable cause hearing."

"At least Tiffany has Aslan."

"Yeah." Savannah tapped Madeline on the shoulder and nodded toward the door.

Jaime watched them walk out. As she turned back to the judge, her gaze ran over those gathered in the gallery. What had she just seen? Her uncle? Yet when she looked again, he was gone. She blinked a couple times and looked again. Yep, definitely not there. Maybe Grant's "warning" was making her imagine things.

"Ms. Collins, you may call your first witness."

"I will only have two, Your Honor." First the dignified woman walked Detective Thomas through why the police had been called to investigate the alleged sexual abuse.

During her testimony, Jaime and Chandler took Tiffany and Aslan back to the anteroom where the child had waited earlier. Madeline flipped through a magazine in one corner, while Aslan yawned as if completely uninterested. Chandler smiled at Jaime over the dog's head.

Tiffany looked around the small room. "How much longer, Mommy? This is taking forever."

Madeline glanced up as if interrupted from a good dream. "I'm not sure how these things go. You'll have to be patient."

"We'll have lunch when you're done." Jaime started digging through her bag. "Would you like some gum?"

"I'd like a Snickers."

Chandler burst out laughing as if caught off guard by her assertion. "I don't have one of those. Do you, Jaime?"

"Nope." She tried to engage Tiffany in some coloring, but the little girl was clearly reaching the end of her patience. Jaime texted Savannah. The natives are restless.

Run her to the restroom. When you're done, we'll be ready for her. Detective Thomas has done a good job.

Okay.

Five minutes later they returned from the restroom, and a sheriff's deputy waited inside the room for them.

"The CA has called her."

"Thanks." Jaime knelt in front of Tiffany. "Now you get to tell the judge what happened to you."

She raised her eyebrows and frowned at Jaime. "Does this mean we have to talk about colors again?"

"No." Jaime tweaked her nose. "The nice lady will ask you questions, and Aslan will be at your feet like last time."

"Okay."

This time they used the door from the anteroom into the courtroom. Judge Thatcher smiled at Tiffany as she walked in with Aslan at her side. "Welcome back, young lady." After Tiffany climbed into the witness chair, he swore her in again. Then he turned his attention to Lacy. "You may proceed."

"Thank you. Tiffany, you did so well earlier." Lacy gestured toward where she sat in the witness chair. "We'll talk for a few minutes if that's all right."

"Okay." Tiffany waited until Aslan was settled at her feet before looking at them. "I'm ready."

"First the judge is going to ask you to repeat some words."

"Young lady, do you remember what the truth is?"

"Yes, sir."

"Do you promise to tell the truth here?"

"Yes, sir."

"All right. Then listen carefully to the questions you'll be asked."

"Okay." Tiffany looked at Jaime, her eyes appearing so big in her face. "You'll stay here?"

"I'm not leaving." At Jaime's words, Tiffany seemed to relax, and her feet grazed the top of Aslan's fur.

Lacy stood and cleared her throat. "Young lady, can you tell me your name?"

"Tiffany Ange." The girl rolled her eyes as if that question was too easy.

"I want to talk about Mr. Corey."

"The man who hurt me?"

Grant popped to his feet. "Objection, Your Honor. She's stating an opinion."

Lacy braced her hands against the table. "Try to be a little more original, Grant. Of course it's her opinion. She's eight."

And then Lacy skillfully and carefully asked a series of questions about how Tiffany knew Corey, leading to what Corey did to her. Then she asked what happened when Corey hurt her. "What happened?"

"When I went to bed?"

"Yes. Was your mommy there?"

"No, she was cleaning the kitchen."

"Why?"

Tiffany frowned as if thinking hard. "Because the dishes were dirty. Corey said he'd help me get ready for bed, but he hurt me."

"Why didn't you get your mommy?"

"He said he'd hurt her if I did."

Lacy paused as Tiffany ran her shoes across Aslan's back. After a moment passed, Grant cleared his throat, and Tiffany jolted. Lacy gave her a soft smile. "Tiffany, what did the man do to you?"

"He hurt me."

"How?" The word was soft but direct.

Tiffany swallowed, and then the story began to flow with her tears. Through it all Aslan never moved, even as Lacy asked follow-up questions. "What else happened?"

"I pretended to be asleep. As soon as he left, I told Mommy."

Jaime's vision clouded with tears. Why hadn't she done the same thing when Dane hurt her? Maybe it could have stopped with one instance of violation rather than repeated encounters.

"What happened next?"

"Mommy called the police, and I met Aslan."

Lacy smiled as the dog glanced up at his name. "What did you tell the police?"

"That I didn't want him to hurt me again."

When Tiffany's words stopped, Lacy let a minute of silence fall on the room. Then she turned toward the defense table. "Is the man at that table the one who hurt you?"

Tiffany nodded, her shoulders hunched as if to protect herself, then said yes in a very small voice. Tiffany's feet rubbed Aslan as if her life depended on his presence.

"I have no further questions."

The judge looked at Grant. "Do you have any questions?"

Grant looked at his legal pad where he'd scratched notes throughout Tiffany's testimony. He pulled his reading glasses off his nose and then tapped the frames against his chin. He glanced at the scowling man with the air of James Dean seated next to him, then at Tiffany. "No, sir."

"Then I will certify this case to the Circuit Court that probable cause has been established and turn this matter over to the grand jury. The grand jury is scheduled to convene at two. Ms. Daniels, do you believe your client can handle answering questions one more time today?"

Jaime wanted to beg Savannah to say no. No child should be asked to do something like that. She'd already bled her story out. But Savannah looked from Tiffany to Aslan. "If the dog is allowed in, I think she'll make it."

"All right, I'd like to try." He turned to Grant and the defendant. "You are both excused." After the two men left, he waved Lacy and Savannah up. "You too, Miss Nichols." Once they were all clustered by his bench, he pushed the microphone out of his way. "Normally, attorneys are not allowed in the room with the witnesses. However, because of Tiffany's age I will allow you to select one person to accompany her and ensure she is not harassed in any way. Whoever it is, I will appoint as her guardian ad litem for the purposes of the grand jury."

Savannah turned to Jaime. "It should be you, Jaime, since she's most comfortable with you."

Ms. Collins nodded. "I agree. I can't do it because of my role, but someone needs to be in there for the child alone."

"All right." Jaime looked at the judge. "Your Honor, do I have authority to end the grand jury hearing if it is too much for my client?"

"Yes. As the GAL you will be there solely to look out for her interests and well-being."

"Then I accept."

As they walked out of the courtroom, Jaime stopped the Commonwealth's Attorney. "Do the hearings usually go this quickly and in such close succession?"

"Not always. However, I detailed a possible plan like this for the judge when I realized the type of testimony she would give. He knew in general what was coming and what might be required."

Jaime glanced up and down the hallway. "Which jury room will the grand jury meet in?"

"One of the deputies will lead you there. First get lunch while I finalize the bill of indictment. Be back here at two thirty."

As Lacy left, Chandler stepped closer. "Ready to break free?"

"This is moving so fast."

"Guess they want to minimize the harm to Tiffany."

She knew that was the intent, but would it work? "Maybe it will make things worse."

"That's why you'll be in there."

The sun was shining when they exited the building. "Let's find a park and let Tiffany and Aslan run while we eat."

Madeline looked green. "I'm not sure I can handle another round of this."

"You won't be allowed in the grand jury room."

"My baby is not going through more questioning without me."

Jaime paused and took Madeline's hands. "I'm sorry, but she will. This is how it has to be if you want to see the man go to jail."

Madeline's face crumbled. "It's too much."

"You're right. But you're giving her the opportunity to do something about the wrong. That is a gift I didn't have, and now the reality is it may be too late. I promise I will stop the grand jury questioning the moment it is too much for her. Trust Aslan and me."

"And if we're wrong?"

"I'll still be here. Chandler and Savannah and everyone else who cares about Tiffany will be with you."

"Aslan too." Tiffany walked to her mom and leaned into her side. "I want to finish telling what he did." Tiffany still refused to say the man's name, but Jaime knew it would be okay.

Grand jury hearings were more casual than competency or probable cause hearings but a key part of determining whether there would be a trial. After their lunch in the sunshine, the bailiff led them to a side room, and when they entered, the grand jury members sat around a table.

For the next thirty minutes Tiffany answered questions from one woman, who must be acting as foreman. She schooled her voice to be kind, but Tiffany faltered as she answered. The girl showed how tired she was as she stumbled over words and timelines.

Jaime split her time between watching Tiffany's nonverbals and those of the grand jurors.

With each answer, the grand jurors' frowns deepened. One woman pressed a hand to her stomach as if for relief from pain.

Finally the questions ended, and Jaime hoped it was only a matter of time before Corey Bowman would be behind bars for sexual assault. Tiffany would be okay because the girl was a fighter with a voice that would not be silenced.

The lights glared in his face, but he kept a serene look pasted in place. His life had led with deliberate pacing to this moment. He had earned the opportunity and no one would take it from him. He would make certain of that.

The young woman across from him rested a legal pad on her knee.

What would it be like to get closer to her?

He reined in his thoughts.

Not now. He would have only the bearing and comportment of the officer he was. The one he would be as soon as the farce of the hearings ended. He locked gazes with Senator Langdon, who'd arranged this little parlay with the media. The coward hadn't once indicated he was in support of Dane's appointment. That was fine. Dane had a long memory and had as much dirt on Langdon as Langdon thought he had on Dane.

It wouldn't be a fair fight, but the good senator didn't understand that.

The journalist glanced down at her notepad. Something about her reminded him of a younger Jaime. The worldly edge tinged with vulnerability reflected his niece as a teenager.

The man behind the camera jarred the room with a loud voice. "Ready when you are."

The woman glanced at him. What was her name? Kathy? Karen? Carmen? It didn't matter. All that mattered was the way she used her beauty to lure him in. Little did she know the power was his. He had learned that years ago with a subject much more appealing and innocent.

"Mr. Nichols."

"Colonel Nichols." He'd earned the rank through years of dedicated service.

She inclined her head toward him. "Colonel Nichols, tell us why you should be the army's next brigadier general."

He answered, the question so softball he didn't need to think. The conversation pinged back and forth, him keeping his gaze locked on her, ignoring the cameras pointed at him from two positions.

"Do the charges filed by the Commonwealth's Attorney of Virginia concern you?"

He schooled his features, kept them controlled. "What charges?"

"The ones that allege you molested your niece." There was steel undergirding her smile, as if she knew she'd caught him off guard.

Not nearly as off guard as he'd make his niece. So far he'd only toyed with her.

No one messed with his career.

No one.

CHAPTER 48

The day was rainy and cold, the breeze slicing through Jaime when she ran outside for a few minutes. Her head still felt clouded from the long day at court the day before, but she was so proud of Tiffany. Now she needed to clear her head and get ready for her own testimony on Tuesday. She called Caroline as soon as she was back in the warmth of her apartment.

"Are you still planning on that picnic at Fort Hunt?"

Caroline sighed. "We're moving it since the weather isn't cooperating. How about we meet at your apartment at three? I can drive."

"All right." Jaime settled on details with Caroline and then spent the next couple hours making a list of every question she could anticipate. She needed to do this so she could relax and enjoy the time with friends—a much-needed break between the stress of Tiffany's testimony and her own.

The drive was pleasant enough, but in the opposite direction of Fort Hunt park. "Exactly where are we going?"

"We've moved it to Almost Home. If the weather cooperates, we can still be outside and have a bonfire. If not, we have the community center to claim."

They chatted about Caroline's apartment. "The fumes are terrible."

"You can always move back in with me."

Caroline shook her head. "I can't sleep on your futon indefinitely."

When they turned into the parking lot of the group home, there

315

were several cars, but only a few that Jaime recognized. Caroline handed two cake pans full of chocolate chip cookies to Jaime, then picked up two more pans filled with cupcakes to carry herself. The icing was piped to perfection with a smattering of fall leaf accents on top.

"Did you make those?"

"Of course not." Caroline shifted the cupcakes and pushed a smile out. "I might be a fan of the Food Network, but I'd need about three days to get something to look this good."

"I've eaten your cooking and it was great."

"Cooking a meal is not the same as baking."

Jaime thought about it a moment. "My birthday cake?"

"Store-bought." Caroline shifted the pans in her arms. "It was a busy week at the court. Please don't tell Brandon these aren't fresh from my kitchen though the cookies are."

"Why?"

"He believes every woman should bake as well as his dear grandmother." Caroline sighed. "Can I help it if I want that man to see me before he decides my worth based on my lack of a flaky piecrust?"

Jaime couldn't resist the laugh that burbled up at the image. "We'll find baking classes."

"Sure. But not tonight." Caroline moved across the stone parking lot with a speed that was surprising for her size.

"Are things serious with you two?"

Caroline skidded to a halt and turned blazing eyes on Jaime. "Of course not. We barely know each other. We're just friends. Anyway, his life is too stressed with things here to worry about me."

But as Caroline's words collided and slid against each other, Jaime could see into her friend's soft heart. She was invested in this man, one Jaime had barely glanced at on the rare occasions their paths overlapped. She'd need to make sure he was acceptable for her friend. Caroline didn't do anything halfway and would easily give her heart away before Brandon considered it anything more than a buddy friendship.

When they reached the long building surrounded by smaller cottages, Jaime slowed. "How many kids live here?"

"Too many but not enough. He's had to close a couple cottages due to budget issues. I couldn't believe it when I came and met a couple girls I used to babysit. They're barely teenagers, and it breaks my heart they're here."

"Why?"

"Why does it break my heart?"

"No, why are they here?"

Caroline shrugged. "Brandon told me they were a little wild after their dad died in a car accident, and no one would take them on. Their caseworker brought them here." She started moving again. "If we don't get in there, we will freeze, and I'm not sure what that will do to the cupcakes."

Jaime followed her friend inside but hung back as Caroline started greeting everyone. Instead, Jaime looked for familiar faces. Andrew and Hayden stood near the fireplace while Emilie and Reid sat at a table surrounded by preteen boys. Emilie looked slightly out of place but very happy, her gaze fixed on Reid as he interacted with the boys. Jaime could practically feel the hero worship from where she stood. As she watched the men her friends loved, she wanted to believe they had found lasting happiness. If they could, there was hope for her.

Caroline set her container of cupcakes on a table, then waved Jaime over to do the same. She introduced her to a hulk of a man. It took everything in Jaime to stand in place and not turn and run, yet as she stayed rooted to the floor she could sense a softness to him. And the look in his eyes as he watched Caroline? She didn't need to worry about her baking ability dissuading the man.

"I'm glad you could come, Jaime." Brandon waved a friend over.

"I'd like you to meet my friend Chandler Bolton. Chandler, this is Caroline's friend Jaime."

Jaime froze as she looked at a man she knew well. There was a nervous energy to him in the way his fingers clenched and unclenched and his knee bounced. He looked like he might dash out of the building at a moment's notice, but not because he was nervous or unsettled. Instead, it was like he had so much energy he couldn't begin to contain it in a space so small.

"Jaime and I know each other." He gazed at her in that familiar way that peered behind her walls, and she felt exposed. Vulnerable. Uncomfortable. Understood. "Can you believe we live in the same complex?"

"Thank you for everything you did for Tiffany yesterday." She turned to Brandon and Caroline. "Chandler's dog, Aslan, was a godsend."

"Tiffany did great." Chandler smiled, and her breath about stopped. "How long have you known this bear of a man?"

"You mean Brandon?" Jaime glanced at Caroline. "I think we've met once."

"That's long enough to become part of this crew." Chandler shoved his hands in his pockets, and Jaime realized she liked seeing him with his friends.

Brandon slapped Chandler on the back. "Something tells me you two are gonna be just fine. Though rumor has it Jaime has been Caroline's friend longer than I've known you."

Caroline slipped back into the group with a pixie grin. "Better believe it. Jaime and I met in the first few minutes of orientation at George Mason. She's been stuck with me ever since."

"Has that been a hardship duty?" Chandler quirked an eyebrow as he said it.

"Not so bad. Caroline liked to bring the snacks. Her cupcakes are delectable." Jaime grinned as Caroline shoved her lightly.

"I am about more than food." She smoothed her hands down her waist, then turned away from Brandon. "I see Emilie waving us over. We'd better go see what she needs." Before Jaime could even say good-bye, Caroline had dragged her across the large common room. "I cannot believe you said that."

"Of course. That's what friends are for. To say the things we won't but need to, or to tease until we do."

"Well, this is not the setting. He does not need that."

"Why not? He clearly likes you. A lot."

Caroline quickened her pace as if she could run. "Don't tell me things that aren't true. Besides, didn't your mama ever tell you the way to a man's heart is through his stomach?"

"Um, no."

"Well, you missed a key part of a Southern gal's upbringing. If it ain't fried and dipped in butter, it's probably not real cooking."

"Then why aren't you the size of a barge?"

She shrugged. "Because my mama taught me all about the kitchen—and portion control."

Caroline kept Jaime away from Brandon the rest of the night, but it didn't mean Jaime's gaze didn't stray to Chandler every other second. There was something about the slightly scruffy five o'clock shadow that matched his shadowed eyes.

Ciara and Daniel Turner walked in, Daniel holding baby Amber against his shoulder as if it was the most natural thing. Ciara's eyes lit with adoration as she watched her husband with their daughter. A flicker of envy blazed through Jaime as she watched. What would it be like to build a family with someone you loved?

She saw Hayden and Andrew share a quick kiss in one corner, and Reid lead Emilie to sit in front of the fireplace. These men knew how to care for their women. It was sweet and oddly touching to watch them cherish her friends.

There was a genuineness to the caring . . . that felt like the way Chandler cared for her.

"How are things with Caroline?" Chandler took advantage of a moment alone with his friend to ask the question.

"I get the sense we'll be buddies for a long time." Brandon shifted his stance. "Until I can get this place back on solid footing, I can't get distracted."

"Seems lonely."

"Says the pot."

"If the shoe fits."

A man Chandler had met a couple times walked up, his khakis pressed and stiff. "Reid."

"Good to see you again, Chandler." Reid turned to their mutual friend. "I think I might have another lead for you. Client needs a write-off."

"Unless it's a million dollars, I'm not sure it's enough." Brandon sighed as he glanced around the room. "I've already had to close two cottages, and I'll close the next two as soon as I can move the kids."

Chandler watched Brandon. He'd never seen the man this down. "Can I do something?"

Reid shook his head. "We don't have funding yet. I've got a few ideas, and this client has a construction company. Maybe he can bring in a couple crews to work their magic."

"Maybe." Brandon looked across the grounds. "There's a lot the state wants done, and all I can think about is the kids we could help. Instead, cottages sit empty while I scramble to find money."

"We'll get there."

The evening passed with Brandon firing up a monster grill

and the guys hanging out with him as he cooked piles of food. Chandler shivered through a game of Frisbee with a few of the pre-teen boys while Reid and Andrew passed a football with a couple others. When they went inside, the women had set out bowls and plates filled with more food. A feast compared to his usual bach-elor fare.

Brandon called everyone together, and they gathered in a circle. "Let's pray." The man looked up and peace settled on his features. "Father, thank You for who You are and all that You've provided. Thanks for these friends, this time, and Your love."

Chandler sensed the person next to him shift and glanced to his left. Jaime wore a settled expression of hope.

"May all that we say and do be to Your glory. Amen."

The group broke for the food, but Jaime stayed rooted in place.

Chandler leaned against her shoulder. "We good?"

"Yeah." Her smile would rival the sun. "I'm still trying to feel my way through faith. It's pretty new."

He took her hand in his and tugged her close, feeling her breath on his chin. He loved how tall she was. The way she fit perfectly with him. And he angled down. Paused to test her reaction. Then leaned in until his lips touched hers. Paused. She didn't move, and then she tipped her head and he deepened the kiss. It was every-thing he'd hoped and more.

No, she was everything he'd hoped and more.

CHAPTER 49

On Monday Jaime headed to Daniels, McCarthy & Associates in time for lunch. Bella brought in salads and sandwiches from La Madeline down the street, and then Savannah, Emilie, and Hayden joined Jaime in the conference room they'd set up for testimony prep.

The moment they finished eating, Hayden brushed the crumbs off her hands and turned to Savannah. "Time to put Jaime through her paces."

The next hours felt like her friends were determined to force her to answer every possible question twice and the highly unlikely ones three times. Then Caroline joined them at four, and they started again.

At six Jaime gave up as her head pulsed with tension. "I'm done. I'm heading home."

Emilie pushed to her feet. "You okay?"

"Sure. Tomorrow I'll expose my deepest secrets to a roomful of strangers and probably a dozen cameras." If she was lucky it would only be a dozen.

Hayden stood and walked to her. "We're going to pray for you."

And they did. They prayed with a power and urgency that humbled Jaime and made her long for that same connection. "You're going to have to teach me how to pray. Right now I feel like Edmund confronting the White Witch, only without Lucy standing by with a magical elixir that will save my life if I fail."

"That's what we're here for." Caroline swiped under her eyes and then took Jaime's hands. "Remember you aren't alone."

Hayden pulled out her phone and tapped a note. "I'll meet you inside the doors at the Russell Senate Office Building. We'll find the hearing room from there."

Jaime nodded because she knew her voice would fail her.

"We love you, Jaime." Emilie took Jaime's hands and paused until Jaime met her gaze. "I will be praying nonstop."

"Thank you." She cleared her throat then gave a watery smile. "I'll see you on the other side."

As soon as she arrived home, Simba begged for attention. It was like he could sense her heightened emotion. The cat who tended to be standoffish stretched up until he was practically standing as he begged her to pick him up. She scooped him up and snuggled him close as she watched a meaningless movie.

Her friends' prayers cycled through her mind. Her faith might be new, but her friends were experts who could guide her if she let them.

TUESDAY, OCTOBER 23

Tuesday morning their prayers continued to give her strength as she dressed in a power suit. The black pants with matching jacket said no nonsense and serious. It fit like a suit of armor and was her uniform for a day on which she needed to feel invincible. She added a silk shell in a ruby tone and a simple gold chain. With a pair of low heels, she would make a statement but hopefully not distract.

A knock at her door startled her. She placed her hand on her heart and then eased to the door. She glanced through the peephole and felt hope well inside. She opened it and smiled. "Chandler? What are you doing here?"

"I'm driving you to your hearing."

"Don't you have to get back to your life?"

"Not yet. The army has crews working on the office space. When I checked on it last night it wasn't close to ready. So here I am."

He ran his hands along his front as if his palms might be sweaty, but nah. Cap wouldn't be nervous.

"That okay?"

"Yes." Her gaze landed on his lips and she remembered the electricity of his kiss. He must have remembered, too, because he leaned in for a quick, not long enough peck.

"You ready?"

"As I can be."

She followed him to the elevator and then to his truck. Before long they were at the Russell Senate Office Building and Chandler found a place to park. He came around to open the passenger door for her, but she didn't budge. "I can't do this."

"You can."

"Please don't say I'm not alone."

He frowned at her with a little jerk of his head. "Why?"

"Because I am the only one who's lived this. I'm the one Dane abused. I'm the one who wears the scars. And if I go through with this testimony I'll be targeted for life. Any internet search will pull up my shame."

He took her hands and massaged them with his thumbs. "No. Everyone in that hearing room will know you are one of the strongest women they have met. You have risen above a wound that would undermine many. You have worked hard to become a woman who is not defined by that time."

"Then why do I still feel like I am?"

———

Her quiet words broke his heart. "Because you need help replacing those voices. God can do it. And your friends will help. I will too. I will keep telling you everything I see in you until you believe me over those tired-out voices in your head. They are lying to you. I will only speak truth."

She leaned toward him until her head rested on his shoulder. He reached around her and eased her into a loose hug. When she didn't fight it, he released a breath.

A minute later she pulled back and then wiped under her eyes. "Thank you."

"No problem."

"Will you stay with me?"

"Absolutely." The fact she wanted him to be there made him want to puff into a larger stance and yell to the world that Jaime Nichols wanted him, a reality he wouldn't squander.

She blew out a breath, squared her shoulders, and transformed into the Amazon warrior he knew rested inside her. "Let's go."

After she stepped from the truck, he took her hand and laced their fingers together. Then they walked together to the building. Inside the doors, Savannah Daniels and Hayden McCarthy waited.

"Ah, there you are." Hayden gave Chandler a quizzical look. "Mr. Bolton. Thank you for driving Jaime here."

"My pleasure."

Savannah studied him, then turned to Jaime. "I've confirmed that the hearing location hasn't changed. Be warned, there's a bit of a media melee. I'm not sure they're in place for you, but you could become the story. Are you prepared?"

Jaime bit her lower lip and then nodded. "It's okay. Let's get this over with." After today it would take a reporter minutes to find the criminal charges anyway.

"Good. Follow me." Savannah led them through a warren of corridors until they reached a large room on the ground floor. The heavy door looked imposing and a man stood at it. "Let me see if I can find Senator Wesley's assistant. Then we'll follow his lead on what to do and where to wait."

Jaime leaned into Chandler's side. "Sounds like a solid plan."

A minute later, Savannah was back beside them with a young man in tow. "This is Andy Gomez."

The young man had swarthy skin and dark hair. He wore a Banana Republic suit with horn-rimmed glasses and dress shoes. "Miss Nichols, thank you for coming."

Jaime watched him as if deciding whether to like him. "Did I have a choice?"

The twentysomething balanced his hands in front of him. "You always have a choice, but thank you for coming voluntarily. I will let the senator know you are here. Until they're ready for you, you can wait on one of the benches against the wall."

Savannah led the way to one, and Chandler placed his hand at the small of Jaime's back as she followed. Savannah took a call while Jaime stayed quiet.

"You okay?" Chandler wanted to read her mind.

"I will be."

She would be, and hopefully she'd keep him close so he could be part of the process.

After what felt like a lifetime but was in reality an hour, Mr. Gomez was back. "They're wrapping up testimony with the prior witness. It will be you and then Mr. Nichols. Come with me."

Jaime froze. "Is my uncle in there?"

The young man looked at her with a duh expression. "He is."

Chandler placed his hands on her shoulders. "This is the moment you've waited for. Your opportunity to tell the truth in front of your uncle and others who can hold him accountable."

She nodded, but her face had blanked somehow, like she heard the words but couldn't process them.

Savannah eased to her feet and thanked Gomez. "We'll be right behind you." Then she turned to Jaime. "You still okay?"

Jaime nodded as her mouth opened and shut without sound.

Hayden took Jaime's hands and said a quick prayer over her.

Following a chorus of amens, Savannah picked up her brief-case and nodded to Gomez to open the door. "Let's get on with this. Nothing like stepping into the lion's den."

Chandler straightened into his don't-mess-with-me stance. "It's not that bad."

Then Andy opened the door.

CHAPTER 50

A barrage of lightbulbs flashed as Jaime looked into the hearing room. Every inch of space seemed to be filled with a body, but instead of distinct people, her mind turned the sight into a kaleidoscope. An array of microphones was plopped in front of the heavy wood table, with reporters crouched on the floor between the raised desks where the senators sat and the table. Dane sat to the side of the table in his dress uniform, looking every inch the military man and hero that most believed him to be. His eyes found hers, and the look bored through her with a malfeasance she could feel.

Jaime stood in the door. "How do I convince everyone about what happened?"

Savannah nudged her toward four reserved chairs at the back of the hearing room. "You tell your story cleanly and simply. No dragging on. Just the bare facts, which are reprehensible."

They were, but as Jaime sank onto the chair and felt Chandler sit next to her, she studied the scene in front of her. How she wanted to change her mind and leave this place. Someone else could dig up information on Dane. If he'd done such unspeakable things to her, he'd surely done other things in a forum that could be uncovered.

He couldn't hide who he was forever.

Were her parents here? She scanned the room, desperate to find them and their support. The kaleidoscope effect made it impossible to tell. She scrambled through her attaché case for a peppermint roller, uncapped it, and held it to her nose. Then she pulled out

328

lavender and swiped it on her temples and wrists. The blended scent wafting toward her was subtle and comforting. Her reminder to breathe.

"The committee calls Jaime Nichols."

As she pressed her way through the crowd, someone grabbed her hand. She startled and turned to find her father and mother sitting on the aisle.

"We believe you, Jaime." Her father's voice was low and husky. "I will struggle to forgive myself for not protecting you. Not doing what a father should."

"I love you. Thank you for being here." She mouthed the words, met her mother's gaze, and then continued forward. This wasn't the time or place to go deeper, but his words soaked into her heart like a soothing balm.

She was sworn in, then sank into the chair behind the table. Her notes trembled in her fingers as she set them on the table. She belonged here. She knew she did. But she could also feel the intense focus of Dane zeroing in on her and stealing her confidence. She shifted slightly so she could see Chandler in her peripheral vision. She needed to know he was there, believing in her and ready to leap to her defense if needed. Her mother and father were there. Savannah and Hayden. They all believed in her.

She wasn't alone.

Dane wouldn't do anything in a crowded room.

She wanted to believe that, but she was actively engaged in destroying his life.

Even if this hearing didn't change anything, the criminal charges would still proceed, and he would have no choice but to respond.

She lifted her chin and placed her hands on top of the notes. Sitting at the witness table, she felt exposed, and she wished Savannah or Chandler could sit next to her rather than behind her.

Senator Schwartz, chair of the committee, turned to Jaime. "Do you have an opening statement, Ms. Nichols?"

Senator Wesley sat next to the chairwoman, but so far he had done nothing more than tip his head in acknowledgment. He had given her a forum. Now was her opportunity to do something with it.

The time of reckoning she'd prepared for.

Now she would rally her words, all the ones Dane had stolen from her, and order them in a way that persuaded the senators that regardless of the length of time between her violation and today, he must be held accountable. A deep breath filled her lungs, then she pushed it out and met the gaze of each senator sitting behind the raised desk. While several were guarded, only Senator Micah Langdon seemed hostile.

"Senators, today you are considering whether Dane Nichols should be promoted to a one-star general. I've been asked to testify about experiences I had with him that affect whether he has the character for the job."

Jaime glanced at her notes, then back at the senators. A couple looked bored, another was talking to an aide, but Senator Wesley and the chairwoman were fully engaged, as if they waited for the truth. She lifted her chin and ignored the cameras and the murmur of voices behind her.

"This is the story of a little girl. One who needed protection while her father served our great country overseas. Instead, this eight-year-old experienced sexual abuse at the hands of her uncle. Every time I was at his apartment, he did criminal acts against me that would shock you."

She licked dry lips and glanced at her notes, which she didn't really need. "Our military is the part of us that we send into the world. They are defenders of the innocent and protectors of our dearest freedoms. My uncle defiled the innocent with violence. He stole my freedom, erecting a prison of abuse and shame. He should not, cannot be promoted to a position of higher authority in our great army."

She told of his abuse, of the nights of terror, until Senator Langdon rocked forward in his chair to interrupt. "This is beyond a stretch. This is a witch hunt, not legitimate testimony. If this really happened, there would be a criminal record related to the allegations."

"Sir, in many states there is no statute of limitations for criminal charges related to sexual assault, and such charges have been filed in Virginia. This is because lawmakers recognize that abuse, especially against the young, takes time and courage to be exposed. In addition, the law in Virginia is clear that a victim can step forward and seek compensation for damages sustained as long as the action is filed within two years of attaining majority or within two years of being diagnosed with harm where the cause is tied in the sexual abuse." She paused.

"And you believe that allows you to come in here today and tell such sordid tales?"

Her blood began to boil. "It's not a tale. It's my life. The easier thing to do is to keep my head down and pretend it didn't happen. But it did happen. Every night I relive exactly what your nominee did to me."

Senator Wesley leaned into his microphone. "This is a time of great awareness of the terrible proclivities in both our military and society at large. What would you like us to know?"

"Thank you." She quickly gathered her thoughts. "In the last weeks and months, we've seen a transformation occur. Women are willing to step forward and expose the crimes that have been committed against them. Some happen in the workplace. Some happen before we enter the workforce. My abuse occurred when I was too young to know how to get help. I'm no longer too young. I have spent years learning how to overcome the damage my uncle inflicted against me. Today I'm here because I believe a man who would commit the kind of crimes he did against a defenseless child could easily do the same again. Senators, carefully consider whether a man who committed the crimes against me that my uncle did is fit for service as a one-star general."

The chairwoman studied her a moment. "Is there anything else you'd like to say?"

"This hearing is a job interview for my uncle and an opportunity to right a past wrong. Ultimately, you must decide whether someone who molested a child is worthy of such a position."

The woman dipped her chin. "Thank you for your testimony."

"Thank you." Jaime rubbed her forehead and then placed her hands on top of the legal pad resting on the table. She tried to focus on Chairwoman Schwartz's words, but it was hard.

She picked up a pen lying next to the pad. Where had that come from? Then she noticed the Wonder Woman logo on the side. She glanced back at Chandler, and he gave her a barely perceptible smile. She felt tears rise behind her eyes. He was here and would be her hero the moment she asked. As she twirled the pen through her fingers, she thought maybe he saw her as one too. Her cheeks warmed with pleasure at that thought.

———

Chandler gave an inward sigh of relief when Jaime met his eyes. He wasn't sure he should have put the pen there, though it had seemed like a good idea at the time. But it was all right. She understood.

She'd taken over his empty places and filled him with the desire to do anything he could to ease her burdens. He liked who he was around her, the way she pulled the best from him. The parts he'd let Rianna's betrayal kill.

His gaze landed on her uncle seated to the side and watching Jaime like a predatory hawk. Chandler had to fist his hands on his thighs to keep from launching out of the uncomfortable chair and giving the man a piece of his mind or something stronger. What he'd done was unthinkable sin. One that only the grace of God could forgive, because Chandler knew he didn't have the strength to do it on his own.

The man sat at his table, gaze locked on Jaime as if his career depended on how the senators took her testimony—and it did. Would he be confirmed as a general after her heartfelt words? The cameras hadn't quit flashing since she started speaking, and her testimony would go viral.

The senators began sparring amongst themselves until Senator Wesley leaned forward and took control. He looked at Jaime with compassion as he spoke. "Miss Nichols, what my colleagues are most interested in is why now? Why after all this time did you decide that this is the time to speak?"

"I filed the charged before I knew he'd been nominated for this position. I knew I was strong enough for moments like this. And I can't live with myself if I don't speak up while he is placed in a position where he could harm someone else." She sighed but kept her gaze firmly on the senators assembled before her. "Sir, it would be easier and certainly more comfortable to have avoided this moment. However, I am compelled to speak up to prevent future harm."

"Do you have any reason to believe he has grievously harmed anyone else?"

"Only that the research tells us it is likely. I'll leave the decision in your capable hands."

Chandler kept his attention focused on Jaime, trying to determine how she was doing. She'd been adamant that she'd handle this alone. As if she needed to slay her demons single-handedly.

Still she had a strong team around her, one capable of standing against evil.

As he watched her he saw a woman as strong as Diana turning into the avenging Wonder Woman. She was taking on evil, and she was beautiful.

The chairwoman knocked her gavel down. "Thank you for your testimony, Miss Nichols. We will give it our full weight and consideration. You are excused."

Jaime sat a moment as if confused about what to do next, then she stood. "Thank you for your time and attention."

CHAPTER 51

A fog seemed to surround Jaime as she followed Savannah and Hayden to the edge of the hearing room. "Is that it? Do we need to stay for the vote?"

"They will probably conduct an executive session first." Savannah nudged her toward the door. "We can talk in the hall."

The only problem was the moment they stepped outside, more cameras waited with reporters shouting questions at her. In a moment Chandler stepped next to her and began clearing a path for her.

"There you are." Caroline's clear Southern lilt sounded like music but so out of place in the cacophony of the reporters. "Make way, y'all."

"Will you give a statement, Miss Nichols?"

Savannah stepped in front of her, further shielding her from the hordes. "My client has said all she will in her testimony before the Armed Services Committee. I suggest you contact your colleagues who were inside for more."

Then Jaime was escorted through the melee and around a corner by her friends. After a few more turns, Hayden opened a door. "We can collect ourselves here." She waved at the receptionist. "Emma, we'll be in the small conference room for a minute."

"Sure thing. Should I let the senator know?"

"Only if he asks. The hearing looked like it would continue for a while." Hayden opened a door, and in a minute the group was standing in a wood paneled room filled with a large conference table and chairs. "The media won't get past Emma."

Before Jaime could register where she was, she was swept into an embrace four people strong. She looked over Hayden's shoulder and caught Chandler standing outside the circle with a small smile tipping his lips.

Caroline squeezed so tightly Jaime was surprised a rib didn't crack. "You okay?"

"I'll know for sure when I read the headlines."

"That's not what I mean." Caroline's gaze was fierce.

Emilie squeezed her arm. "You were so poised and articulate in there."

Savannah stepped back, and Jaime felt like she could breathe. "That little girl is not your identity. The woman I saw today has moved past the horror."

"What do you mean?"

"You are not the powerless eight-year-old who was violated." Savannah's gaze was steady and unflinching. "You are so much more, but still a shadow of what you can be."

Not here. Savannah must have caught the emotion on her face, because she squeezed Jaime's hand and left it at that. Hayden, however, looked ready to tackle it head on. There was that holy zeal in her eyes, the one she got when she was ready to launch into a heartfelt call to action. Caroline stopped her. "Not here, girl." Caroline turned back to Jaime. "Let's get tea somewhere. If I know you, you haven't eaten a thing."

"I didn't dare around the butterflies. Can I say something first?" Jaime took a deep breath. "A couple days ago I did something you have wanted me to do for a long time. After reading a book Chandler gave me and asking some questions, I prayed with Caroline. I'm still new to everything, but I've started the journey toward God."

Emilie's squeal about shattered Jaime's eardrum, while Hayden's "It's about time" made Jaime grin.

"I came in my own timing, Hayden."

Her friend patted her French-twisted hair. "I know, but I'll be delighted to alter my prayers for you." She considered Jaime for a minute, searching her soul. "You'll be fine."

"I know." It wouldn't be easy, but she'd come so far already. She turned to Caroline. "What was that about food? I'm pretty sure my cup of coffee has worn off." She was ready to live knowing life was a bit bitter around the edges with a dollop of sweetness that kept it interesting.

"Remember I learned all your secrets living with you." Caroline waggled her eyebrows, but Jaime smiled. Caroline knew her best and was still here. Sweet, quiet, sassy Caroline.

Emilie looked up from her phone. "I just made a reservation for six."

Chandler stepped back. "No need to include me. I wouldn't want to intrude. And I need to get over to my office." He turned to Jaime. "I'll call you tonight."

As he walked away, she wondered. Could she trust his word? Or would she allow him to get close only to push him far away when he risked entering too deeply into her heart? As she watched him leave, she believed she'd grown past that older version of herself. She didn't want to push him away. He had proven himself a man worth holding close to her heart.

When Chandler reached the Vet Center, he found the cleanup crew packing their tools. The foreman told him they were done and the office was ready. Chandler would let Allison and Beth know they could come back tomorrow if they were ready. They were the ones who had suffered the trauma of being hostages. Meanwhile, he'd take advantage of the locked doors and resulting quiet to put his head down and work through everything in his in-box. It was time to launch back into his work helping veterans. It was a worthy way to spend his life, but as he looked at the pile of work, he knew it'd take time to get caught up. Thank God for dictation software.

Five hours later he'd knocked the pile in half. He'd also determined which items to take home to keep after. Another block of time like this and he'd be back where he wanted to be, but as the clock hit five, he needed to head back to the apartment. He and Aslan would be waiting at her door when Jaime got home.

When Jaime didn't respond to his text, he texted Caroline. Still with her?

No, she left an hour ago.

Where was she headed?

Home

He frowned. Alone?

She insisted she'd be okay

Okay

Thanks for being there for her today. She might not say it, but I could tell it mattered.

Thanks.

338

He had to smile. Caroline the peacemaker, trying to make sure he knew he mattered.

But as he packed up he had a bad feeling about what he'd find when he reached Jaime's. He'd stop at his apartment long enough to get Aslan out and order takeout. Then it would be time to tell Jaime exactly how he felt about her and where he wanted their relationship to go.

The lock didn't take five seconds to trip. Whoever thought it would provide security was a fool.

The apartment looked less cluttered, but that was because the roommate was gone.

Good thing, as he didn't want collateral damage.

His blood roiled as he thought about Jaime's testimony. His niece had woven a sad tale that seemed to sway a couple of the senators, including that patsy Senator Wesley. The man was clean as a whistle despite some of the questionable staff he'd had in the past. There was little to leverage in his background.

It infuriated Dane to think this was a powerful man he could not influence or destroy.

He'd just have to dig deeper into his network. The army was a fraternity, one that reached deep into the fabric of society. It also created an environment where people could do things they wouldn't do in the light of day. Many were noble men like his brother, the boring man who shared parents with him but little else.

Then there were those who liked to push the envelope. They didn't know that Dane was taking notes and photos, but he was. Each one was a potential bullet to coerce people to do his will.

His career proved he could handle any situation, but after Jaime's performance at the hearing, she had to be silenced. Allowing her to spread her lies one more minute wasn't an option.

She'd been warned.

Now she'd left him no choice but to punish her.

When she returned he would be waiting.

She would retract her statement and tell the Commonwealth to dismiss charges or he would handle her.

Nobody messed with Dane Nichols. Nobody.

CHAPTER 52

The relief was immense. Jaime had done the hardest thing she could imagine in testifying before the committee, and now after a late lunch with her friends, she felt so free. This was what all the hard work of counseling and coming to terms with Dane's abuse had led to. His actions would always be a part of her story, but they no longer had to dictate her future.

With the help of her friends and this God she was just beginning to know, she sensed true freedom waiting around the corner.

When Jaime arrived at her apartment, she was ready to collapse on the futon with a book or movie. She might not even turn on the diffuser tonight.

Then she opened the door and froze. The air was already filled with the scent of lavender with an undertone of something that smelled musky. It was a smell she didn't want to remember. The one that assaulted her when she'd confronted Dane at the ball. His signature scent.

Where was Simba, and why was the light she always left on over the stove off?

Something was wrong.

She stepped back toward the hallway and pulled out her phone. She had the phone to her ear, a call ringing to Chandler, when she heard a voice.

"I wouldn't do that if I were you."

The sense of freedom evaporated with that sentence.

Dane.

In her apartment.

How had he gotten in? Even her parents didn't have a key.

She slowly lowered her phone but didn't flick it off, praying he wouldn't notice. "What do you want?"

He stepped into view. Loomed in the space. A hulking frame in the shadows.

Her breath hitched. She couldn't think, couldn't move.

He sensed the power he held. Stepped nearer. "What did you think you were doing today?"

His growl propelled her a step back.

"Telling the truth." Her words squeaked. She needed to be strong. It was the only way she'd survive.

"Close the door."

"No." She couldn't argue with a bully, but she didn't have to obey.

"Have it your way. I can kill you and disappear before anyone knows I was here." His words were so certain, so cold, she didn't doubt he meant them. "I'm very good at my job."

"What job is that?"

"That would be classified, need-to-know information, and you don't have that clearance."

She eased the door shut behind her without letting it latch.

"All the way."

"It is."

"One little twist and your cat's dead." She couldn't see the cat in his arms but couldn't risk her companion. "You'll be next."

She pushed the door until it clicked.

"Good." Dane's voice seemed disembodied, but then he called her closer. "I'll take your phone."

She wanted to whimper but refused to move or speak.

"You have two seconds until your cat is dead."

She slid the phone toward him. "There."

It was small, but that act of defiance felt important. "Why are you here?"

"Because we're going to have a conversation. Then I'll decide your future."

She trembled in the darkness, feeling her old friend fear move in. "No." She repeated the word, this time louder. "No."

"We will talk. Have you seen the headlines, the tickers on the networks?" His voice grated with anger. "You told your lies, and now I'll pay."

"You should." The words were defiant but her tone weak.

"That's wrong. I never did anything you didn't want. That you didn't beg for. So you should pay."

"I have paid every day of my life. I refuse to pay a moment longer for your sins." She felt an energy rolling through her as she spoke. "I am done letting you control my life. How I feel and what I allow to happen."

"Such noble words. Easy to say now that you've destroyed my career with lies."

"You destroyed your career. I just made sure they understood who you are."

"Oh no. Your lies won't stick in a criminal court. Your evidence? Just your word against mine. It won't stand up with the rules of evidence."

"We have more." No need to tell him specifically about the journal and counseling reports. He'd have those soon enough.

"Doesn't matter. No jury will believe you over me."

"But the senators did."

"Not for long. I'll fight back with the best attorneys money can buy."

She startled as she felt a presence wind around her legs. Simba? Dane must have lied about having her cat, and she shouldn't be surprised. He'd made a lifetime of lying, presenting one persona in public and another to her. The man stepped closer. She needed a weapon. Something, anything. But what? The knives were on the other side of the island, and her briefcase wouldn't do much to him. Her thoughts flew in a torrent of desperation.

Then he had her in a headlock, his breath heavy on her face, and she thought she'd be sick. A flashback launched and she screamed. He squeezed her neck until she whimpered. She was tall, but he was taller. He was stronger and there was little she could do.

God? The word screamed through her mind. *Where are you?*

She bit down on his arm and at the same time she stepped on his insole.

Chandler held the phone to his ear, horrified. With his other hand he tugged out his work cell and called 911 as he ran to the security desk in the lobby.

"I need the key to Jaime Nichols's apartment."

The woman behind the desk just looked at him, then listened as he quickly described the situation to the 911 responder. Without another word she handed him the key.

He took off for the stairwell—no time to wait for an elevator.

Within moments he was at her door, barely turning the key before he kicked the door wide and called her name.

"Chandler, stay back!"

Jaime was backed against a wall, writhing to get away, her uncle pressed against her. Chandler reached for the gun he kept in a holster near the small of his back, but Dane spoke without turning.

"Make a move, and I'll kill her now."

Chandler slid his gun free, unclicked the safety, and yelled,

"Jaime, now." He prayed she would understand the order, because he didn't have time to wait for the police to arrive.

He fired.

In an instant her uncle was gone. No chance the man survived the head shot.

Jaime's scream, a sound that had no beginning or end, filled the apartment, and he raced toward her. "Don't open your eyes. Trust me, don't look."

She shook hard as he helped her up and led her around her uncle's body. "I didn't want this. I didn't want this."

"I know, baby, I know."

He led her out of the living area and into the hallway outside the apartment. "We'll wait here for the police."

She threw herself into his arms and sobbed. He held her and wished he could wipe the entire incident from her mind. She'd confronted her demon and won. But the cost would be high.

CHAPTER 53

THREE DAYS LATER

A pile of boxes lined the hallway as Jaime reentered her apartment. Her friends had worked hard since the apartment was released by the police at the conclusion of their investigation, but a shudder rippled through her as she stepped deeper into the space Dane had ruined. Her haven of white had been splattered with his blood, etching into paint what he had done to her.

Her mother put a hand on her arm. "Are you sure you want to do this?"

"We can move the boxes without you." Her father's voice wrapped around her, a blanket of protection that she was only now beginning to accept.

"No, I need to do this." She'd moved in with her parents, back into her old rooms, the ones that had sheltered Madeline and Tiffany. All that remained was to collect the boxes the girls had packed for her. The futon had already been thrown away, Dane's blood embedded in the fabric as it was in the clothes she'd worn. "I need to say good-bye before I move on."

The words would make no sense to her parents, but she knew they were true. She didn't want all the good memories to be overwhelmed by the horror of Dane's death. In his home office the police had found a wall of photos of her. He'd also had photos of her apartment along with one of her books, proving he'd been in her apartment more than just the night he'd attacked. Her impressions hadn't been wrong, even when she hadn't had proof. He'd been there, just enough on the edge to keep her guessing and off balance.

But now he could no longer hurt her.

His power over her was finished.

She stepped deeper into the living room and sighed.

A knock on the door grabbed her attention, and she turned to see Chandler standing there. Her knight in shining armor. The man who knew the worst that had happened to her and was still there. Even now that he'd played an active role in saving her.

She felt a security that was new and something she wanted to settle into as she looked from her father to Chandler. These men were here for her, and they weren't going anywhere.

Kind of like the women crowding behind them.

She'd been so alone for so many years, an island buffeted by the storms of the past. Then the storms had collided with her efforts to make things right. They'd each been there: Caroline as a steady light in the dark nights, a quiet voice when she needed to know she wasn't alone. Hayden with her tangible efforts to help her tell her story where it mattered, never doubting that her pain and experience were real. Emilie, as a steady presence, quiet but there. Always there. And even Savannah, with her help to clear the ethics complaint and then not-so-subtle pressure to come to work with the team.

Maybe today Jaime would let her know that she'd decided to do that. She didn't know what her work would look like, just that she'd restart in the presence of her friends who loved her no matter her background or how prickly she got on occasion.

Chandler stepped closer, a smile lighting his eyes. "You ready?"

"For a new beginning? Yes." Did she dare ask the question? Would he be in that beginning?

"You won't be alone."

That had been his greatest gift to her. He hadn't let her be alone.

Neither had Caroline or her other friends. They'd been there each step of the way, for as much or as little as she could handle.

"Dane can't hurt you anymore."

"I know."

Someday she might really believe he was gone. That he could no longer reach her or haunt her dreams, but for now she would take it moment by moment. One thing she'd learned through all her counseling was that she couldn't rush the process.

"Are you sure you don't want us to move your stuff off-site?" Her father's question was gruff, but now she heard the love that underlay the words. He really did care even when he struggled to show her the depths of that love.

"I don't want to rush away. Living with you and Mom for a bit is a good intermediate solution."

"You need time to breathe." Her mom slipped close for a quick hug. Her phone dinged and her mother glanced at it. "It's Tiffany. I promised I'd bring her home for a bit after school. Sounds like she needs a Happy fix."

They all did. If only Jaime could bottle the feeling that little dog freely gave to people. Between Happy and Aslan, the world would be a more relaxed, happy place. "It's okay, Mom. We're basically done. And Tiffany needs you too. She needs us."

That young girl wouldn't know the isolation Jaime had endured, if Jaime could help it. And if that meant sharing her mom for a while, she would gladly do it.

"Where do you want these?" Chandler stood there looking all Captain America with a couple boxes stacked in his arms.

"Over there." She waved against a wall, eager for the boxes to be dropped so that he could take her in his arms. She was hungry to feel the security that came from knowing he was there for her.

He set them down, and she slid into his arms before he could pick up anything else.

"Thank you." She murmured the words against his flannel shirt.
"For what?"

She loved the way his voice rumbled in his chest. "For being here."

"There's nowhere else I want to be."

She soaked in the warmth of the words. There was a truth in them that she relished. And a promise that she wanted to clutch to her. Instead, she pivoted slightly in his arms so she could tip her chin up. The invitation would be enough.

When his lips claimed hers, she knew she'd found her home.

ACKNOWLEDGMENTS

Many thanks to Victoria Huber, my Savannah, who spent hours with me the first year at George Mason, convincing me I would make it. Victoria also connected me with some fellow George Mason alums who are spending their lives as Public Defenders. One woman in particular generously gave me her time so that I could confirm that I had the law and the motivation right for Jaime. Many thanks, Bonnie! While I have served as appellate counsel on criminal appeals, I have not worked in the trenches of public defense and wanted to make sure I honored those who do. As I conversed with Bonnie, she reaffirmed my impression it is a calling.

I also have to thank the many people who shared with me the experience of sexual abuse and what it did to their families. I knew Jaime had a hard story, but I didn't know it was this difficult until I started digging into her past. Two people read the manuscript to make sure I honored the experience and made it real. Thank you, Hannah and Nick, for helping me honor the experience of survivors.

As I reread this book at the final stage, I realized how much my life has mirrored Jaime's as I wrote it. With each book there is something that I learn, and for *Delayed Justice* I was in a season of asking many of the questions that Jaime wrestled with. God brought certain people along my path to hold me up when I didn't think I had the strength. A huge thank you to Beth Vogt who faithfully texts me each morning with an encouraging Scripture. If you haven't read her books yet, you really must! Thank you to Beth

Nagel for all of the coffee, prayer, and love. And to Kim Lunato, my friend who has known me for years and still loves me. You consistently spoke truth when I needed it. You three have been my Hayden, Emilie, and Caroline this year. Thank you!

One thing I have learned through this season is that God is with us every step of the way, and His greatest desire is for our healing and wholeness. I don't know where you are on your life's journey, but my prayer is that God will reignite hope and joy in your life.

Thank you for joining me on Jaime's journey.

DISCUSSION QUESTIONS

1. Bella tells Jaime that, "sometimes He [God] makes total sense in the moment. Other times, it's only in the rearview mirror that we can see the why of the experience" (page 268). Have you seen this in your life? How would you describe the way you saw God's actions make sense in the rearview mirror of life?

2. Jaime is faced with confronting a horrific past. It's not easy and requires a strength she's not sure she has. Have you ever tried to solve a challenge in your life with your own strength and skills? How did that work? Is there a better way?

3. "When we live with mights, we live with regrets" (page 283). When Jaime says this, she is talking about Chandler's fears that he caused Jake's injury. How does it also apply to her life?

4. Chandler has to be careful with the way he approaches Jaime. What could he have done to demonstrate his care and concern for her? How does his approach mirror the way Christ loves us?

5. Aslan may be a dog, but he plays a pivotal role in the story by providing a safe place for Tiffany. Have you ever had an animal like Aslan? One who seemed to be able to communicate with you?

6. Chandler is a strong hero but not quite typical. He's wounded by his past and things that happened on his last tour of duty. Now he's trying to take what he's learned and help others. At one point in the book he says, "It was easy to focus on the fix rather than on Who did the fixing." Which is easier for you?

7. Jaime is slowly wooed over the course of *Delayed Justice* into a relationship with God. She doesn't believe He can love her because He didn't stop the evil that happened to her as an eight-year-old. Do you know people who have struggled with that same question? How would you answer the question?

8. *The Lion, the Witch and the Wardrobe* is a book that plays a key role in this novel. In what way has a novel helped birth or develop your faith?

ABOUT THE AUTHOR

Photo by Emilie Hendrix

As a preteen Cara Putman watched lawyers change legislative opinions at an important legislative hearing in Nebraska. At that time, she wondered if she became an attorney if people would give her words the same weight. An honors graduate of the University of Nebraska Lincoln, George Mason University School of Law, and Krannert School of Management at Purdue University, Cara has turned her passion for words into award-winning stories that capture readers hearts. Her legal experience makes its way into her stories where strong women confront real challenges.

An award-winning author of thirty books and counting, Cara writes legal thrillers, WWII romances, and romantic suspense because she believes that no matter what happens, hope is there, waiting for us to reach for it.

When she's not writing, Cara is an over-educated attorney who teaches law and communications to graduate and under-graduate students at the Krannert School of Management at Purdue University. She and her family live in Indiana, the land of seasons. You can read chapters for most of her books and connect with Cara at her website.

Visit her website at CaraPutman.com
Facebook: Cara.Putman
Twitter: @Cara_Putman